FADE

Finding Home Series

ASHLEY MUNOZ

Cover Design: Amanda Simpson from Pixelmischief design

Formatting: Ashley Munoz

Editing: Sandy Ebel- Personal Touch Editing, **C. Marie**

Content Edits: Amanda Edens

❀ Created with Vellum

To my husband, Jose.
I choose you today, tomorrow and forever. You are the poem that soothes my soul
and keeps my heart humming.

NOTE FROM THE AUTHOR

Fade is considered an interconnected series, so it is suggested to read **Glimmer** first, for a more enjoyable experience.

LANEY

THE SHARP CORNERS FROM THE ENVELOPE PUSHED INTO MY PALM AS I tightened my fist. I needed the small prick of pain to remind me how easy it would be to go to jail if I started acting on all my anger-infused impulses. *Way too easy, Laney.*

The city of Chicago flew by my window as my cab driver turned down another street. I winced at how hasty I'd been, leaving my purse behind at the office. I lightly leaned to the side of the seat, accessing the small pocket tucked along my hip bone. Sweet relief washed over me as I tugged the folded twenty-dollar bill free. I silently blessed Mr. Ashby and all his future offspring for sending me out to get him lunch like I was his secretary and not the lead supervisor on three of his current projects.

"This okay right here, ma'am?" The young driver asked, sounding a little nervous. I realized I probably shouldn't have been whisper-cussing under my breath for the last half hour.

"Yes, this is fine." I handed the twenty to the driver and told him to keep the change. Another rash decision, one I should have thought through seeing as I had no money to get another cab home. But maybe this little chat with Jackson would end well and I wouldn't need it. I got out and stood two houses down from Jackson's then turned on my heel.

The wind was softly blowing against my face, whispering promises of summer and warmth and all the plans I'd made with Jackson, including a trip to London and Italy. The reminder had me squeezing the letter in my hand tighter and putting more force into every step of my discount stilettos. I hadn't realized earlier that when I returned to the office, sushi in hand, I'd have a courier waiting for me to sign for a letter.

A fucking letter.

I reached Jackson's townhouse, a massive three-story monstrosity. He had black iron fencing along the lower part of the stairs and green vines with budding white flowers dangled over the bars. His house made my apartment look like one of his walk-in closets. I didn't have my key and I knew it would be locked, so I pounded my fist against the dark mahogany door.

"Jackson!" I yelled for all his posh neighbors to hear. I was making a scene, but that was obviously what he wanted when he sent the messenger. My fists slammed against the door in angry thuds, the letter pathetically wedged in between them as they sailed in fury.

A few seconds later, the door swung open and Jackson stood there watching me like a confused butler.

"Laney...what are you—"

I pushed past him into his house and ran up the few steps to the middle level, where his kitchen and bedrooms were located. I turned to face him as he shut his door and slowly took the few stairs to meet me. His head looked recently shaved, not totally bald but a close cut just the same; he must have had it done after I left that morning. His sharp blue eyes looked more intense with his blue jersey t-shirt and denim jeans. I ignored that pull in my belly I always felt when I saw this man, like he was a drug or my very own personalized fuzzy, security blanket. He was my home, my life, and my *nothing*.

Not my boyfriend or my fiancé, he was a lover without a label, and so this letter I'd received...I knew what it meant, but I was just hoping I was wrong.

"What the hell is this, Jax?" I held my fist out, the letter jutting toward him. The paper was mangled and scrunched up at this point, but the words written in black ink could still be seen.

His eyes darted to the letter, and a look of shock came over his face, sending those light eyebrows to his forehead. Had he honestly thought he could send it and I would just go along with this, like the last seven months hadn't happened?

"Look..." He drew out the word, bringing his hands to his hips and slightly slouching his shoulders. "I think you know where I'm going with this, Lane. We need space. Glenda mentioned it was a good idea for you to start—"

I stepped forward until I was just inches from him, sucking in extra oxygen as I cut him off.

"Don't tell me what my therapist said to do, Jax. I was there and I'm aware of her suggestions, but that doesn't explain *this* letter." I stepped back a foot or two so I could unfold the piece of mail and started reading it out loud. "*Laney, I'm headed out of the country this week. I think we should take some time apart for a bit. We'll talk when I get back.*"

I tilted my chin up until I was staring at his stupid beautiful eyes. They were soft and pleaded with me to understand him. He drew his hand up to grab his neck as his lips turned down. I took in his posture and the light hint of red that had entered his cheeks.

Holy shit, this is real.

My legs threatened to buckle.

I should have seen this coming. I really should have, but I was blinded by love—reckless, dangerous love that had torn me open and left me vulnerable for when the proverbial shoe dropped between us.

I carefully lowered the letter, all my steam and anger fizzling out in an instant. That look on his face, the one that said he was sorry but it was over...it killed any argument I had left. I knew seven months together didn't mean anything, especially when he'd yet to even define what we were. *So why does it feel like someone is opening my breastbone and physically removing my lungs without any anesthesia?*

"Look, I just think we need to change some things before it goes too far." Jackson's voice sounded distant, as though he was in another part of the house instead of standing right in front of me.

I swallowed my words and, more importantly, my tears. I refused to let him see me cry over this. *Over him.*

"Laney, did you hear me?" That gentle tone wormed its way into my threadbare heart. I was drowning. I'd been dumped before, but it had never felt like this.

"I heard you," I replied coldly, throwing daggers at him with my eyes. If only those things were real and could land a hit. "What's this really about, Jax?" I whispered because just the night before he'd held me after a panic attack and made love to me. I'd woken up in his arms, showered in his bathroom, and left for work, giving him a kiss on the lips. He had looked like he always did this morning: blissfully happy.

Jackson's eyes left my face and searched his so-clean-you could-eat-off-of-it floor. "We're practically a couple, Lane. I told you..." He stopped midsentence, and I stepped closer, assessing his face as he delivered his bullshit answer.

"So, this is about the commitment issue?" My tone came out sharp and like it belonged to someone else.

Jackson's eyes dug into me, delivering the answer he was too chicken-shit to give.

"Why, Jackson? I told you I didn't need a label...I've been here for seven months—why all of a sudden?" Tears burned the corners of my eyes as my voice cracked. Dammit, I didn't want to cry in front of him. I didn't want to manipulate him.

He shook his head back and forth but didn't move a single step closer. "You deserve more than that. You know you do. I won't ever want the family thing, Lane. I won't ever be your boyfriend or fiancé or anything else. I can't commit to you, and this thing between us for the past seven months has been the closest I've ever gotten to it. But I can't..." He stopped again, his jaw ticked a few times, and he dropped his gaze to the floor.

This whole situation had me feeling like I had just fallen through a patch of thin ice I'd purposely jumped on and was somehow surprised by the frigid water. I cleared my throat and turned away from him, needing to move, needing to end this embarrassing scene where he held all the cards of a deck I had stupidly thought we'd split. My high heels clicked along his wood floor as I moved into the kitchen, where I grabbed a glass from the cupboard and poured myself water from the tap.

"I don't want things to end badly between us...I still want to be there when you need me for therapy and for whatever else you need. I just..." His soft words died on his tongue. I was glad they did because I couldn't handle hearing another word about how he wanted to be there for me but didn't actually *want* me.

"My stuff?" I squeaked out while I watched warming beams of sunshine drench his floor. I didn't have much, but that tiny drawer in his closet was still full of my meager belongings. Jackson's face took on more of that red shading, right along his firm jawline. He shifted, his soft blue shirt moving with him. I eyed that shirt and was tempted to tell him to take it off and throw it in with my things because I'd bought it for him. He bent down around the corner and retrieved a small cardboard box. *He already packed my stuff.*

My heart lurched to a stop as that thought slithered through me and I saw my pillow sticking out from the top.

This was really happening. Jackson was leaving me.

My Jackson. My pillar. My person.

I started to breathe through my nose so he wouldn't see my emotional breakdown, so he wouldn't see the devastation in my eyes. He'd never promised me anything. He'd never once said this was forever so I shouldn't have been angry, but the erratic beating behind my necklace was proof that I hadn't quite come to terms with the finality of our non-relationship. I had always assumed I'd have a say in when it ended, had thought I'd be enough of a woman to put my foot down and demand better for myself.

I don't do relationships, Laney.

That's right—he'd warned me, but I was almost positive he was starting to feel how real this was between us...and I stupidly thought he'd change. Heat overwhelmed my face as my stupid assumptions slammed into me.

I carefully set the glass down and stepped forward until I had one hand beneath the box and the other over it, holding it in place. I stepped back to recreate the distance I needed between us. Or rather, the distance he wanted.

"This is slightly embarrassing, but I forgot my purse—could I snag Lance from you, or do you need him?" I hated asking him for his driver. I hated taking anything from him, but I had naively believed this little discussion would end in angry makeup sex and with me on whatever flight he was about to take.

Jackson gave me a weak smile and nodded. "Of course you can. Laney, I'm still here for you if you need anything at all. I want you to know that."

I returned his watery smile and nodded because there was nothing left to say.

2

LANEY

Three months later

"So, are you going to be there?" My best friend's voice was borderline begging, and it made something twist inside me uncomfortably. I finished swiping the crumbs from my small counter onto the floor. I dusted the remnants of flaky specks into the sink and wiped my hands on my pants.

"Ramsey, look...I just don't think I can make it this weekend. I have so much going on with work." *Lie.* "And I don't have the cab fare for it." *Truth.* "Anyway, you know if I could make it out, I would." I cleared my throat and took a big gulp of water, waiting to hear her voice plead with me again through the three tiny holes of my phone speaker.

"Okay, then I'll come to you," Ramsey suggested in a positive tone.

I spit my water out. "What?" I started wiping my mouth with the back of my wrist.

"Yeah, we haven't all been in the same place in over three months. The kids miss you both and it's my birthday, so we will make a trip of it." I could picture my best friend lifting her slender shoulder like this was no big deal. What was worse was she had already heard all my lame excuses as to why it wouldn't work, so I had no leverage left. I slightly wondered on a scale of one to ten how bad it would be if I used her sick mother as an excuse as to why she shouldn't leave. Then I remembered her mother was currently living here in Chicago and slapped my forehead. *Dammit!*

"Um...yeah, okay. I'll do my best to be there," I stuttered while moving over to my living room, a whopping three feet.

"No way. Don't do that, Lane. You will be there. You said you couldn't leave the city and gave me a bunch of stupid excuses, and now I've fixed all that. It's my birthday, and I'm your best friend, so you're going to be there. Besides, we have something to tell you and Jax." Ramsey pushed on with that determined attitude of hers that got shit done. I admired her, I really did, but at the moment, I also hated her.

I let out a heavy sigh as I tipped my face up to the ceiling while cradling my phone to my chest. I wasn't mature enough to explain why I wasn't ready to see Jackson, and it sucked on way too many levels that he happened to be her husband's best friend. If fate had a face, I'd bitch-slap it.

"I promise I'll be there, Rams." I wearily gave in. She had me and she knew it. I missed her and the kids, and I'd just have to figure out some way to work up the courage to see Jackson again.

"Thank you, Lane. I gotta run—I will see you Friday!" she yelled through the phone, huffing a few extra breaths like she was running. She was probably playing soccer with one of the kids. I pressed my thumb to the red end button and pulled one of my pillows over my face.

This wasn't happening.

A loud alarm sounded on my phone that had fallen to the floor, and I sat up fast trying to reach it, ending up awkwardly falling off the couch. My screen showed a reminder that I had an appointment with my therapist, set for this afternoon. *Shit.*

I jumped up, ran to my room, and traded my large sleep shirt and no pants for a pair of jeans and a t-shirt. I tried to take comfort in the fact that I could process everything that had just happened with Ramsey in my session. I needed to think of the small victories. Hopefully Glenda would have some magical words to help me prepare to finally see my fake ex.

"Let's talk goals," Glenda said while walking over to a rectangular white board that was laying against her desk. Attached to it were large lettered words, printed in seafoam green ink.

'Three months', 'Six months', and 'Twelve months' were taped across the top panel.

Kill me.

"Do we need to think that far ahead?" I winced as I saw other little printed cutouts of edgy images and fonts promising me I could do anything I put my mind to.

"We do. You need to start visualizing your future. Three months have passed since you were dependent on anyone for support, and I think you're doing awesome." My therapist smiled brightly at me. Her white teeth looked pristine against her glowing, ebony skin. Ramsey introducing me to her after my incident was the best thing that could have happened to me. I needed someone, and Glenda specializing in PTSD made her my favorite human being on planet earth.

"So, take this home and treat it like a dream board. Start pinning to it what you want to see in the allotted time spans." She pointed with her manicured nails to each section. "And..." She trailed off, setting the board down, widening her eyes and pursing her lips. "I think it's time we add your family to this board."

My eyebrows shot up in surprise. *Where is this coming from?*

"Why? Things are fine with my family." I could hear the pitch in my voice betraying my lie. Glenda saw through it, her eyebrow lifted in question as she leaned forward.

"When was the last time you talked to them?"

If I'd had a tie on, I'd loosen it. "Um...April...I believe." I stuttered through my obvious discomfort.

"It's August...so don't you think you're due for a phone call?" Glenda prodded ever so gently with her words. This was what I was paying her for, but I didn't like it.

"I talk to Leo all the time...in fact, I'm thinking of going to see him in October for his birthday." I had a hint of pride in my voice because even considering going was a big step. My family and I had a tangled past. It mostly revolved around my father, but a few of my brothers had gotten caught up in it. Then once time passed, it was mostly just my finances that stopped me from going home. The phone calls became less frequent because I was ashamed of how poor I had become from pursuing a dream they'd told me not to chase.

"Planning a trip home is a good start. Do they know about your relationship with Jackson ending?" Glenda shuffled a few yellow pages on her legal pad. My breath felt caught inside my lungs. I didn't want to talk about this right now. Or ever.

"Umm... no. In April we were still..." I trailed off, not wanting to mentally drudge back up the month before he ended things. Glenda watched me and continued to purse her lips, like she was holding back her words. I took the opportunity to ask about the birthday dinner.

"So, tomorrow is the dinner with Ramsey and the family," Glenda said softly.

I tucked a few strands of hair behind my ear. Glenda watched my movement and placed her legal pad down.

"How do you feel about seeing Jackson again? I know when he left, things were pretty ugly for a bit." Glenda spoke carefully while picking at the lint on her skirt. Ugly for a bit? What an understatement. The memory of that dark night still clung to the edges of my mind, taunting me to go back. I had called Glenda at one in the morning, triggered to high hell and not able to rationalize my thoughts or panic.

I ended up checking myself into a mental health clinic for two days while I worked through it. Jackson had always been there to help me, and without him, I didn't know how to deal.

"I don't expect to actually speak to him. We haven't spoken in three months, so I doubt we will interact much." I answered plainly as if the condition between Jackson and I were clinical and not emotional.

"But that three-month silence was at your request, correct? He tried plenty of times to reach out to you, even showing up at your apartment and work on multiple occasions. Each time, you refused to speak to him, right?" Glenda verbally inquired like a detective looking for clues. *I should really stop telling her all this shit about my life if she's just going to bring it back up to use against me.*

"That's correct." I straightened my spine, ready to defend my choices...again. Glenda hadn't agreed with my cold turkey plan, but I hadn't been able to deal with Jackson's absence any other way.

"So, what if he uses this dinner as an opportunity to talk to you?"

I stared down at Glenda's plush carpet, which likely cost as much as the total sum of my student loans, and tried to breathe. I wasn't prepared for this question just like I wasn't prepared to see him again. Nervous energy buzzed under my skin as I thought over my answer, but after a few awkward moments of silence, it was clear that nothing was coming.

Glenda leaned forward, grabbing her clipboard again. "Laney, facing Jackson is a big part of your recovery. He's tied to your PTSD in every way. He's your link to Alicia, just like he's your link to coping after Alicia. The fact that he walked away after you were making such amazing progress was regrettable, but at the same time, I've never been prouder of where you are today. You've come a long way, and I think you owe it to yourself to go in with confidence tomorrow. With whatever you decide regarding him, be brave."

I gave her a weak smile and nodded my head. I could do that; I had done it for three months. Seeing him wouldn't set me back...I just needed to dig deep and be strong.

3

LANEY

"*HAPPY BIRTHDAY TO YOU. HAPPY BIRTHDAY TO YOU...*" THE obnoxiously loud song reverberated through the foyer of the restaurant as I hurried in through the front doors. I was so late, so freaking late. Thirty minutes to be exact, which made me the world's worst friend. I should have just called and told her I had cramps; I'd even strongly considered telling her I had an STD. Either one would have been good enough to get me out of a regular dinner, but not a dinner I had already agreed to show up to.

The lobby was packed full of what had to be the world's largest dinner party. At least ten kids were sitting uncomfortably on a long, pristine wooden bench, wearing what looked like Sunday's best. I pressed in further, bypassing the hostess who was frantically writing names down on a notepad while three women stood over her, pointing and shouting about reservations that were supposed to have been made.

I pushed on the backs of two servers wearing white collared shirts. They lurched forward with their trays, and I gave them a sheepish wave of apology. My hip bumped a table close by, making the water glasses shake and silverware clink. *How close are these damn tables?* I continued to push through the overcrowded room, desperately trying to catch the tail end of the song.

I came to a stop right as everyone started clapping. Heads were still turned in our direction, people craning to see who was on exhibition. I could feel my anxiety start to flare to life. There were so many people in the restaurant and so much commotion, so many people who were watching. My heart was thundering as I worked to bring my anxiety under control. The thing about PTSD is that it doesn't make any logical sense. It felt like it'd taken control of my flight-or-fight instincts and now whenever I felt like I might be in danger or even being watched, it kicked in and told me to run. At the moment, it was telling me to turn around and get the hell out of the overcrowded room.

I closed my eyes and quietly whispered the first few lines of a poem, willing my body to calm down, reminding myself that my threat was currently behind bars. I was safe. I opened my eyes and focused on Ramsey. My best friend had just been serenaded by half the restaurant and I'd totally missed it. Guilt lodged itself inside my lungs, like a fat taco shell trying to choke me death.

I tried to subtly wipe the sweat from my forehead as servers still huddled around Ramsey's space. I eyed the table closest to me for a glass of water. It wouldn't be that weird if I swiped a stranger's glass, would it? Just as I was about to grab it, the crowd around the table cleared, and I saw my glowing best friend with a slice of cake in front of her and the hugest grin I'd ever seen. I headed toward her and leaned in for a quick hug.

"Happy Birthday, Rams." I kissed her cheek and took the empty seat next to her.

"Laney! Where have you been? You almost missed everything," she yelled. Ramsey didn't normally yell or exclaim anything, so her bellowing at me had me feeling worse than before. I winced and tried to recover, although I knew there was no coming back from being thirty minutes late to a birthday party.

"Ram, I'm so sorry. The traffic was crazy, and you picked a restaurant on the east side of Chicago. You had to know it would take me over an hour to get here from my place. I did my best, but I'm sorry."

I quickly handed her the gift, hoping to distract her. It worked. Her eyes went big as she turned the small box over. I took the moment to drink the water that was in front of me. It was then that I got a chance to see who all was at the table.

Sammy and Jasmine, Jimmy and Ramsey's kids, were off to my right, next to them sat Jackson, and next to him was Jimmy, Ramsey's husband.

My eyes slowly moved back from Jimmy to my fake ex. Whenever I saw Jackson, I had to control my breathing. He was still completely handsome, his jaw was still all chiseled and model-like, and his eyes were the kind of blue that made you feel like you were drowning in the middle of the arctic ocean.

I drank some more water, trying to control the flush of red that was creeping into my face. Seeing Jackson after all these months was like someone ripping off a bandage and proving that the wound you swore was healed had never even been properly stitched.

"Laney, this is perfect." Ramsey gasped next to me.

I looked down at the small object she held in her hand and smiled at her. "I'm so glad you like it. I thought of you when I saw a post from someone who used their company." Ramsey took the piece of silver and looked at it with reverence.

"What is it?" Jasmine, her eleven-year-old, asked. Ramsey passed the silver medallion down the table to show everyone as I answered.

"It has your initials and birth dates engraved on it, as well as your dad's. It can be put into a necklace or bracelet, really whatever your mom decides on."

Jasmine's eyes lit up as she held it. I glanced up to see other reactions, mainly Jimmy's, but my traitorous eyes landed on Jackson's face instead. He was watching me with his jaw set, his crisp blue eyes gleaming. My face flushed, and I looked away. *What the hell was that look?*

"Nice of you to join us, Laney. Thought you'd bailed." Jackson's accusatory tone cut through the happy moment of gift giving. Thankfully the kids didn't pick up on it or didn't act like they did. Jimmy and Ramsey did though.

"It's fine, no need to even mention it," Ramsey said, waving a hand in the air dismissively, trying to keep the peace. I would be peaceful for her, but I was glaring so hard at Jackson I was afraid my eyes would get stuck.

I took another drink of water and gave Jackson a tight smile. I turned my attention to Jasmine, who had her hair in two tight braids.

"How's school going, sweet pea?" I asked, rubbing her petite shoulders.

She gave me a half-smile and carefully replied, "Good, but, um...how come you don't come over with Uncle Jax anymore? I miss you."

My heart wilted. I could feel Jackson watching me, and I hated how much I wanted to point my non-manicured nail at him and yell for everyone to hear that he didn't want me and it was all his fault. But I didn't, because it wasn't.

The truth was, I had stopped going partly because I had no extra money to make the trip, but also, I would have had to work out an alternating schedule with Jackson, and I refused to speak to the man. "Work has been crazy, sweetie, but I will come visit soon," I promised her, and I meant it. I would figure something out, even if I had to sell my bodily fluids, even if I had to be mature and start accepting Jackson's calls.

One of the servers I had accidently pushed before appeared by my side and slightly bent over me to ask, "Anything to drink or eat for you, miss?"

I looked up and smiled wide, partly because I needed food and partly because he was handsome. "Martini, please, and the steak salad. By the way, I'm really sorry about earlier." I winced again, remembering the bowl of soup that had spilled on his tray because of me.

The cute server gave me a side smile, which lit up his square jaw, and leaned closer. "Not to be inappropriate, but you're welcome to put your hands on me any time you want." He winked and walked away.

I let out a little laugh and looked over at Ramsey, who was holding back a laugh with her hand. Once he was out of earshot, she let it out in a loud burst.

"Oh my God! That was hilarious. You should have seen your face, Lane." She lightly hit my shoulder then sipped her water. My face flushed red, like it had when the server made his comment.

Jasmine giggled next to me and singsonged, "Aunt Laney's got a new boyfriend."

Sammy laughed, but everyone was else was quiet. It was awkward. I would die before letting my gaze snatch up whatever expression was currently on Jackson's face. I cleared my throat, needing a second to myself; I squeezed Ramsey's leg under the table.

"Excuse me for just a second, I need to use the restroom." I stood and carefully navigated the full restaurant until I found a narrow hallway leading to the bathrooms.

Once I was inside, I shut myself into a stall just as a few tears started silently slipping down my cheeks. I was thirty years old and struggling to handle seeing my ex, like I was some sixteen-year-old teenager. The same questions that had run through my head the day he dumped me were still on repeat in my mind.

Why didn't he want me? Why wasn't I enough? Was my PTSD too much for him?

I wiped at my tears and left the stall. I looked at my reflection in the mirror. My red hair looked as flat as a pancake. There was some desperate part of me that wanted to fix it and make it look vibrant, but because that seemed counterproductive, I was tempted to find a hair tie and just throw all of it up into a bun.

I tried to fix my makeup as much as I could, then just decided to let it go. It didn't matter anyway; he didn't want me. I pulled down the hemline of my black dress, fixed the thin straps on my shoulders, and headed out of the bathroom.

I walked a few steps down the hallway before I stopped at the sight of Jackson leaning against the wall. His arms were crossed, and his jaw was set, the muscles in it jumping. I waited for him to say something, but he just stood there staring at me. Frustrated and annoyed, I began to walk away from him—until I heard him say, "Why won't you return my calls?"

I turned back toward him to see his face. I needed to check for signs of drug use, because he couldn't be that dense.

"I've tried several times over the last few months...but you never answer. You ignore my emails and my texts. Why?" he continued, sounding almost...pained.

I swallowed, trying really hard not to cry again. "You left me, Jackson. You dumped me...you didn't want me. That's why."

His eyes narrowed on me before he closed the gap between us. He stood directly in front of me; I could smell his Old Spice and mint scent, and I still wanted to drown in it.

With some misplaced desperation, in a raspy voice, he said, "It was never an issue of me wanting you."

I watched his mouth as they delivered the words I wanted to hear and explored his eyes for the truth I needed to believe, but I came up empty. Jackson was a robot, never betraying any emotion other than frustration or menace.

I tried to concentrate on our positions instead and quickly realized how much I hated how we stood. It was too easy to grab his shirt, to let his arms come around me. I gripped my dress in my fists to hold off the urge to touch him.

"What difference does it make now?" I whispered, glaring at his lips as if their mere existence teased and reminded me of everything I'd lost.

Jackson's eyes searched mine, and for a single second it was like time stopped and we were just two people stuck in a nightmare we couldn't wake up from. Like at any moment the sun would barge into his room and we'd wake up in each other's arms and he'd smile at me and bend down to kiss me like he used to. But this wasn't a dream, and I hadn't been in his arms in three months.

I dropped my eyes to the carpet at our feet, needing to break the moment. I let out a sigh I had been holding in and started to walk away. Before I made it to the end of the hall, I heard him ask, "Can we talk before you leave?"

I paused, and damn my emotions and damn the history I had with this man, because I nodded my head yes then continued back to the table.

Ramsey and Jimmy were the epitome of a picture-perfect family. The scene before me nearly stole my breath. Ramsey in a modest, black cocktail dress, her hair nicely curled. Jimmy in a tailored black suit and his kids each in cute little outfits. Sammy was making goofy faces as he tried the stuffed mushrooms. Jasmine kept laughing but trying to hide it behind her cloth napkin. My chest wanted to open up and swallow them whole, to keep them just like that forever.

Blinking, I pushed through the familiar burn in my throat that was tied to the idea of ever having a family or settling down. I'd never even thought of it until I met Jackson. *The damn irony.*

I started forward, clearing my throat and settling back in with my pseudo-family, eager to hear the news Ramsey had mentioned when she'd roped me into this dinner. I leaned forward to snag the martini that had been delivered while I was away and relished the burn as it slid down my throat.

Jackson filled his seat a moment later while holding a small tumbler of amber liquid. His stormy eyes met mine briefly before he tipped it back. Jimmy gave him a pinched look before turning back to the rest of us.

"Well, should we spill the beans?" Ramsey jokingly asked her kids while raising her hands slightly in an "I don't know" gesture.

Sammy sat up and tucked one leg under his bottom to gain some height, and Jasmine carefully folded her hands on the table and looked between Jackson and me. Suddenly I was thankful I wasn't the only one out of the loop here. The Stenson family had us outnumbered.

"As you both know, we wanted to wait on adding to our family...and you probably also know we weren't even trying. But the Lord works in mysterious ways because we're pregnant," Ramsey said with a huge grin displaying her white teeth. Sammy jumped in his seat while saying "Yes" and dragging out the S sound. I watched the utter joy cresting over my best friend's face and lurched forward until she was in my arms.

"I'm so excited for you guys," I whispered into her ear, holding back tears that would put the Nile River to shame.

Ramsey leaned back and swiped at her wet face then grabbed Jimmy's hand.

"We wanted to ask you both something," Jimmy calmly said, swinging his gaze back and forth between Jackson and myself.

My heart did a little double flip at what he might ask that involved both of us.

"Jackson used to bear this burden alone, but we've actually been talking about having legal documents drawn up to make both of you our kids' legal godparents, their guardians if something should ever happen to us." Jimmy finished explaining while bringing Ramsey's hand to his lips and pressing a small kiss there. They were disgustingly happy. I worked through what they'd said and tried to make sense of it.

Legal guardian? Godparent...me and Jackson. All the terms were slowly filtering through my brain like molasses. My eyes jumped to Jackson's across the table and waited for a response.

Before either of us could say anything, a woman stopped at our table.

"Oh my god! Jackson, is that you?" she exclaimed while gripping his bicep and leaning back to get a better view. She had on a tight-fitting evening gown with sequins and pearls, her neckline dipped to her navel, and her hair was so white it almost blended with the table linen. Jackson flicked his gaze to hers and gave her a tight smile of annoyance.

"Pristine. How nice to see you," he replied with a cold but polite tone.

She leaned closer until her breasts were pushed together and her bronze skin was nearly touching his. "Two months I believe since we..." She not so covertly coughed and continued, "Had some fun. You never called me after Italy though," she whined, oblivious to the confused and rather annoyed stares around the table. At the mention of my supposed getaway with Jackson, I froze.

Jackson looked down and let out a halfhearted laugh. "Now isn't the best time to discuss this. It was nice to see you, but I'm with family." He lifted a hand and gestured toward Sammy.

"Oh, my word. Where are my manners?" She brought her perfectly manicured nails to cover her lips. She was not about to introduce her—

"I'm Pristine, an old girlfriend of Jackson's. It's so nice to meet you all." She gushed and waved at Jimmy—only Jimmy. Ramsey looked feral. Jackson looked like someone had just gouged an eye out, and I'm sure I looked like someone had just told me Jackson had had a girlfriend after he dumped me.

I would be happy for my best friend. I would come to her birthday party and face the man who shattered my heart, but I would not sit there and watch the woman who'd replaced me meet *my* family.

I worked my jaw to the side and gripped Ramsey's hand under the table while leaning toward her ear.

"I love you. Come see me after this. I can't do this."

She squeezed my hand and kissed my cheek. "Of course. Get out of here." She gave me a slight nod of her head and dismissed me.

Pristine was talking to Sammy about sharks, and I swear she was two seconds from pulling up a chair. In fact...

"Here, Pristine, would you like to sit? I was just heading out." I stood and gestured to my seat. She beamed like a newly installed headlight.

"I'd love to, thank you so much!" She squealed and started walking around the kids, but I knew Jackson was going to spoil the fun.

"Actually Pristine, this is a family event. Now isn't a good time. We will have to catch up later." His eyes pinned me in place, as though I was the weirdo who'd just crashed his family event. I didn't stick around to hear what Pristine said. I knew Jackson wanted to tell me to stay since he'd asked to talk to me, but he also had to tell her not to sit, so I took advantage and walked away.

I crossed my arms as I pushed through the heavy glass doors, wincing at the realization that this side of town was going to cost me at least another thirty bucks in cab fare. I loved my friend and I was so glad I'd come here tonight for her, but I was broke as shit. Maybe I could just find a bus or take the train. Once outside, I looked from side to side, weighing my options, then a black car pulled up to the curb. It was a town car like Jackson used to have. Knowing it was for someone with more money than me, I stepped to the side to get out of the way. The driver got out and jogged around the car, heading straight for me.

It was Lance, Jackson's driver.

My heart did a little lurch at seeing him. I really liked Lance; he was just an unfortunate victim in the mess that had once been Jackson and me.

"Ms. Thompson, please allow me to take you home. Mr. Tate just texted that he'd like you to take his car," Lance explained in a faded British accent. He looked the same; I supposed that was no surprise after only three months. His thin, blond hair was losing the battle to gray and was still strategically brushed to the side, and his eyes still had those laughter lines from being happy with his wife for twenty-five years. I swallowed the thick lump of anger and resentment in my throat. I wanted to say hell no, but common sense was practically screaming my current bank balance at me.

Besides, Lance wasn't just an employee of Jackson's; he was a friend. He was *my* friend. I looked at the ground to hide my embarrassment and gently nodded my agreement. Some tiny part of me felt a kernel of hope warm my chest that Jackson still cared about me. I needed to find some way to crush that kernel because I couldn't fall back into Jackson's world, not after he'd nearly ruined mine.

4

JACKSON

For it being August, it was surprisingly chilly, which was nice because the damp air felt good on my skin. It was almost as if my body remembered the last heatwave that had hit the city and relished the cooler weather. The spray from the large fountains in Lake Shore Park added to the cooler moisture as I pushed myself to complete another mile. I had already run the entire park twice, and my head still wasn't clear.

It was like my mind had pressed pause and freeze-framed the moment Laney stood to leave the restaurant. I shouldn't have cared, and I wished that I didn't, but my damn mind was serving up its own form of penance by way of repetition. Laney's face was strained, her eyes were narrowed, and her gorgeous auburn hair had fallen across her shoulders, its red mixing in with the creamy white of her bare shoulders. The way her face flushed and her lip trembled made me want to punch something. I had hurt her *again*.

I stopped mid-step and leaned forward to rest my hands on my knees. I tried to get my breathing under control as I tipped my head to the sky. This part of the park was practically deserted since there weren't many trees to offer shade from the summer sun. I tried to ignore how light it had gotten, knowing it meant I needed to get home and shower. I had a big meeting this morning that I needed to get ready for, but first, I needed to officially eradicate what had happened the previous night and get it out of my system. For the first time in three months, I didn't want to flush it with whiskey, just clean air, sweat, and sunshine.

I pushed past the corner of the park and continued down the bridge, past several other runners, continuing until I came to East Brenton Street. I slowed down and started walking to slow my heart rate.

I tried to focus my mind on the upcoming appointment, on why August Torson would want a meeting with me, why he had picked me out of millions of business owners to meet with and why it *had* to be on a Sunday, the one day I actually took off from work. I could have asked him to reschedule, but I wasn't an idiot and anyone who knew anyone in the big billionaire circles knew if August Torson called you up, you moved everyone else on your calendar around to fit him in, even if it fell on Christmas morning.

I walked toward the black town car and waved at my driver. Lance jumped out to grab the door for me, but I shook my head, reminding him that he didn't need to open it for me.

"Lance, no need." I waved him off, but he beat me to it. I stopped and looked at the opened door and then back at my driver's face.

"What's with the manners today? Last week I was sore from working out and actually asked you to open my door, and you laughed at me while eating a hotdog in the driver's seat." I tipped my head to the side to further inspect my stiff-necked chauffeur.

"It's a part of my contract, sir," Lance replied plainly without meeting my stare.

Sir?

I shook my head and brought my hands to my hips. "Lance, what's going on?"

He gave me a stiff smile but didn't look at me as he asked, "You ready, sir?"

I ignored the door and wiped the sweat from my face. There was AC waiting for me in the car, but I refused to move until I knew what the hell was up his ass this morning. It was Sunday and he didn't normally work on Sundays, so maybe he was upset about that? "You mad that I made you work today? I already told you that you didn't have to pick me up." I tried to argue, but his jaw just set firmer than before.

He stood frozen with the door open. I waited; the sun had now climbed even higher, and the cool air I had felt before was starting to warm.

"Lance, come on man—tell me what's going on," I pleaded, because enough was enough. He finally met my gaze, revealing an angry storm of emotions.

"It's not my place, sir," Lance responded coldly, emphasizing the sir part of his comment.

Fuck this.

I grabbed for the door again, threw it open, and got in the car. I didn't need this shit today, not after Laney and not after the shitshow with Pristine the night before. "Let's get home then," I coldly stated while looking out the window. If he didn't want to talk, we didn't need to.

Lance slowly pulled away from the curb and started merging into traffic, all while periodically glancing at me in the rear-view mirror.

He wanted to say something; I knew he did. "Lance, spit it out. I'm not in the fucking mood for this today," I spat at him then reached for my water.

He let out another long sigh and cleared his throat. "You're a damn fool," he declared with a shaky tone, almost like he wanted to yell but he was controlling it.

"Come again?" I asked, watching his reflection in the rear-view mirror.

"I've seen numerous couples throughout the years of being a driver. I've witnessed affairs and broken marriages, people who are truly wrong for each other. What you and Ms. Thompson had was one of the most genuine things I've ever witnessed." He pinned me with a glare and finished with: "Yet, you let her go."

Of course this was about Laney. They must have had quite the little chat the night before when he took her home, not that Lance was any stranger to my dynamic with Laney since he drove us almost everywhere when we were together. Lance had grown fond of Laney and I knew that, which was why I'd thought she'd accept a ride from him.

I knew she had no money for another cab back to the west side of the city, and I knew she'd contemplate riding the train or bus—both things I couldn't and wouldn't allow. She may have left my life three months ago, but that didn't mean I would risk her safety.

Not any more than I already had.

I ran my hand over my head and prepared to answer Lance's sentiment.

"It's not that simple." I watched the passing buildings, trying to ignore how much that simple statement stung.

"Nothing worth keeping is ever simple. It's not the simple things that countries go to war over," Lance replied softly.

He had me there.

Laney was worth going to war for, but once I'd won her over, what would I say? I was the same bitter, bastard I'd always been. Nothing had changed. She deserved better than some self-destructive asshole who refused to commit. Besides, it had been bred into me.

My father's parting words before I left for college were: "Don't fuck up your life by settling down. Build your empire and remember that commitment is a coffin."

I finally replied to Lance's comment. "You're right. And she deserves better." I glared at the mirror as he pulled up to the curb outside my building. He scoffed and shook his head back and forth. He put the car in park but made no move to open the door or respond.

I watched my friend in the mirror and locked my jaw, biting down all the words I wanted to shout at him, all the things I wanted him to hear from my side of this, but it wouldn't do any good. Everyone loved Laney; I'd already heard an earful from Jimmy when Laney and I first ended things. Or rather...when I ended them.

I opened the door and slammed it shut behind me. Without looking back, I ran up my stairs. I didn't need to deal with this shit before my meeting. Laney wasn't the only person in this situation who'd been hurting.

I PULLED INTO THE RESERVED SPACE IN FRONT OF MY RESTAURANT, Savor, located in the heart of downtown Chicago. I looked up at the tall skyscrapers that seemed to smother all the sunlight trying to reach the lower buildings and smiled. I loved this spot in the city. The building I had leased was a simple two-story design with glass windows and black brick. The signage above the large doors said *Savor* in cursive, gold lettering. This was one of the most coveted spots in the city, which was another reason it had earned its five-star rating. The restaurant had hardwood floors running everywhere, along with floor-to-ceiling windows that let the light spill in. Darker steel ceiling beams gave the restaurant a more industrial feel.

I walked along the rows of tables adorned in white tablecloths and eventually made my way to the back of the bar area where Mr. Torson was waiting with a small glass of amber liquid.

"Hello, Mr. Torson." I leaned forward and shook the thin, short man's hand. The light from the room reflected off his tinny gray hair, exposing his age, which was likely close to seventy or so.

"Mr. Tate, nice to see you." He rose a fraction, shook my hand, and reclaimed his seat. Jesse, our afternoon server, brought us water and a bottle of bourbon, which I assumed was in Mr. Torson's glass. I poured myself a small amount and sat back in my chair.

"So, to what do I owe this honor?" I asked while letting the smoky flavor of the bourbon make its way down my throat.

He waited, looking around the room, before his eyes landed on me. "I've been watching your business, Mr. Tate," Torson began, leaning back in his chair and crossing one leg over the other. "I like what I see in Savor, but I'm disappointed with your second startup, Singe."

I tried to ignore the stabbing feeling in my gut. I didn't get prideful over many things, but my work was at the top of that list. It was no secret that my second startup was a bust, but it still burned like hell to have it brought up by one of the most influential men in Chicago. I leaned back and cleared my throat.

"I'm not in the habit of discussing the private details of my business with strangers."

Torson smiled and kicked his right foot that lay over his left leg. "I think your lack of numbers in Singe are repairable." He gave me a tight smile and continued, "With my help."

I waited for him to continue; I'd be an idiot to turn down his offer of help, in whatever shape that might take. Torson moved his glass to the left as he watched me.

"I have a proposition for you, Mr. Tate. I'd like you to consider turning Savor into a franchise. Keep the name, nix the second installment of Singe. I'll pay whatever is needed to cut the loss."

Get rid of all the work and money I'd sunk into Singe and just write it off? Franchise Savor? I rolled the idea around in my head. Two months earlier, I would have thrown Torson out at his audacious offer, but currently I wasn't in a position to turn down the help. Unfortunately, my efforts with Dyson and Reed had gone up in flames after I fired Laney from the project. Hiring the company to help me start up my second restaurant was how I met Laney, we didn't start off on the best of terms, but after an incident with her building she ended up staying with me... from there, we were already addicted to one another...but she'd removed herself completely from my team after her attack. The seven months we were around each other, we didn't talk about the new startup; it was a taboo subject, and her therapist suggested for her PTSD that we just move on as if what she'd gone through hadn't happened. So, we had, and a byproduct of losing Laney to that project was me drowning in debt with my second restaurant attempt.

As embarrassing as it was that Mr. Torson knew about my failure, I needed to be smart regarding his proposition. "Why exactly would you be interested in helping me?" I asked, while swirling my drink.

Torson's eyes narrowed on me while a thin smile quickly appeared on his slightly wrinkled face. "Let's just say a very old friend of mine put you on my radar, and after looking into the numbers, I feel it could be lucrative for me."

Uneasiness spread through me. What friend? I didn't know anyone in the circles he ran in. My father did, but I hadn't spoken to him in nearly ten years. I didn't want to sound petulant by pressing him for more details, so I cleared my throat and said, "That's a generous offer, but it's one I'll need to think about." I stood as Torson did and we shook hands, but before he left, he gave me a strange look.

"Think about it, but say yes. It will be worth it. I promise."

I nodded, not sure how else to respond, and watched as he went on his way.

There would be so many things we'd have to go over if I entertained his offer, but for now I needed to clear my head from the previous night.

I didn't have any other reasons to stay in the restaurant now that my meeting was through, so I grabbed some lunch and headed home.

I tried to ignore the fact that my three phone calls and six text messages had gone unanswered by Laney. I realized I was coming on a little strong, but she said we could talk and then she left. I understood why she did...fucking Pristine. What kind of terrible luck had I been dealt to have that woman stop at our table? A socialite from a common business circle who'd happened to be traveling to Italy at the same time as me. I was depressed and drunk, and missing Laney. We had planned the trip to Italy together, and I had stupidly gone alone to convince myself I was over her and my relationship with her had been as superficial as I kept saying it was.

It only proved to be torture. So, when Pristine threw herself where she wasn't invited, and one night ended up at my door. Nothing happened, but the words she'd already said would do as much damage as if something had. I was an idiot, I should have never even gone on that fucking trip.

I grabbed the mail on my way in from the garage and headed into my house, hating how much I remembered the first time Laney had walked through these doors almost a year earlier.

I set the mail down on the desk and started my laptop. Tearing into the larger manila envelope, I began pulling a few documents free, realizing I hadn't even checked to see who it was from. I scanned the first page and my blood froze.

FROM THE CIRCUIT COURT OF COOK COUNTY:

IN ACCORDANCE WITH THE PETITION YOU FILED AGAINST ALICIA Miller on December 21st, 2017, case no. 81-C-56987555, the circuit court is notifying you of a change in sentencing. The respondent has been approved to fulfill 1/3 of her original 24-month sentence due to good behavior and clearly indicated remorse. The respondent will still be held to the original terms of her no contact order in the aforementioned case. The petitioner, Tate, Jackson will be legally bound to have no contact with respondent for the duration of the order. The respondent will have a parole officer to ensure she's not living within a five-mile radius of your already registered residence.

If you have any questions, feel free to call the municipal court of Cook County.

SINCERELY,
   Lex Brown, City Clerk
   Cook County Municipal Court

I SLAMMED THE PAPERS DOWN HARD ON MY DESK AND PULLED UP THE contact for the only person who could hopefully explain to me in English what the fuck had just happened. If I understood this correctly, it meant my previous stalker and Laney's attacker was getting out of jail a year and a half early.

5

LANEY

I PRESSED THE BLACK PEN FIRMLY INTO THE YELLOW LEGAL PAD AND drew a large circle, then drew another circle inside of it, and then another, and I kept going until I had consumed half the paper. I let up and started in again on a clean section of the pad, this time drawing triangles. I had been drawing and doodling for close to an hour. That was also how long Brenda the Boring had been droning on about our new HR policy handbooks. I was halfway slumped over on the conference table with one hand holding up my head, the other hand on the table drawing random shapes.

I lifted my head to see if anyone had noticed that I was utterly checked out. Around the table, three of my colleagues were picking at their nails, two of them were nodding off, and at least two more were secretly texting on their phones. No one seemed to notice, probably because everyone checked out when Brenda started talking.

Brenda was a tall, skinny woman, all limbs and loose skin. Her pale skin looked blotchy beneath her bright and heavy makeup, and she had a tight bun at the back of her head with absolutely no fly-away hairs. I wondered how much hairspray she must go through on a regular basis. Her brown eyes looked tired. She probably bored herself to near death all the time. She probably had a medical alert button tied around her neck for when she talked out loud to herself.

I shouldn't have been so mean, but I was tired and annoyed. It had been three days since I left Jackson at the restaurant. It had been three days since he started texting me again, and each day my resistance to communicating with him was getting weaker and weaker.

"Turn to page thirty-seven in your policy handbook and we will review appropriate email conduct," Brenda announced from the head of the table. I was going to die. I really was. I looked around the table, and based on the muffled groans from half the group, I thought maybe everyone else was going to die too. What a way to go out—no big declaration of love or bullets, just a pencil and an HR manual.

I thought about the texts I had gotten from Jackson over the last three days. The first one was expected.

Jackson: *You said we could talk tonight*

I didn't respond. I didn't know how to, honestly.

Jackson: *Dammit, Laney we need to talk*

I still didn't respond, because it didn't matter. He may have felt bad for having me hear that he'd moved on and actually gotten himself a girlfriend, one he took to Italy with him, but he didn't owe me anything. He must have gotten over that little commitment issue he had. Then he called me, left a voicemail, but I didn't listen to it. There was nothing he could say that would fix things between us. He wanted me as a convenient friend, or at least someone who didn't hate him. He seemed conflicted and had for the past three months, but especially now that I knew about his galivanting.

I tried to tell myself I didn't want Jackson Tate, didn't need him and would never give him access to my heart again.

Blocking his number was a big step, but it was one I was ready for. I needed to date someone other than him and get the hell back out there. Suddenly the utter exhaustion from the past year of wasting my time with someone who didn't want me hit like a Mack Truck. My throat burned, and my eyes stung. Right in the middle of Brenda the Boring's speech, I stood up and left the conference room. I needed a bathroom stall and some tissue.

I was wiping snot, gross tears, and somehow a little drool when I heard someone enter the bathroom. They didn't talk or make any noise, just walked into the stall next to me. I ignored them and continued to wipe at my face, but the person next to me wasn't making any indication that they needed to use the toilet.

I paused as goose bumps erupted on my arms. After everything I had been through, I'd learned not to second guess my gut. I hadn't brought my purse with me, which had pepper spray and a flashlight taser in it, courtesy of my best friend. I pulled my hands into my chest, balled my fists up, and closed my eyes. I didn't have a weapon, and it made my throat constrict.

It felt like it was getting darker in the room, but I knew that was just the fear. The person in the stall next to mine finally shuffled their feet before a clicking sound filled the space, followed by the sounds of recorded voices.

I was frozen.

I felt like a little kid again, afraid of the dark after hearing a strange sound in the middle of the night. I forced air into my lungs as tears clogged my eyes. I couldn't do this. A moment later, sound exploded into the silent space.

"You're the best, baby." It was Jackson's voice.

This wasn't happening.

My breathing turned shallow. I knew the conversation that was playing out. He was talking to me over speakerphone in his office, right after I told him I had gotten us tickets to see the playoffs.

My heart was beating so hard I honestly thought it might explode. How was this happening? The only person who would do this was currently serving her time out in a state penitentiary and would be for at least another year and a half.

This had to be a joke...but who would do this?

I needed to get out of there.

I was about to slam the door open when I heard another recorded voice, or rather a laugh. It was creepy and created a chill that ran down my spine. I used the increased volume of the laugh to cover my movements as I opened my stall, spun around to the door next to mine, and kicked it open. There on the silver trash bin, attached to the wall, was a small black voice recorder, but no one was in the stall.

I looked around the bathroom as my chest heaved. My blood pressure spiked, and my fingers trembled. I tried to think of all my therapist's coping techniques, but my mind had gone blank. First and foremost, I needed to get the hell out of there. I grabbed some toilet paper, snagged the recorder, and ran out of the bathroom.

THE POLICE STATION WAS BUSY FOR A WEDNESDAY, AT LEAST I thought it was—I actually had no idea how busy a police station should be on a regular basis. I grew up in a small town in Indiana, and any time I was in our little police office, which was often because my uncle was on the force, there was never anyone in there.

My brothers and I used to play games in the office, hide under desks, use up as much water as possible from the water cooler, and even pretend to drink coffee by pouring in milk, about a sip of coffee, and a small country's worth of sugar. An ache like no other entered my chest as I thought about my brothers, realizing how long it'd been since I had seen them.

"Can I help you, miss?" asked a tall officer. His blond hair was styled handsomely, and his smile brightened the beige room. He also looked like he might have just graduated high school, so I needed to rein in it and stop staring.

"Uh yeah...I need to speak with Detective Gepsy please," I replied with a tight smile. The kid turned around to consult another police officer, one who looked a bit older and might actually be allowed to buy cigarettes.

"He's in his office. Come on, I'll lead you back," Police Kid offered. I gripped my handbag tighter and followed him down the hall and up a small set of steps into a larger office space with sequestered cubicles and glass windows.

There were four desks and a long table with printers and other things set up on it. All the way toward the back of the space was a large office with floor-to-ceiling windows covered in cheap blinds. They were dented and damaged, like someone had pushed someone or something against them...repeatedly.

My tour guide knocked on the door, and a gruff voice yelled in response. "Busy!" The kid's face flushed red as he peeked at me from over his shoulder. He stood there like he wasn't sure what to do next. I was about to step up and knock when the kid went to open the door.

"Sir, sorry to interrupt, but..." He'd opened the door and stopped talking when he saw the arctic glare from the person sitting in front of Gepsy's desk.

I'd have frozen too because that glare was one that had made me want to cry a time or two. Jackson Tate sat in a deteriorating blue chair that had stuffing falling out the sides. He sat adjacent to Gepsy with a small white cup of coffee in one hand and a large manila envelope in the other. His gaze traveled from the interrupting police kid to me and then softened.

"Laney, glad you stopped by. We need to talk," Gepsy said while standing from his desk. He was so bulky and tall his desk looked miniature next to him.

The police kid half-smiled and turned to walk away. I staggered for a second, thrown by Jackson's presence. Gepsy must have noticed my frozen stature in his doorway and motioned to the chair next to Jackson.

"Take a seat. I assume you received this letter as well?" he asked as he reclaimed his chair. That had me walking in, closing the door, and sitting next to the man who'd shattered my heart.

"What letter?" I asked as I pulled out the voice recorder that was still wrapped in toilet paper. Gepsy leaned forward to grab the envelope Jackson had been holding. Jackson's eyes narrowed on me, as though he was searching for something to be out of place. I kept my focus forward, trying not to notice that he wore a plain t-shirt made of that stretchy jersey material I used to love sleeping in. The navy blue one he had on today was my favorite; I liked how well it matched his eyes.

I turned my attention on Gepsy too and watched as he revealed a white piece of paper and began reading off facts and details about Alicia Miller and her sentencing being cut down to a third of her original time. My pulse jumped as I heard the rest of the letter stating that she was being released. Set free.

Freed from the place that kept her far away from me, ensuring my safety.

"Didn't you get this letter as well since you filed your own petition against her?" Gepsy asked, sipping his coffee. I was still digesting the news and didn't have the words to reply. I eventually shook my head to confirm that no, I hadn't heard that the woman who'd attacked me and tried to end my life was being let out of prison after only serving eight months.

Gepsy let out a sigh and laid the paper down then noticed my toilet-papered piece of evidence. "What's that?" he asked, pointing his finger toward it.

I carefully shoved it forward while swallowing the thick lump in my throat. "Someone followed me into the bathroom today at work. Went into the stall next to me and started playing this." I gestured to the thin black device. "When I tried to confront them, they were gone. I brought it to see if you could find any prints." Gepsy narrowed his eyes and grabbed some plastic gloves from his desk drawer. He pressed play on the recorder, and we all heard the same thing I had.

When Jackson heard his voice, he stiffened next to me. I knew without looking at him that his jaw was ticking, and he was doing that thing with his teeth that his dentist told him not to do. Gepsy let the rest of the tape play, most of which was just random conversations collected from Jackson, and then a few from me. None of it made any sense, then there was a silent bit that sounded like blankets ruffling, until the sound of a low moan filled the room. *Holy shit.*

My face was on fire as more moans echoed through the room. That was me, and I knew what was coming next.

"You like that, baby?" Jackson's husky voice filled the room.

Oh my God, I was going to be sick. Absolutely no one needed to hear what was coming next, so I pushed forward to grab the recorder when Gepsy stopped me.

"I'll turn it off. Sounds like it's just recordings of the two of you at various times during your..." Gepsy coughed and stifled a smile before he finished with, "uh...relationship." I touched my cheeks with my cold hands, trying to cool the red that was invading my face. I didn't want to see Jackson's expression; I had no idea how we would handle that level of privacy invasion. This stuff had never embarrassed him before, even when we'd gone through this humiliation the first time, even when photos of the two of us together in bed made their way to my office with the words *Whore* written all over the few hundred copies that had been scattered throughout the floor—but there was a first time for everything.

"We're going to assume this was her. Although, until we can prove it, we can't do anything with it. But it matches her previous tactics," Gepsy said while putting the recorder into a plastic evidence bag.

I didn't respond, but Jackson leaned forward, the defined muscles in his back stretching with the fabric of the t-shirt, and all I wanted to do was run my hand up and down the hard lines. It wasn't because it was a sexual thing between us, but because I naturally wanted to touch him when I felt triggered or like things were spinning out of control. I shoved my hands in between my thighs and pushed my legs together to keep them there.

"So, what the hell is going on with this, Gepsy? Why are they letting her out? She had two separate cases filed against her. Stalking is a class four felony in the state of Illinois, and the fact that she attacked Laney secured not only that felony but two years in jail. I thought this was a sure thing?"

Jackson's voice had raised an octave, and he began pushing his pointer finger into the documents on the desk. Gepsy had handled our original case with Alicia when her stalking started about a year ago. Jackson was helping his best friend Jimmy get out of the motorcycle gang he was a part of, which connected him to Gepsy. I started working with Jackson around the same time, and he'd appointed me as the person of contact from Dyson and Reed to keep him apprised of everything that happened with the company and his restaurant. That was how I met his assistant Alicia.

"Look..." Gepsy let out a sigh and leaned back in his chair. "These things happen, and they're out of our control. It's common for inmates who have good behavior or suddenly show remorse concerning their charges to be up for cutting their sentence down. Usually they have to serve at least a year, but in some rare cases, it can be bumped up. Blame the overcrowded system. She will have a parole officer and will have to jump through a bunch of hoops to stay out of prison, but there's not much we can do about her being let out early." He finished with his hands open, like he was reading a book.

I finally found my voice and said, "Except it seems like she's already broken parole by coming within 100 yards of me. The no contact order is supposed to still be in place, so if she's already tracked me down to intimidate me, what the fuck am I supposed to do? Wait around to be strangled again?"

Fear was taking control. My therapist suggested I stay seated and try to breathe when I felt out of control or like something was too big for me to handle. So, I stayed in my seat, released my hands, and crossed them over my chest.

Jackson watched me with a small furrow of his eyebrows. He knew my triggers, knew what would set me off, knew how unstable I was—all because that psycho had hunted me, hurt me, and messed with my mind. I'd moved out of my apartment because of her, changed all my contact info. The only thing I couldn't do was change jobs because my student loan debt had smothered the hell out of me and I was drowning under the weight of it.

"Look, I can't prove it, but I have a contact who's been feeding me info on a dirty federal judge. Alicia shouldn't have gotten out this early— it's not usually done with the evidence stacked against her. Something about this feels off. I can't prove it, but if this is tied to that judge then yes, you likely are going to be putting yourself at risk for a repeat." Gepsy speculated while watching his door and leaning forward.

My chest tightened and breathing became difficult. The nightmare I had just left behind was coming back for a sequel. She was going to finish me this time, and I wasn't even with Jackson anymore.

"So, what do we do? We can't just sit around like sitting ducks," Jackson said while leaning back and watching me carefully. He looked like he was two seconds from touching me, which sucked because his touch calmed me and I really wanted him to, but the functioning, rational part of my body and brain didn't want him to cross that barrier between us.

"I can't do anything official with the department. Even if I did, there's a chance it would get back to her. Thanks to her knack for hacking, nothing you do electronically will be safe." Gepsy rubbed at his forehead and leaned into his chair. His silver hair was thinning and he'd almost gone bald, but it worked for him. "What I don't want to do is something rash, without thinking. Let's sleep on it, give it a day or two, and I will come up with something. For now, Laney, please consider staying with a friend. I don't want you alone until we figure this out."

I nodded my head in agreement. I knew he was right, but who the hell was I supposed to stay with? I started to list the people who might have a couch or a guest room in my head, ignoring the conversation playing out in front of me. Jackson and Gepsy were talking about something, but Gepsy got interrupted by a phone call. He bid us goodbye, and Jackson and I both left his office. Outside his door, Jackson tugged on my elbow to stop me from walking. No other detectives or assistants were on the floor at the moment, so it was just us.

"Stay with me, please?" Jackson asked, his blue eyes practically begging me to agree. I wanted to. Damn I wanted to, especially because he was my therapy buddy. He knew how to calm me down when things got out of control, knew how to make me smile, how to keep me safe. I hated that I loved him so completely still, and I was still just a number in his phone, a person he could call up and have fun with.

Just another name.

I summoned the memory of when he left me three months ago, thought of Pristine's face from the other night, and pulled my elbow free.

"I have someone to stay with." I walked forward without looking back and pulled out my cell phone. I had one lead, one friend who might help me. It was a long shot but one worth taking if it kept me out of Jackson's house.

I waited until I was free of the police station and free from Jackson to make my call, the reassuring words from the other night making their way through my head: *"If you need anything at all, anything. You call me."* Lance had said it while we shared an ice cream cone the. He'd known I needed to talk, so he had pulled up in front of Scooter's Frozen Custard Shop, my favorite spot.

I spilled the entire night to him like a gossiping school girl. That was just how Lance and I always were, two peas in a pod, gossiping and carrying on. I had gone to dinner at his house with his wife many times and had only stopped after Jackson broke things off with me. I felt like a jerk for letting my situation with Jackson affect our relationship, but I knew they'd help me out. I pulled up his contact info and dialed.

A few rings in, I heard him answer, "Lance Bettany." He must not have looked at his caller ID, which meant he might be driving...which meant Jackson might hear.

"Uh, hey Lance, it's Laney."

It was quiet for a second, then there were a few muffled sounds before he responded again. "Laney, nice to hear from you. What can I do for you?"

I smiled, knowing he'd help me out. "I need a favor."

6

JACKSON

SOME PEOPLE USE NOISE MACHINES WHEN THEY SLEEP. I USED TO LIKE the sound of the water mixed with the city, but after Laney, it was only a fan that could get me to sleep. She needed one every night, and after she slept here so often, I got used to it. However, the problem with having the fan on every night was the phantom warmth of Laney's body next to mine. I wanted her with me. Selfish as it was and always had been on my part, I wanted Laney. I couldn't promise her forever, couldn't offer her marriage or anything, really, except my warm arms and pathetic heart.

I knew that at one point she had wanted me too. I had seen this look in her eye when she would watch me or talk to me. She looked at me like she would wait for me, like she'd wait for as long as it took for me to figure this relationship shit out. I didn't see that look in her eyes anymore, and after she rejected me at the police department, I was surer than ever that she was done with me.

It was almost seven in the morning and I hadn't slept at all. I knew Laney was with Lance and Trina. I knew she was safe, but that damn fan reminded me of her absence in my bed every single time it rotated in my direction. It reminded me that Laney had been stalked the day before at work.

It reminded me that this nightmare wasn't behind us and that if

Gepsy didn't figure something out, there would be no way I'd let Laney live her life without some serious safety precautions. I knew how overwhelmed she usually ended up and how the anxiety would eat away at her stomach until she threw up, how she'd second-guess every single time she entered her office building. I knew all this because I had lived it with her for seven months.

Gepsy had to figure this out.

A second later I heard my phone chime. I rolled over until I could reach it.

Gepsy: *I have an idea, be here by 8*

I lowered the phone and sagged back into the bed. Thank God.

I punched out a quick reply and got up to shower.

I READJUSTED MY BACK IN THE OLD LEATHER CHAIR; IT WAS MISSING the soft stuffing that was usually inside these particular chairs, which made it infinitely uncomfortable. I looked around Gepsy's beige-colored office and read his accolades, awards, and honorable deeds from the academy that adorned the walls. I needed more of a distraction than this.

I had gotten to the station with ten minutes to spare and had been eagerly awaiting Gepsy ever since. I was about ready to get up to go find him when the door opened and Laney walked in with Gepsy following behind her. She was wearing worn jeans and flip-flops, no makeup, and her hair was in a messy bun. Laney going out in public without wearing high heels or makeup was a big deal. She only did it when she was exhausted or really upset and just didn't give a shit. Laney always gave a shit. I knew she likely hadn't gotten any sleep, just like me. Stressed, anxious, and afraid, no one to lay a cool rag on her neck or to help her breathe. No one to whisper in her ear that it was okay or play with her hair.

Gepsy sat down at his desk, facing the two of us. He wore a gray shirt and blue jeans with his badge around his neck. "Thank you both for getting here so early," he said while he arranged a few papers.

I glanced at Laney, but she wasn't looking at me. She was staring at the floor with her arms pulled in tight and her left leg crossed over the other.

"After we met yesterday, I talked to an old colleague of mine and came up with a plan...at least somewhat of a plan." Gepsy folded his hands and leaned forward, watching both of us while we waited for him to continue. "Keep in mind this is just an idea and one that is not sanctioned by the Chicago PD," he said while still watching his screen.

Laney leaned forward an inch, and so did I, still waiting for him to share his plan.

Finally, he finished typing and let us have it. "Witness protection, or something like it...that's my plan, but we can't go through the police database or make this official in any way. Just me trying to help set you guys up somewhere, like a safehouse. The key part to this is that it would give me some time to do a little digging to find out if someone helped Alicia get released early and if she was the one to leave that voice recorder in the bathroom yesterday."

I scratched the back of my neck as the idea settled into my brain.

Witness protection?

Hiding?

"How would we do that with our jobs and everything?" I asked, a little confused.

"Tell them you're off scouting a potential new restaurant location—something, anything but give yourself an out and don't say exactly where you'll be. Set some people that you trust in place and let them know you'll check in twice a week via email," he finished with a shrug of his shoulders. He turned to look at Laney, who still hadn't said anything. "Are you on any projects at the moment?"

Laney slowly shook her head and softly replied, "Actually we're on hiatus for two weeks to go through HR training."

"Perfect, and what about vacation time—do you have any available?" Gepsy asked, typing away on his computer.

"Yeah...I haven't taken any days off since..." She trailed off, carefully lifting her eyes until they met mine. *Since we broke up...*

Gepsy paused, looking between us. Clearing his throat, he declared, "Take a mini vacation. This probably won't take longer than a week, maybe two."

Laney stopped tapping the foot that was hanging off her leg and asked, "You won't say anything, right? She's probably bugged my work again, and I don't trust anyone there."

Gepsy nodded his agreement then asked another series of questions. "Do either of you have distant family or friends you could stay with? Just until we can investigate her moves without tipping her off or causing her to run?"

I slowly shook my head no while Laney shook her head yes. Gepsy ran a hand down his face and leaned back in his chair.

"Laney, what kind of family connections do you have, and when was the last time you saw or talked with them?"

Laney straightened her legs and kicked at a black scuff mark on the floor before she looked up to answer. "My parents live in Plainfield, Indiana, about three and half hours from here. They live on a big farm. I haven't spoken to anyone since my birthday, which was in April." Laney said the last part like she was embarrassed, and I looked over and saw her cheeks flushing red. I knew she didn't like that she was so distant from her family; it was something she constantly beat herself up about.

"That's actually perfect. If Alicia looks back through phone records —" Gepsy began but was cut off by Laney.

"We FaceTime on the computer. We always do. My parents don't carry their phones around with them unless they go on a trip. They always call me from their computer," Laney finished with a hopeful tone, like we'd finally caught a break in this stupid situation we were walking through.

"Perfect!" Gepsy beamed, then asked, "Do you think they would be opposed to housing you two until we can get this squared away?" I looked over to see Laney's reaction because I knew she'd have one. I knew she didn't want to be around me.

"I don't see why it's necessary to have Jackson come with me. Alicia doesn't want to hurt him," Laney argued while gesturing toward me with her arm.

I tried not to look defeated and spoke up to say, "Hey, she may not want to kill me, but I don't exactly want to be kidnapped and kept in her love dungeon."

Laney gave me a glare then rolled her eyes. I rolled mine right back.

Gepsy cut in then, "Look, we have no idea what her intentions are. If we have a place to put the two of you, we can keep you both safe at the same time without using credit cards or passports. The less likely the place, the better, and the less paper trail we leave behind, the better." Gepsy got back onto his computer again and started typing. "So, I'll ask you again: do you think your parents would be willing to put you both up for as long as it will take to get this settled?"

Laney was watching her feet, until she let out a sigh and then responded, "Yes. My parents are very welcoming and wouldn't have a problem with either of us being there for as long as we needed to."

"Excellent," Gepsy exclaimed with a wide smile. "Jackson, we can set you up with a field laptop. It'll encrypt your location, but just to be safe, take it into a neighboring town before you use it."

I nodded my head and looked over at Laney; she was staring at nothing again.

Gepsy watched her too, then kept going. "I can get a message to Jimmy so he'll know why you two won't be in touch for a while. We will leave later today. You will hand in your phones and use burners for emergencies only. I'll monitor both of your phones here so it doesn't tip her off if they're dead. Only you two and of course I will have the number for the new phones. You will be essentially invisible to the outside world." Gepsy finished, stood, and started toward the door, then he threw over his shoulder, "I'll be right back," leaving Laney and me alone in the room.

I looked over at her; she was breathing hard, and her face was flushed. I knew she was barely holding it together. I hadn't touched her in three months, except her elbow the previous day, but I had this strange tingling sensation in my fingers as I got up and carefully squatted down in front of her. She wouldn't look at me, and I knew why, knew I had this coming, knew trust is earned and I'd lost it when I walked out of her life three months ago.

Her emerald eyes clouded with tears and tugged at me to wrap her in my arms. "Hey," I whispered. I gently grabbed for her hand, and she surprised me by letting me take it. "It's going to be okay. They'll find her and put her away for good this time." I tried to reassure her. She sniffed as a few stray tears fell down her face. She wiped at them then pulled her hand back when Gepsy returned. I stood up and walked around my chair, holding on to the back of it. I needed something to hold other than Laney's delicate hand.

He gave us each a small notepad and a pen and said, "Write your lists. Jackson, I'll leave you to meet us at the designated spot at the proper time. Laney, I'll drive you and shadow you as you go to your apartment."

7

LANEY

"What is that?" I asked, pointing at the hatchback with mostly chipped silver paint and dented fenders.

Gepsy smiled wide and dangled a pair of keys from his fingers. "Your new wheels." He tossed the keys to Jackson, who caught them with a confused expression.

"You aren't coming with us?" Jackson hiked his duffle bag higher on his shoulder.

Gepsy shook his head, walked around to the back of the car, and lifted the hatch. It let out a loud groan while Gepsy dug around inside for what looked like a shortened broomstick. He stuck the stick in between the car and the open hatch and waited until it was stable before he stepped back. "This one is sketchy—it'll chop your fingers right off if you're not careful," he warned while loading my suitcase into the back of the car. "Now, remember that you two are keeping a low profile. Only use your burner phones, don't use your family's phones to contact Ramsey or anything okay." Gepsy leveled me with a glare, like I was a child.

I nodded and tucked my pillow further under my arms. We were traveling to my parents' farm to hide out, just the two of us in the car for three hours. *Should be fun.*

"That should do it." Gepsy took out the stick and let the hatch slam shut. "Stop halfway and use cash to fill up, don't use any credit cards. Did you take some cash out of the ATM?" Gepsy asked Jackson, who nodded and said, "Yeah, only two hundred...didn't think that would tip her off if she was watching it."

Gepsy nodded in agreement. "Yeah, that should be fine. Just don't pull any more out while you're over there. You guys need to stick together. Don't separate or do anything stupid." He walked over to where I was standing and clapped me on the back, slightly pushing me toward the passenger side door.

I swallowed my anxiety about being alone with Jackson like a glob of peanut butter and crawled into the old car. It had ripped, faded red leather seats with an old stereo, a large thin steering wheel, and a crack through the windshield. This thing didn't even seem safe or legal to drive around, but beggars and people going into witness protection can't be choosers.

Jackson climbed into the car a few seconds later and started it up; thankfully it turned over without issue. He looked like he was ready to head to the farm in old jeans, work boots, and a flannel t-shirt, complete with a trucker hat. As he pulled away from the used car lot where Gepsy's brother worked, I let out a small laugh.

"Where on earth did you get those clothes?" I eyed him comically while I squeezed the hem of his flannel shirt between my fingers.

He let out a laugh. "What? Am I not convincing enough?"

I laughed but kept watching him as he drove us toward the interstate.

"Completely convincing. I'm just worried about the farmer you robbed and likely left naked, or worse—in your designer suits."

Jackson smiled wide. "I borrowed it from my assistant."

I raised an eyebrow. "Your assistant wears the same size as you and happens to be a rancher living in the middle of Chicago?"

Jackson kept his eyes on the road. "No, but his brother is an actor and has tons of extra 'set' outfits. I went back to the restaurant after our little meeting and bought it off him. They're my only farm clothes, so the rest of the time, I'll stick out like a sore thumb—don't worry."

I laughed and tucked my loose hair behind my ears. My hair had been washed and dried but nothing more, and I wasn't wearing any makeup. I just didn't have it in me to care. I hadn't slept at Lance's house. I'd tried, and their guest room was more than comfortable, but I was terrified, and having anxiety attacks all night tended to add to the insomnia in a dark and twisted way.

Jackson messed with the stereo as he continued driving south. I was in such a crappy mood, and I didn't want to affect him, so I turned my head toward the window, ready to shut down and sleep.

"You do okay at Lance's house?" Jackson asked.

I turned back toward him and gave a weak smile. "You know I didn't." I also hadn't told him I would be at Lance's, so I assumed Lance had spilled the beans. Jackson carefully placed his hand on my knee and squeezed it, but he didn't say anything.

Things between us were so fragile and strange, like trying to push toothpaste back into the tube. It wasn't the same as it used to be, and now when my worst fears were manifesting, I didn't have him to help me through them. I didn't have him at all.

I turned my head again and tried to fall to asleep so I wouldn't have to think about how good his hand felt or how even that small gesture made me feel so secure. It was just temporary, and I was tired of things being ripped away from me. My eyes fluttered shut and I drifted off to the soft sounds of the radio.

THE BLINKING LIGHT IN THE PARKING GARAGE WAS THE ONLY LIGHT I could see. I was walking slowly through the space, looking for Jackson's car. I clicked the button in my hand and heard the chirp a few cars ahead. I heard the echo from my heels clicking on the cement. No one was around, not a single soul. I found Jackson's car and opened the door, eager to get inside and lock it. Once I was secure in the driver's seat, I exhaled and closed my eyes.

But it wasn't silence that met me: behind me, I could hear someone breathing. I opened my eyes, and just as I looked in the rear-view mirror, something wrapped around my throat and pulled. Time stopped; I couldn't breathe. My hands went up to my neck, trying to free it from the cable that strangled me. I saw her face in the mirror, her dark eyes and dark hair. I remembered I once thought she was beautiful, but there was no beauty in her face as her lips twisted to the side and her eyes narrowed with determination as she tried to end my life. I kicked and kicked and tried to scream.

． ． ．

"Laney! Wake up, baby, wake up!" Someone was softly yelling at me.

I opened my mouth, trying to get air into my lungs, but nothing was happening. I couldn't catch my breath and couldn't seem to grasp what was going on.

"Laney, please honey. Wake up. It was just a dream." Someone's hand was on my face, brushing my hair away, and another hand was rubbing my back. It felt nice, but my eyes stayed firmly shut. It was safe there.

"Laney, you're safe. She isn't here, and no one is going to hurt you. Put your hand on my arm and squeeze."

I tried to focus on his voice and do what he said, but it was like my limbs didn't work anymore or I was frozen.

His soft voiced coaxed again. "Come on, this is weirdly the only thing that calms you down when you have one of these dreams."

I did as he said, he moved my hand until it was over his arm, and I squeezed. Slowly, I opened my eyes and stared into Jackson's sapphire ones. He looked so worried, so scared; it was as though he'd taken my very emotions and now wore them as a mask. That was how I knew what we had was deeper than he'd ever admitted.

His eyes always betrayed him. I leaned forward and let in a lungful of air as I hugged him. He hugged me back, and tears fell down my face onto his shoulder. He hugged me tight just like he used to. We stayed like that for a few minutes until I realized we were pulled over on the side of the road.

"What happened?" I asked, pulling away while wiping at my face. Jackson cleared his throat and sat back on his heels. He was crouched down next to me on the ground with my door wide open. "You were dreaming."

I nodded, knowing there wasn't much more to say because my dreams were a therapy issue we had touched on quite frequently. Jackson had pulled me out of far too many bad dreams. I had probably been screaming and thrashing around, which is why he had to pull over. I fucking hated those dreams.

I sat back in my seat and wiped at my face. "Thank you."

He smiled and stood up. "You okay, or should we take a break?" He looked over the roof of the car, likely to gauge where we were.

I looked up at him and squinted against the sun. "If there's a gas station, maybe we can grab some water or snacks so I can stay awake?"

Jackson leaned against the top of the car with his arms bent. "Yeah, I'll take the next exit and we'll stop."

Ten minutes later, Jackson was standing outside, pumping gas into our old beater car, and I was inside buying snacks and water. I kept my face down, trying to avoid any cameras. I hated that I felt like a criminal, that I was hiding from her, but I didn't want her to have any help in ever finding us. I walked back outside and arranged all of our snacks and drinks to where they could easily be reached then waited for Jackson to get in.

Once we were back on the road, the silence in the car was almost deafening. Jackson cleared his throat and situated his shoulders against the back of the seat. He was about two times too big for this small hatchback.

"So, how have you been these last few months?" he asked with a slight pitch in his voice. I tried not to let out a big fat sigh, because I really didn't want to talk about how miserable I had been or how many times I had cried myself to sleep.

Instead I said, "Good, but busy. How about you?"

He took a moment to respond before readjusting his hands on the steering wheel. "Rough...it's been rough..."

So many parts of my heart wanted to hear why his last few months had been rough and ask if he'd missed me, but asking that would eventually lead us back to the topic of the breakup, and I wasn't ready to broach that yet. So, I changed the subject.

"Are you ready to be on a farm? Want any pointers?"

Jackson let out a small laugh and dug into his can of almonds, which was his version of road trip food. Mine, on the other hand, was Fuyuns, Cheez-Its, Red Vines, and trail mix.

"I don't think I will ever be *ready* for the farm, but I would love some pointers." Jackson tilted his head and looked over at me. The bill of his hat was tipped back just a fraction, making him look like he really did belong on a farm.

I sifted through the pile of trail mix for the M&M's and started in. "So first thing you need to know is that no one will respect you right off the bat. You'll need to be willing to put in the work and earn it." I dumped the rest of the trail mix back into the bag.

Jackson noticed and chided, "Stop it. You know I hate it when you only eat the M&M's."

I shrugged and started hunting for more. "You'll probably be asked to clean up horse poop and collect eggs, maybe even move a few hay bales."

Jackson carefully peeked at me before watching the road again. I was sifting through another pile of trail mix when he ripped the bag out of my hands.

"No! Jackson, don't!" I yelled while trying to reclaim the bag. He had it shoved in between his hip and his door, out of my reach, and even if I could reach it, I'd have to get really close to him to do it. "Give it back!" I held out my hands expectantly.

He was still watching the road as a smile crested on his face. "Not until you promise to eat some almonds." He was always trying to get me to eat healthier, which was discourteous because it wasn't like I was pushing my artificial flavors or processed sugar on him.

"No. It's mine. Give it back," I demanded again.

Jackson peered at me again and gave me a grin that said he was going to like what he was about to say way more than I was. "Come and get it."

I knew it.

I'd fucking known he was going to turn this into some game. I let out a sigh and crossed my arms. "Forget it. I'm not in the habit of feeling up man-whores." It was a low blow, but so was taking someone else to Italy.

Jackson waited a second or two to respond, but when he did, his voice was ice cold. "That whole situation looked much worse than it actually was."

I kept my arms tucked in, suddenly chilled and feeling insecure. I took a sip of water from my water bottle and asked, "How so?"

This was petty and sketchy territory. I didn't want to talk about the last three months or why I left or why he didn't come get me or try to stop me, but that damn curiosity that killed the cat was coming for me too.

"Well for starters, she was never my girlfriend." Jackson's face had hardened, his jaw flexed and his lips forming a thin line. He waited a second or two before he kept going. "I took that trip to Italy to try to prove something to myself...it ended up being quite depressing, but Pristine was there with some friends, and she knew me from some social engagements we'd been a part of. I was drunk...but I didn't sleep with her, she wanted to...but I couldn't."

I PULLED AT MY NAIL, TRYING TO ABSORB THE INFORMATION. "YOU'VE been busy too it seems," I quietly replied while turning my gaze to the window.

JACKSON CONTINUED TO WATCH THE ROAD, HIS ADAM'S APPLE MOVING a few times before he finally looked over at me. "Does that mean you've been busy seeing someone or traveling?"

I turned my head and twisted my lips to the side, thinking over my answer. I so badly wanted to lie, make myself look less pathetic, but it wasn't worth it.

"Neither...it's just been work and back-to-back appointments with Glenda. I had to, uh..." I stopped because he didn't need to know the details of my life. It didn't matter.

"You had to what?" Jackson asked, looking over then quickly back to the road. I was so grateful he couldn't focus on me.

"Nothing. It doesn't matter," I whispered, pulling the tag of my pillow. The silence in the car was stifling, so I reached forward to turn on the radio.

Jackson gently grabbed my hand and whispered, "You've never kept secrets from me before...don't start now."

I let out a sigh and tried to pull my hand free, but he wouldn't let go. Irritation simmered low in my belly, his touch burning like a memory ripped from my mind without permission. I didn't think he understood how painful it was for me to be this close to him. I tugged my hand again until he released it, and I breathed through my nose.

"I checked myself into a mental health facility for two days in June..." I stammered, frustrated and annoyed.

He watched the road, and I hoped he'd just let this go.

I shut my eyes and looked out my window.

Jackson continued watching the road as he carefully reached to his side and pulled the trail mix free, placing it back in my lap. The gesture was probably meant as a kindness, giving me what I wanted, but it just felt like he was pulling back, distancing himself again because he couldn't do relationships and I was nothing but a big fat commitment.

———

I WAS FEELING LIGHTER AND LETTING THE ENTANGLED FEELINGS FROM that dream slip free, and they disappeared entirely when we passed the "Welcome to Plainville" sign. Memories assaulted me as we drove past the tire store that still had ugly, chipped paint. New feelings surged as we passed a cluster of new chain stores, including a Target. I nearly pressed my face to the glass as I saw the shiny red T. *I love me some Target.*

Years ago, it was just the Wal-Mart chain we had to shop at; now there were so many choices I wouldn't know where to start. There used to be a Roberta's Taco Shop that I frequented with my friends and even brothers from time to time; now it was a Taco Bell with brand-new purple lettering telling the masses to '*Live mas*'.

My heart thumped rapidly as we drove through the town and drew closer and closer to the outskirts, where my family's farm was located. Jackson glanced over at me and gripped my knee as we started passing farms and ranches. He was probably remembering the few times I had opened up about my family and the culture here I'd wanted to escape. He was trying to be comforting, but it only made me remember how much I had revealed to him and how little he had shared with me.

Irritated by the memory of how stingy he was with personal details, I shoved his hand away. We may have been thrown together for the sake of staying alive, but I was still sticking to a clean break plan regarding Jackson. I considered that saying about how 'home is where the heart is,' and

I planned on spending this time at home getting mine back. Jackson would just be another person there, another body in the house, another person who saw me in my pajamas every day, another person at the dinner table.

Jackson exhaled loudly and straightened in his seat.

I wanted to comment on his obvious frustration, but I saw Mr. Gregory's apple orchard through Jackson's window. It neighbored my family's farm, which meant mine was next. I turned my head, plastered my face to my window, and relished the view of the familiar lavender farm. I saw the sturdy, white vinyl fencing that ran along the fields of purple spreading across the property. Then I saw the house and held my breath.

Two years had been too long.

My family's home was more like a plantation. It had a wraparound porch and was a stark white with dark green vinyl shutters along the windows of the two-story home. Wooden rocking chairs sat under a myriad of hanging flower baskets along the wraparound porch.

We continued driving until we came to my family's driveway. There was no gate or anything to keep the public out because my family welcomed everyone. They did, however, have two large, very loud dogs that roamed the property at all times.

As we drove down the length of the gravel path, Dexter and Duncan ran out to greet us, barking and making our arrival known. Jackson made a little comment as we continued the trek down the dusty path.

"Nice security they have out here."

I looked over and smiled at him. "Their lick is worse than their bite." He laughed, but I was serious. These dogs were older than dirt and for some reason had the world's driest mouths, so when they went to lick you, it was like a rough patch of sandpaper being dragged down your face.

We pulled in behind my dad's work truck and put the car in park. There was another black SUV with Illinois plates that was parked on the opposite side of the carport. Jackson and I both climbed out of the car to see that Gepsy was standing near the side of the house talking to my dad. *What in the hell?*

I turned to gauge whether Jackson was confused as well, but he was already heading toward the front porch. I shifted my body to follow his lead when I heard a loud "My dear Lord! Baby girl, is that you?"

My mother, a tiny Southern woman with fiery red hair and steel blue eyes, was the one who'd yelled at me. She was born and raised in Alabama, and you would assume she still lived there from her deep accent.

I crossed the small patch of dirt that separated the yard and the driveway and continued toward the porch while rubbing my sweaty hands on my worn jeans. I hadn't thought of what I was wearing when I agreed to this. My debutante, pearls-and-heels-wearing mother was going to get that look and then give me an earful about my grubby clothes. I drew closer, Duncan and Dexter running circles around me, barking, begging to be rubbed and noticed, but my eyes were on the first few steps of the porch that would lead me to my mother.

"Laney Laverta Thompson! This is the best surprise you could have given your mama!" My mother wrapped me in a tight hug. She gave those kinds of hugs that you felt in your bones; it was like an imprint. I was sure my bones would indicate the level of love I'd endured while growing up with her. I hugged her back as much as my small arms would allow.

"Mama, sorry to just show up like this, but I'm in a bit of a pickle."

She held me back and glanced past me at Jackson petting Duncan and Gepsy walking with Dad toward the porch. "You in some kind of trouble honey?" she whispered to me, while still watching Jackson and Gepsy.

I let the air I'd been holding in out and answered, "Something like trouble. Let's go inside and I'll explain it to you."

She nodded and went to move around me. "Beverley Thompson. Welcome to our home." She stuck her dainty, manicured hand out for Gepsy.

He took it and gently shook it. "Detective Franklin Gepsy, ma'am."

Mom's eyes darted to mine. It was a look I was very familiar with, and it said, *You have about two shakes of a lamb's tail to come clean, young lady.* She moved to shake Jackson's hand, and he grabbed it and introduced himself.

"Jackson Tate, ma'am. Nice to meet you."

Mom physically relaxed and patted her hair as recognition sank in.

"Oh, I've heard so much about you, Jackson, from my Laney. If I'm not mistaken, you two are an item, aren't you?" She gave him a smile and a wink. *Shitballs.*

Of course she'd remember the few times I'd mentioned Jackson. I pushed down the urge to be ashamed that I'd shared that part of my life with my family. I didn't regret Jackson; I never would, I just wished things turned out differently. I opened the screen door and walked into my childhood home. The smell of fresh bread and lavender hit me as I walked past the small entryway and headed toward the living room.

The wood floors were polished as usual. In the living room were several plush couches with colorful throws. There was a large fireplace with a stone hearth, exposed beams lined the ceiling, and along the walls were floor-to-ceiling windows. There was a long bar with stools that divided the living room from the kitchen. I took a seat on one of the big couches, Jackson made his way in and took the seat next to me, and Gepsy took one of the arm chairs as my mother made her way to the kitchen.

I looked over at Gepsy as he settled his large body into the chair, and I glared. "Thought we were on our own. Why are you here?"

Jackson let out a little laugh next to me and leaned forward, adding, "What I want to know is how you beat us."

Gepsy laughed as he sipped on a cup of coffee he must have been served earlier. "I had to check the place out, and I didn't want it to be suspicious if we all rode together. Plus, I have family nearby, so I am going to visit them. I've been here for half an hour—what took you guys so long?" Gepsy raised his eyebrow at Jackson, who leaned back and pointed a finger at me.

I grabbed his finger and pushed it back toward his chest. "It wasn't completely my fault—you drive slow." I tried to defend myself, but both men just laughed at me.

My mother made her way back into the living room, holding a trey of iced tea. She set it on the coffee table, and Gepsy and Jackson leaned in to grab theirs, but I didn't. I loved my mother, but she took the sweet part of the tea to the extreme and put way too much sugar into it. I wanted to see Jackson's face when he tasted it, because he didn't consume sugar in his regular diet. I realized then that him staying here might kill him after all. He took a sip and started choking immediately. I mashed my lips together to keep from laughing. Jackson noticed and was probably about to comment on my abstinence from the sugar tea when his eyes landed on my father, who'd just walked into the room.

Wayde Thompson was a tree of a man. Tall, all muscle, the only soft parts of him were his eyes. They were a gentle brown that matched his light brown hair. I hadn't seen him in so long. I hesitated for a second before I stood up and walked toward him, and he scooped me into a tight hug. I hadn't always seen eye to eye with my father, but I loved him, and I knew deep down, he adored me.

"Daddy, it's good to see you."

He bent down and kissed my cheek. "Pumpkin. Detective Gepsy was just telling me a little bit about what brought him out here while we were outside."

I let him go and tried not to frown. There were so many things I hadn't told my family and I didn't want to hurt them or step into anything, so I hoped Gepsy would go back over everything he'd said.

Gepsy leaned forward and set his glass down as my mother cozied up with my father on the opposite couch. "I wanted to wait for you two to get here so we could all properly explain the situation without there being any confusion."

I grabbed a pillow and placed it in my lap so I had something to squeeze as Gepsy relayed his info.

"Last December, both Jackson and Laney filed a no contact order against someone who had worked with Jackson as a personal assistant. Unfortunately, Laney was compromised shortly after hers was finalized. The good news is we were able to catch the perp and she was sentenced to three years in prison for class A stalking."

My mother gasped and darted her eyes to where I was sitting. I knew she was simmering with how many details were being left out.

Gepsy took a sip of tea. "Her name is Alicia Miller. Unfortunately, she's being released from prison early, and we have reason to believe she's targeting the two of them again." Gepsy gestured at both Jackson and me before taking another sip of tea and continuing. "Until I have a chance to investigate this, I thought it would be a good idea to get these two out of the city and off the grid." Gepsy put his hands out and started counting on his fingers. "They only have burner phones, which they are only to use to contact each other or me. They are not to be featured in any social media posts of any kind by anyone in your family, and please abstain from telling your local friends they are here visiting or any details of what I just shared. I will leave it up to these two to share more with you when they're ready, but as for now, we appreciate your generosity and willingness to keep them safe."

My mother clicked her tongue. "Well, we're Laney's family so of course we'll keep her safe, and as for Jackson, he's welcome no matter what."

My dad took that moment to finally look at Jackson and leaned forward with a stern face. "I haven't properly met you. Wayde Thompson."

Jackson stood halfway and shook his hand. "Jackson Tate, sir. Thank you for allowing me to stay in your home."

My mom piped up again. "Oh nonsense. You're a guest of our Laney's, and you're welcome as long as you need it. And Laney, it's about time you come and see your family."

I lowered my gaze as I waded through guilt-infested emotions. I had stayed away too long, and I hated that my circumstances were so minuscule that I hadn't been able to visit.

"Well, I'm going to head out and go see some family. Does anyone have any questions about what's going to happen or what's needed?" Gepsy asked while looking around the room. I wanted him to tell me exactly how long this whole situation was going to last, but I didn't want my parents to take it the wrong way, so I stayed quiet.

"Okay then, I'm off. Beverley and Wayde, nice to meet you, and thank you for helping us out."

My dad shook Gepsy's hand and walked him out, and my mom started cleaning up the dishes. I knew both my parents would eventually pull me aside to talk, or maybe they were just waiting for more details to come out. Either way, I was somewhat expecting more of a reaction to this whole thing.

I headed outside after Jackson and Gepsy but stopped midway when I saw that my father was talking to Jackson with his hand firmly set on

Jackson's shoulder and his eyebrows making a solid shelf of determination.

"I'm not sure of the nature of your relationship with my daughter, but if I had my way, you'd be staying up in the hayloft."

I cringed and darted forward to hopefully stop the conversation, but my dad kept going.

"However, my wife seems to think you having your own bedroom in the house is necessary, so I will honor that. If you so much as lay on the same bed with her to talk or tie your shoe, you're up in the loft. Understand?"

I placed my face in my hands and resisted the urge to groan. When I looked up, Jackson was shaking my father's hand and swearing fealty to him by promising there wasn't anything happening between us.

My parents were very religious, so I was sure the idea of a boy who I wasn't married to staying in a room right next to mine had set them on edge. They'd raised us with a very specific set of values regarding relationships. Their hope for us growing up was that we would group-date with some friends, find a good match, then court for a few months, which would turn into an engagement, and by the year's end it would turn into marriage.

My parents wanted me to be anything I wanted but secretly hoped I wanted to get married and stay home, serving my husband and raising my kids. Being the only girl, it was a serious letdown when I confessed my desire to move to the big city and lead a career instead. The only person to follow their desired plan so far was my oldest brother Lawson. He had gotten married at nineteen to his wife, Sarah. They had four children already and hoped for at least three more.

My dad turned to me and smiled. "Well what are you waitin for? Get going after your stuff. Let's not make this take all day," my dad rattled off at me in his own Southern twang. He had been raised Southern as well, down in Texas.

"I'm goin," I said over my shoulder to my dad. I walked behind Jackson as we made our way toward the hatchback. He rummaged for the broom handle and propped up the back. I was still wary of it falling, so I stayed back by a few feet. Jackson started pulling his suitcase out, then pulled mine free along with my other two bags and pillows.

I went to grab mine, but he picked them up. "I got them, just lead the way." He looked like an oversized, Southern bellboy. I held back a laugh as I led the way up to the second floor, where the guest rooms were.

I took in the sights and memories as we climbed the stairs. The walls were still painted a light forest green with several pictures of us kids at different stages of life. I knew down by the bathroom there would be an entire section of wall dedicated to my senior year of high school. I loved that my mother hadn't changed out the pictures or the order. She had, however, added new pictures down stairs. All the pictures of my niece and nephews were down there.

Once we leveled out, I walked past the office, then my brother Leo's room. We passed the upstairs bathroom, which I pointed out to Jackson. "Here's the bathroom, but we will have one in between our rooms too." I didn't look back to see if he saw or acknowledged me, just assumed he got it.

I continued down to the end of the hall and walked into the first door on the left. The room was modest. It had a queen-sized bed with a homemade quilt covering it. A small desk sat in the corner, and there was a sewing table under the large window that covered the far wall. Jackson walked in and laid his suitcase down on the bed. I turned away from him and headed toward the closet, opening the door and clicking on the light.

"There's space in here to hang your nice clothes if you need to."

I turned, walked toward the closed door in the room, and pulled it open. It led into a Jack and Jill bathroom: two sinks, a white countertop, and a wide mirror framing the space. Off to the side was a tub and toilet.

I walked straight through to the closed door on the opposite side of the bathroom, pulled it open, and walked into what would be my room. It had white carpet, like Jackson's room, as well as a queen-sized bed with another quilt.

I'd helped sew the one I would be sleeping under. There were paintings on the wall that my brother Leo had done, a keyboard rested in the corner of the room, and a small desk sat under the much smaller window. My room was a lot smaller than Jackson's, but I knew my mother would throw me out in a second if I tried to take the bigger room. Jackson walked to the bed and set my suitcase, bags, and pillows down. Then he stood back and looked around. I hated that my gut did a little flip at him being in this room with me.

He was standing there in his old blue jeans and flannel t-shirt, looking relaxed and somehow still too good for small-town Plainfield. Seeing Jackson stand in my brother's childhood bedroom made me remember the last time I actually considered Jackson meeting my family.

IT WAS SNOWING IN CHICAGO, AND CHRISTMAS WAS JUST A FEW DAYS away. I had moved back into my own apartment, but I was still staying with Jackson at night. In fact, I was spending a lot of time with him. I had those new relationship butterflies. I was wrapping his Christmas gift in his guest room, and once it was wrapped, he came in and started kissing my neck. I turned around in his arms and wrapped my hands around his shoulders. We kissed until we fell back onto the bed.

"What are you thinking about?" Jackson whispered, while running his finger down my side and drawing circles on my skin.

"I was thinking about what it would be like to have you at my parents' house for Christmas..." I admitted, afraid he might reject me. He stopped drawing circles and went rigid.

"Your parents' house?" he asked, voice sounding like ice had infused his vocal cords. I couldn't respond because I had already thrown it out there and was already too vulnerable. He patted my arm and sat up, then reminded me, "Meeting the parents is a boyfriend thing, Laney. I'm not your boyfriend."

THE MEMORY BROUGHT SOME PERSPECTIVE. THIS WASN'T JACKSON meeting my parents or coming over at Christmas. This was Jackson staying here because of his crazy ex-assistant. I turned away from him and headed back downstairs. I didn't need this. I didn't need him. *Clean break, Laney. Clean fucking break.*

LANEY

I was in the middle of stuffing a large chunk of banana bread into my mouth when someone came up and slapped me on the back. I started coughing violently before snagging the cup in front of me for a drink of water. Alarm bells went off in my head, causing my adrenaline to surge. One of my very large, ugly triggers was people touching me without permission or at least acknowledgment.

"What the hell?" I choked out while hopping off the stool and backing up rapidly. My oldest brother Lawson had his hands up in mock surrender as I eyed him like he was a thief.

"Whoa, sorry sis. Didn't mean to scare you." A sly grin broke out on my brother's handsome face, and I melted. It had been too damn long since I had seen him. I wiped the crumbs from my face and went to hug him. "How the hell are you little sister?" he whispered into my ear as he squeezed. I felt tears building in the corners of my eyes.

"I'm good, but I missed you guys," I said as he released me.

Lawson was at least six foot five and looked like a quarterback. "What brings you back to little ol' Indiana?" he asked while grabbing for the rest of my bread.

I let out a sigh and tried to be as vague as possible. "Just a big fat pickle that I'll explain at dinner." My mother had informed me after we arrived that she'd called a family dinner and everyone would be there.

"Well, whatever the reason, I'm happy you're home," Lawson said with a full mouth. I watched him as crumbs fell to his blue polo shirt and his sock-covered toes. I had a strange urge to hug him again or to run my hands over his light, curly brown hair. He had blue eyes like our mother's, and they still looked wise and mature like they always had, like he was born to be the oldest of five siblings.

"Did Mom make banana bread again?" Zane asked while he walked into the kitchen.

I turned and smiled wide as I watched my brother register that his little sister was back. His smile started small then stretched to fill his entire face. His brown eyes lit up and his tan forehead lifted as he headed toward me. He wrapped me in his arms and squeezed a little too tight.

"Z, you're killing me," I coughed out.

He laughed and let me go. "Damn, Little Five, you look pale as a ghost. The sun shine at all in that city of yours?" he joked while digging into the covered Tupperware my mother kept her goodies in.

"Ha ha, laugh it up, idiot. I'm a redhead and naturally deflect the sun," I argued.

He turned toward me, holding a chocolate chip cookie in his hand. "So...you finally decided it was time to come and visit your estranged family?"

Guilt tugged at me as his words sank in. They were as heavy and hard as being hit with a baseball bat. I swallowed and went to grab my water, ignoring him for a second. Zane was always the most honest of our family, silent most of the time unless he needed to speak his mind.

His black t-shirt had a faded logo of our high school on it, and his slightly darker brown hair was shoved under a dirty blue baseball hat. Zane worked the farm with Dad, whereas Lawson worked the corporate side of things. Zane could usually be found out on the tractor or in the fields somewhere, hauling bundles of lavender.

I tried to make my reply light as I crossed my arms and kicked at some crumbs that had fallen. "I always want to come visit you guys. I just can't always afford it."

Zane moved to the fridge and started digging through it. "Is it because of Dad? Because you know he's sorry..." He trailed off when I started to shake my head.

"No. It's not Dad. I know he didn't mean to do what he did when I left last. I just..." I suddenly felt the urge to cry. I cleared my throat and pushed through it. "I just have a really demanding job, and it's hard to get vacation and the means to get here."

Zane's jaw moved as he chewed on a cookie.

I shifted my stance so I was near the banana bread and tore off another piece before I asked some of my own questions. "So, how's work going for you guys? You still working with Dad?" I asked just to be sure I hadn't missed something.

Zane nodded while staring at the counter behind me, and Lawson grunted, "Not much changes here, sis."

I figured as much, but I nodded and watched the window as I saw another tall figure head toward the house. I smiled and moved toward the door to meet Ty, my third oldest brother. I kept my hand on the door handle until he was about to open it. I swung it open just as he reached for the handle and said, "Welcome, can I take your coat?"

It was August and obviously not coat weather, but the gesture hit the spot as a fat smile broke out on his face. He took two steps forward and swept me up into a tight hug. "Finally, some decent company!" He bellowed while walking backward with me.

I laughed and asked, "Who else has been visiting you lately?"

He stepped back and held his jaw. "Mom's cousins came last month. Stayed for an entire week with that annoying dog of theirs."

I smiled, and we both walked back toward the kitchen. Ty headed for the fridge, looking for food, just like my other brothers had. My mother was an amazing cook, so I didn't blame them. I stood against the cupboards watching as Ty joked with Lawson. I took a second to catalog the differences in my older brothers' looks.

Last time I was there, Ty's hair was spiked oddly with gunky gel. No one knew why he went that route, but I was glad to see it was now soft and styled nicely.

His hair was more blond than brown, and his eyes were a soft choco-late color, like my father's. Out of all my brothers, Ty looked the most boyish. I smiled at how my brothers moved around the kitchen eating and joking with each other. These three were the ones that made living in this town and being a Thompson girl the hardest.

I had at least fifty girls who only wanted to be my friend to get close to one of them.

Last I'd heard, Ty was still single and working with a neighboring farm because if he spent too much time with the family, he'd kill somebody—his words, not mine.

I was about to break into their conversation and ask about his employment when I heard the front door slam shut. My head whipped toward the sound; I waited, cautiously watching the entryway. My apprehension kicked in and my palms started sweating.

Thankfully, a moment later, Leo walked in. A sigh of relief escaped me as I lurched forward and threw myself at my older brother. Leo was the last boy born into our family before I came along. He was the loudest, the most obnoxious, and the black sheep if there was one.

He didn't style his hair, letting it grow longer on purpose until it was shaggy but still somehow stylish. His shirts were usually not washed, or they were wrinkled, as were his pants. He wore ugly work boots with every outfit, he played more video games than most professional gamers, and he had never set foot inside a gym. But regardless of all that, he was my favorite human being.

"You look like hell, sis," he quipped before he pulled a snack-sized bag of Doritos from his back pocket. Regardless of Leo's lack of self-care, he was still handsome, but he was annoyingly oblivious to any girl who had ever paid him any attention, so we assumed he was destined to be a bachelor for life.

"You're one to talk." I hit his belly, and a few crumbs fell from his shirt. My brothers were pigs.

"True, but I always look this way. You usually look fancy-ish and nice," Leo said while wiping his fingers on his jeans.

I smiled and tugged at his shaggy hair that was past his ears now. "The barber shut down or you sporting this look on purpose?" I joked while my other brothers started laughing too.

"Laugh it up, you morons, but when this is long enough to spike like Goku's, you are all going to eat those words," Leo scolded while holding his pointer finger up like he was trying to make a point. He wore a t-shirt that said *This is a holdup* with a picture of a wall.

I wanted to roll my eyes, but I already knew who he'd bought it from and why he was wearing it. Instead I laughed and focused on his hair. "Leo, you went through that *Dragon Ball Z* phase in high school. It didn't work then, it will not work now."

Leo narrowed his eyes and pointed his finger at me. "My hair wasn't thick enough, so the consistency was all off. It's perfect now."

I shook my head and snagged one of his chips.

"Yeah, he'll get it this time," Ty added, completely serious while taking a big gulp of soda.

"You guys are all idiots," I said to the room of boys. They each narrowed their eyes on me then looked at one another with a little nod. *Oh shit, I know that look.*

I slowly started backing out of the kitchen, but I was too slow. Lawson darted forward and grabbed me, throwing me over his shoulder. I let out a squeal and wondered how Jackson was going to deal with all this craziness. It would likely be an adjustment for him, but for me it was perfect. I was home, and it felt better than anything had in a long time.

9

JACKSON

GROWING UP BY MYSELF, THERE WERE MANY TRADITIONS I DIDN'T GET to partake in. Family dinner was one of them. I spent the first half of my life eating dinner alone at the breakfast counter, just so I could be close to whatever nanny was on shift. Thanksgivings I spent at parties with my father, where he looked and spoke to me only when someone asked who the kid was that'd walked in behind him.

So, when I heard that Laney's family was hosting a huge family feast to welcome her home and me by proxy, I was excitedly nervous. I changed my shirt three times and anxiously watched the digital desk clock until it was deemed appropriate to go downstairs. I was hesitant to head down any sooner because I had this nervous energy buzzing under my skin where Laney was concerned.

The smell of chicken and rice had me moving toward the door and braving this new house, the new people, and this new dynamic with Laney. I exited my room that sat snugly at the end of the hall and paused to look at the pictures on the walls. They covered nearly every surface of the hall, with more memories than I could imagine in a lifetime.

Three young boys sitting in a wheelbarrow and wearing flannel coats stared back at me from a small portrait set within in an oddly shaped frame. A tall ten-year-old kid holding a football and sporting a cocky grin. Another where Wayde had a boy on his shoulders while Beverley had another on her lap. I continued down the row of printed history and stopped when I spotted one sandwiched in between all the boys' pictures.

A young Laney, maybe five years old or so, stood in the yard holding a white cat while wearing a blue jean dress. I ran my finger over the sunshine that reflected off her red hair, which was pulled into two tiny pigtails, and smiled. Somewhere in my gut, something strained at seeing her like this. So innocent and young, so perfect.

The strangest feeling hit me in the chest. I wondered if Laney's kids would be as beautiful as her. If her daughter would look that cute. If her daughter would have the same scrunched-up expression on her face or would stuff her cute little legs into cowboy boots that were too big for her, or if her face would lack freckles, just like Laney's.

I dropped my eyes to the wood floor and shoved that image into the same dark box where all my Laney thoughts went. They would only be pulled back out to examine when I was alone and when no one else would ever know that sometimes I imagined a future with Laney. I turned away from the wall and finished my trek to the stairs, blaming my sentimental thoughts on this place.

This whole experience was surreal. The house, the farm, her parents —I'd never wanted this, except for when I was a child, coloring pictures of a fake family in my notebook.

I exited the top floor and began the descent down the stairs until the sound of male voices stopped me. It sounded like a small army was in the kitchen, with various yells and oddly placed laughter set against murmurs and quiet conversation. I waited a moment so I could adjust my attitude to what I was about to experience and who I might encounter.

I knew Laney had four older brothers, so this introduction could go poorly if it wasn't done right. The anxiety of being an only child and not knowing how to blend with families was surfacing, and as badly as I wanted to, I couldn't shove it down. I wanted them to like me, wanted them to accept me. That dark box served up a memory of a lonely childhood and how badly I wanted a family, how desperate I was for a full house with laughter and love.

I heard the clap of someone's hands and a brash "Lawson stop it!"

That was Laney's voice; she sounded like she was being lifted off the floor.

"What's wrong, lil five? Didn't you miss your older brothers?" There was more laughing, and Laney sounded like her voice was strained when she said, "I didn't miss this! Stop it. Lawson, NO! Do not give me a wet willy or I will kick you in the face!" I got over my nerves because I needed to see this for myself.

I walked down the last few steps, toward the noise. In the middle of the kitchen was another man with huge shoulders and a wide smirk on his face, and thrown over one of his shoulders like a sack of potatoes was a groaning Laney.

I ran my hands over the top of my head, hoping to calm my anxieties. Maneuvering forward just a bit, I came to the edge of the living room, where the wood floor continued into the kitchen and the cupboards and shelves started.

The men standing to my left all gave me a curious look, and the man holding Laney stopped torturing her and watched me with the same confused look. Laney was set down, and she pushed at the man who'd been messing with her before clearing her throat.

"Hey guys, this is Jackson. He's a friend from Chicago and will be staying here with us for a while."

All the men in the kitchen shifted their gaze from Laney to me and glared. Everyone was silent for a few seconds, a few of the guys coughing into their fists awkwardly. Finally, the one in the middle stepped forward.

"Lawson Thompson. Nice to meet you." He shoved his hand out.

I smiled, took his hand, and responded, "Jackson Tate." Lawson looked very much like his dad.

I turned toward the brothers who were leaning against the bar and held my hand out. The first one took it. He looked like he wasn't exactly happy to be here. His hair was shoved under a ball cap, and he barely stopped eating his cookie long enough to say, "Zane. Nice to meet you."

I nodded my head in agreement then turned to the man next to him. This one wore a shirt that looked like it was purposely too small for him.

"Ty. Welcome to our home."

I nodded again, and then the last brother surprised me by ignoring my outstretched hand and instead leaned in to hug me.

He clapped my back hard and said, "I'm Leo, the youngest brother and closest in age to Laney over here, and I've heard all about you, man."

For the second time today, I wasn't sure what to say, but thankfully my brain kicked in and grabbed at the few memories I had of Laney talking about her family; Leo was a constant topic of conversation. Leo stood back and smiled, and I pointed at him. "The painter, right?"

He smiled and turned toward Laney, pulling her into an awkward hug while he cooed, "Aww, is my little sister talkin about us?"

I laughed and scratched the back of my neck. "Not too much, don't worry. She's just mentioned a few things here and there about her brothers." I tried to snag a look from Laney, but she had pushed Leo away and busied herself with snacking on carrots. She seemed so comfortable, laid back, and at ease.

It was exactly how she looked in my house. The realization that Laney felt at home with me hit, and I felt like I needed some air.

The brothers laughed and started shoving at each other then started grazing on some food that was on the counter. Laney went to stand near her mom to help with dinner. Leo grabbed a handful of almonds and broke the awkward lull in conversation.

"So, Jackson, do we get to hear what brought you here, or is it a surprise?"

I looked over at Laney to see what she wanted me to say; I wasn't sure what the plan was.

She looked between Leo and me and said, "At dinner, Leo. We will tell everyone together at dinner."

Leo put a hand over his mouth and made a scoffing sound. "Oh shit, are you engaged?!"

Beverly looked over from the oven and yelled, "There will be no swearin in my kitchen, Leonidas Devlin."

Leo turned red and blanched at his mother's voice. "Sorry Ma." He started laughing again while he grabbed a few carrots off the counter. "Seriously though, if you're announcing your engagement, I think Jud is going to lose his mind or break a gasket."

"Mama, you invited Jud?" Laney asked with a groan.

Beverly stopped stirring and clicked her tongue. "I didn't. One of these idiots must have."

Laney let out a loud and exaggerated sigh and searched the room, looking for the culprit.

Lawson ducked his head and lifted his hands. "Okay, okay...it was me. I didn't mean to. It just slipped when I was talking to Dad about it at the office. He was all intrigued that you were back, so I thought I'd do the Christian thing and invite him along."

"The Christian thing, Law? Really?" Laney scolded.

"What's the harm anyhow? He grew up with us," Lawson said with a shrug, and Laney gave him a look that could kill. He continued as though her objection hadn't just happened. "Besides, poor Jud has been pining away for you, sis. He has his hopes all up about you coming back for a visit."

I continued to watch Laney but felt the need to chew something as well so I wouldn't grind my teeth. Laney moved, and I snagged a handful of almonds. Her skin was already turning several shades of pink from her brother's comments.

Zane was next, and he had started laughing. "Yeah, I think I saw a picture of Laney in his wallet one time. That boy had it bad for you, sis."

Laney was about to cut him off when Ty piped up. "Well, yeah I guess he would have had it pretty bad if he was engaged to the woman." The room went silent, and even Beverly stopped stirring as all eyes went to Ty. He looked at Laney, his own face taking on that flushed color for oversharing.

Yeah, that was something I didn't fucking know.

Once the brothers started talking and shoving at each other again, I took the moment to excuse myself to get some air. I walked out the sliding glass door off the kitchen and headed into the back yard. The smell of lavender surrounded me. I didn't know where to go, but I needed to wrap my mind around the idea of Laney being engaged to someone, belonging to someone, planning a future with someone.

I didn't like the shift in my chest that left me feeling like a stone had rolled onto my heart, pinning it so tightly in place that I couldn't breathe. It wasn't the first time I'd felt this way regarding Laney with another man, but this was different than seeing her flirt with someone. Like the waiter the other night...it bothered me more than I cared to admit, but a fucking *fiancé*?

I shoved my hands into my pockets and walked along the perimeter of the yard. There was a tire swing attached to a large oak, and a tree house built closer to the back of the property. There was a large trampoline, and even a playhouse. It was like something from the notebook I kept as a kid. The entire back yard seemed looked like an ad for Toys R Us. Laney grew up here, submerged in it, and it still wasn't enough to keep her here. It gave me some hope that I hadn't completely missed out on life.

The warm breeze blew through the yard, twisting the tire swing all around. I watched the sun set across the yard and thought back to a time I had done this with Jimmy. My first real experience with family had come from his.

I met Jimmy while I was in college. I had made a piss-poor decision one night at the club bar that happened to be operated by the Brass and nearly got my ass handed to me by some of the members. Jimmy stepped in and calmed down the guy whose girl I had hit on then talked them into letting me go without any issues. For whatever reason, Jimmy drove my drunk ass to his dad and mom's house, where he let me sleep off one of the worst hangovers of my life. I later confessed something I hadn't ever told anyone. I told Jimmy it had been my birthday and I usually tried to get drunk to help myself forget that there wasn't a single person in the world who gave a fuck that I'd been born. That year, I'd gone a bit overboard.

After that ugly weekend, Loretta, Jimmy's mom, had invited me back every Friday night for dinner. Even going to school in Indiana, I managed to make sure I was at their house every Friday night, even if Jimmy wasn't there.

They had become my family.

Now, getting to be a part of Laney's was making feel strange and uncomfortable, especially because they seemed so tight-knit. Taking one last look at the sunset, I turned around and decided it was best to just get acclimated to the newness of this situation and embrace it, no matter how awkward it was.

I entered the house and immediately heard new voices. Three kids were running around a petite blonde woman who Lawson was standing next to. He was holding a toddler on his hip while trying to shake a bottle. I searched for Laney amongst the madness and found her near the entryway hugging someone. I stood there for a moment or two watching, and they still hadn't pulled apart. I crossed my arms over my chest and leaned against the wall, fully prepared to wait and see how long they kept at it.

The hug was full body, all arms, and their chests were practically glued together. *How long does it take to fucking hug each other?* The man she hugged looked about my age and had jet black hair. He wore a gray dress shirt, one I could see the outline of his arms through, showing that he clearly worked out—not that I should care whether or not he worked out, but jealousy had my eyes sizing him up.

They finally pulled apart, and he bent in to whisper something in Laney's ear before he squeezed her side and headed toward the table. I had a twisted feeling in my gut that this was Jud, Laney's ex-fiancé.

I walked toward the dining room where a long table with green and white flowered centerpieces and a white table runner sat. It looked like something out of one those shows Laney used to watch at my house about home decorating. I pushed away the ache that roared to life at the memory of Laney lying on my chest while we were in bed and the feeling of her drawing circles on my abs as she scoffed at the TV about certain design choices, or the little sounds she made when she saw a design she liked. I pushed away the memory of her silky hair that fell through my fingers as I stroked it, half watching and half absorbing everything that was just her.

I closed my eyes to clear my mind and focused back on the room in front of me. There were benches on each side of the table and only two chairs at each end. Wayde came in and sat at the head, and Lawson sat at the other end. Everyone started filling in around the table, and I went to grab a spot, trying not to notice that Laney and entryway guy sat next to each other. He kept whispering in her ear, and she kept laughing at whatever he said.

I had done what she was doing a thousand times with other women, with dates. So why the hell did seeing her with him feel so shitty?

I fixated on the plate in front of me as Leo climbed in next to me and Zane climbed in on the other side. Beverly came in a moment later with two large serving platters and started serving everyone. I could serve myself, so I stood up halfway and offered to do so, but not a single person joined me.

"No, silly. You're a guest, take a seat," Beverly said with a wave of her hand.

I looked around the table, but no one seemed put off by the fact that she was serving seven grown men and Laney. Lisa, Lawson's wife, had herself and her family served down toward the end of the table, but otherwise, Beverly had to take care of everyone else.

I had no mother figure to speak of, but I had always helped my nannies with chores while I grew up. My nanny Matlida made sure I knew how to dust a bookshelf and load a dishwasher. I was sure my father had no idea, but as an adult, I was thankful for her dedication to teaching me. With that commitment came an awareness of sharing the workload, and Beverly didn't to seem to share hers.

I thanked her for the chicken and rice, the lush salad, and the bread roll. I was technically a vegetarian, but I didn't want to be rude and decline the offered food. I could eat meat, I just often preferred not to. All plates were covered in food, and I was about to dig in when I heard Wayde's booming voice say, "Let's pray."

Everyone grabbed hands; Leo and Zane grabbed mine. My focus went to Laney's hand that was now inside the hugger's. Heads were bowed around the table as Wayde started to pray.

"Lord, we thank you for this food. Thank you for the hands that made it, thank you for our company tonight, and we pray that you bless us. Amen."

Everyone muttered an amen in response and then started eating. I kept my eyes on my own plate, not sure how to interact.

Finally, once Beverly sat down, Wayde spoke up and asked the table, "Has everybody introduced themselves?" Heads turned from right to left then nodded, all except for the guy next to Laney.

"Actually no." He spoke up around a mouthful of food and watched me from across the table where he was rubbing shoulders with Laney. *My Laney.* "I'm Judson Davis. Call me Jud...I'm a friend of the family." He leaned forward and extended his hand. I was tempted to take it, twist it backward, and tell him to stay the fuck away from Laney, but I leaned up to shake it instead.

"Jackson Tate. Friend of Laney's."

Once we were seated, Wayde spoke again. "So, Jackson, why don't you explain the situation to the table?"

I swallowed the bite of chicken I had taken and looked at Laney, expecting some reaction to being skipped over, but she kept her eyes down.

"Actually, I think Laney should explain the situation. It will have a different impact on everyone if it comes from her," I explained plainly, hoping they'd understand my intentions. Laney's eyes shot up to mine as she tried to hide a smile.

Jud spoke up next. "Can't you just do it?"

Laney flushed light pink and started eating her dinner roll.

What the fuck?

This was not Laney; she didn't let men steamroll her.

Not ever.

She didn't say anything to Jud to put him in his place, so I went ahead and spoke.

"Laney and I are currently in hiding...a form of witness protection, to be specific. We encountered some issues this past year from one of my previous employees. She didn't like the idea of Laney and me spending time together, and she eventually became obsessive. We went to the police to alert them, but nothing could be done until she did something to physically harm one of us. We'd already filed a no contact order and explained what we could regarding her stalking and threatening letters, but no other action was taken. Not until she attacked Laney."

I paused to try to catch Laney's eye to see if she wanted me to continue, but she was just pushing rice around her plate, not meeting my gaze. I looked around the table as I finished speaking.

"Laney was attacked in a parking garage at the end of December last year, with a cable wire. Thankfully Laney managed to reach her taser and was able to get out of the situation and find help. Laney suffered from a crushed windpipe and couldn't speak for over three weeks."

The room was silent, except for the smaller kids at the end of the table laughing amongst themselves, wrapped up in their own conversation. The silence felt tense and thick, like it really could be cut with a knife.

Ty's face was red, his brows drew together, and his jaw ticked...he looked pissed. He threw his fork down on his plate and stood from the table, stalking off toward the front door, through which he exited with a loud slam.

Eyes darted from his departing form back to me then bounced to Laney. Wayde let out a loud sigh when Leo spoke up with a barely controlled tone, "When the hell were we going to hear about this, sis?"

Laney blinked and slowly chewed the bite of food in her mouth before she sipped her water. "Leo, it wasn't that easy. I didn't want you guys to worry," she quietly argued.

"Bullshit!" Leo cut her off and slammed his fists down.

"Language," Wayde yelled, slamming the table with the flat of his hand.

Leo stared at his father. "That's all you have to say? You hear that your daughter nearly died, had her fucking windpipe crushed, and you reprimand me about my language?" Leo shook his head and moved his angry gaze to his sister. "We were texting during that time. I remember you had been distant and weird, but you swore nothing was wrong. You lied to me. You lied to all of us. I can't fucking believe you!" He shook his head in disappointment then stood and left the way Zane had.

It was silent again before Laney spoke up. "Look, none of you know what it was like. You can't judge me for not telling you. I may have done it wrong, but it happened to me, not you. I don't want to talk about this again after tonight." No one agreed, but no one followed up the comment either. Everyone just watched their plates.

Jud seemed to ignore the mood in the room and the way Laney's eyes were watering as he asked, "I understand why Laney needs to be here, but why aren't you staying with your own family? No offense."

Beverley let out a sigh and left the table as well. Laney pushed the food around her plate with her fork and didn't look up.

I looked down at the table as I answered Jud's question. "I don't have any family I could stay with. I have only ever met my mother once. I have no family on her side that I have ever met or know of, and I haven't spoken to my father since the day I left for college. I have no grandparents, uncles, aunts, siblings. I have no one. I'd leave, but I was kind of ordered to stay."

Jud looked down and cleared his throat. Laney was staring directly at me, no expression on her face. I didn't need their pity, which was why I never talked about my history.

Remembering that I did have some family, I spoke up again. "I consider my best friend Jimmy like a brother. His children are my godchildren. They're my family, but I would be putting them in danger if I went there. Besides, the stalker knew about Jimmy and would probably check there first. It was too predictable."

Beverly returned to the table with two pies in her hands and set them down. She leaned in to ask, "Is that Ramsey's Jimmy?" She aimed her gaze at Laney as she asked it.

Laney nodded her head. "Yes, Ramsey and Jimmy got married last January, Mama."

Beverly looked taken aback. "You must have been her maid of honor, right?"

Laney slowly nodded her agreement while lightly clearing her throat.

Beverly searched Laney's face and pressed forward. "But if you were..." She quickly looked down, as if she wasn't sure she should continue. "How did you go to their wedding if you couldn't speak?"

"It wasn't easy," Laney admitted quietly. "Ramsey was a safe place for me, though. At the time, I didn't want to be anywhere but with her or..." Laney's eyes flitted to mine, but she didn't continue.

I knew she was going to say my name, but for some reason, she stopped. I looked at Jud and resisted the urge to call her out on it.

"Ramsey knew what I was going through, and we agreed not to put our lives on hold." Laney continued, "So, I stood next to my best friend in a black dress and scarf to hide the bruising. I didn't need to speak, just sign as a witness."

Beverley's lip trembled a bit, probably imagining how her daughter must have felt during that time. Finally, after a few seconds of silence, she spoke up again and pointed her gaze at me.

"Well, I'm glad Jackson came with Laney. It's been way too long since we've seen her and way too long since we've gotten to meet one of her fellas." Beverly was trying to lighten the mood and change the subject. I appreciated her for that, but I had a feeling Laney didn't want it broadcasted to her ex-fiancé.

"Laney's fella? What does that mean? Are you two...?" Jud had his fork lifted in my direction as he looked in between Laney and me. Laney dusted her hands off and let out a low sigh.

"No, we aren't together Jud. We've never been together," Laney said while giving me a quick glance then putting her focus back on Jud. I knew I didn't deserve anything from Laney, but that didn't stop the hot searing pain I felt in my chest at her dismissal.

We had been something.

When we were together, we were fucking perfect. We just weren't labeled. Why did relationships need labels? I never touched another woman while I was with Laney. I'd start my day thinking of her and end my day consumed with her. She was the only person I looked for in a crowd. She was everything to me...I just didn't know how to show that to her. In my book, that was commitment, but she had just thrown me to the wolves. How could she honestly act like we didn't even know each other after everything we'd been through?

My stomach turned, and suddenly I didn't have an appetite. I folded my napkin and to the room said, "If you would please excuse me, I'm feeling tired after the long trip. It was nice to meet all of you, and Beverly, dinner was delicious. Thank you."

Everyone nodded and said their goodnights, but Jud and Laney kept eating, saying nothing. I turned to leave the dining room and headed for the stairs. I took them slowly, hearing the small murmur of conversation from below. I made my way down the hall and shut myself into my room. I locked the door that connected to the bathroom, locked the bedroom door, and fell face first onto the bed. I'd done everything right to not hold her close, made all the right choices to keep her at arm's length, to protect my heart. Yet here I was feeling broken.

LANEY

VIDEO GAMES HAD BONDED LEO, TY, AND ME TOGETHER AS KIDS. Lawson was six years older than me, so we didn't get a ton of time to connect. Zane was close behind him, making him five years older. Ty was only three years older, and Leo was closest in age to me, older by nineteen months.

Leo and I called ourselves twins when we were kids, even though I had red hair and green eyes and he had brown hair and blue eyes. We spent our summers in the tree house or down in the creek catching frogs, but every now and then we would convince Ty to hang out with us, and when we did, we'd play video games. It didn't surprise me that the two of them reacted more strongly to the news of my attack than anyone else.

I needed to apologize, because if the tables were turned, I'd be so hurt. So, after I loaded that small tote with three different game systems from my childhood, I exited the garage and headed toward the back shop, which had been converted into a huge game room for us kids when we were younger.

There was a pool table, a pinball machine no one ever played, a foosball table, and a fifty-five-inch flat screen TV that was surrounded by deep, leather couches. I had painstakingly texted Leo and Zane on my ancient burner phone, asking them to meet me here, but I wasn't sure if they'd show. It was the night after our big dinner debacle, and my brothers still hadn't spoken to me.

I had just finished connecting the Nintendo 64 when I heard voices approaching the shop. I started loading Mario Kart and nervously waited for them to enter. Finally, after I had already started a single-player game, my brothers opened the door. I turned my head to see Ty make his way toward the couch. I wanted him to look at me, see my face—see how sorry I was.

Instead, he lifted his arms over his head and stretched. His white t-shirt with the Chicago Cubs logo on it stretched with him. His light brown hair was covered by a black snapback that also shadowed his face, so I couldn't see his eyes.

I wanted to hug him and force him to hug me back, tell him how stupid I was, but I sat there, waiting while he slowly inspected the coffee table that was loaded with sodas and snacks. I had made Zane drive me down the street to the gas station earlier, where I'd grabbed my brother's favorites. Ty avoided my greedy gaze and grabbed a Pepsi then turned dramatically and plopped down on the couch opposite of me.

Leo stayed against the wall with his arms crossed, his brown hair looking like he'd run his fingers through it a few times. He wore a shirt that had a T-Rex and the words "I ran out of Rux to give" printed on it. I knew his friend Travis had made it for him because Travis was *that guy* who made everyone t-shirts and came up with the sayings himself, convinced he'd come out with the next funny shirt that would turn into a viral meme.

I stood and walked over to Leo with my peace offering in hand. Ever since we were kids, Leo loved Snickers bars, and any time one of us wanted to bribe him or get on his good side, all we had to do was give him one.

I handed him the bar, and he eyed the candy then lifted his gaze to mine and glared.

"Doesn't disappear just because you start up a game and hand me a Snickers, sis," he growled, pushing past me to sit next to Ty. I swallowed my pride and went to sit on the couch across from them, hoping to fix the mess I'd made.

"Look, I screwed up. I'm sorry. I was in a bad place with the PTSD. I was depressed and scared. I should have told you guys...I'm really sorry." I looked down, fighting the urge to cry. They didn't need to be manipulated by tears; they needed honesty from me.

It was silent in the room except for the sounds coming from the game. I waited, the urge to cry getting stronger and stronger with every minute. Finally, Ty stood and walked over to me. He watched me carefully before he scooped me off the couch into a tight hug.

"Don't you ever do that again. We would have taken care of you, Laney." He set me down and stole the Snickers bar from my hand, sauntering back to the couch. "Seriously, though..." He paused for a second, looking at the ceiling. "I'm sorry that shit happened to you." His eyes landed back on mine. "I'm so damn proud of you for using that taser." He took a huge bite of the Snickers and watched the screen like he hadn't just gotten emotional and sweet. I swallowed the lump in my throat and nodded.

I didn't want to talk about it anymore, but I knew I needed to stop being so afraid. I glanced over at Leo, who still hadn't forgiven me, and I sighed. "I hate that I have to be here." Leo's eyes snapped to mine as I continued. "I was planning a vacation and wanted to come for your birthday in October. I had it all planned out. I was going to throw you a huge bash at Dawson's, pay Gena from the Sugar House to come and give you a fake lap dance with baked goods."

Leo snorted and broke his angry demeanor. "What was she going to do, hold up a cupcake and scone while she sat on my lap fully clothed?" he joked.

I grinned and started moving the controller with my thumb, moving Princess Peach through Bowser's Castle. "Pretty much, and I was going to invite Mom just for fun."

"Mom?" Leo's eyebrows came together in confusion.

A bubble of laughter erupted out of me. "Yeah, so I could record the look on her face when her precious Gena, who bakes the best pies in the county, sat on her son's lap while holding those treasured baked goods."

Ty pulled his hat down to cover his face while he laughed, and Leo shook his head. Leo finally reached for the rest of the Snickers bar Ty was working his way through and finished it off. Then he stood, walked over to where I was sitting, and paused. I looked up at him, expecting him to scoop me up too, but he turned around and farted in my face instead.

"Goddammit Leo!" I screamed while leaning back into the couch, covering my nose. He was laughing, Ty was groaning, and when I could breathe again, I looked up to see that Leo was smiling. I supposed for now, I'd take it as progress.

MY FEET HIT THE GRAVEL ROAD WITH MORE FORCE THAN NECESSARY. I didn't normally push my limits like this, but the last mile of running on this road made me reflect on all the emotions I had been at war with this last week. My breathing was heavy and my calves stung, but I kept pushing. I normally ran two miles a day so I was in decent shape, but I ran at a pace that didn't break me or cause me to struggle. I maintained, never pushed.

Jackson was half a mile behind me, and that was another reason I was pushing. I didn't want him to catch up to me, not that he had tried a single time over the last four days. The first time I woke up at six, I pulled on my running gear and headed out the door only to find Jackson already running down the road. I had forgotten he ran around this time every morning.

My thoughts went back to the first night we arrived, that dinner where Jackson revealed more to my family in a mere few hours than he had to me in seven months. It stung, ripped, and tore at me in a way I hadn't felt before. I battled with wanting to barge into his room that night and fight with him, make him hear me, force him to acknowledge how much he'd hurt me, but I saw on his face how hard my comment hit when he left the table. *Good.* He was in the same misery I was then.

I pushed harder, feeling like a ten-year-old again trying to outrun my brothers. Jackson's speed had picked up. *Is he actually going to try to catch up with me today?*

The sun was already up and shining down on the green world around us, all the farms alive and busy. I rounded the corner to the straightaway that led back to my road and slowed for just a second to catch my breath. I squeezed my side as I jogged, the crunch of gravel and steady movement of feet sounding just behind me. This whole avoidance thing was stupid, but I refused to be the first to break it. Other than the necessary hellos and "Clean towels are here," Jackson and I hadn't spoken to each other. If Jackson wanted to talk to me, he could make the first move.

The last four days may have been awkward for us, but it hadn't been for anyone else. My brothers had adopted Jackson as one of their own, inviting him to play football in the back yard, watching car shows at night, and including him in all the regular chores. My mother asked what sort of food he liked to eat and promptly took off to the garden to gather all the veggies she could when she learned Jackson was a vegetarian. Otherwise, he stayed in his room and avoided me—which was fine. I had lived without him for three months; it didn't bother me that he was avoiding me or that he was so close *all the time*.

My face warmed at the reminder of what had happened the night before. I had walked into our joint bathroom, exhausted from cleaning out the horse stalls, pulling weeds, and helping in the kitchen, so I'd forgotten to lock both doors. I had stripped my clothes and tied my hair up right as Jackson's side of the door opened. He looked just as tired as me, having been put to work on some of the new fences Dad needed help with.

Jackson was still pissed at me, but the way his eyes heated and slowly moved over my body proved he wasn't over me—or it verified that he was just another guy who liked boobs. Either way, I'd still argue that Jackson wasn't over me.

Finally, giving up my attempts to outrun him, I slowed my pace to a walk. Jackson gained on me, and then when I thought he might slow down, maybe talk about the previous night and how he hadn't left the bathroom right away or about how I hadn't told him to, he continued running at a steady pace right past me. I watched his back. He wore a navy-blue t-shirt that was soaked down the middle. I closed my eyes to get images of all the other times I had seen Jackson sweaty out of my head.

He continued running until he turned down the driveway to the house. Duncan and Dexter ran up to him, jumping, licking, trying to keep up. I decided to go a different route and walked from the road through the grass until I came close to our property fence. I climbed up, threw one leg over, sat at the top, and then threw my other leg over and jumped down. I loved the lavender fields, had liked to walk beside them and gently run my hand along the tops as a kid.

The sun was shining down directly on me, drying all the sweat on my body from the run. It was already in the high eighties and it was barely seven thirty in the morning. The roosters were still waking up everyone within a five-mile radius, and the sound of grasshoppers and groups of bees buzzing sounded through the air.

I took a second to stand in place and breathe the air in, to center my soul and allow it to sync with the pace of the farm. I loved how slow and unhurried things felt here, how peaceful and safe it was. I opened my eyes, taking in the purple fields, the whitewashed barn off to the side, and the house. My eyes skipped over a few outlier structures around the property until I found my Tree Guardian.

My parent's property had no shortage of trees, which was something I'd loved as a child. I had named and climbed almost every single one of them, at least all the ones that bordered the lavender fields. My favorite was the huge weeping willow that sat between the house and the nearest plot. When I was little, I decided it was a 'she' and named her the Tree Guardian. I'd climb her with my pellet gun and pretend we were protecting the lavender together.

Just as I stood a few feet away from my tree and was looking for the right place to put my hands and feet to scale it, something hit my face. Immediately after the splat, I heard laughter, distinctly male *snickering*.

I wiped at my face, searched the ground for the offending object, and found the tattered pieces of a pink water balloon. *Those little shits.*

"Go, go, go. She saw us, dude. Run!"

I smiled, knowing this meant Leo had officially forgiven me. I started running after the two of them. They were only wearing their basketball shorts, but each had at least three more water balloons in each arm. My brothers were notorious for pranks, usually big ones. It was their love language in a weird way, so this was like them giving me a big hug.

"You guys can't outrun me, you idiots!" I yelled at their backs. They knew I was faster, but I had no weapon or anything to throw at them. Once we neared the side of the barn, I veered off and ducked into the chicken coop.

I gently walked through and grabbed a few eggs out of the hen's boxes, then I climbed out and continued my run. My brothers were rounding the house, toward the back yard, which meant they were headed toward the tree house, where they'd have the vantage point.

I ran hard, going the opposite direction, cutting them off halfway. We nearly collided in the back yard as I caught up, but the two of them evaded me by dashing around the playhouse and the tire swing. I focused on the tree house, knowing that was their end game. Leo saw where I was headed and went to cut me off, but before he could start climbing, I threw an egg.

Children, that's what we were. Immature little kids, but I fucking loved it.

"Ouch, Laney! Shit. Don't throw eggs—you know what Mom said about that," Leo yelled.

I smiled, feeling alive for the first time in months, and went to throw another when Zane threw a water balloon at me instead, this one hitting me in the chest. "Dammit, Zane!" I bellowed, frustrated by how hard he'd thrown it and how badly my boobs hurt. I aimed at his face and threw an egg.

"Shit," he groaned, dropping his water balloons and grabbing his nose. Leo threw a balloon at me as he scaled the tree, but it bounced off my hip and broke on the ground instead.

"Ha ha!" I laughed at him and aimed the egg for his man area. It was a low move, but so was a surprise water balloon attack before breakfast.

Just as I was about to throw the egg, I heard a clear, sharp voice cut through the air. "Laney Laverta Thompson, throw that egg and you'll be making breakfast the entirety of your stay here."

I stopped mid-throw and dropped my arm, slowly turning around.

My mother stood on the back porch with her hands on her hips. She was already wearing a light blue house dress and house slippers, and her hair hung in low curlers.

"Which one of you started this?" my mother asked while crossing her arms, her Southern tone cutting through the summer heat.

Both my traitorous brothers pointed their fingers at me as if we were children again and not in our thirties.

I rolled my eyes and yelled at my mom, "Mama, you know they're lying. They always lie!" I emphasized the last part as I glared at each of them.

My mother huffed and turned around but yelled over her shoulder, "You kids get cleaned up and come eat some breakfast, and no more horseplay."

Leo mimicked my mother's voice while he taunted me, "Yeah, Laney Laverta. No more horseplay."

The three of us started slowly making our way to the house, but just as we were about to hit the porch, I took the egg I still held and smashed it on Leo's head. I took off for the door, barreling through before they could catch me. I turned to look back for just a second to gauge how far I had until I was safe, and then I ran straight into Jackson's chest.

His arms went around me to stabilize my steps. I stood there, caged in his embrace for a beat, then looked up at his face, but just as I did, Leo caught up and smashed a water balloon over my head. As the water sloshed down my face and onto my already soaked shirt, I expected Jackson to let go or rear back, but he surprised me by tightening his grip. I tried to catch his expression, but his eyes weren't on me; they were pinned on my cowering brothers, who also caught the look.

"Just remember, boys, Laney has backup this time. And I like surprises." Jackson smiled with a wide grin, showing all of his teeth, then lowered his arms. Before I could comment, my mother walked into the laundry room.

"That's it! You both are on breakfast duty for a week!" she yelled, pointing a finger at Leo and me.

I peeked back to see where the third participant was, but Zane had snuck into the broom closet and was barely holding the door closed. I narrowed my eyes and mouthed, "Coward." He smirked and held up his finger to his lips, telling me to be quiet. My mother was turning to leave when Jackson spoke up.

"Actually, Beverley, would it be possible to take Leo's place on breakfast duty with Laney?"

My mother pursed her lips and tilted her head, looking at Leo with egg still dripping from his hair, and let out a sigh. "Oh fine. I don't care, but this one owes me a chore. And Zane, don't think I don't see you in that closet—you will deliver a few things over to the McKinney residence. Jen is back, and I want her to have a nice care package."

Zane groaned from the closet, and Leo laughed.

"Now, Laney go shower, and Leo go hose yourself off outside, because there's no way you are walkin through my house with that egg dripping off your noggin."

Leo rolled his eyes and turned around to leave through the back door.

I turned my focus on Jackson now that there was some distance between us. "What was that about? Thought you were freezing me out." I headed toward the living room.

Jackson gave me a bored look while he headed in the same direction. "Insurance, in case you decide to go all silent again. This way, I'll be guaranteed to get to talk to you while we make breakfast over the next week."

My stomach dipped at his words, at the fact that he wanted to talk to me...that the last few days had affected him like they did me.

"Me? You froze me out," I argued, pointing at my chest. I winced at how immature I was coming across.

Jackson's eyes narrowed playfully. "I don't recall starting this little moment of silence between us. By the way, how was that ride you took with Jud the other day?" he asked, showing the smallest bit of irritation.

"So that's what this is about?" I asked, now trying to ease up a bit with my tone. I hadn't considered how the whole Jud surprise would be handled by Jackson. Although, at the same time, a part of me didn't care.

Jackson shook his head and smiled like he had a secret. It was unnerving, especially when he leaned in to whisper, "Lane, I still need to shower, so unless you want a guest, hurry up and get yours over with." He smiled, devoured my body with his eyes, and then turned back toward the kitchen, leaving me stunned, confused, and aroused.

11

JACKSON

FOUR DAYS. THAT'S ALL IT TOOK FOR ME TO CRACK AND SPEAK TO Laney. The week passed at a frustrating pace, dragging in the monotonous daily chores and routines. I enjoyed spending time with Laney's brothers, but they each reminded me of her in some small way, and those little reminders were maddening. Leo was the worst, having the most resemblance to her with the way he made jokes, laughed, and even ate his food.

It was like a pinprick to my chest every time one of them would do something she'd done before, something that took me back to a memory I had with her. It didn't help that Laney was everywhere, but not anywhere I could touch her, have her, or even talk to her. The gap between us just kept growing with each day we didn't speak.

What made it worse was how Laney would wear these cute-as-fuck outfits, and not Chicago, fashionable outfits either. These were ranch clothes. She wore these frayed jean shorts and tank tops, complete with a baseball hat she sported atop two braids that fell down her back. Sometimes she even threw that mass of hair up on her head, letting little pieces of red, silky perfection frame her face.

Laid-back Laney was stunning and created this desire within me that I couldn't understand or even rationalize. All I knew was that at night, I thought of that baseball hat and how badly I wanted her in my bed wearing nothing else.

Then she went and rode a horse with Jud, and I was close to breaking. I was on fence duty with Zane and Ty when the Laney and Jud rode by. I was sure Laney had no idea what it would do to me to see her with him, laughing and joking together, nor did she likely care.

The previous night had been the final straw, when I accidently walked in on her about to take a shower. My respect for Laney and for her parents was all that had me leaving that bathroom; otherwise I would have taken the six steps that separated us and claimed her.

"So, what are we making this morning?" I sidled up to Laney and peeked over her shoulder. There were several brown and green eggs in front of her nestled in a glass bowl, and a package of bacon sat on the counter. It was our first morning making breakfast as a team, and she looked exhausted, still wearing her sleep shorts, slippers, and baggy shirt.

"Bacon, eggs, and biscuits," she said in a raspy voice while crossing the kitchen to grab a cup of coffee. I surveyed the ingredients, noticing there were actually three packages of bacon, not just one, and the bowl had at least twenty or so eggs, but I didn't see any flour out for the biscuits.

"What will we need for the biscuit portion of the meal? Want me to pull anything out and prep it?" I offered, still scanning the kitchen counter for possible baking elements.

Laney brought her red cup up to her lips and sipped while she shuffled back to where I stood. Her hair was doing that framing thing again, making her face look like it was encased by little flames. I wanted to tug on the ends that had fallen and were now resting against her bare skin. The shirt she was wearing kept falling off her shoulder; it was a man's and obviously too big for her. Some very insecure part of me needed to know it wasn't one of Jud's old shirts.

Laney and I still hadn't touched that topic other than what I'd said to her the day before. I didn't know how to bring it up, how to ask why she'd never told me about Jud when I'd never told her anything about my past. I couldn't be frustrated with her over it, but my stomach strained for details.

My body belonged to Laney; she didn't know it and I didn't understand it, but at this point, it was just a medical fact. I didn't want to fight it anymore. My eyes sought her out. My feet walked to wherever she was. My hands itched to touch her. Even my calves burned from trying to catch her every morning.

"I have a secret plan for the biscuits," Laney whispered and looked around, like she was worried we'd be caught. I knew most everyone's schedules from running each morning, but now that it was the weekend, I wasn't sure what to expect.

"Okay, are you going to share the secret with me, or do I have to guess?" I whispered back, taking advantage of the need to be discreet and leaning in close to brush her ear with my lips. Laney shivered, grabbed the loose part of her top that had sagged, and righted it.

I stepped back and tugged on hem of her shirt. "Where'd you get this anyway? It barely fits you." I started grabbing the packs of bacon and slicing them open.

Laney shrugged while she grabbed a large skillet from the top cupboard. "I have no idea. It was in the closet. Probably one of my brothers, or my dad's." *Not Jud's.*

I crossed over to the skillet and started laying strips in the pan then Laney grabbed my wrist.

"No way. I am not that cruel. You can make the biscuits."

I looked at her, confused, not sure what she meant, but her eyes kept bouncing between me and the bacon. I laughed. "Oh, because I'm a vegetarian?"

Laney nodded and let my wrist go. "Doesn't seem very nice to make a vegetarian cook...you know...meat." Her face flushed while she awkwardly shifted her weight from one foot to the other. Laney was ridiculous and adorable, and I missed her so fucking much.

"Okay, I can do the secret biscuits." I smiled while stepping back a foot or two, because if I got any closer, I was going to kiss her.

I watched with rapt attention as she verified the coast was clear and pulled out a black bag from the bottom drawer. Because she'd gotten in my head, I also glanced around to be sure no one was coming.

She pulled free a large yellow box: Bisquick. I tilted my head. "Biscuits in a box?"

She nodded and grinned. "My mother would kill me if she knew I was cheating, but her recipe takes ten times longer. I had Leo sneak this in yesterday." She handed it over. "Now mix, and if Mama finds out, I'm blaming you."

"Look at you two! This food looks amazing," Beverley beamed while grabbing Laney's face with her hands and squeezing.

"Oww, Mom, let me go. I won't have any face left if you keep squeezing," Laney begged through mashed lips.

Beverly let go and laughed, waving her hand. "Hogwash, you're fine."

Zane came in through the front door with large work boots all untied, a wrinkled t-shirt, and disheveled hair. "Mornin everyone," he said in a raspy voice, sounding just like Laney, while he headed toward the coffee pot.

"Morning," everyone mumbled back. Wayde was already in the dining room with the newspaper and a cup of coffee.

Beverley had started setting the table and yelled over her shoulder, "Zane, go wake your brother. He still owes me some chores from that egg stunt y'all pulled."

Zane ran upstairs, and a few seconds later, the sound of knocking echoed down the hall, along with "Get up! Gena from the Sugar House brought donuts!"

A few thumps later, someone's feet were pounding down the stairs. Leo slid into the kitchen wearing white socks, boxer briefs, and a black t-shirt.

"Where's Gena? Where's the donuts? Did you guys leave me the Boston cream one?" He started looking around the kitchen while mumbling about flavors and types of donuts.

I bit back a laugh as Zane finally walked back in. "No, idiot. Ma wants you to set the table." Zane hit the back of Leo's head and walked off. Laney started laughing into her shirt, to hide her face.

Leo looked around and let out a groan, "Zane*iack*, that was cold, even for you, man. No man taunts another man with donuts. That was just mean." Leo stalked off carrying a plate in each hand.

Beverly had edged near the counter holding the pan of biscuits, eyeing them distrustfully. Her face was all contorted as she picked up one and began inspecting it closely. I glanced over at Laney, who was trying not to watch her mother but failing. A few seconds passed, but eventually Beverly lout a loud sigh. "Laney Laverta, did you honestly think I wouldn't notice?"

Laney didn't look up from the eggs she was plating while she softly retorted, "I'm not sure what you mean, Mama."

Beverly scoffed. "Really, baby girl...you sure?"

Laney made a noise of lightly agreeing while rubbing at her collar-bone like her lie was stuck under there, trying to break free. "Mama, Jackson handled the biscuits—ask him."

Oh hell no.

She was not pinning this on me. "I just did whatever Laney told me to do," I argued, holding up my hands.

"And what exactly did Laney tell you?" Beverley asked, eyeing me like a criminal. I looked over at Laney, who was giving me the look: the big eyes, the thinned lips. She even shook her head when her mother wasn't looking.

"I don't know, just followed a recipe, ma'am," I said and hurried out of the room.

"I will find out, you two! Just know I always find out," Beverley boomed from the kitchen.

Leo, Zane, and Wayde all fell into a fit of laughter as I sat down and put my hands over my head. These Thompson women would be the death of me.

LANEY WAS BAREFOOT AS WE WALKED THROUGH THE LARGE GRASSY field behind her house used for pasturing the horses. She promised they wouldn't bother us. I hoped she was right because horses scared the shit out of me. I kept glancing up to memorize their positions in the field as we walked.

It was hot as hell and my clothes were sweaty against my skin, but I didn't own a pair of shorts, except for the running ones I had brought. I wore tennis shoes, but I was starting to envy Laney in her bare feet and bare legs, walking in her tiny shorts and tank top.

I missed her skin, missed her legs, missed the way they used to wrap around me. *Shit...focus on horses...biscuits...barns.*

Laney was picking away at a flower in her hand but had yet to speak. She wanted to talk, but so far, we'd only walked. The black horse in the field lifted its head as we got closer, sniffed, then started grazing again. Laney finally dropped the flower, or what was left of it, and turned to look at me. Her red hair was brilliant under the sun, all loose and wavy, and my fingers itched to touch it. I watched her green eyes instead and waited.

"Look, I'm sorry. I'm sorry for saying we weren't anything to each other the other night. I was just trying to protect my heart because you hurt it so badly. That's no excuse, and I shouldn't have said what I said, especially to Judson." She watched me carefully, taking in every inch of my face as she waited for me to respond.

I looked at the ground as I considered what she'd said, kicking at a clump of dirt. "What's the story between you two anyway?" I watched the black creature continue to eat the grass near his feet, nearly positive he'd gotten closer.

Laney shifted on her feet. "Jud and I met in Sunday school when I was eight. He was the first boy I ever had a crush on." She looked up to the sky and closed her eyes as the warm breeze brushed past us. I watched her, completely enraptured by the length of her throat and the perfect hue of her creamy skin. "He became good friends with my brothers, so I essentially grew up with him. He was my first kiss, my first boyfriend, my first...everything..."

We had started slowly walking toward the horses, but I just kept watching Laney's toes as we moved through the grass.

"It was our senior year that things got weird between us. He kept talking about how he wanted to get married and how lucky Lawson was that he had met Sara and they'd already started having kids." Laney stopped about ten feet away from the massive equestrian creature and toyed with the stem of a flower. "It's not that I didn't want to marry him. I loved him, but there was something I wanted more than him. When he proposed, after graduation...I said yes, but I was conflicted. Things here at home were stressful. I had investigated college options, and all of them would take me away from home. My dad and I were fighting so much that he finally said if I was going to leave then I couldn't have a dime from them to do it." Laney's eyes went to the grass, and her tone had softened.

I was feeling something hot rise up my throat as I pictured eighteen-year-old Laney trying to chase her dream and everyone here try to hold her down. She should have had support. She should have been given everything to pursue those dreams.

"Dad wanted me to take the very reasonable proposal I had gotten from Jud and settle down...do the right thing. That's what he kept telling me. *'Don't expect us to give you any money to go chase tail around Chicago like some party girl'*...that's another thing he liked to say a lot. My mother never stepped in to defend me. The only person who did was Leo. He told me to get the hell out of there and chase my dreams until I owned them." Laney grabbed her elbow and looked past me. "I went to Jud and told him I wanted to go to college and live in Chicago, said I wanted to travel and experience things. I told him I wanted him to come with me and we could get married and do college, travel—all of it. He gave me an ultimatum, told me if I wanted Chicago then I didn't want him, so I handed the ring back and moved away."

We kept walking through the field, the silence lighter now that she'd exposed part of her past to me.

"My father and I didn't speak the day I left, except for his harsh reminder that I'd regret leaving...that I'd regret the city and not to ask him for any money." Laney slowly made her way toward the black horse. I let her grab my hand and pull me forward until my fingers touched the soft nose of the creature.

It was enormous, its fur so glossy under the sunlight. It had the softest hair and the gentlest brown eyes.

Laney stroked its side and talked softly to it. "Hey there, Loki. How's my boy?" She pulled a carrot out of her back pocket and laid it flat in her palm under the horse's nose. I didn't move; once it showed its teeth, I was frozen. I watched as Loki ate it, then Laney patted the horse's neck and whispered in its ear.

"I'm sorry you went through that," I whispered as we stood arm to arm in front of the horse. She smiled at me, pulled another carrot out, and handed it to me; I tentatively took it. She guided my hand, making sure it was flat, and when the horse neared, she held my wrist in place. Loki gently took the carrot without harming me. I moved closer to pet its neck, like Laney had done. I smiled.

"It's okay. I don't regret it, and things with Jud...they're complicated," Laney confessed, which gave me pause.

"Complicated as in you still have feelings for him?" I asked, trying to keep my tone easygoing. Laney furrowed her brows like she was concentrating, but before she could answer, we heard: "Janey, you back here?"

I turned my head to see Jud walking toward us. I moved away from the horse.

"What did he just call you?" I jokingly asked Laney.

Laney rolled her eyes and quietly said, "It's our names mixed together. People used to call us Janey in high school. That or Lud, but I liked Janey better...anyway, it's dumb. I'm not sure why he's doing it now."

She moved from the side of Loki so she was within eyesight of Jud. He smiled as he got closer and broke into a jog.

"Hey, I was looking for you," he said, slightly out of breath.

Laney wiped her hands on her shorts and gave him a smile that didn't reach her eyes. For some reason, it eased the panic building inside of my chest.

"Well you found us. What's up?" she asked, and I didn't miss how she didn't say he found her, but us. I smiled and continued to pet Loki.

Jud watched me pet the horse then looked at Laney. "I wanted to see if you want to go out tonight? It's Saturday night, and you know what that means down at Dawson's."

Laney let out a little scoff. "Judson, I'm supposed to be laying low. If I walk into Dawson's on a Saturday night, it will be the opposite of laying low."

Judson started laughing. "I know, but I haven't seen you in ages, and from the sounds of it, you could use a good night on the town."

Laney looked over at me, squinting against the sun. "What do you think?"

I glanced at Jud. He was wearing sunglasses so it was difficult to gauge his reaction, but I assumed he was pissed that Laney had just included me in their plans.

"I think we were told to stay put and lay low...I think there's a psycho looking for us and going to a bar isn't a good idea," I chided, looking straight at Jud. What a fucking moron, suggesting she go out, knowing she's in hiding.

Judson looked at me with his mouth turned down. I knew he didn't like this, but I didn't care.

"You've been here for over a week, Lane. Come on, just come out with me. We won't broadcast that you're here. You can wear a wig or a disguise...whatever you want."

Laney caressed the horse's ear before looking back at Jud.

"If I do go anywhere, Jackson has to come with me." She glanced at me quickly then looked away, like she was embarrassed to have to include me in her plans.

Jud waited just a second before he smiled at Laney and said, "Great, maybe Jackson can ride with Leo. I'll pick you up at eight tonight, Laney. Gotta go!" Judson ran off before Laney could tell him no.

12

LANEY

I WAS STARING ABSENTLY INTO THE STANDUP MIRROR IN MY temporary bedroom. The sun was setting outside, and streaks of red and gold were shattering the shadows that lurked in the corners of my room. I didn't even realize how late it had gotten until one of the golden beams blinded me by reflecting off the mirror.

Jud would be arriving soon to pick me up, but I wasn't focusing on him or his request to take me out. I was still focusing on the fact that Jackson had asked about him. Jackson had never really asked about my past before; he always listened if I talked but never went out of his way to ask. It was unsettling.

There were a million times when we used to be together that it seemed like he wanted to ask or say something, but he'd always just clench his jaw and change the subject, like conversations like that would move us into couple territory.

I let out an exaggerated sigh and adjusted my dress. I had run by the outdoor mall with my mom and Jenny. Jenny was our next-door neighbor growing up, and her mom had been my mom's best friend, but she'd died when Jenny was twelve. Since then, Mom had stepped in as unofficial mother to her, and we'd essentially grown up with her. It was good to see her again and spend time with her. Last I'd heard she had moved to Cincinnati to teach. We shopped for a while and I picked up a few things, including this little black thing and a dark brunette wig.

I was hesitant to wear it because I didn't want to give Jud the wrong idea. I was wearing this for me, for being home again and for just feeling good. And some very small part of me reminded me that I might also be wearing it for Jackson.

I closed my eyes tightly, angry with myself because I was being an idiot if I thought Jackson's moment of curiosity meant he would suddenly be the relationship kind of guy. Because he wasn't.

He was the type that recognized what he wanted but was too damn afraid to embrace it. This was supposed to be about me getting my heart back, not about offering what little scraps I'd gathered back to him. Yet, every time I thought of dancing with Jackson tonight, I couldn't put these stupid metaphorical butterflies flying around in my stomach back in their metaphorical cages. I wanted him to want me again, and I wanted him to ask me. I was a fucking glutton for punishment and exactly back where I had been before he'd walked out of my life three months ago.

My fingers itched to dial my best friend and demand she verbally kick my ass into gear regarding Jackson.

He was so good at pretending with me. He had fooled me so many times. It always felt real with him, and now that we were here, I needed more. More details. More truths. More touches. More of everything from him.

"Laney, you ready?" my mother called through the bedroom door. I blinked to clear my thoughts, grabbed my wallet, and headed for the door.

"Yep, all done." I peered at my mother, who'd pulled her hair back and exchanged her shoes for big fuzzy slippers. I smiled at the reminder of her and my dad's Saturday tradition: Western and Waffles night.

For as long as I could remember, they'd shoo us kids into the game room or our bedrooms, right at eight p.m. They didn't want to be bothered while Mom made them chicken and waffles, then they snuggled on the couch and watched a variety of westerns. I always loved watching the two of them cuddle up, sharing a blanket, my father stroking my mother's hair while they watched John Wayne strut across some dirt-covered field.

"Have fun tonight, sweetie, and be careful," my mother said while she gently placed a few curls that had fallen out of place behind my ear.

We walked down the hall next to each other in a tight silence. I knew she wanted to say something, but I wasn't going to be the one to force her. Once we reached the steps, she turned to me and grabbed my hands.

"I've cried myself to sleep every night since you've been back." She looked at the ground. I swallowed the lump of emotion that was climbing up my throat and waited. "I keep picturing you in that garage... I keep seeing you thrashing about and reaching for the thing around your neck. I keep tryin to push it out of my head, but you're my baby girl and I can't believe someone hurt you."

She reached up and started stroking my hair as tears rushed down her face. I pressed my fingers under my eyes to keep my own at bay.

"I know I couldn't have been there, but I wish I could have been a support to you afterward. I would have come to you, sweetie. I would have cooked and cleaned for you...I would have done whatever you needed." She sobbed while pulling me into a firm hug.

I'd known this moment was eventually going to come, but I hadn't been expecting it to happen right as I was about to go dancing for the night. I let a few tears fall for how badly I had wanted my mom back then, how badly I'd wanted my family but how stubborn and ashamed I'd been about letting any of them know what happened. They had told me if I left the farm and moved to that city, something was bound to happen.

They'd warned me, repeatedly. I didn't want them to know they were right, to know there was evil in the city and it'd found me. I had Jackson, and he was all I had needed at the time. I could feel that reserved part of me take center stage, the dormant, quiet, good daughter persona coming back strong.

My mother finally stopped sobbing and pulled away. I smiled and grabbed her face, wiping at her wet cheeks.

"Mama, I love you so much. I'm so sorry for not telling you. Please forgive me." It was all I could think to say to fix this fracture that was between us. I knew it hurt her, and just like with my brothers, I knew it would have hurt me too if they had done it to me. I just didn't know how to go back in time and fix it.

"It's okay, baby. I love you, I just need you to know how much sometimes." She kissed my cheek and turned to run downstairs, leaving me alone at the top. I breathed in and out a few times and tried to get my emotions under control.

Below I heard the screen door open and a loud "Janey, you ready?"

I winced at the name he chose to use again and let out a shaky breath. Running down the stairs, I plastered on a fake smile for my friend Jud, who looked at me like I wasn't his friend at all. He looked at me like I was much more...exactly the way I used to look at Jackson.

Shit.

Dawson's was a small bar with peeling blue paint all along the outside. It had worn-out, faded windows and the best burgers and fries in the entire state. I had grown up sitting in the ripped-up booths in the back, then eventually graduated to the stools that ran along the wide bar in the center of the room. Jud opened the door for me, and the smell of beer and grease filled my lungs; I happily breathed it in.

I missed this place.

There were still pictures of people breaking records all over the walls, only local heroes, but all the pictures dated back to as far as anyone can remember. Some were newspaper clippings of high school football teams, others were fish that had been caught, their weights breaking all sorts of accounts.

There were mementos all over the walls, and none of them had been dusted. Old man Dawson was nearly blind and thankfully not cooking anymore, but we all loved him. We didn't care about the places unkempt appearance; in fact most everyone knew to bus their own tables and even wipe down surfaces before they sat down to eat.

Jud placed his hand on the small of my back and nudged me toward the open area in the rear part of the bar. My anxiety regarding loud places and crowded rooms was flaring to life. If Alicia was in town and watching us, it would be too easy for her to sneak in unnoticed. This was a terrible idea.

I played with the long ends of my faux hair that covered my red coloring. The style had the brunette strands falling to my midback, and it was twisted into a half-updo with small curled strands that gently framed my face. Judson pressed me further toward the rear of the building.

The back was a huge party scene on the weekends, or at least it had been in the past. There was a huge dance floor with a stage, and stools lined the outer edges of the space, along with a few pool tables.

The lights were already low as the room filled with people. I could feel my heart beating so hard I wondered if it were possible for it to dislodge itself. My eyes scanned the room, desperate to find a certain pair of sapphire eyes. My stomach twisted with worry when I saw that he hadn't arrived. He was supposed to stay with me, and although he hadn't agreed with this idea to go out tonight, I knew he wouldn't truly let me go without showing up.

"Here." Jud handed me a beer and gave me a seductive smile. I smiled back, happy to be near his familiarity. It may have been years since I was considering marrying him, but those laughter lines around his eyes were the same, just deeper. The strong frame of his jaw I used to run my hand along was still the same. Even his woodsy scent hadn't changed.

I took a sip, watching the room, and a moment later, Leo and Jackson walked in.

I tried not to react or care that Jackson had shown up, but that anxiety-ridden wave of destruction was crashing down on me, demanding I cling to the one person who made me feel safe. Jackson had on the outfit he'd worn the day we arrived, his trucker hat covering his eyes and his flannel shirt making him look like a local.

I turned away from him, trying to calm my nerves and rid myself of the need to be near him.

"You guys ready to have fun tonight?" I turned to see my brother Leo rubbing his hands together and watching the room, like he was hunting. I rolled my eyes.

"Sure, let's have fun, brother. I dare you..."

Leo's hand went up fast as lightning to cover my mouth. "Don't even think about it, little sister. I will not be accepting any dares tonight." Leo smiled at me and slowly lowered his hand.

I bit my lip and stayed quiet. I'd wait for my other brothers to show up and then trap Leo into hearing our dare.

We Thompson kids had a rule: We never backed down from a dare. Truths we could pass on, but dares were not optional.

Jackson looked between Leo and me a few times before he picked up on it. "You guys don't turn down dares?"

"Nope," Leo said with a pop of his lips. Jackson gave me a heated look. My face flushed; I knew what he was thinking about. The memory pinged in the back of my mind like a TV channel.

"STOP IT, JACKSON." I PUSHED AT HIM AS I CONTINUED STIRRING THE spaghetti noodles.

He grabbed at my waist again and pulled me toward him. "Why?" he whispered into my neck.

"Because, kissing you was a one-time thing. I'm not getting involved with the guy who gave me a place to stay. It's messy," I said as I watched the boiling noodles. I tried to cook for Jackson as much as possible, to show my appreciation for giving me a place to stay.

He lightly lifted my t-shirt and started dragging his thumb down my ribcage. "Laney, please. Kiss me. I've never had to beg a woman before. You're hurting my ego." His chin was resting on my shoulder now.

I laughed because the idea of his ego shrinking was thrilling. "Good. You could use a downsize."

He spun me around and moved me toward the sink, then caged me in. His face was close to mine as he whispered, "Please."

I shook my head no, determined to keep things platonic between us. I couldn't risk having nowhere to go again, and I already knew Jackson wasn't a one-woman kind of guy. He looked down at our bare toes and let out a sigh. I thought he'd give up, and I was honestly glad.

He was hard to resist.

We'd had one kiss the weekend before, on his couch. I kissed him. He kissed me back. The next day I stole his car. What we had was complicated to say the least.

Just when I thought he'd move away, he stared me down and said the last words on earth I thought I'd hear from him.

"I dare you."

I blinked and scoffed, "You what?" I tried to push him away, get some air, because I didn't turn down a dare. Never had.

He laughed and grabbed at my hands. "Come on, Laney, I dare you. I'm not proud that you've forced me to childish antics, but here we are." He finished with widening his arms. I thought about running away, but I stood my ground and stared into his blue eyes instead. He smiled at me, knowing he'd won.

"Fine, but only if you swear not to ever dare me to do anything else again," I told him firmly.

His face faltered, then he flashed another smile. "Deal." He stood still as I stood up on my tippy toes, wrapped my arms around his neck, and pressed my lips to his. That kiss was a catalyst for us.

It wasn't just a kiss, as much as I needed it to be. It was so much more and sadly broke down any remaining defenses I had left.

"LANE, LET'S DANCE." JUDSON BROUGHT ME BACK TO THE PRESENT with a tug on my hand. I half-smiled at Jackson, who had his eyes pinned to where my hand was enclosed in Jud's. I pushed my hair behind my ear, wishing it were just as simple to push some of these uneasy emotions away.

I followed Jud out to the dance floor, and the music was loud as we moved to an upbeat country song. I smiled up at Jud; he was taller than me, but shorter than Jackson. His inky, black hair was messy and to most girls it would seem sexy as hell, but sadly, not to me. I had grown accustomed to running my hand over Jackson's shaved head and found the lack of hair soothing.

The more I looked at Jud's hair, the more I remembered how greasy it got. I looked into his eyes instead. His lips were curved into a grin, his eyes heavy-lidded as he watched my mouth. He looked at me like I was still his girl and he was still my man, like we were going to get married and have three kids and a dog named Jumbo.

The song switched, and we started swaying to the slow melody as Jud's hands moved to my sides then wrapped around me. It took me back to the last time we'd danced together. It was at my brother's wedding. I was such a different person then, so strong and brave, so sure of what I wanted in the future—even to the point of laying down my future with the man I loved to get to it. I could sense that Jud wanted to say something by the way he kept clearing his throat and positioning his torso closer to mine.

Not wanting to hear what he might say, I let go of Jud's shoulders. The song changed a second later, covering my awkward blunder. With a tense look, he grabbed my hand and walked us back toward our stools. I noticed that Jenny had shown up, wearing a navy blue summer dress and brown cowboy boots. She had bought the dress while we were out shopping. I wanted to go over and tell her how good it looked, but Jud tugged on my hand, leading me away from her.

Ty and Lawson were standing there with Leo and Jackson, laughing and drinking beers. Jackson looked at where my hand was, inside Judson's. There was no emotion this time on his face, just the intensity of his scrutiny. The side of his jaw ticked as he lifted his gaze and moved his eyes around the room. I wished I could say I knew the myriad of expressions he was displaying, but I had never seen Jackson jealous.

A fire started in my belly at the thought of Jackson being jealous over me, a total inferno of excitement and joy. Feelings I shouldn't feel, emotions that would only confuse me and leave me disappointed—yet I couldn't extinguish it.

I hated that he made me feel like a teenager again.

I walked away to grab a beer from the front, just to shake the feeling. I felt like I was unraveling. For once I was feeling emotions that rivaled the fear that always seemed to be surging through me.

I walked up to the bar and found old man Dawson. He had his coke bottle glasses on, his watery brown eyes homing in on me.

"Laney Thompson, as I live and breathe," he said in a raspy voice. His white hair was stuffed under an old Cubs cap, and his large belly was barely concealed under a massive Hawaiian shirt. He had tan cargo shorts on and white, bargain brand tennis shoes.

"Your hair is different, and you look so much older," he said, trying to asses me from behind the counter.

I let out a sigh as I walked toward the opening of the bar and let him wrap me in his large arms. "How you are doing, old man?" I felt his body shift as he laughed.

"Who you calling old man? Why just last week a pretty thing flirted with me, asked me to get her a drink."

I stepped back and watched him as he tried to put on a proud face. "Sure she wasn't just giving you her drink order, because you know... you're the bartender?" I said while slapping his belly.

He doubled over like I'd hurt him. "So mean, damey Laney. That big city sure has changed you." He held his hand over his heart, faking a heartbreak. "Ya, ya, ya...so you say. But I've always been this cheeky." He laughed as he made his way toward the draft beer, and I leaned over the bar and folded my arms. "So, how long are you here for, darlin?" he asked while pouring me a large mug I knew he wasn't going to let me pay for.

I let out a sigh. "Not sure, a few weeks. I'm kind of hiding from someone," I quietly admitted while looking around. Most of the customers were in the back, just a few older ones sitting on the stools around me.

Dawson handed me my beer, and as I went for my purse, he glared. I stopped and started sipping my beer instead.

"Hiding from who?" he asked while drying his hands on a towel.

I cleared my throat from the foam that coated my tongue. "Long story, Daws. I caught the attention of a crazy secretary stalker for this guy I worked with in Chicago."

Dawson's eyes went large. "Leave it to you, Little Five." He started shaking his head as he walked back toward the kitchen. I giggled at his pet name for me. Little Five was what everyone who knew our family called me, and Damey Laney was what Dawson called me after he helped shoo off more than a few boys over the years due to unwanted glances. Dawson always claimed I was his damsel in distress.

I sauntered to the back and found Leo up on the stage singing karaoke. I knew he'd been dared by Lawson, and I hated that I'd missed seeing it. Leo hated getting dares, and as a result, we dared him more than anyone should ever be.

He was belting the chorus of some 90s pop ballad when I noticed Jackson was off in a corner laughing with Zane and Lawson; Jenny was standing close to Zane, as usual. The two of them were inseparable. We were all shocked she and Zane had never become an item. Ty was leaning up against the wall sipping on a beer, watching the floor. He caught my eye and lifted his drink, and I smiled and headed over. I didn't know where Jud was.

As I got closer, I heard them laughing about what song they were going to get Leo to sing next. I leaned against the wall next to Ty and just watched as the guys pored over a large binder full of laminated lyrics. Jackson had a small glass of what looked like vodka, which was odd as he didn't normally drink anything but whiskey or beer when he was out.

My attention was stolen when a group of five guys headed in our direction. All were wearing a variety of flannel and Carhart. Three of them looked like they could benchpress my father's tractors.

I gripped Ty's forearm as the group got closer and whisper-yelled so he could hear me over the music. "Is that Andrew Ebely?"

Ty kept his eyes on the group and nodded. Then he slowly set his beer behind him and turned his baseball hat backward. *Oh shit.*

That was the universal Thompson sign for "Shit's about to go down." I stayed put, waiting as the mood in our little corner shifted. Lawson saw them approaching and stood up, rigid as a telephone pole. Zane let out a low whistle while cracking his knuckles. The guys were standing just feet away from our little mismatched group.

"Lookie here. It's the Thompson crew." Andrew Ebely scoffed while spitting his wad of chew into the cup in his hand. *Ewwww.*

I tipped my head down, hoping he wouldn't notice it was me, but I wasn't fast enough.

"Oh, and look..." He gestured at me with his hand while glancing over his shoulder at the mangy group behind him. "It's their Raggedy Ann sister too."

Andrew Ebely was a bully. We'd known him our entire lives, and we'd never once gotten along with him. He used to throw gum in my hair, dead frogs, spiders—whatever he could find. He made my brothers' pranks look pathetically weak.

I hated him. I assumed he hated me too, but my junior year, he asked me to prom, confessed this long crush he'd had on me and everything. I coldly and proudly turned him the fuck down and reminded him that I had a boyfriend. He'd thought if he told me how he felt, I'd dump Jud.

Asshole.

His eyes skated over me, perused my bare shoulders, and drifted down my legs. On instinct, I crossed my arms to try to conceal my chest.

Jackson shuffled a foot or two closer to where we were then cleared his throat. "Can we help you with something, or are you just going to stand there and stare at her like a fucking creep?"

Andrew's gaze swung to Jackson and his eyes narrowed. "Just wanted to remind the Thompson boys here that regardless of their beloved little bitch—of—a sister's homecoming; this is our turf. Last bet at the tables confirmed it." He spat again, and my stomach rolled.

It wasn't exactly easy to see all my brothers' expressions, but I knew the name Ebely had called me wasn't going to fly.

I heard the song switch over on the speaker system. All the guys behind Andrew stood their ground as he laughed at the fact that no one was moving. *Okay, maybe they are going to let it go...*

"That bet ended a month ago, Ebely. Now get out of here before we make you pay for that comment you just made about our sister," Lawson very calmly explained to Andrew. Jackson had moved, now just a few feet from Ty, from me. I could see him clearer now; his jaw was ticking —no surprise there since that was all he usually did—but I noticed his fists were clenched too. Jackson didn't fight, at least as far as I knew. He was the reputation guy, the calm, cool, business connection guy. But seeing him now, next to my brothers, he looked like he was country grown.

Andrew started rubbing at his overgrown facial hair while the guys behind him laughed. "What? You guys don't like it when we call your little flirt of a fucki—" His words died on his tongue as Jackson took two large steps forward and threw his fist right into Andrew's face.

Holy shit.

I ducked as all hell broke loose around me. The guy behind Andrew stepped up and Zane stepped in, throwing a punch. Lawson was throwing punches at another guy. Ty was on the ground, punching some-one. Another guy came from across the bar and broke a pool stick over Jackson's back. I gasped, worried he was hurt, but he didn't even act fazed by it. He had two ass-wipes attacking him now, but not a moment later, Leo came running from the stage, yelling like Goku from Dragon

Ball Z. He had a beer bottle in his hand and broke it over the head of the guy who'd hit Jackson with the pool stick.

It was madness. Chaos. And I loved it.

I stayed crouched against the wall until things got too crazy. Jenny was ducked down too, across the room. When I had a clear chance, I crawled over to a safer table and secured a place underneath it, and Jenny joined me, covering her head. Now the entire bar was in on the fight, and no one was safe. A few other women had joined us under the tables as the men went all *Fight Club*.

Old Laney would have joined in. She would have jumped on Andrew the asshole's back and pulled his overgrown hair. I hated the fact that I might have done that if I didn't still feel so defective inside. It felt like Alicia had taken something from me and I couldn't figure out how to get it back, like she'd stolen my fire and now I was just a watered-down mess.

As it was, I was barely containing my panic at the whole bar being in chaos. My stomach tightened as people moved around us. My reflexes were telling me to curl into a ball and protect myself until the danger was over, but the old part of myself that was tied to this life begged me to remember how it used to be, to remember how alive I used to feel when I was amidst chaos like this with my brothers.

An air horn went off and the music died out, followed by Dawson yelling.

"That's it. Ebely, you and your idiots get out. I know you started this shit. You always start it. You're banned for two months this time. No wiggling your way back in either."

Andrew and his idiot friends mumbled a few complaints, swiping at some blood, but eventually followed Dawson out of the bar. Some of them had to be carried out by other guys. People started righting chairs that had been knocked over and tables that were tipped.

Jackson had a pretty ugly cut on his lip, so I scrambled out from under the table and grabbed his hand, leading him to the bathroom. He followed silently and perched on the counter. He watched as I wet a paper towel and carefully placed it against his lip.

"This is going to swell. You need ice."

He let out a low laugh. "Worth it."

I caught his eye and frowned. "Was it?"

He narrowed his gaze at me in confusion and caught my wrist mid-wipe. "The Laney I knew would never have asked that." He pushed off the counter until he was towering over me. I felt his stare like a branding iron. "In fact...the Laney I knew would have thrown the first punch the first time that fucker called you a name." His lecture and firm gaze made me feel small.

I hated that he was right. My eyes burned with unshed tears over the person I wasn't anymore. He knew it better than anyone though.

I didn't respond, but he whispered, "She doesn't get to take everything from you unless you let her. Stop being a doormat. I can't figure out if it's this place, your family, or just the fact that Alicia is out of prison, but I miss you...the old you. I miss your fire."

A tear slipped down my cheek at his admission. He searched my face, like he was waiting for that spark to ignite the second he called me out. Like, just by saying it, the fervor would magically come back. He'd been gone for three months; that fire had slowly left me over the course of trying to stand on my own two feet, and then she'd been let out and any progress I'd made from the first attack had vanished. I lowered my head and swiped at my tears. I didn't have any words for him, and I didn't want to be around someone who saw me so clearly. I turned away from him and exited the bathroom, running directly into Jud.

"Whoa...what the hell happened? I stepped outside to take a call and—"

I shook my head. "Jud, just get me out of here please."

He carefully held my shoulders and looked at me, and Jackson came out of the bathroom a second later. I didn't look at him. I didn't want to see his face as Jud pulled me into his arms and walked me outside.

JUD'S THUMB RAN ALONG THE INSIDE OF MY ARM, HOVERING OVER MY tattoo. I watched the movement and swallowed the lump of guilt in my throat. He'd been carefully touching me all night, and I hadn't stopped him, mostly because he hadn't crossed any lines or done anything but skim my arm, hand, and face. Still, it didn't change how horrible it made me feel.

We were walking this line that Jud kept erasing. Each touch, each laugh, every tug of my hair, or joke was him kicking dirt over that line I'd drawn in the sand.

I went with him to his house.

It sent a message.

One I wasn't aiming for, but just the same, I knew what he wanted.

I was lying in my dress, barefoot on his oversized king-sized bed. He had *SportsCenter* playing in the background and all the lights off in the room.

He sat up on his elbow, bare chested, and traced a line from my eyebrow down to my neck. I knew where this was going.

I knew what would happen if I let his finger travel down to my shoulder and pull on the strap of my dress.

My breathing was ragged as he kept that finger moving up and down my neck, until he hovered over my collarbone.

I watched his eyes as they heated.

"You're breathing hard," he said, laying his hand over my heart.

I tried to even it out by taking a deep breath. "Yeah, guess I'm nervous."

Jud laughed. "About what? You know me. There's nothing to be nervous about."

I nodded and placed my hand on his chest to stop him from getting any closer.

Jud's blue eyes looked gray under his dim lights. They traveled from my collarbone to my lips and paused. He slowly took the hand that was on his chest, brought my fingers up to his lips, and kissed the pads of my fingers.

"Jud, stop." I breathed out, pain slicing at my heart.

He leaned back a fraction, concern weighing down his expression. "What's wrong?"

I tried to collect my thoughts and keep the tears that wanted to fall at bay. "You have to stop trying stuff because nothing is going to happen between us."

"Why isn't anything going to happen between us?" he asked in a light tone while bringing my fingers back to his lips.

"I can't do this," I whispered as a few tears sprang free and ran down the sides of my face. He carefully watched me, then let out a sigh and lowered his head to rest on mine. His lips were too close to mine, and I knew if I wasn't careful, he'd...

His warm lips gently fused with mine and pressed for access. I refused to give it to him. I pushed at his chest until he was releasing my lips and sitting up. I sat up so we weren't horizontal anymore.

Jud ran his fingers through his hair and groaned. "Why did you agree to come back here? I thought..." He broke off and looked away from me. "I thought things were different this time."

I peered over at him and wrapped my arm around my middle. "Different how?"

"Different like you were ready to settle down and that's why you came back...why you came over tonight," he whispered while watching the wall.

I looked away from him and let out another sigh. "Jud, I came here tonight because we're friends. I miss you and wanted to spend time with you. And I'm back because I have to be."

"Bullshit." He shook his head and glared at me. "You came here because you miss us. I know you do. It's why you came to me and not him," Jud yelled while pointing at his chest.

I didn't want to hurt him.

My stomach twisted, and my heart was filled with lead. I'd left with Jud to forget. I needed a distraction and something to take me back to an easier time, a time when my heart didn't hurt, when my mind wasn't solely caught up in a man who didn't know how to love me.

Judson had always known how to love me.

I wanted to agree with Jud, wanted to let him help me forget, but I couldn't. I looked down at my hands and prayed time would pass so I wouldn't have to be honest with Jud.

"Is it him? I thought you guys weren't together..." he asked, while carefully pulling my chin up.

More tears spilled down with his question. "I love him, Jud. I wish so badly that I didn't. I wish I could erase him from my mind and my heart, but it doesn't work like that. He's stuck in there, in my very bone and marrow, and I don't know how to get him out. What's worse is that he doesn't even want to be there." I sobbed, violently wiping at my eyes.

Jud picked at a piece of lint and flicked it from his fingers. He waited a second or two before he pressed me for more details. Finally, he exhaled and asked, "So you do want to settle down, just not with me?"

I swallowed the truth of that statement and looked away from Jud. I hadn't considered whether or not I was ready to settle down, but the thought was planted now, and I hated the image that ran through my head.

Jackson holding my hand while we watched our kids play with Sammy and Jasmine, my belly big and round with Jackson's baby...

I blinked to get rid of the picture and the spike of adrenaline it brought. I shook my head and answered, "Jud, I'm not ready to settle down. Not yet."

Jud slowly met my gaze and frowned. "Then when?"

I didn't have an answer because I hadn't considered the 'when' question. When *would* I be ready to settle down?

I smiled and shook my head. "I don't know. But Jud, when I am ready, I don't think it will be here."

He looked away, his jaw ticking as he nodded in understanding.

13

JACKSON

I AGREED TO GO TO DAWSON'S KNOWING LANEY WAS GOING WITH someone else, knowing she wasn't mine. She's always been free to do what she wants, and she doesn't owe me anything. I did think I might get a chance to dance with her, but seeing her with Judson was painful and had my rage simmering.

He held her close, like they were lovers, like he knew her body as intimately as I did. I hated that they had a past that could rival my own with Laney. To ease my mind and my body, and so I didn't punch Judson in the face, I kept close to the Thompson brothers. I tried to ignore how gorgeous she looked even with that darker hair and how Jud kept watching her with that stupid look on his face, like he was ready to claim her like a fucking animal.

The two of them dancing together, him holding her and her clinging to him...they made a good-looking couple. The way the lights danced along her dark hair and the way her hand moved up his back...I thought back to the last day her hands ran up my back like that, the last time I had held her like Jud was holding her.

. . .

MAY WAS EXACTLY ONE MONTH LONGER THAN I HAD PLANNED ON KEEPING Laney, but her birthday was in April and I was being selfish. I wanted to see her face when she saw the birthday gift I had gotten her.

Laney had never allowed me to purchase her things that would improve her life like a car or a better apartment, but every now and then she'd indulge in the finer things if it included me. So, I had bought us tickets to a secluded cabin in Canada. She had no idea where we were going until our flight. She loved that cabin, and I knew by the way she thanked me that she was starting to love me. I needed to let her go...

Laney deserved to one day get married and have kids. I knew her PTSD wouldn't last forever; she'd get through it and lead a happy life. I knew I was clinging to the fact that Laney needed me, and I in turn gave in to the notion that I needed her. But it wasn't right.

I was selfish and my time was up. Like an asshole, I had a courier deliver the letter to her, hoping I wouldn't have to see her face as I walked away. I had booked a flight, planned to get the hell out of there, but I should have known better.

THE LOOK ON HER FACE HAD STUCK WITH ME, LIKE A SCAR I WOULDN'T let heal. I had to stick to my belief that one day she'd find someone better. The realization hit that the guy she deserved was probably Jud, and it sliced through me like a blunt knife.

I leaned forward, placing my head in my hands. I thought about the stupid fight and what that asshole Ebely had called Laney, how he'd looked at her. I couldn't keep whatever this was that tied me to her shut off anymore. Why she hadn't said anything infuriated me. The fact that she was so reserved here bothered me. I knew about her PTSD and had walked through her behaviors and personality in the throes of it, but this was different.

She let everyone walk all over her.

Her dad had barely spoken three words to her, and her mom only talked to her when it had to do with meal prep or cleaning. She was only really seen by her brothers, and a part of me wondered now if that was why their pranks were so harsh—to remind Laney that she was noticed and that she mattered. I wouldn't take back what I'd told her because someone needed to do it.

I doubted Jud would tell her that her fire was missing or that she used to be someone who could make men like Andrew Ebely piss their pants with some of her insults. I did, however, regret the fact that she'd ended up in Jud's arms instead of mine.

I worked out until midnight then tried to work on a business proposal, but without access to the internet, I didn't get far. I was waiting, and I hated that I was waiting. Laney still hadn't shown up. I finally broke down close to one in the morning and called her. The funky melody jingle from the burner flip phone rang out from the direction of Laney's room. Not wanting to wake anyone up, I ran through our adjoined bathroom, found her phone, and quickly silenced it. She had left her phone, which wasn't a great thing since we were technically in hiding. *Shit Laney.*

I paced my room for another thirty minutes before I finally collapsed on the bed, coming to terms with the fact that she had spent the night with Jud. She was moving on or back; whatever it was, she was moving beyond me. I pushed away the anger I had no right to feel and closed my eyes, wishing I could tear out my own heart if it meant I wouldn't feel this torture anymore.

I tried not to picture Laney with Judson, tried not to imagine how he had probably talked her into going back to his place, how he moved his body just enough to convince her to kiss him, probably talked about old times until she was putty in his hands—anything to remind her of the mess she'd left behind, the fucked-up, emotional mess that couldn't commit to her. She was probably in his arms right now, trying to figure out why she ever left in the first place.

It was hard to swallow, and my body was burning up. The Thompsons had air conditioning, but they turned it off at night, saying the night breeze would do just fine. I was hot as hell and sure I might be dying. I walked into the bathroom and splashed cold water on my face. I had to get the image of Laney in bed with Jud out of my head, had to remove the fear in my heart that I had lost her, regardless of how absurd it was that I'd never actually had her to begin with. I wished I could get my father's voice out of my head, wished I could just be the person worthy of her heart, of her life. But his voice was there, taunting me, warning me...

"Jackson, before you leave for college, let me tell you one thing. No woman, no person is ever going to love you. Not really, not fully. People are liars and fakers. Pour your time into your work, build your empire, because at the end of the day, it's the only thing worth having. Everyone else and everything else will fuck you over."

I was starting to feel the truth of his words tied around my neck, like a stone about to drown me in the ocean.

I needed to push Laney away, get her out of my system, get away from her. I had to fix this, because I was sinking.

14

LANEY

JUD LIVED JUST ALONG THE OUTSKIRTS OF TOWN, BEFORE THE MAIN road led to farmland. It was convenient, because by city standards, he was only a few blocks from my parents' house. I snuck out of his suburban home around one in the morning—which, for the record, was a damn stupid idea. I snagged a pair of Crocs—yes, Crocs—socks, and a sweatshirt from Jud. Otherwise I would have made my idiotic trek in high heels and a tiny dress.

I may not have been thinking clearly, and I'll admit that. My mind was full, muddled, and confused. Images of Jackson and me together with kids was playing on repeat in my head, and with it was a memory...

JACKSON HELD ME IN HIS ARMS WHILE WE LAY IN FRONT OF HIS FIREPLACE. We'd made love and didn't want to go back to the room, so we decided to sleep there. My face was tucked into his neck while he drew invisible words into my back.

It was perfect.

"Jax?" I whispered into his skin. He stroked my hair and hummed his acknowledgment. "Have you ever thought of having kids?"

Jackson stopped stroking my hair and froze.

Panicked, I corrected myself. "Not any time soon or anything, I just mean ever. In your lifetime...I mean." I fumbled over my words and winced at the delivery.

It was quiet, and all we could hear was the sound of the propane that lit the fire, blazing behind the glass.

Jackson let out a heavy sigh and continued writing things into my spine. "No. I have Sammy and Jasmine. I won't ever want more than that."

WANT. THAT WAS THE WORD THAT STUCK OUT IN THAT MEMORY MORE than any of the others. Jackson would never *want* more than that. The same pain I felt then surfaced anew and felt just as ugly in the dark hours of the morning as they did in the glow of firelight.

Twilight was proving to be a good distraction. As addled as I was, the orchestra of frogs and grasshoppers was enough to get my mind back on where I was, and I was about halfway home when fear started to sneak under my skin. The grass swaying in the wind had me peeking over my shoulder and my steps quickening. My breathing hitched a bit as I looked around. *God, how stupid am I?*

I broke into a soft run, as much as Jud's Crocs with socks would allow, and willed my body into submission. My organs ached with how tight my chest felt. My heart was racing and I couldn't seem to catch my breath, but I kept moving, rolling the long sleeves of the sweater up my arms and pushing harder. I mentally went back to therapy sessions and started repeating over and over, "I am safe."

But I didn't feel safe. I needed to get off the main road and into the field. I knew these fields, and I'd know how to evade someone in them. I tried to focus on something that would help me through this, something that would make me feel fearless. I thought of Ramsey.

"HOW DID YOU DO IT, RAMS?" I ASKED SOFTLY. WE WERE LYING ON HER bed, the TV playing something in the background, but all I wanted was to slip under the covers and sleep. It had been two weeks since she returned from her honeymoon. Jackson had forced me out of the house, worried my depression was going to consume me. He said it would be good for me to see Ramsey. Ramsey had gone through her own trauma, so she'd know how to help me deal.

"I find something, anything that ties me to normalcy...could be a pen or a hair tie. I squeeze it and tell myself I'm okay, I'm not in danger, and even if I am, I'm a fighter now, not a victim," she whispered back, buried under the covers with me, holding the top of the sheet up like a roof. She allowed me to be broken with her, like we shared the same scars. In a way, I think we did. When she was abducted... something in me shattered. When she had her breakdown in the club...I felt that same brokenness obliterate me. I broke with her, and I knew she was breaking with me too.

I LOVED HER SO DAMN MUCH AND WISHED SHE WERE HERE WITH ME. I searched for something to tie me to this moment, not the ones where fear ruled me. I crouched down, picked up a rock from the gravel road, and squeezed it as I walked.

I zigzagged through corn fields and bee-lined toward my family's farm. I kept track of the little milestones as I went and internally marked how much further I had to go: the Smiths' boundary boulder, the McKinneys' tree swing that sat on the edge of their property, and finally my Tree Guardian, standing there tall like a beacon. My breathing evened out as I made my way up the porch. I wiped at my face and blotted away the evidence of my almost breakdown.

I waited a second, catching my breath. The fear hadn't fully ebbed, but some small part of me needed to rationalize that I was safe.

I knew *she* wasn't here. I knew *she* didn't know where I was, but some very tiny part of me thought of her like the boogie man. If I was alone, she would find me. Somehow, some way. Which made my next revelation even worse.

I pulled on the door and found that it was locked. *Fuck.*

I scanned the porch and began pulling up the mat, used what little light I had from the barn lights to check inside and underneath flower-pots, but the spare key wasn't anywhere. I wanted to cry and scream, but it wouldn't do me any good. Our house had a firm rule: come home after curfew, and the door will be locked, and no one will open it. I didn't even know if Jackson was inside, or if he'd gone home with the someone after I ditched him. I could climb up the side of the house or throw rocks at Leo's window, assuming he was home. I was even tempted to stand there and pound on the door until someone opened it.

But I was exhausted, and the only option I felt I had was to sleep. I turned on my heel and headed for the barn instead. I snagged a battery-operated lantern off the shelf then crept past the livestock and headed for the hayloft. After climbing the rickety ladder, I found a small setup in the corner and smiled.

I knew my brother Leo used to escape the house when he had someone over, and although it totally grossed me out to be sleeping in my brother's possible hookup location, at least I'd be warm. I shook out and flipped the large quilt that lay over the small cot then turned the fluffy pillow over, pulled up the hood on my sweatshirt, and curled into a ball, praying sleep would claim me fast.

I'D KNOWN SLEEPING IN MY BROTHER'S COT MIGHT BE A BAD IDEA, BUT I had been tired and made poor decisions. Now as I tried to open my eyes, I knew I had made a colossal mistake. They wouldn't budge. *Oh my God! My eyes will not open and they hurt.*

My heart rate shot up and my breathing was coming in and out in tiny gasps.

Shit, this was bad.

I was frozen, immobile, and terrified. Why couldn't I open my eyes?

I grabbed at my face and started feeling. There was something sticky that clung to my fingers as I pawed away at my eyelids.

Near the foot of my bed, I heard male giggling.

I screamed and pitched forward. Half my brain was telling me it was okay, saying the male giggling at least wasn't female, but my brain was in fight-or-flight mode. I held my eyes, feeling tremors rack my body.

"Forever...forever with me today, tomorrow, until I am no more," I whispered, trying to regain some grasp on what the hell was going on.

The giggling stopped, and I heard shuffling feet.

"Please don't hurt me," I sobbed as I held my core.

This wasn't me.

This was some pathetic version of me. Ramsey wasn't a victim anymore, but I was. That was all I was ever going to be. Alicia owned me, mind, body, and soul.

"Shit, Laney. You okay...why are you whispering poetry to yourself?" I heard my brother Leo whisper. He must have lowered himself until he was eye level with me. He touched my hair and started stroking it. "Seriously Lane...what the hell is going on? We always joke with you...are you okay?"

I tried to rein in the sobs that were caught in my throat and the embarrassment that was burning me from the inside out. I tried to wipe at my eyes, but the dried dirt or whatever it was wasn't moving. My eyes burned, then suddenly a cold wave of water hit me right in the face.

"Fuck, Zane. Why did you do that?" Leo yelled. I was gasping, grappling for the blanket to wipe at my face, oddly grateful for the cold and the aid it offered to help me see.

"Sorry, she just seemed like she was going into shock or something, so I thought the water would be like slapping her in the face. Plus, she seems to be freaking out over not being able to see," Zane argued from a few feet away. I could somewhat see now; my vision was fuzzy and blurry, but it was better than the darkness.

I was about to explain what was happening with me when I heard a sharp and clear, "What. The Fuck. Is going on?" That was Jackson, and he sounded lethal.

Leo sounded taller when he said "Jack...calm down, dude. You look pissed as hell," Leo calmly begged.

He did? I needed my sight back.

"Don't tell me to calm down. What the hell are you doing to your sister?" Jackson screamed. I cringed, even though his anger wasn't even aimed at me.

"It was just a prank, just some harmless fun. We were trying to reenact the whole Jesus heals the blind man thing," Zane explained.

"But without the spit," Leo quickly added, like that would make it better. I could see Jackson stepping forward and breathing hard. His jaw was probably ticking too, but I still couldn't totally make it out.

"Do you have any idea what she's gone through?" Jackson asked, voice deadly calm.

No one responded. Leo cleared his throat and looked down as Jackson kept going.

"A stunt like this would fucking terrify her. You essentially blinded her while some psycho is out there possibly on the hunt for her life. If I didn't like the two of you, I'd fucking kick your asses. Don't ever do anything like this to her again." Jackson scolded them in that eerie calm voice that made me think of Rick Grimes from *The Walking Dead*.

Another chill racked my body, and I pulled the blanket closer. My brothers mumbled apologies as they walked past Jackson and headed down the hayloft, leaving Jackson and me alone.

Jackson walked a few steps until he was sitting in front of me. I could slightly see him, but my eyes were still messed up so his form was a bit blurry. I let his fingers drift over my calves and his thumb rub gentle circles into my thighs. I looked down and realized there was rope tying my legs together. I was so shocked about my loss of sight that I hadn't even noticed my asshole brothers had tied me up.

Fuckers.

It took him probably longer than it should have to untie me, but I didn't care. I liked his closeness, and with everything from the previous night and this morning hanging over my head, I wanted to push forward, curl into his chest, and have him hold me. I was free a moment later, and his hand wound around mine as he pulled me up and asked, "You okay?"

I tried to laugh, but it came out as a cough instead. "Oh yeah. You just witnessed my entire childhood, summed up into one moment."

Jackson was quiet.

I could make out his body shape but not much more than that. I nudged his side and tried to laugh. "Wanna help me get revenge?"

He let out a sigh. "Laney, this isn't funny to me. You didn't see what you looked like. Do you have any idea what it did to me to see you like that? Your eyes covered in that shit, and you tied up in a dark hayloft?" His voice cracked, and my heart flipped. I always forgot Jackson was affected by this too. I always ignored how things with Alicia hurt him—not on purpose; he was just better at hiding all of his pain.

"I'm sorry you had to see that, Jax. I'm okay." I rubbed his shoulder, trying to reassure him.

He ran his hand over his scalp and let out a sigh. "Here, let me help you down and into the house so you can shower. Your mother informed me that we have church." Jackson spoke quietly and led me down.

"Church? What is it about lying low that my mother doesn't understand?" I asked through a scoff.

"From what I understand, she says if we can go out drinking and dancing then we can go worship God as well." Jackson smirked while leading me down the ladder.

I knew I didn't have a choice in the matter, because when one was under Beverly's roof, one obeyed her rules and participated in everything she wanted you to.

We made our way past the animals and into the house, and thankfully my mother didn't see me sneak in. The mud, last night's dress, and Jud's sweater would have been way too much for her.

"What happened last night?" Jackson asked as he pulled out a fresh towel from the linen closet. I let out a long sigh, not exactly eager to talk about my evening.

"I fell asleep in the hayloft." I started to take out my hair, and large chunks of mud were caked in some of the strands.

Jackson still had his back to me as he sorted the washcloths. "What time did you get in? And why didn't you just go up to your room?" he asked, a little confused. He was in basketball shorts and a white t-shirt; he must have been about to go running.

"I walked home and got in around one. The door was locked, so I just slept in the loft," I said as I shimmied out of my dress. I was in my underwear and bra when Jackson finally turned back around. He drew in a sharp breath as his eyes settled on me.

"What are you doing?" he asked is a raspy tone.

I stared at him a moment, locked away in a different time with those blue orbs staring back at me all hungry and electric. I wasn't meaning to undress in front of him; it was just something I did out of habit. I stopped though, suddenly feeling awkward that he noticed. He'd seen me naked a thousand times and knew my body more intimately than anyone else, and he'd walked in on me stark naked just a few days earlier.

"I'm getting in the shower, Jackson. No need to be weird about it—you've seen me naked before." I reached in to start the shower.

He looked down at the ground, red coloring his face. "I'm not being weird...it's just my body isn't sure what the rules are with you anymore, especially not after you've come home in another man's sweatshirt after spending the night with him," he quietly said.

There was obvious pain in his tone by the way it cracked, and it did something to me. It was like something cracked open inside of me. My mind toward Jackson had been that he had walked away coldhearted, distant, but it was like he couldn't bear the idea of me moving on.

I looked down, embarrassed by what he was insinuating with Jud. I should have rushed to tell him that nothing had happened, but he seemed to have already made up his mind. I just waited for his next move.

He continued watching the floor, ignoring me, and whispered again, "We have church with your family in less than an hour."

He turned and left the bathroom.

***

"FORGIVENESS ISN'T FOR THE PERSON WHO HURT YOU AS MUCH AS IT IS for you. It sets us free and gives us the opportunity to move forward instead of staying stuck in the pain of the past." The preacher's voice echoed through the small church and seemed to ricochet into every broken part of my soul.

I grew up attending church, but it had been a long time since I set foot in one. I trained my eyes on the large cross hanging on the wall above the baptismal pool and tried to turn my brain off.

I didn't want to think about forgiveness because some people didn't deserve it. But then again, there were others who did. I considered what it would be like for my heart if my standards and dignity decided to switch sides and forgive Jackson. But what was I even forgiving him for? Being himself?

I peered down the long pew my family was seated in and tried to catch Jackson's eye, but he was successfully ignoring me. When we'd walked into the building, he had purposely fallen back so Leo and Ty were between us on the bench. I'd wanted to tell the two of them to shove off and switch me places, but that would have given Jackson the wrong impression. As of right now, he thought I'd slept with Jud, and that was putting a necessary wedge between us. I needed the distance from him; I knew that I did.

Or rather, my heart did.

A few moments later we were all standing and singing along with the choir, going through the hymnals. As we sang about amazing grace, I closed my eyes and thought of Jackson's voice from that morning, the pain in it when he found me in the hayloft and when he thought I'd slept with Jud.

I gripped the hymnal book a bit harder than necessary as I considered what it would feel like to have Jackson lie to me the way I was currently lying to him. Sometimes omitting the truth was just being irresponsible with it, like being inebriated when operating a vehicle or heavy machinery. It was wrong of me to let Jackson believe I had slept with Jud. It wasn't fair, and he deserved better. Wedge be damned.

I kept trying to catch his eye, to let him know I wanted his attention, but he wouldn't budge.

Finally, the service ended and we all started facing each other and chatting amongst ourselves. Jenny was one row back, sitting with her dad and uncle. She was watching my brother Zane with the same expression I often had when I looked at Jackson.

I followed her line of sight and tried to see what she was seeing: Zane with a scruffy, day-old beard, nice dress shirt and slacks...and messy hair.

I shook my head, trying to focus on Jackson and the truth I needed to share. I tried to elbow my brother in the ribs to get him to move, but he was too tall, and the pew was too narrow. Suddenly, someone was tapping on my shoulder. Jud was standing there in a nice pressed shirt and slacks. The obnoxious gaggle of men behind me stopped talking as soon as he approached.

"Lane, what in the hell happened last night? I woke up and you were gone," Jud pressed, sounding worried. His narrowed eyes searched mine, his eyebrows drawn in. I wanted to see Jackson's face so badly. This all looked so wrong.

"How's your head, Jud? You hit it really hard last night," I practically yelled, interrupting him. Hopefully I could get everyone focused on the fact that Jud was maybe crazy or hurt, definitely not in his right mind.

Jackson cleared his throat and took off from the group, making his way through clusters of people until he was outside. I turned to see my brothers' faces, and each of them narrowed their eyes and glared at Jud. Then they turned that arctic glare on me. *What in the hell?*

I cleared my own, dry throat and explained to Jud what happened. "Sorry, I just needed to get home." He watched me carefully and nodded, then got pulled away by his mother to talk to someone else. I grabbed my purse and trudged outside too. The sun was high, and the air was thick with heat.

I didn't look for anyone as I fully intended to walk home, but just as I crossed my arms and set off toward the edge of the parking lot, my brother's blue pickup truck pulled up next to me.

Jackson stuck his head out of the window and yelled, "Hey."

I slowed my walk and watched him, squinting at the sun. "Hey," I said back.

He had sunglasses on so it was hard to see his expression, but he kept looking toward the street instead of where I stood.

Finally, he asked, "You hungry?" His hand was drumming on the door through the open window. I didn't allow myself to think about it; I just walked around the pickup and crawled inside. I settled in and buckled while Jackson pulled out of the parking lot and headed toward town.

15

LANEY

WE RODE IN SILENCE UNTIL WE ARRIVED AT A TINY BREAKFAST BISTRO called Perk it Up. It was a whitewashed building with a beach vibe. Colorful flower baskets hung near the entrance, along with a tall surfboard and bench. I hadn't ever been to it before, but I liked the breezy feeling inside and the smell of bacon that assaulted my senses as soon as we entered. Jackson and I settled into a small table in the back corner, him wearing his trucker hat and me donning the wig from the night before. He eyed a vinyl menu and continued to ignore me. I wanted to talk, to get everything out in the open, but I was so hesitant because I believed he'd heard his own form of truth. It would make it seem like I was just trying to cover it up now.

"What's good here?" Jackson suddenly asked from across the table. He didn't normally ask for suggestions on food because he knew exactly what he liked to eat, regardless of what was 'good' on the menu. I was so surprised he'd broken the silence—and in the strangest way possible— and I didn't notice when the waitress showed up. She went red in the face and then started fumbling over herself as she watched Jackson. She wore a green tight t-shirt, a white apron secured over it, and black pants. Her hair was up in a high ponytail, and her face was painted, complete with fake lashes and durable lipstick that wouldn't budge all day.

"Hey," she said breathily as she leaned over the table to turn Jackson's coffee cup over, practically shoving her breasts in his face. She was about to pour him coffee without asking if he wanted any when he put his hand over his cup and gave her another sweet smile.

"Can you get her coffee please? And for me, just water."

She thinned her lips and poured my coffee.

"Looks like you've got an admirer, Jackson..." I jokingly said over my steaming cup. I didn't know why I said it. His business was his own, but he already assumed Jud and I had slept together, so I figured I'd just make a joke out of it.

He smiled and continued to look over the menu, but he didn't respond. We stayed quiet for the next few moments, then his new waitress friend came back with a pitcher of water.

"You ready?" she asked him, ignoring me. I laughed and sipped my coffee. She glanced toward me, while Jackson fought a smile.

"Go ahead and take hers first," he told her.

Janelle, as her nametag identified her, turned her blonde head my way and narrowed her eyes. *Yeah, she is totally going to spit in my food.*

"I'll just have coffee, thanks," I replied as our waitress stared down at me. It was Jackson's turn to laugh, which seemed to break whatever silent spell he'd been punishing me with. Janelle left in a huff, and Jackson turned that smile on me.

"So, how did things go with Jud last night?" he asked in a sarcastic tone while taking a sip of water.

I swallowed my bitter coffee and answered, "Fine. We went back to his place and watched some TV. We...uh, talked."

Jackson watched me too carefully. His scrutiny was unnerving.

"Talked?" he asked, slowly drawing the word out.

I nodded. "Yeah. We talked about how he needed to stop trying to kiss me and how nothing is going to happen with us. Then we talked about how he thinks I'm ready to settle down."

Jackson sipped his water and clenched his jaw for a second before he launched into a new series of questions. "So, are you ready to settle down?"

Someone in the kitchen must have dropped a load of dishes in the sink, and the perfectly timed clatter that went along with Jackson's question made me jump.

I let out a breath to calm my nerves and answered while watching the table. "It hadn't been on my mind until Jud brought it up." I laughed at the idea, shirking the odd feeling the noise had created in my chest, and drank more coffee. Janelle came over to deliver Jackson's meal and refilled my coffee before she shot off again. I thought Jackson would move on from the topic since he wasn't a settle-down guy and didn't care about this stuff, but he started in again.

"So, you agree with him? You think you're ready?"

I watched him carefully as he swallowed and went for more water. I considered telling Jackson a lie or not answering at all, but after that morning, I was ready to just be honest with him.

"A week ago, I would have told you no." I looked away and toyed with the sugar shaker. "But..." I lifted a shoulder. "I don't know. Being back here, it kind of makes me think I am."

Jackson watched me carefully as he took a bite of his egg white omelet. "You're ready to settle down in general or settle down with Jud?"

I sat back and let out a sigh. "Not with Jud." I smirked at him, to make sure he was hearing me. "I think I am finally ready to accept that I might want that life. Not here, but being here has made me realize I might be ready for the whole family thing." I looked out the window. "It's a shame it'll never happen though."

"Why wouldn't it happen?" Jackson asked around another bite of food.

I let out another sigh. "You don't want to hear this, Jax." I laughed and winced at how pathetic it sounded.

He sat up taller and pulled his hands in under his chin, narrowed his gaze on me, and whispered, "Try me, Laney."

I focused on his blue eyes as I readied my heart to be honest with him. I leaned forward and said, "Okay, assuming I actually get past my PTSD...I want to settle down, raise my kids down the street from my best friend. I don't want to *have* to work. I want the option, and I want a man who wants babies and a big house, a big yard. I want the works." My face burned at my admission.

A large family had just entered the small bistro, and the sounds of chairs scraping across the hardwood floor echoed through the room. It felt like forever before Jackson responded to me, but eventually he did.

"Why aren't those things you could have?"

I held in the urge to roll my eyes, scoff, or throw my hot coffee in his face. *Fuck*, it should have been so damn obvious at this point, but screaming that I wanted to settle down with someone who would never settle down was completely out of the question.

"My student loans, for one." I pulled my hands into my lap and began digging my nails into my leg. I didn't like what this conversation was pulling out of me.

"What about them?" Jackson asked while scrutinizing me.

I pressed my nails more firmly into my leg. "Well, they're a lot. I didn't get financial aid, didn't get scholarships...my student loans total nearly a hundred and fifty thousand dollars, Jax."

He raised a shoulder and finished off his omelet. "What? This imaginary guy would never love you if you came with debt?"

My face burned as I worked through my justifications. The truth was I knew if I found the right guy, none of those reasons would matter, but it seemed like solid enough logic if I placed something like a student loan in front of it.

I shrugged, hoping he'd let it go.

Jackson had his fist under his chin, listening intently. He leaned forward. "So, you want me to believe you want to marry a billionaire, have him wipe out your debt, buy you a house down the road from Ramsey, then knock you up with a bunch of babies?"

I laughed and let out an airy sigh. "That about sums it up."

Jackson wiped at his mouth and took a sip of his water then let out a heavy sigh. "I don't believe you."

My eyes snapped to his.

Blue. Hard. Unrelenting.

"What?" I whispered.

He leaned in closer. "I don't believe your bullshit reason for thinking you'll never get that. There's some other reason you don't think you'll get it." He snagged a sugar packet, shook it, and tore open the corner.

I watched his movements as my face heated. "What do you mean?" I asked, not sure how to proceed with his accusation.

He scoffed. He tilted the bag of sugar, poured it on the table, and drew the shape of a heart into the powder. "There's something you aren't saying."

"Okay," I scoffed and rolled my eyes.

He watched me and continued to draw. "So, what is it?"

"Nothing."

"Come on, you talked to Jud—talk to me. Why don't you think you'll get it?" Jackson purred and drew the letter L into the sugar. I looked outside and shook my head in frustration. He knew. The asshole knew what I was going to say, but he wanted to hear it.

The waitress brought our check, thankfully breaking my precarious moment and giving me the opportunity to end this emotional conversation. Jackson smiled at Janelle once more, and she returned his smile. I looked out the window again to try to focus my mind on something other than the fact that Janelle had slipped Jackson her number. He cleared his throat and stuck the scrap of paper into his wallet.

We exited the restaurant and were headed toward the truck when Jackson tugged on my elbow and said, "Are you going to tell me?"

I scanned the sidewalk for someone to get me out of this moment. I didn't want to give him what he wanted. I blinked back a few tears and finally gave in.

"What, Jackson? What do you want to hear? That the man I love doesn't love me back? Or that I won't ever settle down because the only person I have ever pictured a life with doesn't want one with me?" I pulled my elbow free and started to walk away. Jackson didn't have a single emotion playing across his face at my confession, and that might have stung worse than having to admit to him that I was pining after him.

I fumbled with my purse as if to hide the hole he'd just torn open inside of me with his annoying questions. Making me admit that out loud was a bastard thing to do.

I felt a gentle tug on my elbow when I charged past the truck.

"Here, take the truck. I have a few things to do today," Jackson said quietly, like he hadn't just heard my little confession back there. Shame simmered in my belly.

I was a fool.

He handed me the keys and threw his thumb over his shoulder in the direction of downtown. "I'll make my own way back."

I nodded dumbly, not sure why he'd even asked me to breakfast, not sure why I was feeling so empty all of a sudden. I carefully climbed into the truck and drove away.

I DIDN'T WANT TO GO BACK HOME, OR ANYWHERE THAT JACKSON might go for a while, so I drove toward my brother Lawson's house, hoping Sarah wouldn't turn down a nice afternoon of sister-in-law conversation. I was dying to talk to Ramsey, dying to cry into the phone while I told her how much Jackson's actions had just crushed me. She would get it. She was the one who'd put me together after Jackson left me. She knew how much I loved him and how badly I wished I didn't— but I couldn't call her. I couldn't see her because Alicia was hunting me… again. With or without someone to talk to, I needed to get over this man once and for all. I wanted to be past this pain, but being tied to Jackson here while we waited this thing out was torture.

16

JACKSON

THE LITTLE TOWN OF PLAINVILLE WAS TURNING OUT TO BE JUST AS IT sounded: plain. I found myself missing the speed of the bigger city. I missed how the tall buildings offered shade, and I especially liked how I didn't often run into people I knew if I chose to randomly stop in at a Starbucks.

I'd only been sitting at a table for roughly fifteen minutes when someone pulled up a chair and sat down across from me. I looked up from the small work laptop Gepsy had given me and stared at the last person on earth I wanted to see. Jud was leaning back in his chair and had casually kicked his leg out to the side. His face was blank, pale, and bored.

I blinked and waited for him to explain why he'd interrupted me and sat down, but he just sat there and watched me. Growing tired of whatever the fuck was happening with him, I sighed and asked, "Can I help you?"

Jud smirked and leaned forward. "Just trying to find it."

I shut the laptop, knowing this conversation wasn't going to be a pleasant one. "Find what?"

Jud rubbed his day-old scruff and laughed before meeting my eyes. "Whatever it is Laney sees in you."

This fucker.

I gave him my best shit-eating grin and tried like hell to hide my insecurity. "You'd have to bed me to find out, sweet Jud. You ready for that kind of fun?" I winked and started packing my laptop.

He locked his jaw and looked through the glass windows before he replied. "Yeah, well all I know and care about is whose bed Laney was in last night."

I was tempted to check my chest to make sure there wasn't a gash across it. I had worked all morning to get the image of Laney and Jud in bed together out of my fucking head. I kept my grin and 'I don't give a shit' attitude in place, taunting him.

"Must be something she found unsatisfactory in your bed if she left it for a cot in the hayloft," I replied, while fastening the bag over my shoulder and heading toward the glass doors. I didn't need to look back to see that Jud had followed me out. He was steaming; I could sense it from the sound of his breathing behind me. I had no vehicle, so I just started walking in the general direction of the farm.

"Fuck you, Jackson. You think you can give her anything? Do you have any idea what we've been through? There's a reason she's back here, and I have no plans of losing her again," Jud yelled while shoving my shoulder. Why I turned to hear him out at all, I have no idea. What was this, high school?

I smiled, shaking my head. "Jud, you're misplacing your anger on me, man. Laney and I aren't together," I said with a hint of disgust because there was so much about that sentence that made me sick.

"The fuck you aren't. She won't even look at another guy when you're around. She *acts* like you're together, and that's what pisses me off." Jud slowly encroached on my personal space.

I stepped back, because I didn't want to get into a fight with him.

"Jud, you convinced her to sleep with you last night—why are you acting like she won't give you the time of day? Laney isn't acting like shit where I'm concerned, so go grab a tampon and get over yourself." I shouldered past him and grabbed the leather strap to keep my hands busy and from forming fists. Jud moved until he was in front of me again, and his eyes had gone wild.

"That's just it..." He laughed sarcastically. "She wouldn't do shit with me. She had her reasons, but I can't help but think it has something to do with you."

I tried to make sure my face didn't break into a joyful smile, but I was happy as fuck to hear that nothing had happened between them. Instead I moved past him again and spat my next words at him. "What the hell do you want from me, Jud?"

Jud stood his ground, even as I passed him, and said to my back, "Let her go. She's holding on because some small part of her thinks there's hope with you. Everyone else can see there's not, but she's blinded by whatever it is she sees in you. She's clinging to someone who won't ever give her what she needs."

I spun on him as my anger boiled to the surface. "I did fucking let her go! It was the hardest thing I've ever done. I did it for *her*. I walked away for *her*!" I had my hand pointed at my chest, and I could feel a vein in my forehead throbbing. "You're the one who needs to let this shit go. Laney doesn't owe you anything. You need to move on."

I turned around and kept my face forward. Jud walked away, and I continued toward the farm, trying to push the feeling that had just invaded my chest away. His words were like little needles that had pierced my skin. I couldn't shake them or lose the feeling of each one as they pricked me and drew blood. I thought about what Laney had said that morning. I thought about how she'd admitted to wanting a life with me, wanting a future with me, and I had just stood there like a prick and hadn't said anything.

Let her go. Let her go so she can and will move on. Let her go to someone who will give her what she needs.

I blinked against the sun and tried to erase the words Jud had just spewed at me. I was selfish to the core. As far as I was concerned, I had let her go and she'd come back to me. If she wasn't ready to let the idea of us go then I wouldn't either. I'd spent the last three months miserable and alone.

The revelation hit me in the chest, shredding whatever was left of my pride.

I wanted Laney.

She was mine in whatever capacity I could have her. Jud would have to learn how to deal with his heartbreak, because I wasn't giving her up.

"Here." I shoved the small piece of scrap paper at Leo as I headed toward my bedroom.

He looked down and smiled. "Is this Janelle Taylor's number?"

I shrugged, not sure of the waitress's last name, and grabbed my doorknob. "She was the one you were talking to last night at the bar, right?"

"Yeah...we go way back, but I've never asked for her number before." Leo continued staring at the scrawled ink on the slip of paper.

"Well, she gave it to me with the breakfast ticket. I don't plan on using it, thought you guys might know each other better by the way she was flirting with you last night. Use it if you want."

"I most certainly will. Hell, that girl has been on my radar for a while now." Leo rubbed his jaw while staring at the ticket. I laughed and opened my door, but before I went inside, I looked over at Laney's.

"Leo, where's your sister?" I casually asked, trying to downplay how badly I needed to know the answer. I never should have left her that morning, and I never should have left her the night before. On my way home, I'd realized how reckless it was that Laney had gone home alone. Now she was alone again, and we were supposed to be together. If Gepsy knew, he'd be pissed.

"Last I heard, she was over at Law's house," Leo said while pushing into his own bedroom. I sighed with relief. At least she was safe and with family.

I took a shower, feeling the need to wash the interaction with Jud off. Once I was done, I headed downstairs and spent time with Wayde, watching preseason football. I tried to hide how frequently I examined the large wall clock and how every time the screen door opened, I checked to see if it was Laney walking through.

By the time dinner rolled around and the house was full of people, I was getting worried. Both Sarah and Lawson were at the farm, laughing and joking, happy to be free of any kids for the evening. Zane had invited their neighbor Jenny over, and she was also looking around for Laney. Leo was eating his weight in chips and dip, and Beverly was joking and laughing, as was Wayde. They all seemed to be having a great time.

I wasn't.

I stood up and clapped Leo on the shoulder. "Hey, I'm going to head into town and check on Laney."

Leo stood up and wiped his bean-dip-covered fingers on his jeans. "Hold up, you can take my bike. Sarah accidently blocked in your little hatchback."

I winced. I hadn't even thought to check that first.

"You know how to ride?" Leo asked.

I smiled. "Yeah."

I had learned how to ride a few years back thanks to Jimmy. I followed Leo out of the house, past the barn, until we were nearing the carport that had an old truck and a covered bike under it. He took off the canvas cover, revealing a dual-sport Suzuki dirt bike. I held back an unmanly cringe. I wanted to tell him I'd only ever ridden nicer classics, but I was too desperate to care about how different a dirt bike might feel.

"She's a little touchy when it comes to turning, so if you can help it, don't do it," Leo said plainly, while putting gas into the front, just above the seat.

I bit back the need to voice the questions and concerns I had and realized I was in way over my head where Laney was concerned. I hadn't seen her all day, and I hated how much I missed her. After everything with Jud and him confirming that nothing happened between the two of them, and how I had just ignored her confession...yeah, I fucking needed to see her.

"Okay, no turning," I said simply, and Leo smiled and handed me a white motocross helmet. I slipped it on my head and tested the bike around the yard a few times before I took off down the driveway, heading toward town.

17

LANEY

It was dinner time and I had been at Lawson's all day. I had suggested that Sarah go to a movie and catch up with some of her girl-friends so I could spend some much-needed auntie time with my niece and nephews. Lawson was out at the farm with my parents; apparently Sunday night was game night with my dad and brothers.

How nice for them.

"Now, Jonah what did we agree to?" I asked with my hands on my hips, looking down at my seven-year-old nephew.

He took off his hat, sat on his but in the chair, and grabbed the kid-sized fork. "No acting like a barbarian at the table."

I nodded and smiled. "Thank you. Now if you eat up, I'll make sure you get a double scoop of ice cream."

He smiled at me with almost all of his glorious baby teeth still intact; he was missing three on top. His messy brown hair was falling onto his forehead. I looked over at his sister, Livie, and resisted the urge to play with her spiral curls. She was four and rebellious as shit. Her little arms were crossed over her chest, and her hair kept falling across her face.

"Livie, baby girl, eat. Come on, don't you want some ice cream later?"

She shook her head. "Don't care, don't want to eat tis stuvid foob," she said in her four-year-old language. How did parents do this? This was not easy.

I sat down next to her and smiled. "It's just mac n cheese, don't all kids like mac n cheese?"

She shook her head defiantly and drew out a "No" like I was being ridiculous. I looked over at Tommy, the five-month-old, and Grayson, the two-and-half-year-old.

God, how did Sarah do this every day? At least the other three were eating. I gave up on Livie and settled for her eating an oatmeal cookie. It was healthy, right? I had started a movie and was about to clean up dinner when I heard the doorbell ring.

I went to open the door and found Jackson standing on the doorstep, hands in his pockets, a sly grin on his face. "Did you even look to confirm it was me?"

He said it jokingly, but it was like a rubber band snapped and I came back into my body. I had so easily fallen back into a role I used to fill with being back home. I had finally started to relax enough to not even consider looking through the little peephole to check who was at the door. I swallowed thickly and turned away. What if it had been Alicia? What if she had tried to hurt the kids?

"Hey...it's okay. It's fine. She doesn't know where we are. We're safe... it's okay." Jackson started cooing and rubbing my back. I had placed my hands over my face to try to calm down. I had been making such stupid decisions lately. I was angry with myself for it, frustrated and alarmed that I was likely going to end up dead because of it.

"What are you doing here, Jax?" I asked, trying to move past my frustration.

I wasn't ready to see him yet, but I didn't have much of a choice.

I walked further into the house, watching as two of the kids waddled and rolled around the living room. I crossed my arms over my body and looked up at Jackson.

"Need a ride home after all? It's kind of late, but I'm not sure how much longer Sarah will be tonight." I tried to explain so he would just leave and maybe walk home.

"Actually, Leo needed someone to get the truck, and I volunteered.

Sarah is out at the farm with Lawson hanging out, playing games. She doesn't seem to be in a hurry to get back."

Hurt found its way in between my ribs. I supposed I shouldn't have been surprised that my family didn't seem to care that I was stuck at the house with the kids; I had offered, after all. I just hadn't thought it meant I would be here all day and night. Now everyone wanted to hang out together, without me. I went to get the keys to the truck and handed them to Jackson in a daze.

"Here you go. Tell Leo thanks for the truck and I'll see you later." I turned away from him and headed into the living room to snuggle the kids.

I thought Jackson left, but a moment later, he was plopped next to me on the couch with his sock-covered feet propped up on the coffee table.

I looked over at him in surprise. "Jackson, you can leave. Take the truck and head out, sounds like I'll be here for a while."

Jackson laughed. "Yeah, which means maybe you need some company."

I huffed out a laugh. "Have you seen how many kids are here? I've got plenty of company...you can head back if you want." I hesitated, not wanting to say this but also knowing I needed him to see that I would call someone if I needed to feel safe. "Look, Judson lives like one block over...if there's any trouble or I feel unsafe, I know he'll be here within minutes." I reached forward and grabbed a toy then handed it to Grayson as he waddled toward me.

Jackson was staring at me with his jaw set. "Is that what you want?"

I didn't look at him as I answered, "I don't *want* you to stay just because you feel obligated."

I laid my hands on my sundress and grabbed a handful of fabric to try to center myself. Jackson turned to look at me then stood up and headed for the kitchen. The sound of water caught me off guard.

I turned around and found him washing dishes. I got up and walked in to relieve him. "Hey, stop it. I'll do those. Go on now, head back to game night." I moved in to take the pot from him.

Jackson held on to the dish and turned his body away from me, letting out a heavy sigh. "Stop it, Laney." He rinsed the pan and gently laid it in the porcelain sink. The light above our heads illuminated his sharp facial features. His simple *I am a lyin, hear my lore* shirt I knew he bought off Travis made Jackson look playful and fun. I wanted to poke him in the chest and ask how many he'd bought off the small entrepreneur.

Jackson dried his hands on the towel and faced me. "Stop suggesting Jud. I'm here with you, and we aren't supposed to be apart. I know I fucked up letting you go last night and today, but I'm here and I want to stay."

I watched the muscles move under his shirt as he pinned me with a heated glare and reached for another dish that was next to me. The pan in question caused Jackson to reach across my body, bringing our faces close.

His eyes roamed mine as he whispered, "I'm sorry for being an idiot. Just give me a chance."

I didn't move. I didn't breathe. I just waited as the heat between us grew. Jackson's gaze dropped to my lips, and I was transported back to the night when I had heard those same words fall from his lips.

"Just give me one chance, Laney."

I had given in and told him he'd only get one...

Ever so slowly, his face grew closer to mine—until a loud "MANNA TIME" interrupted us.

We broke apart and glanced over to see Jonah standing on the kitchen island with a sleeve of Ritz crackers high above his head. The bag was open, and he was tossing broken pieces of cracker to the younger kids like he was feeding pigeons in a park. Jackson and I moved in unison.

"Get down!" I yelled while Jackson laughed and calmly said, "Nice idea, bud. Let's try it from the floor."

I looked at Jackson in confusion. How was he the super cool guy under pressure? My heart was hammering at the idea of Jonah falling or causing the baby to choke. Jackson helped Jonah down by grabbing at his waist and setting him on the floor. Jonah abandoned the crackers and started running around the living room. I let out a sigh and peered back over at the pile of dishes.

I grabbed the scrubber brush, handed it to Jackson, and said, "Fine. Suit yourself. I'm going to go start their baths."

"PLEASE LIVIE, PLEASE LET ME GET YOU DRESSED." I WAS SITTING ON her floor with fresh pajamas in my hands, she was still wrapped in a towel, and her golden curls were drenched.

"No," she repeated, for the hundredth time. I was about to cry or cuss, not sure which one, but something was happening in my chest. Just then her bedroom door opened, and Jackson walked in.

"Hey sweetheart, what's going on?" he asked, squatting down in front of Livie.

She wiped some of her curls away and started to cry. "I want my mommy."

Jackson leaned forward so that she was sobbing into his shoulder. What made him so special? Why couldn't she just have told me that? He wrapped her in his arms and stood up with her. The sight of him with a little girl in his arms nearly took the air out of my lungs. It was like getting a glimpse of your wish list being granted for someone else.

"Now, I happen to know your mommy misses you but really wants you to get some sleep so she can snuggle you in the morning. So, will you get dressed for me?" he whispered into her hair. Livie nodded her head yes.

Jackson sat her down in front of me then turned away while I got her dressed. Once she had her pajamas on, she grabbed a book from her little bookshelf, went up to Jackson, and handed it to him.

"Read to me pwease?" she requested with a sniffle.

I was seriously freaked the hell out. Had she met him before? How on earth was she asking him and not me, her blood relation? I sat back and watched as Jackson snuggled on the bed with her and cracked open the book. His voice was so soft and tender, as if he'd read bedtime stories a million times. It made me wonder how involved he must have been with Jimmy's kids when they were little. I knew Jimmy's wife had abandoned them, and Jimmy basically didn't have anyone except for his dad and Jackson.

I got up to check on Jonah; the two youngest were already in bed. Jonah was slashing a foam sword from side to side as he lay in his. I walked further in, gently took the sword from him, and turned out the big light. He watched me as I made my way to his side.

"You going to pray with me tonight Aunt Laney?" he asked in his little seven-year-old timbre.

I nodded my head yes, remembering how many times I had prayed as a child and in Sunday school.

"Dear Lord, please protect Jonah tonight. Give him good dreams, and protect his daddy and his mommy on their way home. Amen."

Jonah smiled and nodded his head, then reached his hand out to grab my own and started his own little prayer. *Okay.*

"Lord, help the world. Help my chicken to live tonight, please help Livie to be nice tomorrow, please help there to be worms in the morning, please let my mom make me my favorite food tomorrow too. Please let me be able to get a dog soon, help Laney and Uncle Jackson to have a baby soon. Help Grandma to know how to make those yummy cookies again, and please help Tommy not to eat dirt anymore. Amen."

I ruffled his hair and kissed his forehead. "Thanks Jonah, but you know Jackson isn't your uncle, right? We aren't married, and we won't have kids, buddy."

He shrugged his shoulders then, with a yawn, said, "He looks at you like Daddy looks at Mama. I think you should ask him if he wants to marry you."

I laughed but stopped as soon as I noticed Jackson's tall frame filling the doorway. His jaw was doing that jumping thing, and his arms were crossed with his fingers digging into his skin. I looked back down at Jonah, ruffled his hair one more time, and then left.

Jackson was already downstairs picking up the toys. I'd started to help him when he stopped and looked at me. I stopped too, not sure if he wanted to say something about what he'd heard. Knowing he was probably going to launch into why we wouldn't ever work, I readied my heart and said, "Look, about what Jonah said, I don't think he meant—"

Jackson cut the space between us and grabbed my waist, cutting off my words. Our bodies were flush, his mouth hovered close to my lips, and his forehead pressed to mine.

"I can't keep doing this, Laney," he whispered, sounding pained. I swallowed, not sure how to respond.

"Can't keep doing what?" I breathed out, trying to control how hard my chest was rising and falling.

He pulled me closer to his body and moved his hands up my back. "I can't keep seeing you and not touch you. I can't stay away from you because it hurts. I wonder what you're doing all day and who you're with. I can't keep doing this. I need you."

His words ended in a breathy panic as his lips crashed into mine, desperate and hungry. I wrapped my arms around his neck and matched his intensity.

All the resistance I had built up over the last three months was gone in an instant. My defenses were down, and my heart was for the taking. I should have pushed him away, should have said no, but my entire body was screaming yes. I felt like I had been trying to hold back the tide, and I was damn exhausted. I wanted Jackson, I missed him, and I would sort this mess out tomorrow. For now, I was letting this happen.

My body was working from memory. It remembered the feel of his strong arms around me, the feel of his hot breath on my neck as he trailed kisses down to my collarbone. It remembered the feel of his lips and the taste of his tongue, things I had gone without for so many months, things I wanted back in my life.

I kissed him and let my hands roam over his head, up his back, under his shirt. His moans were setting me on fire, until I was letting out little moans of my own. I was sure he was going to throw me down on the couch any second then I heard keys jingling and the deadbolt unlocking. We broke apart and Jackson took a few steps backward while holding on to his neck.

My brother Lawson walked in, Sarah on his heels, and both looked at us like we were guilty. I looked at Jackson and felt my face betraying everything that'd just happened between us.

"Jackson came by to get Leo's truck," I blurted in a panic, out of breath and flustered. My face was probably red from making out with Jackson, and I felt like the thirteen-year-old babysitter caught sneaking her boyfriend in. I stood up and went to grab my things, and Sarah walked over and pulled me into a hug.

"My goodness, Laney, you have no idea how much I needed the day off. I can't thank you enough." She hugged me tight with her little chicken arms and then released me. I smiled and purposely kept my eyes away from Jackson, horribly aware that we would be alone in Leo's truck in less than five minutes.

I waved my hand around the house as I responded, "It was no trouble, they were great. Jackson helped a ton. I wasn't sure about their bedtime routine, so I just winged it."

Her blue eyes furrowed into confusion and she glanced at Lawson, who was talking to Jackson. "I texted you a bunch today—did you not get any of them?" she asked while taking out her phone and checking it.

I looked over at Jackson then at her. "I never gave you my new number, Sarah—how were you able to text me?"

She looked even more confused than before as she put her hand on her hip and shifted her weight to one foot. "No, I texted your old number, or the one I had in my phone at least. Look." She shoved her phone into my face, and there on the screen were over twelve messages to my phone number that had been sent throughout the day. Several were pinged locations of where Sarah was, including one of my parents' house. *Shit. Shit. Shit.*

I slouched over the counter, trying to catch my breath. Jackson was there in an instant, looking at Sarah's phone, the same look of worry painted on his face.

"Shit. Laney, we need to call Gepsy. Now." He grabbed my arm, reached for Leo's keys, and started herding us toward the door.

"Wait, what's wrong? What did I do wrong?" Sarah started to ask, worry lining her voice. Lawson was there next to her rubbing her back.

"Nothing, you didn't do anything wrong, Sarah. We ditched our phones in Chicago because of our situation and the fact that her stalker is trying to find us. She'll have our location by morning now," Jackson replied because I had no words or air in my lungs.

She brought her hand up to cover a gasp and tears gathered in her eyes.

"I'm so sorry. I didn't...I didn't know," she sobbed.

I finally found my voice. "Sarah, it's okay. It's not your fault, but we have to go."

Lawson looked stern, not sure what to do. I walked back and hugged them both, then let Jackson drive us, hopefully to the next town over or.

18

JACKSON

As soon as we were in the truck, I took a second to think about our situation. Even if Alicia knew where we were, she wouldn't be able to get to us in a house full of people. I calmed down and carefully drove the few miles to Laney's parents' house. As soon as Laney knew where we were headed, she frantically looked at me then the road.

"Jackson, what are you doing? You can't take me home. She's crazy, and what if she..."

I grabbed for Laney's hand and put it over my heart. "Laney, she can't get to you at your parents' house, and we can take tonight to figure out a plan. It won't make a difference if we head to a different town—she already has your parents' address. I'd rather be there and be alert than leave and give her a chance to sneak in."

Laney relaxed at my words and sank into the seat. I wished I could take the pain in her eyes away, wished I could turn back time to that moment Alicia first met Laney. I wished I'd never hired Alicia in the first place. Jimmy had warned me not to, and I'd ignored him because I was an idiot and didn't care at the time.

We pulled into the driveway and parked the truck. Laney climbed through my side to get out, never letting my hand go.

I walked into the house with Laney holding my hand, trailing behind me. It was late, so all the lights were off. Leo was in the living room and jumped up at hearing us enter.

"Finally!" he roared as he came closer. Once he saw Laney, he stopped and then looked at our hands, then my face. "What's going on? Laney, what's wrong?" He rushed closer and was still trying to see if I was the cause of the ghostly expression on her face, but he was thrown off by the sight of our hands tangled together.

"Leo, its fine. Sarah..." Laney's voice broke then she gripped my forearm and stood closer to me, like she was drawing from my strength. "Sarah accidently texted my old phone number with this location, and the crazy chick who's stalking us will know where we are now."

Leo stood back with a puzzled expression on his face. "Shit, so she knows where we live and that you're here?" he replied, like he was trying to piece everything together, and Laney nodded. "How exactly would she know that?" he asked.

"Our phones were kept on, with Detective Gepsy. Alicia has likely been monitoring them, so as soon as those location pings came through, she saw them," I carefully explained, all while Laney's grip grew tighter.

Leo turned away from us while pulling out his cell phone.

A few seconds later, he was talking into his phone while pacing the room. "Zane, get your ass to the house tonight, and plan on staying here for the next few nights. I'll explain when you get here. It has to do with Laney." He hung up, ran his hand through his hair, and then put the phone back up to his ear again. "Ty, you need to sleep at the house tonight. Yeah, get here quick."

Leo turned back toward us, walked toward Laney, and pulled her into a hug.

"You aren't alone anymore, sis. We'll get through this together this time. Let us help you."

Laney let go of my hand, put her arms around her brother, and let him hug her. I stood back and watched her beautiful countenance crumble and tears stream down her face. My chest caved at the look of Laney finally having people around her to lean on. It had just been us for so long, too long, and if I could have given her what she needed then it wouldn't have been so hard, but I couldn't.

The reminder of our kiss flashed in my head, and I hated myself. I was a selfish asshole who should have just kept my damn body to myself. Laney deserved to move on. She deserved family and support, and more than just me. I walked upstairs to give Leo and Laney a moment alone and tried to shut myself away from the growing need in my gut. I needed her, wanted her, but could never have her. It wasn't fair.

I needed to stop toying with her emotions.

———————

THE SOUND OF SCREAMING WOKE UP ME AND HAD ME JUMPING OUT OF bed. It was dark and disorienting, but I knew who it was. Laney was screaming as if someone was gutting her. I opened the bathroom door that joined our rooms, but the door was locked. I ran back around to enter through the main hall and found Leo running toward her room as well as her mother, worry etched into both their faces. Her main door wasn't locked, thankfully, so I opened it and tried to make sense of what I could see. Her room was dark, but her body was moving and shifting while she was screaming.

"Please, someone help me. Help me. Someone, God. Please someone help me."

I ran to her side and gently shook her. "Laney, wake up." I tried to hold her, but her arms shot out in defense, while she screamed.

"No, please don't. Don't, please don't." Tears were streaming down her face. Her mom and Leo were standing closer as she thrashed about.

Remembering the last time this happened, I told Beverley and Leo, "Get me an ice pack, cold water, and a fan."

They both took off down the hall as Ty, Zane, and Wayde made their way to her room as well. I kept gently patting her face to get her to wake up. Beverly came in a moment later, hooked up the fan, and handed me an ice pack. I gently laid it on the back of Laney's neck and sat her up until she could feel the cool air on her face.

"Laney, baby, wake up. It's okay." I whispered in her ear as I stroked her hair. I placed her hand on my forearm and felt her grip tighten. That was good. That meant she was coming out of it.

She finally stopped moving and cracked her eyes open. She sat up and leaned her head back against my chest. Tears streamed down her face as she drank the water Leo handed her. Once she was able to regain some composure, she cleared her throat.

"Sorry you guys, sometimes..." She broke off and looked at the wall.

She was struggling, so I spoke up to help her. "She has PTSD. It happens every now and then and causes her to dream." I looked down at Laney's pale face, and she slowly nodded her head then cleared her throat to try to speak again, but it came out in choppy sobs.

"I was buried alive...in my dream. I was in a coffin."

I tightened my arms around her, forgetting my earlier reasons for being noble and letting her go. She turned her face into my chest. Beverley finally spoke up and seemed to be struggling with not comforting her daughter. I wasn't sure how to allow that to happen and still comfort her too.

"Let's clear out and give Laney some air, y'all." Beverly looked at me and gave me a weak smile, then herded everyone out of the room. I sat there for a second longer, rocking Laney, making sure she was okay.

"She won't get you again. I promise." I kissed her head and prayed I wasn't wrong. Laney nodded her head in acknowledgment, then whispered to the empty room.

"Take me to your bed, Jax."

She didn't have to ask twice or even say please; I knew her well enough now to know she didn't want to lie back down in the same place where she had her nightmare. I picked her up and carefully carried her to my room. I laid her down on the bed then walked to shut my door and turn off the light. I got under the covers and pulled Laney to my chest. I held her in the dark for a while until I finally asked the question that had been on my mind for the last three months.

"How did you handle the dreams, those three months alone?"

Before she left, Laney and I had attended her therapy sessions together, so I knew how to support her, but I had wondered nearly every night we were apart how she was dealing with the night terrors.

She exhaled. "It hasn't been that bad. If I did have one, I'd eventually wake up and figure it out. I'm sure my neighbors have complained a bunch about my screams and whatever, but my landlord has never said anything."

I was very careful not to kiss her neck like I used to, and I was careful not to get her distracted with better, more pleasant ways to fall asleep like I used to. Memories battered me as I thought back to then.

"OKAY, I HAVE THREE BOWLS. I FIGURED THREE WOULD BE ENOUGH." I carefully carried the tray of cereal into the bedroom. Laney was sitting cross-legged in the middle of my king-sized bed, her hair a tussled mess of red on top of her head. She wore my t-shirt and nothing else, which instantly had me thinking about how soon I could take it off her. She smiled when she saw me and sat back against the headboard.

"Jax, you didn't have to do that." She laughed and blushed at the same time, sending another urge to strip her bare straight to my gut.

"I know how you feel about your sugary, milk-induced therapy. I don't mind," I explained, setting the tray on the bed and pulling her hand toward me. I situated our bodies until she was in between my legs, laying against my chest.

She reached for the ceramic bowl and began pushing the cereal into the milk. "Do you think eating Cocoa Puffs at three in the morning is a bad thing? Like it could lead to Alzheimer's or something?" she asked around a mouthful of chocolate puffs.

I laughed and bit back the rather long monologue I wanted to go on regarding the sugary cereal and how eating it period was a problem, that the time of day likely didn't matter. Instead, I kissed her head. I turned the TV on and handed Laney the remote, letting her pick the show. I didn't care much for TV, but I usually liked what she picked, so I just rubbed the skin that was exposed on her body and relaxed into the bed.

We sat watching The IT Crowd *in silence. The side table lamps were on, and the fan was pointed directly at her. From the outside, it probably looked like we were having a romantic moment, but Laney and I knew how strategically broken this whole scene was. She'd woken up screaming, sweating, and swinging at me. It took me ten minutes to wake her up, to make her realize she was safe and remind her that Alicia was in jail.*

The lights would stay on until the sun rose. The fan would stay on high for the rest of the night too. The cereal helped her to calm down, and the TV helped her to focus on something other than the nightmare she'd had. Laney and I had played this scenario out nearly every night since the attack, and for as much as I wasn't a commitment guy, I didn't mind it.

I wanted to be the one to hold her and brush her hair back from her face. I wanted to be the idiot asshole walking down the Costco cereal aisle, stocking up on boxes like I was getting ready for the damn apocalypse. It was all worth it because when Laney sank into my chest and rested her head in the crook of my neck, rubbing the veins on my arms, it was always fucking worth it. Every damn time.

Eventually, when our competition for who could touch the most exposed skin first won out, we'd turn toward each other. I'd lay her down on the bed and distract her from the dreams, from the pain, and remind her of what's good, of what's worthy of her memories.

THE FACT THAT LANEY WAS ALREADY FAST ASLEEP AND HADN'T touched my arms once or pushed into me a single time told me all I needed to know.

She'd learned to cope on her own and no longer needed me.

19

LANEY

I STARED AT THE BACK OF MY SISTER-IN LAW'S BLONDE HEAD WHILE SHE made breakfast. She felt terrible, like this was somehow her fault. It wasn't, but she had still insisted on coming over this morning with all the kids in tow to make me breakfast.

She was sweet.

Jenny had agreed to come hang out today too, which made me glad. I had run into her on my walk that morning; I was tired after the previous night and didn't have the energy to run. Without Ramsey, I was going crazy and felt extra clingy toward Jackson, and I was eager to cut that habit real quick, especially after I woke up in his bed all alone.

I didn't know what I expected. I supposed I had expected things to be like they used to be. Memories of waking up with him after a bad night had drifted over me as I lay in his bed that morning.

JACKSON HAD HIS FACE IN MY NECK AND TRAILED KISSES DOWN MY shoulder. His hands were around me, flat against my stomach as I stirred awake. The night before had been bad, the dreams so real. He had done everything my therapist suggested to help wake me and comfort me.

I opened my eyes, watched the sun dance across his wall, and smiled. I loved waking up in his arms. He kissed my earlobe next and then made his way back down to my shoulder.

Then he whispered in my ear, "Wake up, baby. Let's go find an adventure to give you something else to dream about tonight." Then he got up, grabbed me, and carried me to the kitchen, where he made me breakfast, then we did exactly as he suggested. We went and found an adventure. He booked us two tickets to Florida, where we spent the entire weekend.

I RUBBED AT THE TATTOO ON MY WRIST THAT I HAD GOTTEN THAT weekend and tried to draw the same strength from it that I had then. Its black, curving letters said *Brave enough to dream.*

"Laney, do you want some coffee?" Sarah's voice broke into my thoughts and brought me back to sitting at the breakfast nook, alone. I had a large sweater on over my tank top; it was a cloudy day, and I was cold. I nodded my head yes to the coffee and let my eyes drift outside, looking for Jackson. I didn't know where he was; I assumed possibly talking to Gepsy or making arrangements. He wasn't here, and I had woken up a little after seven.

I hated that I was angry with him, or more that I was angry with myself. I'd let him kiss me, and I had kissed him back then asked him to take me to his bed. All we'd done was sleep, but still, I had thought things might be different this morning.

"Good morning, sweetie," my mother said hesitantly as she made her way inside from the back yard. I internally winced at how scared my mother must have been when she saw me like that last night. Trying to calm her worry, I smiled brightly at her.

"Hey Mama."

She busied herself with setting the eggs on the counter and sifting through the fridge for something. I was zoning out as different people buzzed around the kitchen. Sarah set a plate of eggs, bacon, and toast in front of me. I smiled up at her and was about to say thank you when she set another plate of poppy seed pancakes in front of me. *Holy carb overload.*

I didn't usually eat a ton for breakfast, but I was feeling emotional, so I grabbed my fork and dug in. Twenty minutes later and nearly full to the point of explosion, I stood and walked over to my sister-in-law and hugged her.

"Sarah, thank you. You know it's not your fault, right?"

She was washing dishes, because apparently making a monster breakfast wasn't enough. She took a second before she turned toward me. When she did, she had tears in her eyes.

"Laney, we love you. The whole family loves you so much, and we worry about you. We worry the big city is going to swallow you whole and we won't have you anymore. I know it's not my fault, but it doesn't change how bad I feel."

I rubbed her back and pulled her in for a hug. I couldn't change the fact that she felt bad, but I could try.

"Laney, I need you in here," my mother cried from the laundry room.

Shit, laundry duty. I resisted the urge to groan like a teenager.

"Okay, be there in a second," I yelled back, purposely making my voice sound further away than necessary. I took the longest route possible to the laundry room, which included going upstairs, then back down, around the kitchen, living room, three bedrooms, then the kitchen pantry before I finally made my way into the laundry room.

I hated doing laundry.

As a kid, growing up with a bunch of brothers, I was always put on laundry duty because it was a "girl chore" according to my father.

I had to wash their nasty football uniforms, and t-shirts, and underwear. It was the worst. I turned the corner to the room and stood inside the doorframe as I watched my mother fold a load of whites.

"What's up, Mama?" I asked, hoping she just wanted to ask me a question instead of wanting my help.

"Here, honey, help me for a bit, will you?" She extended a basket full of jeans to me. I concentrated on keeping my eyes straight so they wouldn't roll to the side. I hated how immature I had become since coming home. We folded in silence for several minutes. The laundry room had two long counters on either side of the space, along with bars for hanging items that sat above the counters. I was done with half the load of jeans when my mother spoke up.

"Did you know your father and I nearly divorced just two years after we got married?"

I turned around to face her, shocked and surprised by her admission.

"What?" I asked in awe. My parents were the poster children for what a perfect marriage should look like, or so I thought.

She kept folding white shirt after white shirt.

"It's true," she admitted while still looking down at her load. I took a pair of jeans and pretended to fold them, until she continued.

"We were so young when we got married, I really had no idea what I was doing. Your father was a great guy with good intentions but had about zero experience with communicating with women." She shook her head and lightly laughed. I kept moving the same pair of jeans around in my arms as I waited.

After a hearty sigh, she continued, "We were both raised listening to the same sermons, the same teachings about a woman's place being in the home, in the marriage...her *godly* place. I believed it, wanted it, but walking it out was so much harder than I ever imagined." She sighed again then stopped folding and turned toward me. "Your father was raised believing women shouldn't have more of a voice than a man, unless it was in private, away from the public eye. I was lonely because he left so often, doing work, and when he wasn't working, he was spending time at church and with his family. I was just expected to stay home, keep busy, and wait. It got to be too much, and every time I tried to talk to him about it, he would remind me about my place in the home."

She kept wringing a white washcloth in her hand while looking down. My heart was beating so fast; this was information that had never been shared with me.

"We argued so much I started to believe he didn't actually love me. I got pregnant with Lawson and I was so sick, but your dad, he didn't soften...and I felt so alone. Just because the bills were taken care of didn't make it any easier to do everything by myself. It came to a boiling point when I told my friend I wanted to leave your dad.

"She encouraged me to go back and reason with him, not hold his culture against him. So, I did, and once your father realized I was serious about leaving, pregnant and everything, he agreed to change." She looked up at me with tears in her eyes. "He changed, but there hasn't been a day in our marriage that hasn't been work, Laney. It has taken work to get here, and it takes work to stay here. I decided I wanted this to last, and so it does." She turned her back and continued to fold the clothes as if she hadn't just dropped the bomb of the century on me.

"Why are you telling me this, Mama?" I quietly asked.

She turned again and smiled at me. "Because I see you and Jackson working, but you're working in the wrong direction. You put in the same effort and the same amount of dedication to your relationship, but you're putting it in all the wrong areas. If the two of you chose to focus it on bein and stayin together, you'd last an entire lifetime. I'm sure of it. That boy's in love with you, sweetie. Whether he knows it or not, he's head over heels for you."

My face was burning as she took it in her hands and watched me.

"When he finally figures it out, don't turn on him, honey. Don't hold his culture against him." She kissed my cheek, then pulled me into a hug and whispered in my ear. "I'm so glad you had him, during everything. I'm so sorry we weren't there for you. I hate that we didn't know about it, but I understand why you didn't tell us. Just don't keep us in the dark anymore, okay?"

She was crying, and so was I. I nodded in agreement with her and hugged her again, relishing the feel of her strong arms around me. I wanted to remember this moment and hang on to it. I wished there were a way to make it as permanent in my heart as it was to brand my skin with a tattoo. My mother had never opened up to me about her struggles with our "culture."

Things I'd battled against my whole life, she always just acted like I needed to see the sense in. It changed so many things for me to know she struggled with the same things. I had a deep respect for my faith, but I hated the way I was raised—like women had more work to do in the home than men, like we were only put on earth to serve them.

When I looked at my mother and my sister-in-law, I felt bad. They reared children and kept the home together, and now I knew how much work it took. It wasn't just something my mother said yes to lightly. She had to work at this life as much as I had to work at mine. It gave me a better perspective of her choices and this life she led, and it gave me a ton more respect for her.

"TWENTY SAYS YOU CAN'T DRINK THAT," MY BROTHER LEO TEASED while looking at the fresh container of cow's milk on the kitchen table.

I laughed like it was no big deal, even though it was, and said, "You're on."

I took the container and held it to my lips, ready to chug it down, then I stalled. I just needed a second to sort out my thoughts. I had a thing about fresh cow's milk; it freaked me the hell out. To this day, I wasn't sure why, but the thought of warm cow's milk fresh from the udder was gross, and I had never been able to stomach it. It was something my family knew, but I was feeling courageous.

Or I just *really* couldn't turn down a dare. Leo leaned closer, Zane ran over to join in the fun, and Ty turned toward us from where he sat in the living room.

"Do it, Laney, do it!" he yelled. Then all my brothers started yelling it in unison. I closed my eyes and let the warm milk slide down my throat. I took in two big gulps before I started to choke.

"Ewww, gross, Laney," Leo yelled as I started to sputter the milk all over the table.

"What is goin on in here?" my mother demanded from the stairs.

Shit.

Leo looked scared too. "Nothing, Mama, just Laney wanted fresh milk for some reason," he said while watching my face as he lied through his teeth.

"Yeah, she kept saying she wanted to chug the whole thing," Ty piped up. *I am going to kill them.*

I looked to the last person who might possibly come to my defense and wiped the cream from my mouth.

"Yep, crazy Laney," Zane said through a laugh.

That was it.

I lunged at them. "You liars!" I screamed, hitting the table and knocking the milk over and down onto the floor. I ran, Leo and Zane ran. I slipped on the milk and fell flat on my ass. All three of my brothers were laughing as Ty jumped up from the couch and the three of them ran outside. I started to wipe myself off as my mother came to stand over me.

"Clean this mess up, Laney Laverta, and then go grab some more milk. This was supposed to be for Jenny." Her hands landed on her slender hips, and I blinked up at her and tried to get up.

"Wait—what do you mean go get more? Like from the fridge?" I hoped against all hope.

My mother smiled at me. "No, sweet girl, from Tilly. Quick now. Jenny needed that milk yesterday." My mother made her way toward her office. *Shit.*

Milking a cow was way worse than drinking the milk from one. I would be paying my stupid brothers back for this. I angrily made my way toward the front door without changing, because what was the point? I threw the door open, cursing under my breath, then stopped when I saw Jackson coming up the steps.

We hadn't talked since the night before, since the kiss or the sleeping in the same bed, hadn't discussed him leaving that bed. I crossed my arms over my chest and tried to ignore the fact that I had cow's milk all over myself.

He smiled as he looked down at my clothes. "Headed somewhere fun?"

The afternoon clouds had finally parted, and the sun was shining through, making him look all dreamy and shit. I looked toward the barn, past the house.

"I'm milking Tilly. My idiot brothers." That was all I was able to give as an explanation while I walked past him. I just wanted to get this over with.

Jackson followed me.

"Well, can I help?" He sounded excited. I stopped and looked up at him. His tree height was never as frustrating as it was when I tried to be irritated with him.

"Why do you want to help?" I asked, genuinely confused.

He smiled and pushed some of my wild, milk hair behind my ear. "I just do," he whispered. Butterflies took off in my stomach as though some idiot butterfly catcher had forgotten to shut their cages. I thought I had a lock on those stupid winged creatures to keep them from having free reign. I walked past him and didn't respond. If he wanted to help milk Tilly, who was I to stop him?

20

JACKSON

I watched as Laney sat on the small bench next to the brown dairy cow. She had her hands on the udders, working them back and forth to squeeze the milk into a stainless-steel bucket, just like something from a movie. I was leaning against a pillar watching with my arms crossed. I had never seen someone milk a cow, and it was intriguing.

She finally lifted her head up and asked, "You going to help or just stand there?"

She sounded irritated, which I didn't blame her for. I had taken off this morning. I hadn't wanted to leave, but I also didn't want to cross any lines with her, and if we'd woken up together, we would have crossed at least a few.

When I talked to Gepsy, he told me they had someone following Alicia and they would know if she made any trips this way or did anything suspicious. It made me feel more at ease and I knew it would help Laney to feel more relaxed as well, but I hadn't had the opening to tell her. Her brothers must have done a number on her for her to be this irritated.

I bent down next to her, waiting for instructions. Laney grabbed my hands and placed them over her own on the cow's teats. The cow shifted and tried to walk forward when I accidently squeezed too hard.

"No. Gentle, like this." Laney moved my hand until it was positioned perfectly on the udder, then together we worked the milk out. Laney had me next to her, which was uncomfortable, so I stood up and got behind her, caging her in with my arms, then I repositioned my hands with hers. I could feel Laney's breathing change now that she was pressed up against me.

We milked in silence. I liked being this close to her, just as I had liked being with her the night before. This place was doing something to my self-control, demolishing it with every new day I was near her.

All that could be heard in the barn was the swoosh of milk as it went into the bucket and a few of the cows mooing from their stalls. The bucket was half full, and I figured our time doing this was nearly done. Over the course of the day, I'd had some time to think about Laney and my situation. Since I was losing this battle against her, I toyed with the idea of giving in.

So, before any more time passed, I pressed my nose to Laney's ear and asked, "Will you go on a date with me?"

She froze.

Stopped moving entirely.

We stayed like that for longer than I wanted. Worry of rejection began to fill in all the silence between us. I shifted behind her, about to get up when she finally turned her head toward me and blinked.

"What?"

"Go on a date with me," I clarified with more certainty this time. She started to move, to stand up, and I moved with her.

"When? Why?" She looked around as though the answers could be found in the walls of the barn.

I smiled and took a step toward her. "Tonight, and because I want to eat dinner with you." I took another step and grabbed her hand as I whispered, "And kiss you again."

She flushed red, like I'd known she would. She tucked a few loose strands of hair behind her ears. "Jackson, we shouldn't."

I gripped her chin lightly and bent down to kiss her, but she took three steps back. I stepped closer, closing all the distance she'd just created. "We should. I'll ask Leo about his truck. Be ready by seven." I kissed her quickly on the lips and walked away before either one of us could back out.

THE CANDLE ON THE TABLE KEPT GOING OUT. I WASN'T SURE IF THAT was a sign or not, or if I even believed in them, but we eventually needed to ask for a new one since it provided the only lighting. Laney stared down at her half-eaten lasagna, pushing pieces of meat around her plate. I looked down at my salad and took a drink of water.

Things with us had never been this awkward, but I had also never officially asked Laney on a date before either. Laney was wearing a sexy black dress I was struggling with because she'd told me it was her mother's.

Her hair was curled with pieces that fell around her face, and with the new light from our working candle reflecting off her cheeks, she looked stunning.

I cleared my throat, trying to clear the air and the awkwardness between us. She looked up and stared at me.

"So, what are we supposed to talk about on this date?" Laney asked while snagging a tomato off my salad.

I smiled at her. "I don't know...what do you want to talk about?"

"How about we talk about where you went today?" she asked around the tomato in her mouth.

I smiled and pushed my plate closer to her. "I drove over to Romeoville to make some business calls and talk to Gepsy."

She watched me with a curious glare. "What did he say?"

"That they're watching Alicia and have tabs on her, so we don't need to worry." I waved it off like it was nothing, hoping she'd be reassured.

"Good, that's a relief," she answered with a mouth full of food, again.

I smiled and went to grab her hand that rested on the table. "Yes, it is."

She stopped chewing and looked down at our hands. She swallowed, drank some water, and gently pulled her hand back. "Yes, well maybe we should be getting back. We don't want Leo to get upset about his truck."

I didn't want to push her, and I knew this whole dating thing was a big surprise since I had been so anti-dating our entire time knowing one another. After I kissed her, something had just broken open inside of me. I was tired of not having her, and if I needed to play by her rules, I was ready to win.

"Okay, if that's what you want," I said gently while motioning for our server.

Laney looked back down at her plate. "I think it is," she admitted weakly. She was trying to keep us somewhere safe, where she wouldn't get hurt. I understood that, and I knew it would only take some time to wear her down. I hated that I knew this about Laney, hated that I was so selfish that I was willing to risk her heart for a little reprieve from being away from her, but I couldn't take it anymore.

We paid the check and drove the few miles back to the farm. We walked upstairs together and stood by our separate rooms as we watched one another. I stepped forward, and as soon as I was close enough to kiss her, she opened her door and walked inside, shutting it in my face. I rubbed my hand over my chin and turned toward my room. She wasn't ready and maybe she never would be, but I wasn't going to stop trying.

"Jackson?" Something was shaking me. "Psst. Jackson, wake up." More shaking and louder whispering.

I blinked a few times and found a dark room and someone standing above me. The moonlight was shining through the window and highlighted Laney's hair and fair skin. I tried to sit up, but she placed her hand on my chest.

"Did you mean it?" Laney asked while still whisper-yelling at me, trying and failing to be quiet.

I cleared my throat. "Did I mean what?"

She was running her hand down her braid and playing with the ends. "Did you mean our date? Did you mean to date me—was it real?"

What time is it? I looked around for a clock or something to tell me how early or late it was. We'd gotten back from dinner at nine, and I had fallen asleep instantly.

She must have gotten where my thoughts were headed as she sighed and crossed her arms. "It's eleven thirty. Now answer my question."

All at once I realized Laney was sitting on my bed, next to me, and in silky pajamas that left little to the imagination. I reached for her, and she moved.

"Jackson, did you mean it?" She stood, sounding more adamant.

"Yes Laney, I meant it. That's why I asked you," I explained, hoping it would be enough to convince her to come to bed with me. She nodded her head and pulled on my hand.

"Come with me," she whispered.

I stood up in my boxers and t-shirt, and she handed me some jeans and my tennis shoes.

"Where are we going?"

"To the river." She was pulling on jean shorts, boots, and a sweater over her pajamas. I stood up and watched her in the dark, so tempted to just pull her to bed and take off all those clothes she'd just put on. Laney turned around and walked toward my door.

"Let's go." She gently pulled it open, and I followed her out, unsure of exactly what we were doing.

21

LANEY

I was a fool, a dumb, stupid fool, but I couldn't help myself. I was leading Jackson by moonlight to my favorite part of the river, a place I would go often as a kid, even at night. Obviously, my parents had no idea, otherwise I would still be locked in my room from being grounded for all eternity.

As we made our way through the field and past the set of trees that bordered our property, my heart pounded in my chest. I had lain awake after my date with Jackson, thinking all this over.

He meant it. He had meant to take me on a real date where he tried to kiss me at the end. My heart soared at the thought of him wanting to have more with me. It was soaring for an entirely different reason when I realized I wanted more with him tonight too. I climbed down a few rocks and looked back to watch Jackson scale the small hill. He was light on his feet, and you wouldn't know he had lived in the city his whole life. Or had he?

I didn't actually know. The sound of water rushing downstream filled the air as we drew closer to the river.

We walked the length of it for a few minutes before I finally turned off the path and headed closer to bank. There was a small cove where water pooled and sat peacefully, like a miniature lake. The embankment was all lush and green. I pulled the blanket from under my arm and laid it down, pulled off my boots, and carefully made my way toward the water. Once my toes were touching, I took off my clothes, revealing a bathing suit underneath—something Jackson probably hadn't seen earlier.

He hadn't had the luxury of bringing one because I was too focused on his answer to my dating question. I threw my clothes behind me onto the blanket and watched Jackson's eyes take me in. He started at my painted toes, which were now dipped in the cool water, slowly made their way up my thighs, and then settled on my stomach, which was his favorite part of my body.

"THIS RIGHT HERE." JACKSON SAID WITH A MUFFLED VOICE. HIS FACE WAS buried in my stomach and he kept blowing raspberries into my skin, making that awful fart sound. I was laughing and kicking at him as he continued to torture me.

"Jackson, stop!" I breathed out, begging him to stop because it tickled.

I was still laughing when he finally stopped and resurfaced. His face was bright and happy. I held his jaw in my hands and gently kissed his lips.

"There you are," I whispered to him. He smiled and threw me over his shoulder, then gently slammed me on his bed as he made another assault against my belly.

"I love your belly, Laney. I think I'll just live here." He laughed while trailing kisses down to my stomach.

"Live here? How's that gonna work?" I laughed while rubbing my hand over his buzzed hair.

He looked up at me and smiled. "Well, it starts with me not letting you get up." I smiled, my heart beating through my chest. I wanted him to keep me, to hold me, to have a place with me. Jackson gently laid his head on my stomach and relaxed.

SPLASHING BROUGHT ME BACK TO THE PRESENT AS JACKSON MOVED closer to me. He had taken off his shirt and was standing in just his boxers. Goose bumps erupted on my arms as I scanned his muscular form. I had seen him without a shirt so many times, but here under the moonlight was something different. He had the perfect chest. Sure, he had those washboard abs he worked so hard for and those big, solid-as-rock pecs, but it was the fact that Jackson didn't have a single strand of hair on his chest that made it perfect.

It was all bare and smooth. The only hair he had was a small amount that trailed down from his belly button. I took in a shaky breath as I adjusted to the sight of him and tried to calm my heart rate as he took my hand and led me into the water. The little pool was deceivingly deep. Before I knew it, we were up to our waists, and Jackson started to swim around.

It was a warm night, and the cool water felt amazing as I started to glide through it too. After a few minutes of swimming around each other, I finally asked him a question.

"Have you ever lived anywhere but the city?"

He swam closer, his body gliding next to mine as he let out a breath. "Nope. I've been a city boy my whole life. I went camping in college though, so I've had *some* experience with the outdoors."

I stopped swimming and stared at him. "College? No one took you as a kid?" I pushed my hands through the water and tried to make my way closer to him.

"No, there wasn't anyone around to take me," he replied easily, as if it was no big deal.

It was though.

Going camping as a kid was a rite of passage, and how come no one had been around to take him?

"What about your dad?" I asked carefully. I tried to remember the details he'd shared at my family's dinner table about how his mother wasn't in the picture and he didn't have any extended family.

Jackson stood on his feet and looked up at the moon. He waited a while before responding, but when he finally did, he stared at me and then lightly splashed water to the side.

"My father and I have a complicated relationship. He wasn't exactly present through my childhood." Jackson let out a small sarcastic laugh and launched back into the water. I watched him submerge, knowing the subject of his dad was closed.

I frowned as I watched the dark water at my fingertips. I wasn't ready to end the conversation, especially if he wanted to 'date me.'

"Complicated how?" I lightly splashed him, hoping he'd continue.

Jackson let out a sigh and placed his hands on his hips. "He wasn't exactly present while I grew up. His only advice to me was to never settle down."

He likely couldn't see my face, but it was twisted in confusion.

"Then why would you take his advice if he wasn't present...or really even an active participant in your life?"

Jackson turned toward me and ran his large hands through the water. "I don't think I actively did it...it's just that I..." He stopped talking and narrowed his gaze. He took a few steps closer to me, which made my body warm. "Uh...Lane, you remember when we were in Florida that one time?" The slow sound of water dripping surrounded us as he drew even closer.

I turned toward him and smiled.

Of course I did. Was he serious? It was one of the best weekends of my life, but no way was I telling him that.

"Yeah" was all I surrendered.

"Remember how you thought that shark was following you?" he joked. I rolled my eyes because Jackson made fun of me all weekend for that, but it was true.

"Yes Jackson, I remember," I said while I let out a sigh, wondering where he was going with this.

He circled around me as he swam and asked, "Remember that night, how you thanked me for saving you?"

I could feel the warmth of that moment from all those months ago still rooted in my body, like it was sitting idle in my bones, just waiting to surface again. I had been stupid that night in Florida, vying for Jackson's affection and attention. He hadn't saved me, but we'd both pretended like he did, and we had a very steamy night of gratitude.

"Yes, I remember that too," I murmured.

Jackson was so close now that I could feel the warmth from his skin in the river. I looked up into his eyes and saw the reflection of the water in them. He reached for me, his fingers brushing my jaw.

"Why are you asking, Jax?" I whispered, fighting those damn goose bumps that only surfaced when he was this close to me.

He put his arm around me and pulled me close. "Because you have a leech on your shoulder, Lane."

I didn't even think, just jumped into Jackson's arms while I strained my neck to the side to try to find the damn thing.

"Get it off!" I yelled at him, not caring who heard because: death. I was scrambling his human tree height like never before. "Jackson get it off!" I was nearly crying now.

"I am. I am. Just calm down and hold still." He lowered me enough to reach my shoulder. I felt a pull and a pinch, then heard something drop into the water. No way was I going back in. No freaking way. I stayed crumpled against Jackson's chest, and he slowly walked us back to shore with little giggles erupting from his throat.

"It's not funny, Jackson," I scolded, and he laughed harder. "It's not funny!" I said again.

"It is a little bit," he joked.

"Have you never seen a leech in this part of the river before?" he asked incredulously.

I stared at him in shock. "No, I haven't. Do you think I'd willingly go into leech-infested waters?"

He laughed again, placing his t-shirt over my head to keep me warm. I'd had these grand delusions that after we came to the river and felt the water and the magic of the moonlight, we'd kiss again. He'd finally open up to me about his life, and we'd make love on this blanket.

But the damn leech ruined whatever moment we might have had. I was positive there was no way Jackson would open up again, and there was no way I wanted him touching me after that stupid thing had been on my skin.

I pulled my knees up to my chest as Jackson pulled on his jeans and shoes. I found my boots, shook them out, and pulled them on, and did the same with my shorts. Then we headed back to the farm. The whole thing was ruined, just like our date had been.

"I WANDERED LONELY AS A CLOUD..." I WHISPERED OUT LOUD TO THE white wall of the shower. The hot water pelted my back as I tried to regain composure. For some reason, the leech, the turn of events from the date, and the lack of things going as planned at the river had caused me to surf the unruly waves of anxiety, and I wasn't dealing very well. Feeling anxiety usually triggered my PTSD and then spun everything out of control.

I tried to rationalize that it didn't matter, that things were fine, but the events of the night reminded me of losing Jackson in the first place, and deep down, I still believed he'd left me because of my trauma.

"It floats high over vales and hills..." I tried again, louder this time. My voice was shaky, but no one would know from the cover of the loud shower.

The poetry wasn't working.

I'd already recited this entire poem in my head ten times. Now I was reciting it out loud. The next step was yelling it, and I wasn't prepared to do that.

I crouched down in the middle of the shower, wrapped my arms around my legs tightly, and closed my eyes.

"When all at once I saw a crowd..." I said louder, into my knees. I couldn't hold off from crying, and I fought to rise above the agony that it caused me. Every time I shed a single fucking tear over this shit, I felt like I was giving *her* power. I needed to get out of my head, out of my memories, out of the images of Alicia's dark hair in the rearview mirror as she pinned me to the seat with the cable wire...images of how her lips were the color of blood as they thinned into a solid line from the force it took to choke the life out of me.

"A host of golden daffodils...beside the lake..." I shuddered and paused. Each word was getting harder to push out, and all I wanted was to sleep. The water had turned cold, but I didn't move. I was frozen in place.

In time.

I was back in that car, in that garage, alone as she choked me. I felt my lungs squeeze and constrict as I fought to breathe. I needed the next phrase of the poem. I needed to force the words past my lips, but no words would come.

I let the sound of defeat wrap around me. I was getting so much better, so much stronger, but now I was backsliding, and it hurt. It hurt my lungs. It hurt my heart…if only I could get the next words out.

"Beneath the trees, fluttering and dancing in the breeze." Someone's voice cut through my negativity.

My head shot up and I scanned the white walls, but all I saw was the curtain and soft glow beaming overhead from the light fixture. My heart was pounding as anxiety took more territory in my chest. I was frozen until a hand gently pulled back the curtains and Jackson stood there. Our gazes locked, his blue eyes at war with the pain I was sure he found in mine.

He paused, watching for a second, then reached over me and turned the shower off. He then dipped down, wrapped a large, yellow towel around my body, and lifted me from the tub. I let my head fall into his neck, let him carry me to his bedroom.

The darkness of the room was like a welcome beacon of hope. I didn't want lights or exposure. I needed to hide.

I felt safe with Jackson. He laid me on his bed, under his covers, wearing nothing but my towel, and continued to recite the words of William Wordsworth to me.

"Continuous as the stars that shine and twinkle on the milky way, they stretched in a never-ending line along the margin of the bay," he whispered into my skin as he pulled me against his chest.

My face was soaked from tears. The shower. The memories.

Every time I got into this place, Jackson would read poetry with me. We eventually landed on this one poem: *I Wandered Lonely as a Cloud.* Focusing on each line, sharing it, he'd take a few and read them, then I would. It was huge reason I had fallen so deeply in love with him. He had me when I felt lost; he always knew how to lead me back to sanity.

I turned around in his arms and watched the dark contours of his face. There was a soft glow coming in, likely from the barn light outside. The breeze from his cracked window was soft, and my body was buzzing from anxiety and adrenaline.

If I was going to be lost tonight, it was going to be in the arms of the man I loved. I was fucking tired of caring about whether he loved me back. I was too damn selfish tonight to care. I leaned forward and lightly pressed my lips to his. He matched my slow rhythm and moved his hands until they wrapped around me in a hug. It felt like he wanted to be careful with how he held me, like at any moment, I might disappear.

I didn't want him to feel that way, didn't want that weakness between us. I pushed forward and pressed into him more firmly, letting my hands grip the planes of his back. I dug my nails in as hard as I could, encouraging the animal inside of Jackson, with which I was well acquainted, to take over.

He pulled away from me and let out a groan. He shifted our bodies until he was hovering over and staring down at me. He traced the outline of my lips with his finger and slowly lowered himself until he was resting between my legs. His hard length pressed against my center, teasing me. I let out a small breath and waited for him to move, but before he did, he whispered, "I know what you want."

He carefully kissed my ear before he continued, "But I can't be rough with you tonight. I *won't* be rough with you tonight. Tonight, you're mine in an entirely different way." He carefully kissed the space next to my eyes and slowly moved to my nose. "Tonight, it's your heart that I want to own." He sat up slightly and watched me. "Let me love you tonight, Laney."

I stared at him, not sure if I'd heard him correctly. I didn't want to second-guess it. I nodded and let him lower his mouth to mine, let him slowly push that velvet length into me until we were both staring at each other, our breaths stilling. I let out a shuddered breath as he froze completely, watching my lips widen as a shuddering breath left my lungs.

"I've never had anyone that was just mine, Laney," he whispered against my lips as he moved inside me.

My eyes rolled closed. He felt too good.

"I want you to be mine...I've always wanted you." His hand moved down to my hip, holding me in place as he went deeper inside me. His breathing was ragged as he moved in and out of me, so slowly and so perfectly that I was shattering inside, completely unraveling. I let him have me in a way he'd never had me before, with an intimacy I'd never experienced. I let him love me with his body, and it was the most perfect kind of therapy. He was my healing. My atonement. My second chance.

22

LANEY

I KNEADED THE DOUGH BETWEEN MY FINGERS MORE VIOLENTLY THAN I was supposed to. My mother noticed and came over to slap my hands.

"Laney, stop that. You're gonna knead all the yeast out."

It was what she always said when I over-kneaded or was too rough with her bread. I dropped the dough, moved around the kitchen to where the veggies were set up, and started dicing.

I didn't want to talk, didn't want to think, just wanted to focus on the task at hand because I was living in a bubble and I didn't want it to pop.

Yes, a perfect bubble made up of all my hopes and dreams. It had been three days since that night I spent with Jackson. We'd woken up the next morning, a tangled mass of naked limbs and blankets. I looked at Jackson's face and saw that he was smiling. He'd said the last thing I ever expected to hear come from his lips.

"So, this is what dating you feels like? What the fuck was I waiting for?" My heart took off, soared, and hadn't come back down since.

Every day after that we had spent together. At night, I'd sneak into his bedroom, where we'd escape outside and find some adventure to go on. Guided by moonlight, we'd ride horses, watch Netflix in the tree house, or play Zelda while I sat in Jackson's lap in the game room. We were living out one of those rom-com movies, and I was terrified that the other shoe was going to drop.

Jackson snuck kisses in every chance he got. He'd find some way to touch me, pull me into him, get under my clothes. God, he was frantic and crazy, and I loved every second of it—but the anxiety was bubbling up inside of me like an overheated pot of water.

Anxiety from having to face the reality that we were still in hiding from Alicia...the reality that we had real lives to return to at some point, and with that the anxiety about whether or not Jackson would pull the plug on us.

Mom looked at me from over her shoulder; something was on her mind. Maybe she knew Jackson and I had been having sex. That was a big no-no in her house unless two people were married, and even then, I wasn't sure. Jackson and I were as quiet as church mice every time we were together, and we ensured there wasn't even any bed shaking or rocking. So, if she knew, she was a wizard.

She kept looking over at me, and I kept ignoring her. Thankfully, a few moments later, Leo, Tyler, and Zane came inside with Jackson on their heels.

"I'm serious!" Ty yelled as he ripped open the refrigerator door. I looked over at my mom to see if she was going to say anything about the fact that dinner was in less than an hour or the fact that we were in the middle of cooking it. She didn't.

"You are lying!" Leo said while looking at Ty from over his cup.

"There were elk up there last time I rode up. Scout's freaking honor," Ty swore while holding up two fingers pressed together.

I rolled my eyes because I knew what was coming next.

"Prove it!" Leo bellowed.

As usual, they were going to have to verify it to each other.

"We need an extra person to prove there were actually elk. You get ugly when you lose," Leo said while eyeing Jackson.

Crap, they were going to rope him into this. "What am I, chopped liver?" Zane asked while holding his hands out.

I tried to cut in and use the off-kilter moment to warn Jackson, but as soon as "Leo, don't" left my lips, Leo cut in.

"Jackson, ride up with us."

I lowered my head back down to watch the carrots and celery.

"Up where?" Jackson asked curiously.

"Ride up to Slide Mountain with us. It's half an hour there, half an hour back—we'll be back in time for dinner," Leo promised.

Yeah right. Everyone knew there was a reason it was called Slide Mountain. The ride was all up hill, and the horses couldn't take that kind of altitude with huge, man babies on their backs. It was going to be a two-hour ride at least.

"I'm not very good on a horse," Jackson said weakly.

"It's fine, we'll put you with Maya. She's our easiest horse and works with kids." Leo affirmed his statement with a clap on Jackson's shoulder then he, Zane, and Ty started vacating the kitchen while Jackson watched me.

I smiled at him, giving him the okay and relaying that it was fine. He walked over and lightly touched my neck. I knew he wanted a kiss, but I wasn't sure what our PDA status was, especially in front of my mother. He was about to leave, and something in me snapped. I reached for his hand and stopped him.

He turned and glanced at my mother, whose back was turned to us. I searched his face, waiting for him to dip his head and kiss me, but he was waiting for me to confirm that it was okay. I stood on my tiptoes and pressed my lips to his.

He pulled me into his arms and hugged me, kissing my head. It would have to do.

He smiled at me once more and left through the front door.

When had we become like this? Like a couple? It felt strange, but perfect. I liked that he cared, and I liked that he'd looked at me before he followed them out. My nosey mother kept watching us and refused to say anything.

It was dinner time, and no one was back yet, so my mother ate a salad and rushed off to her bible study. My father was still working with Lawson, so I was alone in the house aside from them being locked away in the downstairs office.

I was picking at the chicken pot pie my mother had made from scratch and trying to count the number of lines in the wooden table.

Truly exciting stuff.

The front door opened a moment later, revealing Jud. He had shaved his face and his dark hair was shorter. He looked good, handsome, and holy Lord, he smelled good.

"Hey Laney, what are you doing here all alone?" he asked as he came and sat next to me.

"Jud, I kind of live here. For now, at least. What are you doing here?" I asked while picking up a bite of chicken and stuffing it into my mouth. He watched my mouth, like I'd just spouted off some magical spell or something.

Finally, he blinked and looked away. "I came to see if you wanted to hang out."

I stood up and got him a plate then dished him some food, hoping it would make him look at me less. "Okay, here, have dinner with me."

He smiled and started eating his food while I grabbed him a drink.

"Thanks, that was great," Jud said while dusting his hands off. He didn't move to pick up the dishes or put anything away though—not like Jackson had done at every meal so far. Jud was from the same culture as my father, where women's place in the home was to make it, keep it, and sustain it, alone, or in any way that was necessary. At one point, I had wanted that life, had dreamed of it. Then one day realized I wanted to make my own damn money and didn't want to keep a home or be the only person to clean it.

Once I was done with the dishes and putting all the leftovers away, Jud had moved into the kitchen, standing against the counter near me. He was really close. I took a few steps back and cleared my throat.

"Jud, what are you doing?"

He watched me and moved his jaw back and forth. I shifted from foot to foot, because his silence was making me uneasy.

He cut the silence by stepping closer and pulling me into a kiss. I didn't kiss him back, but that didn't stop his lips from moving over mine or his tongue from pushing for access into my mouth. I pushed at his chest to break the kiss.

"Jud, what did I tell you last time you tried this?"

He pinned his forehead to mine and whispered against it. "Laney..." He tilted my chin up. "Give us another shot. Please?"

I moved around the kitchen and went to a different counter to get some distance. I crossed my arms over my chest and tried to reel in my crazy Laney vibes.

"Jud, I am with Jackson." I didn't want to waste time on pleasantries or making him feel better. He needed the truth.

He laughed and ran a hand through his hair.

"Laney, open your eyes! He's not serious about you. Everyone can see it. You're the only who seems to wear blinders where he's concerned."

I swallowed, pulling my arms in tighter across my chest. "Well, it's different now," I said firmly. He laughed again, and I clenched my fist. I wanted to punch him.

"Do you hear yourself? *It's different now.* Are you sure?" His condescending tone chipped away at me. Did he know something I didn't?

"Yes, I'm sure, Jud. It's different."

He stalked closer. "So, you two are together then? Official and dating, serious? Or is he going to flip the script on you and pretend nothing is going on between you two?" Jud asked with a wicked smile on his face. What the fuck did he know that I didn't? Whatever it was, it hurt, and I hated Jud for making me feel it.

I looked down. "We're together."

He walked backward and smiled. "Whatever you say, Laney. Just double-check, and if he's not as attached as you think, come see me. I miss you. Hell, I still want to marry you."

I kept my arms glued to my chest as he kept flinging words at me, words that would have flattered me ten years ago, but not now. Now they just pissed me off. He acted like I needed him, like he was doing me a favor by wanting me. What a dick.

"You should go," I bit out, swallowing all the words I wanted to scream at him. Instead, I turned and went upstairs.

Things were different this time with Jackson. They had to be. There wasn't a way that things could be this perfect between us and not be real. I tried to reassure myself, but panic settled into my ribs and began cracking them, separating them like I had just been hit by a sledgehammer.

I$_T$ W$_{AS}$ A$_{LMOST}$ M$_{IDNIGHT,}$ A$_{ND}$ T$_{HE}$ G$_{UYS}$ H$_{ADN'T}$ M$_{ADE}$ I$_T$ H$_{OME}$ Y$_{ET.}$ I was stressed, and borderline pissed. Jackson had taken his phone and had responded vaguely to all my texts.

Good

Fine

Be back later

That all started around nine at night, and once my parents went to bed, it just got worse. Finally, my phone dinged with a text from a number that I didn't recognize. It said: *Dawson's—come get him.* My stomach twisted with anxiety as I pulled on my flip-flops and ran downstairs, snagging my mother's keys on the way.

Dawson's wasn't far, thankfully, but it still took me at least ten minutes to pull into the gravel parking lot. The thought that the mystery texter could be Alicia settled in my stomach, but I knew my brothers wouldn't just leave him, so they had to be somewhere.

I flung the door open and searched the area for my brothers and Jackson but couldn't find them. I walked further in, until I was in the back and saw Jackson slumped on the bar, a glass of amber liquid next to him. He looked pale and like he was about to pass out. I searched the room to see who might have texted me, then finally found Leo talking to a group of women by the stage.

I walked up to him with my arms crossed. "What the hell Leo?"

He raised his hands in mock surrender. "At least I texted you and didn't let him do anything stupid, like go home with that blonde that keeps trying to talk to him."

I looked back to where Jackson was and saw the tall blonde, who was wearing practically nothing, leaning into his space and trying to talk to him. Off to the side, I noticed Zane and Jenny talking. He was leaning over her, trapping her with his arms on either side of her head. He looked like he was talking to her about something important because his face was all red and she was crying. A second later she pushed past him and ran outside. Zane pulled at his hair and slowly followed her. *What in the world is going on there?*

I turned back to Leo and glared at him. "What happened? You guys were supposed to go elk hunting or something and then come back."

Leo shook his head back and forth and brought his hand through his messy hair. "When we got back, Jackson got a voicemail that surfaced after being out of range. Once he listened to it, he asked that we come here instead of returning to the house."

I turned my head back toward Jackson and then nodded at Leo, releasing him from my questioning. I slowly walked back toward Jackson and gave the blonde a dirty look, warning her to back off. She flipped her hair, narrowed her eyes, and walked away. I tugged on Jackson's arm and helped him stand up.

"Laney. Baby, it's you," he said, voice raspy as he laughed a little. He was so, so drunk.

"Yep, let's go home, big guy," I said while trying to hold up his body weight with my shoulder. He slouched against me as he followed me out. He kept laughing intermittently and hit his head on the frame on his way into the car, but eventually I got him buckled. I knew it wouldn't do any good to ask him about what had pushed him to drink tonight, but sometimes his lips were looser when he was inebriated.

"Jax, who called you tonight?" I asked while I gripped the steering wheel more firmly.

He let out a loud sigh and said, "Gep. Said my dad is dying. I need to go see him."

I looked over at him, but his head was against the glass and he was nearly passed out. I felt this warm, cracking sensation work its way through my heart as I thought of what must have gone through Jackson's head when he got that voicemail. Jackson hadn't gotten around to telling me any more about their relationship after the other night, but I knew this still had to hurt. I reached over and grabbed his hand, but he was already asleep.

23

JACKSON

SOMEONE WAS KNOCKING ON THE DOOR, AND I WANTED TO KILL them. My fucking head was pounding, and my throat was on fire, not to mention the state of my nauseated stomach. I tried to sit up and get my bearings, not sure how I'd even made it back to the farm. I noticed I was lying on a towel in the bathroom that connected my and Laney's bedroom. I looked around and saw the toilet just a few feet from me. *Shit.*

Must have been that kind of night then, which meant Laney had probably helped me.

I groaned, stood up, and turned the hot water on in the shower. I stripped my clothes and showered, brushed my teeth, and then dressed. The knocking was coming from outside the house. I noticed and saw that Leo, Zane, and Wayde were putting in more fences. Shit, I should have been out there helping them. I checked the clock in the room and saw that it was almost ten thirty. I went to pull open my bedroom door and found Laney standing there with a bag of Taco Bell. The smell made my stomach turn, but I smiled at her just the same.

"So, is everything okay?" Laney asked while swinging her legs back and forth. We'd walked outside and decided to spend some time in the tree house while I ate and let my hangover slowly ebb away. I took a drink of water and nodded my head, not entirely sure how much she knew. I needed to make flight arrangements soon and get to New York to see my dad. My silence must have bothered Laney, because she let out a sigh.

"I mean, last night you said your dad was...dying. I just wanted to know how you're doing with the news?" she gently asked while rubbing my thigh. I could have definitely gone for some hangover sex right then, but not like this.

I wanted Laney in every possible way, but I didn't want her to see this mess. She didn't need to be a part of it, so I deflected. I just needed some time to sort this shit out and figure out how I felt about it before I opened up to anyone about it.

"I'm fine. Nothing really to talk about. Just have to make some arrangements is all."

She watched me as I ate another taco. Her green eyes narrowed, and her lips formed a thin line.

"Jax. ...come on. We're together now—that means you have to talk to me about this kind of stuff."

I watched her, feeling my jaw tick as I bit back the urge to defend myself. I pulled my hand free and cleared my throat.

"Lane...I need time to process this on my own. Please just leave it."

She swallowed and kept watching me, but eventually she gave me a small nod. She pushed that gorgeous red hair out of her face and released a breath. "When are we flying out? Have you talked to Gepsy about that yet?"

Shit.

This was not going to go over well.

"I'm going alone. I need to process this by myself. I should be back in a few days, but honestly I don't know what I'm walking into or why he even wants to see me."

I tried to explain, but it didn't do any good. I saw the second her hopes of us actually having a normal relationship evaporated. Her shoulders slumped, and her face turned red. She didn't say anything, just nodded her understanding.

I was so fucked up. Some very broken part of me didn't want her understanding. I wanted her fire. I wanted her to somehow physically reach into my chest and make my heart work right. I wanted her to tell me she was coming regardless of my reasons and my arguments. I wanted her to push me. I wanted her to be the Laney I'd fallen in love with in that boardroom.

But that Laney was gone and had been for some time.

I tried to nurse that part of her back to life, tried to get it to come back, but here, she was even further out of reach than normal.

Laney slowly slipped down the ladder until she hit the ground then walked toward the house without looking back.

———

THE SMALL FLIP PHONE WAS OPEN ON THE BED, ON SPEAKERPHONE AS I moved around the room, packing my things.

"I can secure you a ticket, just get a ride to the airport. Stick with the loaner phone and check in when you can." I nodded my head, forgetting Gepsy couldn't see me.

"You sure Laney will be safe here without me?" I wanted to double-check so I knew I was doing the right thing. I may have wanted to process this shit on my own, but it didn't stop me from being worried about her.

"Yeah, I think this will throw Alicia off and have her focus on New York instead of Indiana. She'll assume you guys are together," Gepsy reasoned through the crackle of the outdated phone.

"Okay, I'll get a ride to the airport, just text me the flight details." I could hear Gepsy clicking away on something on his end of the line.

"Will do, be safe."

I closed the flip phone and threw it on the bed then began rubbing my forehead. I needed to go find Laney and clear the air with her. I needed to say goodbye to her, and the thought made me feel uneasy. I wanted to tell her about this part of me. I wanted to open up this broken and dysfunctional door in my life and let her see inside, but I was afraid she'd deem it beyond repair and write me off.

I had told Laney a few nights ago about the notebook I had kept as kid. I thought back to that night and how much truth she'd gleaned from me.

I STARTED THUMBING THROUGH SOME OF THE CURRICULUM BOOKS WHILE Laney started taking books out. Laney and I offered to help Lisa when she came fumbling through the door with boxes.

I took out two more large books about algebra and geometry, likely aimed for the eleventh grade, and set them into a pile. Under that pile was a black spiral notebook. It looked so much like the one I had carted around as a kid that a smile broke out on my face.

"What's that?" Laney asked, walking over to peer over my shoulder.

I smiled at her. "Looks like Lisa's old notebook or something."

I flipped through the pages, shamelessly invading her younger self's privacy. There were pages of colorful drawings. She must have been young when she did it. Butterflies, a house, a dog, and about a million different variations of hearts filled the pages. Laney smiled too as we looked at the old notebook.

For some reason, I muttered, "I used to have one of these, a notebook I drew stuff like this in. I took it everywhere with me."

"What happened to it?" Laney asked. Her warm breath fanned my check due to how close she was standing to me. I closed the book and set it down, trying to rearrange the feelings it had brought up.

"I don't know. I stopped drawing in it at some point...didn't keep track of where it ended up."

SHE'D ASKED ME WHY I HAD STOPPED DRAWING IN IT AND I'D TOLD her I assumed it had gotten lost, but the truth was that I had stopped dreaming, stopped wanting all the things I colored in that book. The two parents, the siblings, the multicolored dogs, the tire swing, the trampoline...the life I dreamed of.

I didn't want to tell her the reason why.

I didn't want to tell her I'd found my mother when I was twelve years old. I wasn't ready to share that when I took a bus across Chicago by myself, wandered into one of the most dangerous parts of the city, and knocked on my mother's door, I found a shell of a woman who laughed in my face.

I couldn't explain the hole that had been ripped open inside of me when I learned that my mother had only gotten pregnant with me to trap a wealthy man, and when she learned that he couldn't be trapped, she threatened to abort me. My father paid her off, with the terms being that she agreed to continue with the pregnancy then walk away after I was born. He paid all her doctor bills, provided for her diet regimens, and even had a private room secured for delivery.

As an adult, I learned to push past the twist of anger and pain that began to lace my heart from that point on. My father's only redeemable quality was that he didn't want me dead, but he was never a father to me. I supposed in his defense he didn't know how to be one. I was sure Laney could argue that as an adult maybe I could get past my fear of abandonment, relationships, and women, but I'd argue that point and further explain that when I met Jimmy, he was a happy man, in love and blissfully ignorant to heartache.

He loved his kids and his wife, and then his wife left him. I'd watched as the one person I looked up to, the only person I knew who'd actually achieved the whole perfect family image got fucked over.

I watched as he drank himself into oblivion more nights than I could count, saw how his father and I were the only support system he had when his one-year-old cried for hours for a mother who wouldn't come home. I sat in the hallway with my best friend as he cried into the carpet, not understanding why his daughter wouldn't speak or eat. I was there pulling him off some dumb-fuck MC member who'd started a fight with him, trying to get him to see how bloody the guy's face was, how close to death he was. I watched as his whole world was ripped away from him.

The answer Laney was looking for wasn't a good one or a pretty one. It was made up of a thousand moments where I lived and breathed abandonment. Loneliness was all I'd ever known, and honestly, I welcomed that shit with open arms, because the alternative was too fucking ugly. I would never recover if I opened my heart completely to someone only to have them leave me. At least with my mother, I had been oblivious to her disregard for my life.

With Laney, if she woke up one day and realized how shitty I was at being a husband or a father—fuck, I'd die if she left. I wasn't built like Jimmy; I'd never be strong enough to recover and dust myself off. I didn't have a badass father figure to help show me how to do it either. So, laying those dreams down and losing that journal was a form of survival.

Something told me Laney would never understand my reasons, not coming from this world, so it was better this way, better if she just accepted that I was a selfish asshole who couldn't commit. I held my chest as I headed out of the room, suitcase in hand, ready to say goodbye.

24

LANEY

"Again!" Jenny yelled, slapping her sparring gloves. Her golden-brown hair swayed back and forth as she jumped in place. Something about her in this element made her seem invincible, like a warrior. I hopped in place too, mimicking her movements while shaking out my fatigued legs and arms. I had in a mouthguard and wore two red boxing gloves on my hands, along with yoga pants and a racerback tank. Sweat was seeping out of every possible pore of my body and my breathing was ragged, almost to the point of wheezing. After the tree house incident with Jackson, I had needed to hit something. So, I'd walked over to Jenny's house, and she had driven us here.

I had been sparring with Jenny for an hour and a half, and I was way too proud to admit that I was exhausted, especially because Jenny had yet to even break a sweat. I had taken a few self-defense classes after the incident with Alicia, but my instructor had told me that what'd happened to me wouldn't have been helped by self-defense, so I had stopped going. I still wasn't sure why he'd told me that. He could have just encouraged me to get really good at kicking ass so I could scare off attackers, but it was like he gave up on me.

Jenny didn't though.

She informed me that she worked as an instructor at a local gym in Cincinnati, which explained her Amazon-like muscles and endurance.

Punch, punch, squat, punch, punch, squat. It was a combo I had now perfected. Jenny finally threw her sparring gloves down and picked up some boxing gloves, then joined me in the ring.

Jenny hit me, her punch hard as hell. It took me a second to recover, but I loved it. It pushed me to hit her just as hard. We were so lost in the dance as we worked around each other that we didn't notice we had an audience. Tyler, Zane, and Leo were standing outside the ring, yelling at us, shouting about who should hit who. Jud had shown up too, on the opposite side of where they were standing. His presence grated my nerves because he'd proved me wrong with Jackson.

I was still focused on the sparring, easily ignoring all the men who'd shown up, until I heard a voice say, "Come on, Laney, you're faster than this." I turned my head so fast that Jenny clocked me good. I spun backward and fell over.

Jenny yelled out, "Shit."

Then ran over to me and helped me up, everyone yelling, "Oohhhh." Jackson laughed, and Jud ran into the ring to help me up. The fact that Jackson was watching me made me remember the last time we'd sparred together. It was a month after the attack.

"Hit me, babe," Jackson encouraged while slamming his gloves together and dancing around me. We were in his regular gym in downtown Chicago. He had paid to rent the entire thing out so I would have space and time to work with just him.

"No, I don't want to hurt you," I replied weakly. I was a mess, and I didn't want to punch or hit anything, I just wanted to sleep. Depression had gripped me and held me after the attack. I'd taken a sabbatical from work and basically hung out in Jackson's house for the whole month with the shades drawn. My savings went up in flames because of it, but I had to get away from everyone.

A month later, Jackson was finally forcing me to move past the incident. It wasn't that she'd just attacked me with a cable wire, trying to choke the life out of me. It was that she had methodically stalked me. She'd entered my home and painted the word whore on my walls, had sent me horrific pictures in the mail.

She'd messed with me mentally, following me, prank calling me, pretending to be a client at work so she could leave a picture behind of Jackson and me together from the day before. She was evil and manipulative, and it scared the shit out of me.

"Laney, honey, hit me." Jackson egged me on, and I finally tried to match what he was doing and stepped up to hit him. He gently hit me in the arm instead, then danced in a circle around me. I moved to hit his arm like he had mine. "Hit me harder, Laney," he pushed.

I let out a sigh and tried to do what he wanted but just ended up crying and throwing my gloves on the ground.

He came over and held me, kissed me, and told me, "It'll get better, baby. You'll get stronger, and one day you're gonna kick my ass," he joked, and I laughed through a steady stream of tears.

THE MEMORY FLASHED BEFORE ME AND FILLED ME WITH RAGE AT WHAT we had, what he always gave only to take it away from me. Without thinking any more about it, I motioned for Jackson to join me in the ring. He smiled and laughed, shaking his head side to side. I waved him forward.

"Come, on, let's go."

Jud looked between us and shook his head no. "Laney, that's not a fair fight,' and its stupid. Jackson will hurt you."

I ignored Jud's comment and watched Jackson as a slow smile worked its way over his face. He was wearing a thin t-shirt that said *The Great Wall of Fine Ya* with a picture of the Great Wall made up entirely of bills. The sight of him in another one of Travis' shirts pushed me over the edge.

He was at the back wall until he found some gloves that fit him. The guys were all yelling "Oooooo" again with their hands around their mouths like little trumpets.

Jud was yelling, "No way, you guys. This is stupid. I'm not letting you box with Laney."

I glanced at Jud, anger rolling off me now, and spat "Fuck off" at him.

I'd never talked like that to him before, but I was so angry that he was suddenly trying to protect me when the night before he hadn't cared about how careless he'd been with my feelings. Jud took a step back as hurt flickered across his face and a nice red color filled his cheeks. I focused on Jackson again as he laughed and continued wrapping his hands. The ring was just a set of flat, black mats with white tape to indicate the boundaries. Jackson stepped inside, and Jud eventually walked out as Jackson and I danced around each other.

Everyone was silent as we gently hit each other's gloves. I knew Jackson would never hit me hard enough to hurt me. I, however, had quite a bit of aggression to take out on him.

I lightly tapped his gloves, and he danced back. Working from memory of the afternoon spent with Jenny, I pranced forward and took a hard swing, catching him off guard. He moved to the side and gave me a strange look, like he was surprised. I advanced again and punched him, putting all my strength into it. He took it, danced away, and raised his arms, like he wasn't sure what was going on.

I jumped around the manmade ring and waited. Jackson watched me and smiled. It was that damn smile I used to love. It was the one he used when he thought I was being cute, the one he used when he wanted to make love to me.

Tears burned the corner of my eyes as the hopelessness of our relationship set in. It hung around me like a heavy blanket. I was in love with him, and he'd never love me back. He was good to me and protected me but would never be *with* me. Hurt propelled me forward until I was completing the jab I had perfected earlier. A loud pop filled the air as Jackson went down, and I realized what I'd just done.

I'd hit him as hard as my tiny arm would let me, right in the nose. His hands went to his nose as he eyed me warily. Jenny ran up to him, as did Zane and Leo. I tore off my gloves, threw them in the ring, and walked outside.

The warm air didn't help at cooling the sweat that was dripping down my face, but I had to get out of there. Tears were already streaming down my face as I sat on the concrete steps thinking over what I'd just done. I had never hurt anyone in my life, especially not someone I was in love with. I heard the gym door open and close a second later. I knew it was Jackson without even seeing him. He was quiet as he stood against the metal railing.

"Want to tell me what that was about?" he calmly asked, still holding a white napkin to his nose.

I turned to look at him and gestured to his nose. "You okay? Is it broken?"

He didn't let up in the intensity of his stare as he shook his head. "Just a little swollen."

I nodded and looked down, not ready to answer his question.

His jaw ticked. "You and I have sparred plenty before, Laney, but you've never attacked me."

Guilt pricked at my gut. I scrubbed at my sweaty face, trying to rein in my emotions, then thought *To hell with it* and let it all out.

"Jackson, I'm in love with you and it's the most painful thing I've ever experienced." I shook my head, eyes full of tears as I stared at the loose gravel near the stairs. "I thought when you asked me on a date that you'd changed your mind." I looked up to watch his face then continued, "I thought you could picture it for once. I thought you could see me in your future...I thought..."

I stopped as my voice caught, and my words became strained.

"I thought it was real this time. Even after all the millions of times you acted like you loved me but never said it, all the times you acted like the perfect boyfriend but wouldn't be it...I thought this time was different for you."

Jackson looked down at the steps, his hand busy holding that damn bloody cloth, and his jaw ticked. I hated that I wanted to yell at him to stop grinding his teeth, but I kept quiet and waited.

Slowly he looked up. "Is this about the thing with my dad?" he asked, his tone reverent. He was utterly clueless, and my heart broke even more. I scoffed and shook my head back and forth at his ignorance.

"No, this is about your inability to include me in your life, Jackson. It's about how you always push me away when we get anywhere close to acting like a real couple."

My hands were set on my chest. I didn't even realize it; it was like they went there on their own to protect what was left of my heart. My voice was starting to shake with how loud I was yelling this at him.

His face stayed neutral and he didn't respond, because he knew I was right. Nothing had changed for him. This was just as casual for him as it had been three months ago when he left me.

Things were silent for a few breaths before I continued.

"Couples open up with each other. They cry on each other's shoulders when a loved one is dying. They pull the other one along for support and strength, but you just keep pushing me aside."

I dropped my hands and watched his face as the silence ate up the words he was supposed to give me. He was supposed to defend himself, argue with me, tell me I was wrong about us, about him.

But he didn't.

He stood there, like a piece of art...staring at me, and as usual giving me absolutely nothing. I shook my head again and looked past him.

"I'm done, Jackson. I'm done hoping one day you'll want me the way I want you. I'm done waiting for you to realize we would be perfect together. I'm just done, and I only want to be free of you," I whispered, ignoring the redness that had started to shade his face.

I walked to Jenny's car and got in, hoping like hell she'd figure it out. She, along with everyone else, was right around the corner where the big garage door was wide open, listening as I laid my heart down in front of Jackson, only to have him ignore it. Jenny saw me and followed me. At this rate, I was more than ready for him to go to New York. I needed space from him; I was done with this entire scene.

25

JACKSON

WHEN LANEY MOTIONED FOR ME TO JOIN HER IN THE RING, I honestly thought it was going to be a fun mix of jabs and dancing around each other. I knew she might be upset with me from earlier, but when she landed the first punch, I realized I was wrong.

She was sending me a message.

By the third hit, I knew it wasn't just a message; it was goodbye.

She was done.

I followed her outside and knew what was coming. I had seen Laney get pissed at me enough times. As her words flew at me, I was barely holding it together.

She loved me.

I had told her to let me love her the other night, but we'd never talked about it and she had never said it back. When she said those words, something was set free and locked down instantaneously in my heart. She had too much access, too much room to hurt me. So, I kept my face passive, unaffected, so she wouldn't see through me.

I let her say everything and let her walk away.

This was best.

A clean break for us. I wouldn't be changing any time soon, didn't know how to love her the way she deserved. I had to remember that this was always better for us. She would find someone, marry. My heart would crack, and my breath would hitch, especially when I saw her pregnant or holding her kids or kissing her husband, but eventually I'd get over it.

Eventually the pain would fade.

I WAS ABOUT TO BOARD THE PLANE TO NEW YORK. I HEARD THE CALL for my flight and walked down the ramp toward the gate. I had arranged a taxi to take me to the airport after I said my goodbyes to Leo, Tyler, Zane, and Lawson, who all told me to come back and not to be a stranger. I hugged Beverley and shook Wayde's hand, thanking them repeatedly. Laney hadn't come downstairs.

I knocked on her door but didn't get anything. I wanted to write her something. Call her. Leave her a voicemail. Anything to not leave with things so broken between us, but then again, I needed the end. I kept wavering between which pain would be more bearable. Eventually I landed on Laney just being rid of me for good and getting the chance to move on.

The plane took off and I watched through my window as everything began to diminish into little dots, and then there was nothing but darkness.

THE FACILITY MY FATHER WAS STAYING IN WAS TOP TIER AND FULL OF ridiculous amenities. I supposed that was the entire purpose of hospice, though, to help keep the patient comfortable until they passed. I wasn't ready to walk into his room yet. I stared at the numbered plaque outside the dark, mahogany door that bore the number one. I laughed to myself at how my father had managed to get himself into room number one as if it were as prestigious and isolated as him. I closed my eyes and exhaled, then pushed the door open.

My eyes slowly adjusted to the large size of the room, the hardwood floors, the nice accent walls and light fixtures. The recessed lighting in the room was dimmed, but it still lit up the space nicely. The large, floor-to-ceiling window showcased the entire city of New York and let in a decent amount of light. Finally, my eyes landed on my father's body in the center of the room. He looked withered and skinny, lying in an elevated hospital bed with tubes and IV lines connected to him. His hair was white, and so thin it was barely visible. I didn't recognize him.

His eyes were closed, and for just a second, he looked peaceful, even kind. But my father was neither of those things, not even in death. The rest of the room was tailored accordingly to his high-profile budget: marble kitchenette counters, private bathroom, large-screen TV placed flat against the wall. I walked around his room and waited—for what, I wasn't sure.

I heard an exhale and movement behind me, then I heard his voice, low and weathered.

"Son. You came." Not a question, because he knew I would.

I turned around and faced him, slowly moving closer to him. "Yes, sir. I was told it was urgent," I replied flatly.

My father moved his body forward, then started coughing and wheezing. I looked out the window, afraid to feel the vulnerability this moment created.

"Jackson, I need to talk to you," he barely whispered through his labored breathing.

A male nurse wearing white scrubs walked into the room and started typing on the computer. He then moved to the IV bag and continued checking my father's vitals and documenting everything. "I think you should put the breathing mask on, Mr. Tate," the nurse suggested.

My father waved him off, as if he were a pesky fly.

"I need to speak with my son." He managed the statement with more labored breathing, and the nurse looked up at me with a slight frown. His eyes reached mine for only a second before they dropped back down; it was the unmistakable look of pity, which meant my father was about to die.

That revelation shifted something inside of me, especially now being here, seeing him. There were thousands of unspoken words between us, regrets, anger toward him, questions I wanted answered. Now looking at him so pathetic and weak, I just wanted to say goodbye.

The nurse left us alone and I moved closer to my father's bed, pulling up a chair. My father watched my movements and then reached out to grab my hand. As weak as he was, his grip was iron tight.

"Thank you for coming, son." My father relaxed his head back on the bed. I nodded at him, still unable to speak. "They aren't sure how much time I have left, but I wanted to spend what was left of my life with you. I have a lot to make up for and I know I won't be able to make things right in a few days, but I have to try."

I scanned his face as he spoke, unsure if I was really hearing that my father wanted to try to fix things with me—my unfeeling, unshakable father who believed people who allowed weaknesses into their lives were themselves weak. I swallowed the lump of disbelief and said the only words I could think of. "Yea, I'll stay."

26

LANEY

RAIN WAS HITTING THE GROUND SO HARD DIRT WAS KICKING UP FROM the gravity of it. They were huge drops pouring down as I tried to ride Loki back toward the stable. I had snuck out and saddled him before anyone woke up. I climbed down and led him into the barn, took off his saddle, and combed him down, then refreshed his oats and water and put him away in his pen.

Zane was standing inside the door waiting for me.

"Dad's looking for you," he said around a wad of chew. It was one of the many things he hid from our parents and only did when he went out to do "chores."

I brushed the residue of the oats from my hands and nodded at him. "Where's he at?"

I asked, watching the monsoon transform our yard from the barn door. My father and I hadn't really spoken about anything since I'd been back, not about the past or what had happened to me. We just revolved around one another in a strained existence.

Zane spit his tobacco out and turned to look at me. "In the house."

I nodded again, and we waited in the doorway as the rain pounded down.

"So, you gonna ever talk about what happened between you and Jackson?" Zane asked while sticking a long piece of gum into his mouth.

I gave him a look from the side of the doorframe I filled and crossed my arms. "You ever going to talk about what happened between you and Jenny?"

He rolled his eyes and looked away, then let out a heavy breath. It seemed neither one of us was too eager to run through the rain back to the house.

"Jenny and I have a complicated past," Zane said while watching the stray pieces of hay strewn across our path. His eyebrows creased as he crossed his large arms over his chest. "I told her I loved her two years ago. The next day she left for Cincinnati. She never once called me, emailed me...nothing. Then she came back and acted like..." He trailed off and then watched the rafters. "She acted like nothing ever happened. So, that's how I acted too, like nothing ever happened, and we fell back into our same old friendship...like I never said I love you, like she didn't ignore me for two years."

I watched my brother's face, saw the pain in his eyes and the frustration that was there. He rubbed his jaw as we watched the storm together, not continuing about Jenny.

I exhaled, ready for my own confession. "Things with Jackson have always been confusing. I fell for him, knowing he wasn't the commitment kind of guy." I kicked at the dirt near my shoe as I tried to order my thoughts well enough to explain this. "We ended whatever we did have about three months ago. Then all this happened and we kind of fell back into the same rut. Then Jackson took me on a date. Like a real, monogamous, I-want-to-date-you date."

I looked up to watch Zane's reaction. He was standing with his arms tight, a baseball hat on his head, still wet from the rain. I swallowed my anxiety over this topic and continued.

"We were together for a few days. Then he found out about his dad... and he shut me out. Didn't want me to be a part of it or for me to go with him." I shrugged my shoulders, internally wishing I could shrug the feeling I had over Jackson completely away.

"That sucks, sorry sis." Zane leaned forward and pulled me into a hug. I hugged him back and buried my face in his shirt, letting my tears over losing Jackson fall free. Our little magical time on the farm was over.

Zane let go and I stepped back, wiping at my face.

"Let's watch something tonight, just me and you," Zane suggested.

I looked up at him. "You mean it?"

He nodded and put his arm around me, leading me through the rain to the house.

———

ONCE I DRIED OFF, I FOUND MY FATHER IN HIS OFFICE, ON THE bottom floor. He had a silver laptop perched in front of him, and a small glass of what looked like whiskey next to him. My father didn't drink to my knowledge, but after my mother surprising me, I wouldn't put it past him.

"Hey Daddy, you wanted to see me?" I asked while walking further into his office.

I took a seat in one of the deep, cushioned chairs in front of his desk. My mother had decorated his office, so it was a mixture of green, leather, and animal parts. A few antlers lined the walls, and a rabbit skin, an elk head, and even a few fish were displayed around the room. He had a large bookshelf near his window that held philosophy texts, spiritual guidance books, bibles, a concordance, and theology tomes, and if a space wasn't filled with a book, it was filled by a photo of one of us kids.

Most the room was covered in pictures of him hunting with my brothers and uncles, but there was one he kept on his desk, and it was of me. I was ten and holding a fish. Something blossomed in my chest at seeing that photo of me so close to his workspace. Sometimes I lost sight of how my father cared for me.

"Hey sweetheart. Yes, I did, thanks for coming," my dad responded while shutting his computer and finishing whatever was in the cup.

I itched to lean forward and smell the cup just to see if I was right about the alcohol.

"I wanted to discuss somethin with you," my father said with his Texan drawl.

I crossed my legs and leaned forward. "What's up?"

My father paused, pursing his lips and drawing his hands together. "I haven't handled your return home well." He exhaled and moved until he'd walked around his desk, then leaned against it. "When your brothers were born, I felt like father of the year every day." He chuckled. "With them it was so easy to know how to talk, how to discipline, and how to love them." He watched the carpet at his feet as he continued. "Then you came along, and everything changed."

His brown eyes had little flecks of gold in them as they flitted over my face. He slowly crouched beside me.

"Right from the start, I thought I was going to break you. Physically or emotionally...like one day you'd just leave, all because of me."

My throat was tight at his admission and my eyes stung, but I kept quiet, hoping he'd continue and help heal some of these old wounds I still had.

"You were always so beautiful...like your mother, and I always just wanted you to be safe. From me, your brothers, anything that could hurt you." He paused, watching his feet. I could see his Adam's apple move a few times before he looked back up at me and continued. "When you wanted to leave...it felt like I had failed, like I had broken you, and I knew your mother was going to blame me. Heck, I blamed me."

I moved forward to place my hand on my father's face.

"Dad...stop it. It wasn't you or anyone. I just needed to try something on my own." I shrugged trying to lighten his load.

He placed his hand over mine. "I know, but then you came home, and I didn't handle it right. I kept all that news about your attack...about your—"

He stopped talking and swallowed. Tears were gathering in his eyes, and at the sight of them, mine were unleashed.

"You got hurt, baby girl. I wasn't there to protect you. You came home, and I didn't wrap my arms around you and tell you I love you and I'm glad you're okay." His chest shook as a sob escaped him. A tear cascaded down his face, and my heart broke open. I had never seen him cry or be this vulnerable.

With a strained voice, he continued, "I'm so proud of you. I'm so honored to be your father. I'm so sorry for how I've handled this...can you ever forgive me?" His face was red and wet from tears, and so honest.

I pushed forward, threw my arms around his neck, and hugged him as tight as I could, letting all my tears for my father fall free. All the moments where he wouldn't talk on our video calls. All the birthdays he wouldn't call on. All the things he should have said while I was growing up. I chose to forgive him.

"Of course, Daddy."

I let out a sigh and relaxed into his shoulder, feeling like some piece of me had just clicked into place.

I needed this. I needed him.

My father rubbed my back and sat back before he exhaled and smiled. "Now, onto some business matters," he said, smiling down at me.

I smiled and sat back in my chair. He stood, walked back around to his desk, and pulled out a large red folder, then leaned forward and placed it in front of me.

I took the folder and opened it. There was a stack of papers kept together by a large, silver paper clip. The front page held a group of numbers and a mass of highlighted portions. I flipped through a few more pages, and the pattern of yellow highlighter and numbers continued.

"What is this, Dad?" I asked while keeping my eyes on the paper.

"That"—my father pointed at the folder—"is the evidence of a sinking ship."

I snapped my head up. "What?"

My father leaned back in his leather office chair and explained, "Your mother doesn't know. She has no idea we're going to sink unless we make some changes."

I sat up taller, trying to rein in the thousands of questions I had. "What are you talking about?"

Dad nodded his head in agreement but pulled at his chin. "We have steep competition and zero marketing at the moment. One of our clients is on the fence about moving forward with us because they found another supplier for a fraction of what we charge." Dad rubbed at his face and leaned forward again. "We need to make some changes and fast."

I set the folder down and closed it.

"What are you going to do?" I asked softly. I had never observed my father in a bind. He'd always had a plan, knew the next ten steps, and always had a huge buffer in his bank account. He was a pillar.

Dad reached forward to grab the folder that was in front of me and let out another sigh. "I want to hire you, honey."

"Excuse me?" I leaned as far back in my chair as possible.

"I know it sounds crazy, but hear me out," he pleaded with his hands up.

I waited, because even before he explained himself, the seed he'd just thrown out had already taken root.

"I know you love the city and have a great job. Don't say yes because you feel bad for us or because you think we're trying to manipulate you. I need someone who can handle our marketing, and I don't want just anyone. You know I prefer to hire family, and I prefer someone who is capable and competent." Dad leaned in. "I know you have some debt you've been trying to pay down, but I imagine that might be problematic living in the city."

I nodded my head, saving my words for what was coming next.

"So, here's my proposal, and I want you to take some time to think it over. If you agree to come on with T. Lavender Farm & Co, within the next six months, I will give you a signing bonus of a company house in any place you'd like to live. If you choose Chicago, we'll support that, as long as you agree to work remotely. Or you can move back here and work close to us, which we'd love—you know that. You can live anywhere, and we'll pay for your living expenses for the first three years of your employment."

I leaned forward and tried to grasp what I'd just heard. "Dad, you just told me you're struggling—how can you even afford to pay me?" I tried not to stare at my ten-year-old self on his desk. What would she do in this situation? Ten-year-old Laney was fearless and brave.

Dad got up and walked around his office, grabbing another file from the cabinet on the back wall. He took the paper from the file and set it in front of me while leaning against the edge of his desk.

"Our current financial status and shares. I'm just planning ahead. We aren't sinking yet, but we will be if I don't make some changes—one of them being that I invest in you."

I stared down at the zeroes and numbers among the page. *Holy shit, they're loaded.*

"We can actually offer you more than you are currently making at Dyson & Reed," he conceded.

I sat back and looked at him curiously. "How do you know what I make?"

"Jackson told me," Dad enlightened me, all serious with his arms crossed and his nice dress shirt tucked into his jeans. I waited for him to explain why he and Jackson had been discussing me, but he never did.

"Why would Jackson say anything about how much I make?" I asked.

Dad exhaled again and watched the wall behind my head. "I asked Jackson whether or not he thought you'd be interested or if you'd say yes. I also wasn't sure if he had any plans for you back in Chicago."

I resisted the urge to scoff or roll my eyes at my dad asking that question. Of course he asked Jackson before he thought to ask me. I tried to remember what my mother had said about his culture and calmed down.

"Dad, this is crazy. Are you seriously offering me a job right now?"

He stood up and walked over to the window then turned and addressed me.

"I really am, sweetie. You can work anywhere, and you'll be making more money. It will give you some time to pay off your student loans and settle down somewhere." He moved closer until he was standing right next to me. "I won't lie...I am hoping you'll take this and move back here. Your mother and I miss you, and whether or not you want to admit it, so do your brothers."

I needed to think this through. This decision would change so many things. Mostly, it would be officially closing the door on the idea of Jackson. It would be me moving on, because if I said yes, I would move. I wanted to tell my father about my issues with Jackson and tell him about my heartache. I wanted my father to tell me it was all going to be okay.

Instead, I cleared my throat and told him. "I'll think about it, Dad. Give me a week."

27

JACKSON

They say people don't change; the people around them just adapt. I've always believed that saying, because I've never had any proof to the contrary. I'd known my fair share of assholes, jerks, and bastards, each of them with someone who agreed to adjust to their bullshit behavior.

Knowing Laney would inevitably become one of those people if she was ever with me had me pushing her away. Laney didn't need to adapt; she needed someone who would not only change but shift the fucking moon and stars for her. Changing wasn't in the cards for me, and I wouldn't have believed it was possible for my father either, but I was starting to witness it for myself.

He'd asked me to stay and so I did. I sat there next to him, waiting for him to explain why I'd come all the way to New York to say goodbye to a total stranger. Once the nurse left, my father coughed then turned his head feebly in my direction and wheezed out his confession.

"I was wrong, Jackson." He waited and let out a heavy sigh, as though this conversation was as painful for him as the disease in his lungs. "I have many regrets in this life, but how I treated you is by far my greatest." He paused, reining in whatever else he had to say. "I was raised with a monster who hurt me as a child."

He coughed, holding a rag to his mouth, and blood spread through the white cloth.

He leaned back and continued, "I swore once I left home that I would never have a family, and if by some accident I did, I would be sure they knew the value of being alone."

That sounded like an accurate description of my childhood growing up.

I flicked my gaze over to the door of the room, half tempted to leave on that note, not even sure why I came. Memories of how lonely I'd been ran through my head. Memories of how left out, how ignored, how fucking desolate my childhood had been thrummed through me. I was angry at my father. Really fucking angry.

He must have noticed; his frail hand came to mine but stopped. He swallowed and coughed a few more times before he continued in a whisper.

"I am so sorry, son. I was so wrong." His eyes started to water, and his breath turned shaky and unstable. He took two big breaths as if he was summoning all the strength he had left to pour into this moment. "I was wrong, Jackson. I am alone on my deathbed, and it's my own fault. After all the money and all the women, all I have are regrets. I am sorry for what I taught you, what I put you through." He leaned forward to grasp both of my hands, using some supernatural strength. "You need to love someone and let them love you. Let them hurt you, let them hold you, and let them know they matter to you. Experience all of it, because I allowed none of it, and loneliness is the worst kind of pain you'll experience from loving someone."

I swallowed the lump of grief that was making its way into my throat. I barely knew my father, but this confession was gutting me.

He closed his eyes. "I've left you everything, son. I've watched you from afar, and I am so damn proud of you, of your restaurants and your achievements. I reached out to ask a friend of mine, August Torson, to meet with you. Take his help and take the money I've left you and invest it into something that will matter. Whatever you do, Jackson, find someone worth coming home to." He coughed again and let go of my hand.

I thought over my father's confession. I weighed it and tried to let the words sink into my heart, but it wouldn't take. I wanted to forgive my father, but the years of anger that held me captive wouldn't give.

I was stuck.

Stuck in anger, in hurt, and in rejection. I wanted more from my father. I wanted a reason why I wasn't wanted, why he resented me so fucking much he couldn't even get me Christmas presents. With his massive fortune, he didn't think to gift his son anything but the basics for surviving. I wanted to know why he felt like it was okay to leave me home alone, night after night. Why he didn't hug me or tell me he was sorry when I got hurt. Why he didn't teach me to ride a bike or how to shave. Why he was gone for so much of my life. I needed more than his apology, and I hated myself for it.

I pushed through three days of visitations with my father.

Each day giving forgiveness a shot. Each day agreeing to talk to him, to tell him about my life.

The only thing I had worth talking about was Jimmy, my godchildren, and of course, Laney. I told him all about my time on the farm with Laney and her family. He laughed when I told him about my feisty redhead, the one I'd agreed to let go of. I kept her close to my heart in each of our conversations.

"Sounds like I'd like her," my dad said on a laugh as I recounted how I'd originally met her. My smile wavered, because I had no idea if he would or not, but over the last three days, that forgiveness had worked its way into my chest and eventually caught.

So, when I asked my dad if he wanted to watch something with me and he didn't respond, something like panic swelled within me. I quickly looked over at the same time the machine started beeping. Three nurses ran into the room and asked me to step aside. I stood against the wall and clenched the TV remote in my hand. I held my breath waiting for the beeping to even out, for the sound of the air moving through the ventilator to turn back on, but none of that was happening.

I looked out the window and saw the sun reflecting off the skyscrapers. It was so fitting that an empire like the city of New York was his last and final audience. They laid my father flat and took his oxygen mask off.

He was gone, and he took those last three days of bonding with him.

Three days I got with my father, three days to hear his stories and get to know him.

———————

I STARED OUT AT THE DARK CITY FROM THE FORTY-FIFTH FLOOR OF MY father's building and thought about how much he probably loved this view, how every day he'd looked out at this city and how it'd probably pushed him to climb higher, push harder, and be stronger.

All for himself.

I blinked at the city lights and turned from the glass wall toward the kitchen, where I finally turned on some lights. My father's condo was opulent and expensively decorated. His kitchen faced the entire living room, with chrome and marble fixtures and floors. Not a single glass or piece of silverware was out of place.

That reminded me of a phone call that was in order; I'd need to let his housekeeper go. I'd have to sell the condo, or I could keep it for any future business I might have in the city. Torson's offer made more sense now, and my pride aside, it was a good idea.

It clicked into place for me, all of it: the weight of my father's life, his rejection, and his death. It hung around me like an invisible burden that wore me down and threatened to crush me. I'd always wanted his approval and his acceptance, and to get it and lose it all so quickly tore at me. I tried to deny the waves of pain that crashed over me. I tried to push it away, but it came back in full force. I threw the glass of scotch I was nursing across the room against some piece of artwork that likely cost more than someone's home.

Hot tears streamed down my face as I pictured my father dying on that bed, bleeding out all his regrets and shame. It all tasted so bitter on my tongue. I didn't want his fucking money or his fucking advice; I didn't need any of it. I just wanted the chance to know him, to talk to him, to see him at Christmas, to call him and wish him a happy Father's Day.

I sank to the floor and hung my head in my hands as ugly sobs flowed from some deep, dark place within me, some place I hadn't let hurt in so long, some place I kept fortified and protected.

A high-pitched ringing echoed through the room, interrupting my thoughts and the moment entirely. I stood up and headed toward the sound, finding a thin black phone connected to the base, lit up and ringing. I carefully picked it up and answered, "Hello?"

"Jackson?" My best friend's voice filled my ear.

"Jimmy?" I parroted, to be sure it was him.

"Yeah, it's me, man. I just wanted to see how you're holding up."

I looked around the room and ran my hand over my head, wondering how he knew to call me and how he got my father's number. My best friend and I had been through some shit together, and he was no stranger to how I felt about my father.

My silence must have spurred him into an explanation. "I figured you'd be there...at his house. Don't ask how my dad got the number, but he did. He's worried about you, I'm worried, and Ramsey's pregnant-worried, which means she's driving me crazy. So, I need you tell me if you're okay so I can give her the thumbs-up."

I let out a sigh, wishing I could summon the humor for picturing a panicked Ramsey. There was some space inside of me reserved for family that had been wounded long ago but repaired by Jimmy and his family. I loved Jimmy like a brother, so having him hunt me down and call me was fucking everything at the moment.

"I'm okay," I managed to get out in a raspy voice. Jimmy waited, and when I slid back to the floor with the phone attached to my ear, I continued, "He told me he regrets how he treated me." I watched the glass wall in front of me.

Jimmy made some sound on his end. "You think he meant it?"

I nodded my head to the empty room. "I think he did...and he told me to find someone to love." I paused and decided that was all I was going to say; it was all my lungs would allow on the emotional subject of my father's death.

"That messing with you?" Jimmy asked, perceptive as always. I let out another heavy sigh and let all the shit that'd happened with Laney surface, glad I could finally talk to him about it.

"I don't know how to love someone, Jimmy. I'm so fucked up—how could I put someone through that?"

Jimmy made a slight humming sound. "So you'd rather just assume you aren't worthy of someone loving you?"

I felt it.

The offense in his tone...it began to rise inside me, dying to defend myself.

"It's not about being worthy. It's about not being selfish enough to put someone else through that shit. I'm a fucking mess, man," I yelled at him, feeling pushed and prodded by his accusations.

"Bullshit," Jimmy argued. "It's about you being afraid—afraid if you tell Laney you love her, she'll say it back, and then you're in that fucking painful place you didn't ever want to be in again, that place where someone could walk away from you."

I stood up and started pacing the floor. I was seething as Jimmy laid out my insecurities before me.

"Fuck that, Jimmy. You know it's more complicated than that," I spat at him.

He let out a sigh. "Jax, I love you like a brother. You know I do, and you know this isn't the first round we've gone regarding Laney. I argue because I want you to feel what I feel. I want you to wake up with the woman you love every morning and feel how fucking magical it is to know she's yours. I want you to one day have the privilege to rub your wife's belly, swollen with your baby inside. I want a niece, a nephew— fuck, Jackson, I want us to get that happily ever after. I have it, and I want it for you to. So, stop being so fucking hardheaded. I have no idea what's been going on at the farm, but if there's even a chance at anything with Laney, fix it. Make it happen. You deserve some happiness." He finished with a sigh.

I didn't respond while I thought over what he'd said. I could hear Jasmine in the background trying to get Jimmy's attention.

I just stood there, watching the city as his words sank in. Finally, being pulled away by his kids, Jimmy ended the call.

The realization of those secret hopes I'd had as a child for a family, a wife, and children floated through me, and it caused me to ache. I wiped at my face and headed for the top floor, where I knew some empty boxes waited for me. I wanted to pack this place up and leave it behind me, just like the memories of my childhood.

I grabbed the steel railing and jogged up the two flights of stairs until I came to the loft on the top floor. It was lit by the city lights.

I put my hand out and found the light switch, the soft glow of recessed lighting filling the room. I found a few boxes near a glass desk that had papers, a laptop, and a familiar-looking black notebook on it. I zeroed in on the spiralbound book and strode toward it. I carefully picked up the relic and cradled it in my hands; I had thought it was lost years before after I left for college. I pulled the office chair out and gently sat down as I opened the book.

Color jumped out at me as I surveyed the artistic stylings of my younger self. There were pages of my pretend family, all my fake siblings and my fake pets, my fake parents. I flipped the page over and saw the picture of a tree fort with stick figures inside it, and the memory of holding Laney all night in hers surfaced. I smiled because this whole journal felt like a weird photo album of my time with Laney at her family's farm. A trampoline where all my siblings and I jumped...one where we ate dinner as a family...one with horses and sheep, a big barn with hay inside.

Those hot tears had returned and with them something foreign I had never allowed myself to feel before, something I was too afraid to allow into my life. For the first time ever, I felt hope. I felt the beginning instead of the inevitable end. I felt full, and I pulled on that feeling and tugged it close until I owned it. I was so tired of running and worrying about things fading, and I'd never considered what it would be like to have something last. I shut my journal carefully and stood, walked over to the boxes, and started back downstairs. I had a flight to book.

28

LANEY

"IT IS NOT," ZANE RUMBLED FROM BESIDE ME WITH HIS HAND IN THE popcorn bowl.

I laughed and popped a piece in my mouth as I retorted, "Yes, it is!"

Zane watched the screen as another alien ripped into someone's flesh.

"It's a human wearing a costume, I swear." I tried to convince my brother, but he shook his head to argue with me again.

He was finally following through with his movie night with me. We'd curled up on the couch to watch some alien movie marathon.

I was loving it because I planned to exact revenge on my brothers tonight for all the pranks they'd been pulling on me lately. I just needed him to fall asleep and somehow convince Leo and Ty to come down, and I'd be all set.

"There's no way that's a human, sis. You're crazy," he spouted off again around a mouth full of popcorn.

I shook my head with a smile on my face. "You'd be surprised how detailed those costumes can get, Mr. Thompson. Don't be so surprised that your little sister is smarter than you," I joked while moving my blanket to cover my toes.

Zane laughed while reaching for his soda. "You know if Mom came down right now, I'd blame you for the movie choice, right?"

I rolled my eyes and reached for his soda, hoping he'd share.

He released the can and eyed me with disdain. "Seriously? Can't you go get your own?"

I shook my head while I sipped it. "The fridge is too far."

The front door opened, and Leo and Ty piled into the room. "Make the nachos, idiot, before Mom wakes up," Ty whisper-yelled at Leo.

Leo headed for the fridge, and I propped myself up and cupped my hands over mouth like a trumpet as I yelled, "Grab more sodas!" Both men stopped and glanced at me before milling back around the kitchen. Leo nodded at me and grabbed three sodas.

Once Leo and Ty settled in on the chairs and other couches, we continued our marathon for three more hours. I was barely keeping my eyes open, but I was determined to get my revenge tonight. It was almost one in the morning and Leo was nodding off; the other two had passed out. I had texted Jenny to give her a heads-up.

She was going to head over as soon as the coast was clear. The sleep aids I'd slipped each of my brothers' sodas should help in keeping them out so we could fulfill our master plan. I glanced back at my brother and his eyes were closed, his head was back, and we were set. I texted Jenny and carefully got up from the couch.

I grabbed the spray bottles from the bag I'd brought down and started filling them with water. After the fourth bottle, I heard a light knock and tiptoed over to the slider door to pull it open.

Jenny stuck her head in. Her bangs were pulled back with a colorful clip, and she wore jean shorts and a tank top. "Are they for sure asleep?" she whispered.

I took the bag from her and nodded my head yes. "I gave them the pills too, so they shouldn't wake up."

That seemed to appease her, and she started unpacking the boxes of hair dye. We started with Leo, using the small brushes, and applied the dye all over his hair. He was going to have green hair when this was done.

We set the timer and moved on to Ty. I carefully moved his head side to side as Jenny painted his hair, and we followed suit with Zane. I watched Jenny's movements as she worked on his hair. She had chosen a bleach for him, coloring his hair blond versus the blue and green like the others. In the end, it would probably make him look better. I pondered it and wondered if she still had feelings for him.

I wanted to ask about the night at Dawson's, but it wasn't the right time. By the time Leo's timer went off, we were finished with Zane. We used the spray bottles to carefully wash the dye out, using a towel to catch the colors that ran. My mother would kill me if I got hair dye on her couches. Leo didn't move a muscle, so we had a fairly good feeling that the sleeping pills were working.

We moved our way down the line, rinsing the boys' hair. It was getting late and fatigue was starting to set in. Jenny didn't show any signs of being tired, but I knew she had to be exhausted.

We were nearly done with Zane's hair. Jenny was bent over the front of him, wiping away some residue when his eyes snapped open. She froze in place, her hands still near his hair, and he reached up and gripped her wrists, holding her in place.

I froze, standing perfectly still behind the couch, where I was out of Zane's eyesight. The two of them stared at each other, and Jenny's breathing changed into something labored and somewhat loud. I realized Zane was trying to pull Jenny closer to him and she was resisting.

His face turned serious, and he lifted an eyebrow and tugged harder until she landed flat on his chest. Then he kissed her, hard and unforgiving.

I closed my eyes and tried to disappear. I didn't know what Jenny wanted me to do, but this was awkward, and I definitely didn't want to watch my brother make out with someone. Decision made, I slowly turned and crept away until I had cleared the kitchen and then made my way upstairs.

I had no idea what was going on with those two, but I'd catch up with Jenny in the morning. I shut myself in my room and went to take a shower. Once I was done and ready to crawl into bed, I plugged my phone into the charger and noticed a missed text message. Butterflies took off in my stomach; it had to be Jackson. I flipped the phone open and pressed the button to select the text.

My hope sank like a rock in water. It was from Detective Gepsy.

Laney, I tried to call you earlier but didn't get through. I talked to Jackson already—everything is clear to go home. We got her.

I double-checked the call log, and sure enough, there was a missed call from Gepsy's cell. It was over. They'd caught her, and I could go home. A strange feeling came over me; it was relief, but also reluctance. I liked being home, liked being near my family. I wasn't ready to go. I put the phone back without responding and sank into my bed. I'd decide in the morning.

———

THE MORNING CAME WITH THE USUAL FARM SOUNDS: CHICKEN, COWS, birds. I stretched and snuggled further into my blankets. It was summer, but I had a fan and was obsessed with blankets, no matter how warm it was. I had just closed my eyes and welcomed at least another hour of sleep when I heard yelling coming from downstairs. My eyes snapped open as the yelling got closer, as did the sounds of someone running up the stairs.

Shit.

I jumped out of bed and ran toward my door, locking it just as the sound of fists hammering it down echoed through the room.

"You can't hide in there forever, Laney!" Leo yelled.

I slowly backed up and watched the door. They knew how to pick the lock, and they knew how to scale the house to get in through the window.

"Seriously, Laney? Blue?!" Ty bellowed, referencing his new hair color.

I laughed to myself and suddenly wished Jackson was here to see my revenge.

"How come Zane got a normal color? Do you like him better than us?" one of them yelled; I couldn't tell which one.

I crawled back into bed. I was safe for now, until my mother left. They wouldn't do anything to break the house while she was around.

"You have to come out sometime, and payback is a pregnant dog, little sister," Ty yelled through the door.

I winced and pulled the covers over my head. I thought about the text from last night. Suddenly it didn't feel like such a bad idea to head home.

I hadn't texted or called Jackson, but the strange thought that Gepsy could have been hacked had squirmed into my brain. So, I tried to call Jackson and got his voicemail. I lowered the cell phone, defeated, and tried to swallow the frustration that came with it. A second later, the phone vibrated with a text from him.

Sorry, can't talk. Everything okay?

I shot out a text: *Yeah, just wondering if you're heading home.*

He texted back a few seconds later.

Yeah

I supposed that was enough to convince me it was time to go home.

29

LANEY

THE SOUND OF GRAVEL CRUNCHING MADE ITS WAY THROUGH THE OPEN windows of the living room. I pulled the white curtains aside and peeked out, and sure enough, the green and white taxi had pulled up in front of the house. I turned around and faced my family. They'd all shown up to say goodbye, including Jud.

The boys got over the hair dye the second I announced that Gepsy had given me the all clear. My mother along with Leo tried to persuade me to wait a week, but I insisted I needed to get back to work.

"You'll be back for Thanksgiving, honey?" my mom asked while pulling me into a tight hug.

"Yes, Mama. I'll be here."

She let go, and I moved down the line to my brother Lawson and sister-in-law; they both hugged me and kissed my forehead as he said, "We'll always be here for you."

I nodded my head in understanding, my throat feeling tight as emotions swam through me.

Ty was next. He messed up my hair then pulled me into a solid hug. "Love you, sis."

"Love you too," I responded while rubbing his back.

I stood in front of a blond Zane, who was smirking and had styled his hair all messy. I knew it—he looked better with lighter hair.

I went in for a hug, and he pulled me tight and whispered in my ear, "Not sure how much you saw last night, but please don't bring it up to Jenny."

I nodded into his shoulder, and he pulled me back and fixed me with a stare that was deadly serious. I met his eyes and said, "I promise."

Leo was at the end of the line, and he was smiling. "Miss you already, little sis. I might come to visit you here pretty soon."

I smiled and hugged him fiercely.

My brothers carried my things out to the taxi, where my father waited. He stood tall, like a mighty oak tree, and watched me carefully make my way down the steps. Once I was close enough, he pulled me into a hug.

"Think about my offer, sweet pea. I love you very much." He kissed the top of my head and waited a second, not ready to let me go. I stood there in his arms and let my emotions run rampant. It felt so good to have him on my side and in my corner. Finally, he let me go, and without another glance, I got into the cab.

A moment later, the door on the opposite side of the car opened and Judson got inside.

"What are you doing?" I asked while wiping at my tears.

"I'm riding with you as far as the edge of town. I need to clear the air with you," he said while watching me intently.

I didn't respond, just watched as trees passed us and my family's house got further behind me.

Jud let out a long breath. "I'm sorry, Laney." His face was pained and his eyes soft. "I was an ass. I shouldn't have said those things, and it was a really shitty thing for me to do." He pulled his hand through his hair. "I want to be your friend. After everything, I don't want things to end like that between us. I was just jealous."

He watched me, waiting for my response. I swallowed the emotions that had surfaced at having to say goodbye to everyone.

I reached for his hand. I wanted Jud to be my friend and things to be okay with us.

"Jud, I forgive you, but you have to stop waiting for me." I pinned him with a pleading look.

He wrapped his hand around mine and tugged me toward him until he was hugging me. "I know, and I will, I promise."

The car arrived at the edge of town and pulled over. Jud handed the driver a few dollars, and he waved goodbye. I wiped at a few more tears as the cab pulled away and drove toward Chicago.

My parents had given me cab fare because there was no way my dad was going to let me drive that hatchback alone. It would have embarrassed me to take money from them, but I honestly couldn't afford it, and none of my siblings or parents were able to drive me.

The trip took forever, and since I was determined to not fall asleep on the way because of nightmares, I had consumed a dangerous amount of coffee. I was jittery and jumpy and daydreaming about what Jackson must be going through and what it would be like to accept my father's offer. I'd still be in marketing and using my law degree whenever Dad needed it, and I could live wherever I wanted.

That was the most appealing part of his offer. I thought of renting a house near Ramsey, getting to be there when she gave birth and getting to put down roots close to her as her kids grew up. That was what I wanted.

I wanted to be near my best friend and grow old with her. The thought made me feel all warm and fuzzy, like my gut was telling me it was the right thing to do. I could pay off my student loans, and I'd do it on my own.

The taxi pulled up along the curb outside my apartment building. Once I paid my driver, he offered to walk my baggage up to my door.

Home sweet home. I relished the smell of lilac and linen that filled my apartment and reminded me of home. Once I put my luggage inside, I locked the door and kicked off my flats. I stretched my arms above my head to get out the tightness from the trip and headed for my bedroom.

Just as I turned the corner of the hall, something hard hit my head. I flew forward, hitting the floor with a thud. The pain was excruciating, and my vision blurred. I grasped for the wall but there was blood, so much blood.

I couldn't move.

I saw a wisp of black hair hovering above me; I reached for it, right as everything went dark.

30

JACKSON

THE FLIGHT BACK TO PLAINVILLE WAS NEVER-ENDING. I HIT DELAY after delay after fucking delay. The engine, the drink cart, someone was sick, the fuel—the reasons as to why the delays existed seemed to be endless, and I was exhausted.

I hadn't called ahead, because I wanted to surprise Laney. I kept thinking over that text she had sent, wondering if I was going home. I was trying to play her game. Obviously, I knew she didn't mean Chicago. I wasn't ready to explain that I considered her my home, but I needed to let her know I was coming back just the same. So, I tried to stay vague.

The cab I'd ridden in for over an hour pulled into the Thompson's driveway as Dexter and Duncan ran around it, letting everyone know someone had arrived. I got out and grabbed my luggage just as Beverly walked out of the house.

It was near dinner time, so I was sure an unexpected guest alarmed her. I waved my hand at her to put her at ease.

"Hey Beverly, sorry to arrive unannounced." I paid my cab and walked closer to the porch.

She held her arms across her chest as she watched me. "Jackson, nice to see you again."

I climbed the three steps to the porch and smiled at Laney's mother. "It's nice to be back here. I was hoping to surprise Laney."

Beverley's face fell, her brows drawing together, creating a few wrinkles on her perfectly smooth forehead. "But, Laney went back home. Gepsy contacted her and told her the woman had been caught." Beverley's blue eyes searched mine in confusion.

The fuck?

I pulled out my burner phone, flipped it open, and dialed Gepsy. I noticed Beverly observe me with concern. She had grabbed the pearls around her neck and began pulling at them as if she needed something to feel other than the worry that was likely building inside of her.

The phone rang a few times before I heard Gepsy's gruff voice answer, "Jackson, what can I do for you?"

I tried to steel my voice and stay calm, especially in front of Beverly.

"Gep, did you contact Laney to tell her the coast was clear?"

Silence for two-longer-than-eternity seconds.

"No. Did she already leave?" Gepsy's voice had risen and sped up, like he was rushed and worried.

Shit. This is not happening.

I rubbed my forehead and was suddenly thankful that Beverly was standing in front of me.

I put the phone on speaker. "Gep, I'm here with Laney's mother, who saw her last. She can give us the timeline."

Beverley looked taken aback and searched my eyes frantically. "What's going on? Is everything okay?"

Gepsy answered, "Mrs. Thompson, please stay calm, but I didn't contact Laney about coming back, which means it was likely her stalker. We need to know exactly what time Laney left and how she got back to Chicago."

Beverly blanched and covered her mouth with her hand. She looked back toward the house and then began explaining. "Sh...she left here this morning, around 9:30 in the morning. She was picked up by a cab. We gave her money...she...she must have arrived around noon or so."

Beverley stammered most of her words, but she got them out. I understood that she was scared, so I nodded my thanks to her.

"That's perfect, thank you, Mrs. Thompson. We will be in touch once we have information," Gepsy said before he hung up.

Beverly started to cry a moment later, and I pulled her into a hug.

"She's going to be okay, isn't she? She has to be okay," she sobbed into my chest.

I wanted to tell her yes, tell her it was going to be okay, but I was terrified. I tried to think of the fastest way to get back to Chicago. I already knew the nearest airport was over an hour away because I'd just come from it. A cab would take too long. I needed to get to Laney.

I remembered that Beverley had a brand-new Mercedes Wayde had bought her. "Beverley, I need to get to Chicago immediately. Can I borrow your car? I'll make sure it gets back to you in one piece. I just have to get there."

She quickly nodded her head. "Of course." She turned and dashed into the house.

I followed her, thankful no one had spotted us; questions would slow me down.

She handed me the keys. "I just filled it up yesterday, so you should be good to go."

"Thank you. I'll be in touch as much as I possibly can." I turned to leave, but Beverley grabbed my arm and hugged me again.

"Find my girl, Jackson. Please," she pleaded as tears spilled down her cheeks. I nodded, grabbed my things, and headed for her car.

I ARRIVED AT LANEY'S APARTMENT BUILDING IN RECORD TIME, BUT two hours was still too long. It was now close to eight at night. The flashing red and blue lights were bright against the dark night. I jumped out of the car and ran upstairs. Laney's door was open but had yellow caution tape across it. There was a team inside, brushing for fingerprints and taking pictures. My heart wanted to stop beating and just give the fuck up, because I had failed her again.

I lifted the tape and took a tentative step inside, looking around. Sure enough, someone saw me and yelled, "Hey! You can't be in here."

I stopped and looked around. Laney's luggage was near the door, her purse, her pillows. It was all there, and there was blood on the floor, near the hallway.

"Hey, did you hear me?!" someone in a blue jacket yelled at me. I turned around and headed back for the door just as Detective Gepsy walked up.

"It's okay, he's with me," he said to the officer.

"Gep, tell me Laney is resting peacefully in a hospital right now," I said in a raspy voice as I glanced at the blood again.

Gepsy let out a strained breath. "Jackson, you know I don't want to turn you away, but maybe you shouldn't be here for this."

My eyes shot to Gepsy's. That sounded a whole lot like Laney was dead. I shook my head and ran my fingers over my freshly buzzed hair.

"Gep, sounds like you have no idea where Laney is, that or you do and it's not good news. What the fuck is going on?" I begged while pinning him with a glare.

Gepsy walked back out into the hallway, and I followed him.

"Nothing was called in, Jack. No neighbors heard or saw anything. I have no idea how she moved Laney. My gut tells me she has Laney alive somewhere. This is a game to her. She plans and teases, and she wants a big finale."

I rubbed my chin, thinking the news over. He was right, and maybe if I tried to reach out to Alicia somehow, it would throw her off her game and make her reveal where she had Laney.

"What do we do?" I asked while watching the outdated brown carpet at my feet.

Gepsy adjusted his gun holster. "We flush her out, pull the info we gathered on her over the last week or so, and find her."

31

LANEY

I TRIED TO OPEN MY EYES, BUT THE BLINDING PAIN I FELT FORCED ME to keep them shut. I was lying on my back, hands pinned beneath me. I twisted my wrists and felt cold metal.

Handcuffs.

There was a distant sound of a TV soap opera playing somewhere behind me, probably from a bedroom. I could tell by the melodramatic music and the overly dramatic dialogue between the characters. I didn't hear anyone walking, talking, or any other noises, so I finally forced my eyes open. I winced at the bright light that assaulted me.

The room came into view; I was lying on a kitchen floor. There was an outdated stove to my right, a yellow fridge next to it, and molting wood cupboards, half of which were torn out. I turned my head to the left. I could see the living room; the carpet was pulled up, and replacement windows rested against the wall. This place looked like an apartment that was in the middle of a renovation.

The realization finally sank in that Alicia had attacked me...again, and for some reason, she was keeping me alive.

My head pounded as I tried to gather more details about the space, but the pain was overwhelming. I heard footsteps, and a second later someone was standing over me. Her inky black hair was longer than I remembered. She wore tight black jeans, big combat boots, and a tight white shirt that had red splotches of blood on it. Her skin was still pale, and her blue eyes were bloodshot and irritated. She leaned in close to me and pushed my hair out of my face.

"Good, you're awake." Cinnamon breath fanned my face.

That smell—it made me want to puke.

My insides were trembling as all the memories of Alicia ran through my skull. My heart was beating erratically as fear tried to grip me and keep me from speaking, breathing, or even moving. I wanted to shut my eyes and pretend this wasn't happening.

I tried to turn my face away, but she grabbed my chin and held me firm.

"You just couldn't stay away, could you?" She gritted her teeth, spit flying from her mouth and landing on my cheek. She let me go and sauntered out of my eyesight, creating an entirely different kind of fear.

I rolled over to try to see her while she stalked around the room. After I took a few sharp breaths to push past the fear, I managed to whisper, "What do you want from me?"

Alicia came closer and was now holding something, I tried to adjust my head so I could see it, but she returned it to her pocket too quickly.

"Did you know he once took me on a date?" she asked while she held her nails in front of her face, examining them. "We'd gone on one fucking date before he met you."

She placed her hands on her hips. With the movement, I noticed scars on her wrists. She continued walking around the apartment while she went on.

"Not everyone would get all this." She waved her arms around the room. "They wouldn't appreciate the dedication and the love I have for Jackson."

She bent down until she was eye level with me again. "You never even loved him, did you? You used him...played with him and messed with his head," she whispered, while stroking her finger down my face. She grabbed my hair and pulled me closer to the living room. "See those carpet rolls?" She lifted my head until I could see the ugly, blue rolls of carpet that sprawled around the room. "They get thrown from this window into a large dumpster tomorrow morning. No one will check the dumpster, Laney. They just scrap it. Your dead body will never be found, and no one will be able to prove I did it. Kind of like how I dumped you in a laundry bin and no one batted an eye at me hauling you out of your apartment." She smiled and laughed to herself. "Although, the laundry service outfit helped."

The sound from the back room changed to a new anchor speaking. I couldn't make out what the report was on, but it added a frantic vibe to the room.

Alicia continued on her little tirade. "You see, I made frequent trips to your apartment while you were over in Indiana, playing house. So, no one thought it was strange for me to leave with a rolling laundry bin, because I had done it nearly every day the week before."

Oh fuck.

She stood up and kicked at a mark on the floor, close to my head. "You know, I thought I could wait it out, especially when you did break up. I thought after a few weeks, he'd move on from you. But the more I watched Jackson, the angrier I became, because he wasn't getting over you."

"What in the hell are you talking about? You were in cell block D when he and I broke up." My voice was raspy, as though my throat had completely dried up.

She laughed bitterly, throwing her head back. "That's right. You don't know, do you?" She shook her head in disbelief and leaned closer, her thin hair moving forward, over her shoulder. "I graduated top of my class from Caltech." She moved closer to my body, gripping my hair. "I was drafted by the CIA for my ability to bypass firewalls like they didn't exist and hack security feeds in the most inaccessible places. It's allotted me some friends in high places." She said it on a sigh, like this was boring her.

My mind spun as she spewed her ridiculous bullshit. Why the hell was she working as a personal assistant if she was CIA? I swallowed some of my fear down and adjusted my body on the floor.

"You're so full of shit," I whispered.

She stopped walking around me and leaned down again, pulling my hair. "You don't believe me?"

I tried to shake my head, but it was futile. "You worked as a PA—why would I believe you?"

Alicia let my hair go with a forceful push of my head back toward the floor. "I don't owe you shit, but I can guarantee you Jackson's entire home is wired. His computer is monitored, and everything he does, every move he makes—I not only see, but I hear." She stood up, stepping on my hair that was lying in a mass around me. "Did you know he wrote you letters while you two were broken up?" She looked down at me like we were two friends having a fun conversation. "Fucking letters, Laney. What kind of man writes letters?" She started laughing, throwing her head to the side.

She walked around the island, toying with something in her hand.

"I met Jackson long before I worked for him. He doesn't remember, which is fine, but I have been following him and keeping tabs on him. We went to school together before I transferred to California. He was my study partner for an English course we took. He didn't realize what we had then, but I knew one day if our paths crossed again, we'd be together." Her voice transitioned into something soft as she continued. "When I moved to Chicago, I knew it was fate. I knew I'd find him again. I watched him for a bit, and when I saw he was looking for an assistant, I applied. I was still in training with the agency and had..." She stopped talking for a second and started whispering to herself. I couldn't make out what she was saying.

She started hitting her head repeatedly and then cleared her throat. "I was in training. They hadn't said yes yet because they wanted to be sure I was a good fit. I was special to them. That's what Tom said."

Tom?

I froze, trying to let her little episode play out. I didn't know what to do. She could bash my head in any second, or just slit my throat. I didn't know who Tom was or anything else she was talking about, but I knew if she was actually CIA, she'd have gotten a hell of a lot longer than standard prison sentencing for what she'd done, and she wouldn't have been released on good behavior. Even if she did have friends in high places, that one would be hard to pull off.

"You were in jail, so how did you manage to watch him?" I asked, because what she had said about Jackson writing me letters had snugly made its way into my brain and wouldn't budge. She laughed, a full-on giggle erupting from her wicked lungs.

She turned and bent back down to whisper in my ear. "Tom got me out three months before that notice was even sent out to you or Jackson. So, you guys have been prancing around like morons with no clue that I have been watching you." She shoved me toward the carpet roll.

I wanted to shut down, but instead I tried to shift my body into some kind of defensive position because she'd confirmed that she was going to kill me. She'd had so much control over me for the past year. I pushed my eyes together and tried to press into the confidence I had somewhere buried within me. Somewhere deep inside me, there was an unbroken Laney. She was fierce as fire. I needed that.

I was tired of Alicia winning, of her controlling me through fear.

So, with everything I had in me, I pushed down the fear that had consumed me, and then I focused.

The first thing I needed to do was get out of these cuffs. Alicia was facing away from me for the moment, kicking at the carpet roll I'd eventually be rolled up in. I kept my eyes on her and slowly rolled away so I could get my knees under me.

It was proving to be rather difficult. In fact, the more I tried, the more I just fell back flat on my back. Alicia let out a sigh and pulled the item from her pocket that she'd stashed earlier. It was a syringe with the cap still on it. I'd have bet a billion dollars it wasn't a flu shot.

I closed my eyes for a second and tried to calm down. I had to stay calm and push the fear back. She had the upper hand, but she was crazy as fuck and unstable. She'd be easy to taunt, to push over the edge. I just needed to hit the right buttons. I started moving my wrists around, trying to pull the cuffs off. If I could create a cut or get some blood and create lubrication, I might be able to slide them off. I had freakishly small wrists.

Alicia rolled the syringe between her fingers and continued to stare out the window.

"So, your plan is to kill me and...what? Jackson suddenly falls in love with you because I'm gone?" I yelled at Alicia's back, while trying to free my wrists. I pulled them back as far as they could go and bit the inside of my cheek to keep from crying.

Alicia spun around and glared at me. "Yes. It will break whatever magical, fucked-up spell you have over him."

I rolled my eyes. "Seriously? That's what you honestly think? You're an idiot." My left wrist twisted and tugged, I could feel a pinch and a burning sensation throb through my arms. Tears threatened to fall as I kept tugging back and forth. I could feel liquid between the cold metal and my skin. Alicia hadn't tightened them enough; my wrist would be free in less than five minutes.

She reeled back, "You think I'm wrong? He was a self-absorbed player, which was fine because eventually he would have seen me for what I was and wanted to settle down with me." She pointed forcefully at her chest; her eyes had gone wild.

Yes, lose your shit, crazy. Put that syringe down and come over here.

"He would have asked me out on another date, but then you showed up." She pointed at me and gave me a seething glare.

I wanted to spew back at her how wrong she was, how Jackson didn't want me, how I had wasted seven months of my life with him, but she wasn't sane, and it wouldn't do me any good. I needed her to lose her mind and come after me, preferably without that death liquid.

"He would never have wanted you, Alicia. He could smell your crazy from a mile away. He never liked you, and even after I'm dead, he won't want you," I spat at her.

That was it—I saw the rage ignite in her eyes. They narrowed, and her lips thinned as she moved forward. "I'm going to kill you, you fucking bitch!"

"Come get me, crazy!" I yelled as she drew closer.

My wrist was free—enflamed, raw, mangled, and bloody, but it was free—and Alicia had left the syringe behind somewhere. She wanted to physically hurt me now. She went to grab my hair, but I reached up and gripped hers instead, pulling her to the ground with everything I had in me. She fell awkwardly with a loud scream.

I didn't waste any time. I jumped up and kicked her with my bare foot as hard as I could. Then I grabbed her head and thrust it against the floor. She rolled away from me. I crouched low, scanning the linoleum for the syringe. *Where did she put it?*

As she crawled away from me, she kicked backward, and her boot collided with my chin, knocking me back.

Tears welled in my eyes with the piercing pain in my jaw. I pushed past it and stood, searching for a weapon. *Fuck that boxing instructor for giving up on me—I could really use some self-defense skills right now.*

I tried to remember the drills I'd gone through with Jackson and with Jenny, but it wasn't as clear as it should have been in my head. I needed a weapon, not my fists. I wasn't strong or skilled enough.

Alicia pulled the syringe from her pocket and flicked off the lid. "I'm going to shove this needle into your heart and then I'm going to cut you open and see which you die from first." Her black hair was tousled and tangled, blood dripping down her face.

A silver box cutter was to my right; I saw it just barely under a piece of cardboard. *Thank you, Jesus!*

If I reached for it, she'd lunge with the needle. I needed to get to it without setting her off.

"See, that's your problem, Alicia—you're so goddamn stupid." I straightened and moved my hair out of my face.

She looked taken aback for a second. I kept going, slowly making my way toward the box cutter, which she thankfully couldn't see from where she was—at least I hoped she couldn't.

"If you inject me and cut me, there's no way to tell which one actually kills me. There's no way to measure it."

She was watching me, not where I was maneuvering to. I slowly shuffled to the left, putting the island between us.

She scoffed, her blue eyes sparkling as she fixed her hair. "Doesn't matter. I'm going to shove this needle inside of you then let you feel every single cut and slice until you bleed out."

She lunged, but there was too much space between us. Instead, she started scrambling over it.

I GRABBED THE BOX CUTTER FROM UNDER THE CARDBOARD AND THRUST the blade into her neck with every ounce of strength I had. She froze and dropped the needle.

I pushed the blade further into her body, feeling the thick blood run down my arm. I could have let go, seen if there was any chance of survival, let her live—but I just kept pushing as hard as I could.

I pushed all the anger and fear I'd been stuck in for the last year into that box cutter. I had no words to speak as the light slowly left her eyes, as she slowly sank to the floor while her blood continued to flow out of her body.

Everything ached, and all I wanted to do was cry.

The soft sounds of the TV drama coming from the other bedroom filled the air. I had backed up against the wall and slowly slid down it, watching Alicia's body continue to bleed onto the carpet rolls that were supposed to hide my body.

I was trembling. My fingers wouldn't stop shaking, and my teeth were chattering. I wrapped my arms around myself as tightly as I could to try to keep from shaking, but once my hands were within my eyesight, I saw the red and my stomach turned.

I needed to get out of there. I needed to find a phone. Adrenaline was still coursing through my veins as I searched the apartment. I got up, my bare feet freezing now and barely able to move me down the hall. My wrists hurt, but I kept fumbling to the back room, toward the sound of the TV. There on a rickety TV tray was a rectangular, black cell phone. With trembling hands, I picked it up and dialed for help.

32

JACKSON

"MORNING, MR. TATE." TRINA, THE CHARGE NURSE, WAVED AT ME.

I waved back. "Morning, Trina." I set the carrier of coffees down on the counter and handed her one. She smiled and gracefully accepted. Her dark skin looked beautiful with her fluorescent lipstick, her deep purple scrubs matched the color perfectly.

"You know, if Ms. Thompson doesn't agree to see you today, I am giving you my daughter's number," Trina whispered adamantly.

I laughed and shook my head. "If she doesn't see me today then I'm going to break in there." I leaned in closer. "Don't tell security." I winked, and she winked back while shuffling her papers. I had gotten to know Trina well over the last few days, while Laney was in the hospital.

Each day Laney refused to see me was starting to wear me down. Laney's entire family was here visiting. Zane, Ty and Leo were all staying with me at my condo, whereas Wayde and Beverly had gotten a hotel, wanting to be closer to Laney. I didn't understand why Laney was still in the hospital, but Leo had explained that her wrists had suffered so much trauma that it would require a few days to be sure no infection set in.

I had a big bouquet of flowers with me, just like I had every other time I'd come to visit. I knew Laney just needed time.

I arrived before anyone else, including Beverley.

When Laney *was* ready, I wanted to be the first one to see her.

I had just sat down in the waiting area, near Trina's desk, when I heard the door open near the hallway entrance, where Laney's door was. I focused on the opening in the room and waited to see who was coming toward us.

Ramsey walked out a second later, wiping tears from her eyes with a white Kleenex.

I stood up and walked over to her. "Rams? What are you doing here?"

I turned my wrist and saw that it was seven fifteen in the morning. She sniffed and stood up taller. She had her hair braided back and a pair of black yoga pants on. Her belly was finally starting to pop, just a little bit.

"Jax." Ramsey tried to talk, but her expression contorted into what could only be described as an ugly-cry face. She pushed forward and threw her arms around me.

I hugged her, feeling her chest heave and her body shake. A second later, we broke apart, and she continued wiping at her nose.

"She needs you. She won't admit it, but she does. She called me last night telling me she wanted to talk to you, but she wasn't sure how to let you in without hurting herself," Ramsey said through choppy sobs.

I'd never seen Ramsey this emotional.

I nodded, not sure how else to respond.

Ramsey kept wiping at her face, then pulled out her cell phone. "I need to get back. Jimmy has a conference, so I'm all alone with the kids."

I nodded, knowing Theo was likely not far to help if she needed it. "Call me if you need anything." I hugged her goodbye.

"She's waiting for you. Just go in there and talk to her," Ramsey whispered before she let me go and walked down the hall.

I tried to hide my excitement, but I practically ran to Laney's room. The large door was a teal color, with a small window cut in the shape of a rectangle. I peeked through the glass but couldn't see if Laney was awake or not. All I could see were her toes, covered by a white blanket.

The sound of the door swishing open was all that could be heard as I padded through the white room. Laney's red hair was braided to the side, likely thanks to Ramsey. Her face was pale, and she had a bandage on her forehead and her two wrists. Otherwise she looked okay.

I crept closer, until I was near the foot of her bed, and waited.

She slowly opened her eyes; those green emeralds were so watery and red.

Emotions crept up my gut and lodged into my throat as I watched her lie there.

"Ramsey told you to come?" Laney asked in a whisper.

I nodded, not trusting my voice yet.

She let out a small sigh. "I'm sorry I didn't see you the first few days. I just..." She broke off and moved her eyes to the window. It was already a stunning day, with the sun shining and zero clouds in the sky.

A tear slipped down her face as she continued, "I needed time."

I nodded again, understanding that she needed time, but still didn't speak.

"When I went through this the first time, I leaned so heavily on you that I didn't know how to be alone. Those three months we were apart were the hardest of my life." Laney was whispering, but she couldn't have been louder if she were screaming.

I swallowed the worry that would leak through my voice if I tried to talk.

"I realized this time that I need to learn how to do this on my own. I need to get some coping skills that don't involve you, Jackson, especially because we aren't together...and we won't be." More tears slipped from her eyes. She made no move to wipe at them.

I shuffled until I was next to her. "No. I came back to see you in Plainville. I have things I want to tell you. I want to be with you." I tried to explain in a rush. I tried to pull Laney's hand into mine, but she pulled it free.

"Please, Jackson. Don't make this harder for me. I just need time." She stared at me like I was a stranger, like she didn't even know me.

I wanted to argue with her, push her. I just needed to lay it all out there.

"Can we just..." The door opened, interrupting me. Detective Gepsy walked in, holding a *Get Well Soon* balloon. I narrowed my eyes at him in confusion.

"Gep? What are you doing here?"

He set the anchor to the balloon down on the counter. "I wanted to go over some case info with you two. I figured you'd be together and thought two birds...one stone." He held up one finger.

Laney cleared her throat and tried to sit up. I sat with my elbows on my knees but didn't make any move away from Laney's side.

Gepsy cleared his throat and started in. "Here's what I uncovered during this investigation..." He took a big breath and shoved his hands into his pockets. "Alicia Miller was approached by a recruiter for the CIA after she graduated. The recruiter was a man by the name of Tom Jenkins. Alicia started training with Tom, and while she mostly did a few practice sessions regarding her computer skills, there was a physical element to her training that he was in charge of as well. We believe Tom developed an obsession with Alicia.

"She wasn't accepted into the academy once it came time for her testing. Results showed she seemed to be mentally unfit. Tom hid the results from her and fed her lies about how special she was, and he exclusively worked with her. Tom, however, was still a part of the agency and had connections to get Alicia out of prison early. He's currently in custody and will be processed for aiding a felon, providing prison contraband, and a few other things."

I looked at Laney, who looked as confused by the contraband bit as I did.

Gepsy clarified, "Tom provided Alicia tools and gave her access to certain things in prison that she could have used to escape. She hacked a few databases with his help, which helped change her trial date and the notes that were left about her, making it look like she was being recommended for early release."

I looked back over at Laney; she was silently crying.

I cleared my throat. "Thanks, Gep, for everything. For helping us and getting us out of town."

I stood up and shook his hand. His eyes softened as he looked at Laney. She didn't move or say anything, just kept watching us.

Finally, before he turned to go, he said, "Get better soon, Laney."

"I will. Thank you. I need some rest." She smiled and flicked her eyes to the door, dismissing us.

I wanted to continue our conversation and tell her to talk to me, ask her how much time she needed, but if she needed rest, I would let her. I followed Gepsy out of the hospital door. I would give her time. That was the one thing about Laney and me—we were good with time, like wine or some shit. We would be better after a little time, not worse.

33

LANEY

I LISTENED TO THE RAIN AS IT HIT THE WINDOWS OF MY FATHER'S office and pulled the blanket tighter around me. He'd shown up with a big U-Haul truck two weeks after I was attacked and moved me back home.

"Laney, are you listening?" Glenda asked from the screen off to my right.

We were doing a Skype therapy session, and so far, I wasn't being a very responsible participant.

I turned my head toward the screen and swallowed. "Yeah, sorry. I'm here."

Glenda let out a sigh. "Laney, it's been three weeks since your attack. It's also been three weeks since you've opened up about what happened in that room. We need to talk about it," she pleaded gently, her beautiful dark skin all shiny and glow-like under her lamplight.

I sighed and repeated the same thing I had the six other times we'd talked about this. "There's nothing to discuss. She died. I lived. That's it."

Glenda's lips thinned, but her eyes remained hopeful. She was so damn patient with me. "Laney, you killed someone. You haven't talked to

Jackson since you left, and he was a major part of this story. We need to start talking about that."

I blinked and focused on the photo my dad had of me on his desk. Glenda was right; I wasn't processing anything that'd happened. I wasn't processing that I had cut Jackson out of my life or that I'd left my job or that I'd killed someone.

I just slept and ate enough to stay alive, but that was it. I focused on that little picture of me in a sloppy ponytail, that stupid fish in my hands. I focused on how good I had felt back then, how happy I was that my dad had finally taken me fishing instead of just the boys. I wanted that again.

I wanted to be happy again.

I thought about how close I'd gotten to getting my fire back, only to have it extinguished by Alicia's death.

"At night, I dream about her. The dream is always the same...I'm sticking the box cutter into her throat...blood is everywhere, but when I look at her face...it's not her. It's me," I quietly said and then looked down at my hands. Sometimes when I looked at them, I still saw the box cutter there, still saw the blood staining them.

"What do you think that dream means?" Glenda softly asked while slightly leaning forward.

I shook my head. "I don't know."

I didn't.

I really didn't know what the hell that dream meant, but I hated it every damn time.

"Laney, do you regret killing Alicia?" Glenda asked firmly.

I looked up from my hands and watched her as I thought over the answer. "No. I'm glad she's dead. I'm glad she can't ever hurt me again."

That truth probably stung worse than any guilt I felt over killing someone.

"Do you think there's a part of you that was left in that room when she died?" Glenda prodded.

I took in a sharp breath. "I think so. I think Alicia won some small victory there, and it's something I'll never get back."

Glenda made a sound of acknowledgment. "Laney, you know that what you did was self-defense...it wasn't murder. You were going to be killed if you didn't fight her." Glenda reminded me of this like she had every time we had gotten this far.

I nodded, knowing she was right but still not believing it.

"What are you doing to cope this week?" Glenda asked, like she had the last two times. She asked every week what I was going to do to cope and get through the PTSD and depression that had set back in.

"I'm going to start running again, with my older brother Zane. He's agreed to be my running partner. I'm also agreeing to go out twice this week with the guys to do something social," I explained while trying to keep the grimace off my face. The running I could get back into, but the social scene wasn't something I wanted to jump into.

"Have you considered following through with your original plan? The one you said you had before this happened?" Glenda asked while looking over her notes.

I looked back outside at the rain and thought of what I had planned. "I still want to move to Belvidere...I'm just not sure how to start the process," I admitted weakly.

Glenda sat forward and pulled her hands together in a straight prayer-like fashion. "Laney, look. You know what you need to do. You're a brilliant woman, and I know you know how to look for a house to rent. You already have a job with your dad's company. He already agreed to pay for your rent and give you money up front for the move. Do you think being around Ramsey and the kids might be good for you?"

I pulled the blanket that was around me tighter and held my breath. Ramsey wasn't currently doing well with my situation. She'd been pushy about coming to stay with me for a week after I got home, but she was a mom now, a wife.

She couldn't just pick up her life and visit someone for weeks on end at the drop of a hat. She stayed for three days before I booted her back home. But honestly, I hadn't wanted her to go. Having her to talk to, having her know what it was like to process shit like this was therapeutic. My family loved me, but none of them knew what I was going through.

"Maybe. Maybe it's time for me to move on," I lightly said while looking back at the screen.

"What about Jackson? Are you ready to discuss him and why you cut him out?" she asked while leaning back in her chair.

I thought that over and realized I wasn't ready to talk about him. For some reason, the pain surrounding my heart where he was concerned was more poignant than the pain surrounding me killing someone.

So, I responded truthfully. "Jackson knows I need space. He knows I need my heart and mind to heal. Things with him are just too unstable, and I need to be around things that won't change on me. I need to be around people who won't change their minds about loving me. He can't promise me that."

Glenda waited a second, then lightly nodded. "Then I suggest you let your coping this week revolve around house hunting. Get yourself to Belvidere, Laney. Start the next chapter of your life."

34

LANEY

"You need to hit it harder, Laney!" Cal, my boxing instructor, yelled from the ropes. I squared off with my opponent, a tall blonde girl who was built like a tree not in height but in width. She was all muscle.

They said she was one of the best people to spar with, but I questioned who had determined that. I pounded my gloves together and shuffled to the left, then punched with my right arm. She dodged. I came with a left hook and caught her chin. Her head snapped back.

"Good, Laney, good. That's what I've been talking about. Now, take a break and get down here," Cal encouraged from the side.

I carefully hit my opponent's glove, indicating I was done, and nodded at her. I started peeling off my gloves, headgear, and mouthpiece.

"See, told you that you would eventually get it." Cal beamed from beside me. He was right; it had taken six months to get me here, but I'd made it. When I had first joined the gym, I'd told him I didn't want to spar with any females.

I had been coming to Cal's gym four times a week and doing video sessions with Glenda.

Jimmy had recommended Cal to me, said he had gone to his gym a few times to work out and told me he'd be a good fit for me.

Cal was a large man, corded with muscle. He had dark tattoos you could barely make out on his equally dark skin, but if you got close enough, you'd feel the pain behind each one. His amber eyes held an intensity I needed to get me back on track.

He was built like a boxer, lean and sleek, but he was also married. I drooled over him the first few sessions, then his gorgeous wife showed up and I promptly straightened out and stopped ogling him. Now, after all these months, both he and his wife were good friends of mine.

I had built myself a small community here in Belvidere, and it felt good. I still had nights where I cried myself to sleep for what I'd lost, what I could have had, and the part of me I'd left behind in that apartment, but I pushed through it. I was still taking some medication to help with my PTSD and nightmares, but again, I was pushing through it.

I had a two-bedroom, cottage-style home with a small fenced-in yard. It had a single-car garage I didn't park in because of the punching bag and gym I'd had Jimmy help me set up. Whenever I couldn't sleep, I'd go and hit something or lift, and it helped.

I got out of the shower at the gym and dressed. I didn't check my phone very often these days, just when I got home. Tonight, however, was mini pizza night at the Stenson house, so I dressed and climbed into my new-to-me Jeep.

My dad had bought it for me for Christmas, and I hadn't argued. They were doing better than before with the marketing skills I brought to the table, and they just needed the peace of mind that I was okay.

I started the car up and drove the two miles from the gym to Ramsey's house. I always had a slight pinch of longing when I pulled up to her house. She was living my dream out: beautiful home, husband who loved her, kids, one on the way. I still had that small kernel of hope inside of me that I might have it someday.

I opened the door because after being over almost daily, I didn't knock anymore. "Hello?" I asked with a singsong voice as I made my way through the entryway.

I could hear playful laughter from upstairs, where the kids likely were. There was a light murmur of conversation and dishes clanging in the kitchen. The Stenson house was a three-story, suburban dream home. The living room alone was the size of half my house. There was a full, wraparound couch in the living room, and a huge eighty-inch monstrosity of a television hung on the wall above the mantle. Strategic lighting fell over the space and the cushy, white carpet.

I looked for new photos on the walls, because Ramsey had mentioned they'd had a maternity shoot a while back and had been waiting forever for the canvas prints to arrive. I still didn't see it hung up, but Jasmine and Sammy's school pictures were on display.

I moved further inside and heard Ramsey talking loudly. "I know, but she won't even listen to me, Jimmy. She is being unreasonable, and I love her like a sister, but I am about to slap some sense into her."

I stopped mid-step. *What the hell?*

Who else did she love as much as me? She had to be talking about me —what had I done wrong?

I crept closer, praying the kids wouldn't run down and blow my cover.

"I know, babe, trust me. I had to put the poor guy back together, but there's nothing I can do about it, or you, for that matter. She's made it clear that she doesn't want to see him, and we need to respect that," Jimmy softly responded to his overly pregnant wife.

She was due in nearly two months and was a little emotional lately. "That's not good enough." She cried and threw something metal down on the counter. "I want to be able to invite him over at the same time as her. I want to have a birthday party for the kids where they're both present. I want this baby to be loved by them both. What are they going to do when I go into labor? Just assume that Laney has dibs?"

I had crossed my arms now. *Hell yes I have dibs.*

"Babe, I have no idea, but there's no sense in getting so upset over it. There's nothing you can do about it," Jimmy cooed again.

He was so gentle with her, I wanted to scream. She was being unreasonable, not me.

"Like hell I can't. I am going to put my foot down. I am telling her tonight that Jackson will be here for Sammy's birthday next weekend and she will be here too, and if she's not then..." She stopped talking.

I wanted to hear what would happen if I didn't show up. Would she kick my ass? Never speak to me again? Good Lord, she was being ridiculous. I rolled my eyes and carefully walked back outside, not wanting to get into it with her right now. I felt good after the gym and didn't want to come down from that high just yet.

I drove back home, trying to sift through everything I'd heard. It had been six months since I had seen or talked to Jackson. I had told him I needed space in the hospital, but a few days after I got home, he started calling. I wasn't ready to talk to him. A week went by until he finally showed up at my front door.

THERE HAD BEEN A RAINSTORM, A BAD ONE THAT KNOCKED OUT HALF THE power in the city, and I was struggling really fucking badly that night, especially when I heard a knock on my door. It was 8 p.m. when I carefully pulled my door open after checking to see who it was. The backup lights in the hall showed Jackson's face.

Jackson barged right through, which set me on edge. He was drenched from head to toe. I didn't offer him a towel or anything. I'd let him say his piece then I wanted him gone. He wiped at his face, his blue eyes so striking against the candlelit darkness of my apartment. He had a box with him; it was wooden and had little carvings on it. He had nothing else, just the box and his wet self. I waited as he stepped closer to me.

"Laney, I have to talk to you. Why won't you take my calls or see me?" he asked, sounding desperate, like he was crazed and going out of his mind.

I looked at him, standing in my sleep shorts and tank. "Jackson, I need space...I need time to heal. I told you that." I delivered the words evenly, like saying them didn't hurt.

He shook his head back and forth. "No, you don't. You need me, and I need you. We need each other—that's how our fucked-up dynamic works."

"Jackson..." I whispered, while putting my hands on my head.

He cut me off and stepped forward. "I have things I need to say to you. When I said I was coming home, I was talking about you, Laney. You're my home..." He trailed off, not able to finish his sentence.

I turned away from him and let out a sigh. "Jackson, I can't do this right now."

He got closer to me, erasing the gap between us. "Yes, you can. I know you can because you love me and I love you and we are supposed to be together."

I couldn't tell if he was crying, but his voice broke, and it made me want to shatter into a billion pieces.

"I don't want to be confused anymore," I said, shaking my head.

"There's nothing to be confused about. I want you. I want this." He stepped forward and grabbed my hands in his.

Tears started falling down my face. I was finally getting what I wanted from him, and I couldn't accept it.

"Jackson, when I look at you, I see her. You are my only connection to her. I killed her. I killed someone. The dreams are back, the nightmares, all of it—but I can't let you back in because when you decide to leave again, I'll never be okay. I love you, Jackson, too much. I need to be away from you. I need to work through this without you." I was sobbing as the words left my mouth. This was so much harder than I'd ever imagined.

Jackson shook his head back and forth before lowering his eyes in defeat. "Don't do this. Give me another chance, give us another chance." He panted, like he'd run out of breath any second. "Some things happened with my father, and I want to tell you about them. I want to talk to you. Please," he begged.

God, everything in me wanted to tell him yes, believe him, let him hold me and keep me, but I knew too well that I would just let him be my Band-Aid and never deal with the real wound of this. I needed to heal. I needed to find myself again.

I didn't respond, and as the silence between us grew, so did the distance. He took a step back, then another. His retreating form was like watching someone pull the muscle from my bones and stretch it over hot rocks. I gripped the chair to keep me in place so I wouldn't run into his arms.

He watched me, his eyes misting over.

He begged one last time. "Don't do this, please don't do this."

I shook my head and let a few more tears fall free. "I have to."

He stood up tall, carefully set the box on my counter, and walked out my door.

THE SOUND OF MY CELL PHONE CHIME BROUGHT ME OUT OF THE memory and back to the wet, cold present.

Ramsey had texted me, asking when I was coming over. I threw my phone into my purse and headed inside. I didn't want Ramsey—or Jimmy, for that matter—to feel like they couldn't see Jackson if I was there, and now that I had moved here, I knew it made it nearly impossible to see him. I let out a sigh as I set my purse down on the entryway table.

I needed to clear the air with him, for the sake of our friends. I felt surprisingly mature about talking to him again. It had been six months, and it was entirely possible and probable that he'd moved on completely from me.

Part of me hoped he had. He was the great love of my life, and if he wasn't over me, I wasn't sure I could convincingly say I was over him. I hadn't dated anyone new, mostly because of all the work I was doing on me. I wouldn't know how to explain to a random date that my heart still burst into hard thumps and frantic beats when I even pictured Jackson's face.

I placed my hand over my chest and closed my eyes. The truth was, he still owned it. I may have told him I needed time and space, but my heart didn't understand those rules or those terms. It still hungered for Jackson, longed for him and hurt for him. But I didn't ask him to wait for me. I couldn't.

For all I knew, he'd finally learned to love, had gotten rejected, then had gone and found someone who knew how to let him in and they were now blissfully together. A bone-deep sorrow came with that thought.

I needed to think about something else. I opened my car door and ran through the rain. Once I reached my front door, I began unlocking the two deadbolts, then quickly shucked my wet coat and entered my security code. Three loud beeps reverberated through my house as two loud barks sounded from the hall.

"Are you going to actually come and see if it's an intruder?" I yelled, securing the front door.

Two more barks met me from my room but no dog. I might have been concerned if this wasn't Maggie's normal behavior, but she seemed to know when it was me and when it was a stranger. We found that out the hard way when my brother Leo showed up for a visit. No, Maggie was just lazy and refused to leave my bed unless it was absolutely necessary or when I asked her nicely.

I slipped off my shoes and with cold feet, shuffled to my living room and pressed the switch on the wall to turn on the gas fireplace. I immediately felt warmer just seeing the tiny flames lick the glass. Rubbing my hands together, I sauntered down the carpet covered hall and entered the first door on my right.

There, curled up in a ball, was my beautiful, black and gold German Shepherd. Maggie had one droopy ear and one that stood tall, a thin, sleek body with prowess and grace. She was such a lady and I totally loved her.

"There you are. Wanna come keep me company while I make dinner?"

Maggie jumped off the bed and walked to my thigh, then rubbed her head against my hand. She never licked me, which was actually quite soothing; I wasn't a big fan of dog saliva.

I opened a bottle of wine and was about to dig into my microwavable meal for one when I turned the tv on and headed for the couch. I curled up under a blanket with Maggie on my toes and found the evening news. It was a larger station based out of Rockford, about fifteen miles away.

I looked down and plucked a noodle from my dinner carton when I heard the news anchor say, "And this is your second restaurant?"

I glanced up while I snagged a piece of chicken and shoveled the food into my mouth.

"Actually, no. *Savor Me* is a franchise I'm starting, based on my first startup. I had a second restaurant that I recently concluded."

I froze in place as I watched the news anchor hold his microphone up to none other than Jackson Tate.

Those erratic beats and thumps in my heart were back at the sight of him. He had a dark suit on with a thin tie, his hair was still buzzed, his blue eyes jumping as he talked about his new venture. My heart was hammering so hard.

Oh my God, was I going to have a heart attack?

He opened a franchise in Rockford? I reached for the tv remote to turn it up, but went too far, falling completely off the couch instead. Maggie sat up and started whining at me.

"I know, I know... Momma's a mess." I muttered to my worried guard dog.

I tried to sit up and ended up having to kick all the blankets off. The remote was under the blankets now, and I couldn't seem to free it.

"Damn you remote!" I cried and finally pulled it free and turned the television up,

"Well, we are certainly excited for this new restaurant to open up here. Many people have considered Savor a destination restaurant when they visit the big city. When is it set to open?" the news anchor asked, nearly finishing his segment.

Jackson looked confident and happy as he proclaimed, "April. I'm trying to finish it in time for it to be a birthday present for someone special to me."

My birthday was in April.

Was he talking about me? What if he was talking about a new girlfriend, what if she was also an April birthday?

He probably had found a new redheaded—April—birthday—wife and wanted to live near Jimmy to raise his new babies with her. He probably took my dream, and I was going to have to sic Maggie on him to get it back.

I stood up and threw a couch pillow across the room. Maggie jumped up and fetched the pillow and drug it back to the couch. I couldn't reach out to him *now*. It would seem like I was only doing it because of the news segment.

I threw myself on the couch and pulled the blanket over my face, but Maggie started shoving her nose under it, forcing me to pull it back. I let her in, allowing her to settle her rather large head into my neck.

The realization that Jackson was just fifteen miles away from me sent a rush through me. He was so close. What if I did reach out? What if I asked him to stop by and see me? Maggie would probably sense he was the biggest threat to my heart and kill him on the spot. It was probably better I forgot about it completely.

35

LANEY

IT HAD STARTED RAINING AGAIN, AND CALL ME NOSTALGIC, BUT SEEING Jackson on tv felt like a big fat sign of some sort. It was past midnight, and I had attempted sleep, but it never came. Plus, Maggie kept laying over my chest like she legitimately was trying to protect my heart. I shoved her off a few times before I just gave up.

The rain poured at an angle against my windows as trees bent under its weight. I had battery operated lanterns on in my room and in the kitchen, just in case the power went out.

I always needed some kind of light on now, slept with a gun under my mattress, and a taser in my nightstand. Maggie was a must when I had rented this house, so when I came home I'd know if something wasn't right, plus she wasn't bad for company.

I slid out of bed, careful not to wake my dozing shepherd and walked over to my closet. It was a modest, non-walk-in, galley closet. On the top shelf, I had a shoebox of important things I had collected over the years. Inside was the wooden box Jackson had left behind.

I never did open it, afraid of what I'd find. Remembering Alicia mentioned that he had written me letters, I thought if there were letters in the box, I wouldn't have been strong enough to read them. I may not even be strong enough now, but I wanted to see them. After seeing Jackson for the first time in months, it was like the box called to me.

I carefully pulled the small box free. I pulled at the golden latch that secured it closed and pushed it back. Sure enough, there were several folded pages inside the box. I lifted them and laid them flat on the desk.

I clicked on the office lamp on my desk and hesitantly started with the first letter, dated the middle of May of last year, a week after we broke up the first time.

LANEY,

It took me a week before I broke down and texted you. Seven whole days where I wondered how you were. Where I stared at the empty space in my bed, where I tortured myself and ate all the cereal you left behind in the house. Seven days of agony and then you didn't respond. I watched my phone for days, waiting and hoping that you'd fix what I broke but you didn't.

I SWALLOWED THE THICK LUMP IN MY THROAT AND FLIPPED TO THE next page dated, May 23rd of last year.

LANEY,

It's getting warmer out. I tried to set up the balcony furniture today on the top floor like you suggested in the Spring, but I couldn't bring myself to do it. I'd sit there alone, and it wouldn't be the same without you. If I could change who I was, change this darkness in me, this loneliness that exists, I would change it for you. I'd trade in this treacherous heart and ask for a new one, just for you. So, it could love you the way it should. I'm sorry I couldn't be the man you needed me to be, Laney. If you knew I loved you, in the only way I knew how to love, would it change things? What good is the love of a broken man who's never been shown it a day in his life?

HE KNEW HE LOVED ME IN SOME FASHION BACK IN MAY? I FLIPPED TO the next page, dated June 11th of last year.

LANEY,

   I almost slept with someone. I couldn't go through with it, but that doesn't change that the pain of not having you is growing to be too much. Have you moved on? The idea of you with someone else kills me. Tortures me.

   Italy was supposed to be our trip. Instead I wasted it, drunk the entire time and trying to push you out of my head and out of my system. If that isn't love, Laney, then what is? I ache for you, think of you and even fucking dream of you. What more do you want of me, you already have everything.

I HAD TO STOP READING. TEARS PRICKED MY EYES, AND IF I HADN'T heard Alicia talk about him writing letters to me, I might almost not even believe these were from him. How could he hold so much back from me? Why would he do that to us? I shut the box and pinned the letters to my work board. I'd pick up on the reading tomorrow.

———

I HAD TRIED ALL MORNING TO IGNORE MY WORK BOARD, WHERE THE letters were pinned. I had reached out to Ramsey already and told her I was fine if Jackson came this weekend for Sammy's birthday, that I would be there, and I'd be nice. She squealed for joy, then immediately started crying.

Now, it was Tuesday. I was going to see Jackson in just a few days and see him with the knowledge of all these letters between us.

I stood up, grabbed my purse, and jumped into the jeep. I needed coffee and to get out of the house. Maggie came with me like she usually did when I went to random places in town.

The coffee hut that I frequented was busy. Three cars were in line on the opposite side of her little business, and the car in front of me was taking longer than it should normally take anyone to get coffee.

Kimber, the barista, was a friend of mine and had actually been the only person in town who'd been over to my house with a welcome to town gift. It was partly why I was so loyal to her coffee spot. Today, she kept poking her head out of the window and tucking her hair behind her ear like she was flirting. She'd laughed and flicked her hand toward the driver, three times.

Maggie whined from beside me.

"I know, maybe we should go, but then you wouldn't get one of those doggie biscuits you love." I absently said to the windshield, watching the sleek black car in front of me.

It was a newer version of Ramsey's car, all the bells and whistles, from the look of the chrome wheels and tread on the tires. I knew about things like tread now because of my Jeep Wrangler.

I rolled down my window to hopefully hear what Kimber might have been saying to the driver, but it only reminded me how decaffeinated and irritable I was.

"Hey, Kimber, the rest of us want coffee too!" I bellowed at her, totally shocked I'd just yelled at the sweet girl.

She turned toward me with a surprised face, her mouth falling open.

The driver turned around too and stuck his head out of the window, staring directly at me.

Demanding, sapphire eyes met mine and it was like cold water to my face. Refreshing all the dry and dated places that had withered and become frail. My heart rate spiked and my breathing turned shallow as Jackson effing Tate stared back at me.

"Shit," I breathed.

I pushed the driving gear backward and put the car in reverse, and as swiftly as possible, turned my jeep toward the main street. I peeled out, and with a screeching tire, I floored it.

"Maggie, if we get pulled over, our stories have to match. I was held at gunpoint, got it? I peeled out of there and..." My words died on my tongue as I spotted the sleek, newer Tahoe in my rear-view mirror. Following me.

"Maggie! He's following us!" I careened past the outlet store and took a hard left, hoping to lose him. I didn't. My heart was thrashing in my chest begging me to slow down and let the only man it wanted to catch it. But the letters were screaming at me to keep going. I wasn't ready to see him and just the idea of it had me feeling crazed.

Maggie slid to the side as I took another left and looped the small city block. No one was behind me now, and I breathed a little easier.

"That was a close one, Mags." I let out a little laugh and slowed down as I got to my street. I pulled into my driveway and unbuckled just as a black car pulled in behind me, blocking me in.

36

JACKSON

KIMBER LIKED TO TALK WHEN SHE WAS NERVOUS. I FOUND THIS OUT three weeks ago when I realized her coffee hut was Laney's favorite spot. I had been going every day, hoping to catch Laney and hoping to get details from the barista. Ramsey refused to tell me where Laney lived, saying it was up to Laney to share that. The only thing she had surrendered was the coffee spot, and that was by accident.

They all just kept living their lives like I didn't exist and I was fine with that—I had taken seven months from Laney when we were together, so giving her time to process how she felt and get the healing she needed was something I felt I owed her.

But now, I was ready to be seen.

So, when Kimber saw what happened with Laney, and I told her I was there in Belvidere because of the feisty redhead, she rattled the address off with ease.

I PUT MY CAR IN PARK AND WATCHED THE WHITE JEEP SIT IDLE IN front of me.

I took in the small, lavender cottage-style home with the white picket fence. The white shutters looked freshly painted, the green patch of grass in her front yard looked well maintained and the yellow door was friendly. This place suited Laney. I remember driving past this house, when I went hunting for her around town; I should have known.

I tried to control my breathing as I opened my door and walked the few feet from my car door to hers. Once I was standing next to her jeep, I saw she had the lock pushed down. I smiled and tapped on her window.

She turned her head toward me slowly and gave me a wicked smile. Her face was absent of any makeup, and her red hair was tied back into a ponytail. The sight of her nearly drew me to my knees.

"Laney, can I talk to you?" I asked through the window.

That evil smirk stayed in place as Laney jotted something on her hand with a pen. She was turned awkwardly toward the window like she was hiding something next to her, her bulky raincoat hiding her shoulders and whatever else she was trying to block.

I smiled and waited, all while my stomach twisted with apprehension. Six fucking months.

Six months of missing her smile, her voice, her skin...it was so much worse than the three months apart because this time around, I knew what I wanted. I was as sure of it as I was my own name.

Laney suddenly slapped her hand against the window, with the word "RUN" printed on her palm in black ink, then she smiled again.

I furrowed my brows for a second in confusion when she leaned over to the passenger door and opened it.

My heart rate jumped, then plummeted when I heard barking. Two seconds later, a German Shepherd rounded the car, snarling at me with all its teeth, warning me away from the jeep.

"Holy Shit!" I backed up a few steps and held up my hands.

"Laney, call it off," I begged, but Laney stayed in the car.

The dog kept barking and had lowered itself in such a way that it looked like it was about to pounce.

Fuck, I knew I needed to respect what message Laney was trying to send. She still needed time and wasn't ready to see me. I kept the dog in front of me as I sidestepped and pulled my door open and got back inside the Tahoe.

I'd give her until this weekend, but after that, her time was up.

As I drove away I felt a smile break out on my face. My spitfire was back. She'd found her fire and it was fucking beautiful.

37

LANEY

I LAID MY HEAD AGAINST THE STEERING WHEEL AND WHINED INTO THE empty car. Seeing Jackson so close was torture. Everything inside my body begged for me to open the door and fall into his arms. But panic had me siccing my dog on him instead. I couldn't believe I had done that, but it was all too much at once.

I headed inside with a proud Maggie on my heels. I couldn't really tell if she was proud, but she looked taller. I decided to make coffee instead, then headed to my back office to start work.

It was fine. Everything was fine, except I eyed the pinned letters, and it suddenly wasn't.

I let out a sigh and tugged at the pin in the cork-board, snatching the rest of the pages. The next one if succession was dated June 15th of last year.

Laney,

Do you remember that time we went to that vineyard, and that couple asked us when we were getting married? How awkward it was for us after that? I pictured you as my wife that day. Imagined what it would be like to have you there as Laney Tate, my wife. I pictured what kind of ring I'd give you, what kind of wedding we'd have. I saw it all. Thought of what our kids would look like, how many we'd have. For a brief second, I wanted it all too. Then fear moved in and occupied me. I want to give you those things, but I don't know how. I don't know how to be the person you need me to be. If I did, I'd be it, be the man who deserved to keep you. I wish I were that man, Laney. I'd die to be that man.

WHY WAS HE DOING THIS? HE WAS THAT MAN, ALL HE HAD TO DO WAS say yes to us, but he just kept pushing. Frustrated, I reached for the second letter and fought the disappointment, realizing there was only one more after this one. This letter was dated June 30th of last year.

LANEY,

I saw you today. I had business with Dyson & Reed… I could have found you, waited at your desk but I had stupidly shown up on your doorstep the night before. You didn't answer. I waited all fucking night for you to open the door, which I knew meant you were out. That you moved on. So, I didn't seek you out when I saw you, I just watched from the shadows, wishing I was a braver man. You looked so beautiful. Your hair was tied back in a ponytail, and your lips were that shade of red I loved. It took all my strength not to walk up to you, then ravish you in the elevator. I miss you, Laney. I hate being home without you. It's not the same now. When I was a child, I always imagined what a real home would be like when I moved out on my own, but now that you're gone, I fear I'll never know. It only felt like home when you were there.

I REMEMBERED THAT NIGHT. I HADN'T GONE OUT, I WAS HOME BUT I couldn't bring myself to open the door and instead I ended up falling asleep in front of it. So close to the man that had healed and shattered me.

I touched the last letter and ran my fingers over the blue ink lines on the folded paper. I wanted to save it. I wasn't ready to be done reading his heart and his thoughts. This was the most vulnerable I'd ever experienced from Jackson, and I wanted it to last longer. So, I put the page in my purse and got back to work.

"WHOA," RAMSEY SAID, LEANING BACK INTO THE SOFA.

I nodded my head, "I know."

We were sitting in her living room. She'd finally taken maternity leave from the bar she owned and was nesting. Currently, she was wearing black sweatpants with orange smudges all over them from the Cheeto's she had been binge eating. She had a white t-shirt that barely fit over her pregnant belly, and her hair was in a pile on top of her head. When Ramsey wanted to grunge it up, she went all out.

I had brought over the letters and let her read them because that's what best friends did. And because I needed her to know where my head was when I saw Jackson again. It was Thursday, and he was expected to arrive tomorrow night, assuming I didn't run into him again.

"Lane, he loves you. Doesn't that change things for you?" my best friend asked, shoving a handful of grapes into her mouth.

Where was she getting all these snacks from? I looked around, rather confused because when we sat down, all she had was a bottle of water.

"It does, and it doesn't. I mean, he said he did that night in my apartment too. It's not that he loves me. It's that he *knew* he loved me back then. He kept all of this from me when I was in agony over it. We could have been together so many times," I explained with my hands spread open.

Ramsey situated her body and put her pink toes up on the coffee table. *How did she paint those?*

I stared at her feet and asked, "Did you get a pedicure? Because I was just over here last weekend, painting those piggy's a dark shade of teal."

Her eyes darted around the room, "Okay, so I thought I wanted the teal but after a day or so, it bugged me. Then I panicked thinking my baby would come early or something, and I'd have to stare at my toes while they were up in those stirrups, wishing I had just taken two seconds to change the color to pink," she reasoned like it made total sense.

It didn't.

I gave her an exasperated look, complete with an eye roll. She smiled and wiggled her toes.

"Here's the other thing," I began again, holding out my hand, ready to count on my fingers. "He gave me these letters six months ago, and I never read them. Surely that's upset him. He was probably expecting me to respond, and when I didn't..." I trailed off, lowering my hand, unsure of what points I had to begin with.

Ramsey tried to lean forward but quickly rolled back into place once she realized her belly wasn't going to allow it.

"Look, that may be true, but I think you owe it to him to have a conversation and bring these up." She held the pages in her hand for emphasis. I glared at the papers and fell back against the sofa.

"I don't think I can, Rams." I sat up, tears working their way out. "I mean, what if he strings me along, then changes his mind?" I shook my head fervently. "I couldn't handle that... it would kill me."

Ramsey had moved to my side and was rubbing my back.

"Honey, that's what love is. You put it all out there, praying it holds together. You put every part of you on the line and risk not having them do the same. No matter what, in the end, if they don't, you'll never get all those pieces back."

I kept crying and through my sobs, said, "I just don't want to lose him again."

Ramsey pulled me into a hug and held me until I stopped.

"It's worth risking if you might get to know what it's like having him for once," she whispered into my hair.

She was right.

It was time to take some risks.

38

JACKSON

"UNCLE JAX!" JASMINE JUMPED INTO MY ARMS SCREAMING.

I spun her around and threw her over my shoulder. "Jazzy, I missed you."

Sammy came barreling into the room and threw himself toward me. "Uncle Jax, it's my birthday!" he announced as he fastened himself to my side, giving me a hug.

I tried to process the fact that he hadn't clung to my foot like he used to. He was growing up.

"I know, buddy. You should see the present in my car." He immediately jumped up and ran toward the front door just as Jimmy stepped into the living room.

"Sammy," he scolded, and Sammy froze in place with his hands up and a sneaky grin on his face.

"Okay, okay, I'll wait."

I walked further into the house and hugged my best friend. "Nice to see you, man." I clapped him on the back.

"It's been too long," he returned while clasping my arm.

"Where's my future godchild?" I placed my hands on my hips, looking around.

"Mommy went shopping for the birthday party with Aunt Laney," Sammy explained.

Just the sound of Laney's name made me burn with nervous excitement.

I WALKED FURTHER INTO THE KITCHEN AND GRABBED A GLASS OF water. It was Friday, and the party was set for Saturday, so I hadn't planned on seeing Laney today, but I wouldn't hate it if I did. I just hoped she didn't have the dog with her.

"How's the franchise going?" Jimmy asked, pulling out a glass bowl of chicken thighs in dark marinade sauce. I watched as he laid each one out evenly in a baking dish. I looked outside and frowned at the rain that had started pouring again. It was still technically winter, but spring was just a few weeks away, so using the BBQ was probably out of the question tonight.

"It's going really well. Should be ready to open in April," I replied, watching the chicken. Truth was, I wanted to be finished in time to host Laney's birthday there and christen the restaurant with it. I had all kinds of plans that involved Laney—whether she agreed to be a part of them was totally her choice.

Jimmy looked up from the poultry and smiled. "I still can't believe you pulled it off man." He shook his head back and forth.

I smirked at him, "Me either, but if she could pack up and move her life over here, I didn't see why I couldn't." I took a sip of water, wishing it was vodka or scotch, anything to prepare me to see Laney. The sound of the garage door opening and a car pulling in, tore us from our conversation.

Jimmy turned his head toward the door, and I stood there, looking like an idiot. My chest was on fire, my palms were sweating, and I had the sudden urge to vomit.

Six fucking months.

I heard laughter, and Ramsey's voice flutter in a muffled tone through the closed door, then I heard Laney's voice. I couldn't make out what she said, but I heard her voice, and it cut through me. She was the branding iron, and I was pliant skin, ready for her burn.

The door swung open, and Ramsey's belly was the first thing I saw. She was huge and that saying about pregnant women glowing was totally true, she looked radiant. Her hair was braided back, and a long, black shirt flowed over her body with leggings underneath. She saw me and smiled, her light blue eyes dancing, and as she drew closer, tears started to fill them. She held her arms out as she waddled closer to me.

"Jackson, you're here."

I pulled her into a hug as more tears cascaded down her face.

"Of course, I am," I said dryly. I didn't want to get emotional right now; I was barely holding it together as it was.

A second later, a brilliant shade of red caught my eye as Laney walked through the door. Her pale skin made her red, curled locks look like fire. Laney wore tight jeans with boots and a large sweater. Her green eyes were lined with dark makeup that made the color in her face pop and seem more intense, like looking at the sun for too long.

She was different, a little darkness lingered with her now. A bright part of her had faded, not gone out but diminished just the same. Not in the way she looked but something about her essence. Laney called to me when she was near, like there was an invisible line that always connected us. So, to me, she carried something darker with her now. Like a second skin she couldn't shed. I hated myself for what she went through, what she was forced to become in order to stay alive. She bore the scars, but I carried her wounds in my heart.

But there was a fresh fire under there too and that made this dark-ness she carried seem more like a weapon instead of a defect.

Laney carefully set the shopping bag in her hand down, then straight-ened, all while cautiously eyeing me. Jimmy and Ramsey were quietly talking to themselves, and the kids were downstairs with Theo, so it was just the two of us for a moment.

She slowly walked toward me. I did the same, meeting her halfway. She nodded her head at me before speaking up,

"Hey."

I smiled at her and responded, "Hey."

We stood there for a few seconds before I acted like I was looking around.

"What?" Laney asked, looking too.

"Just making sure no ferocious German Shepherd was lurking around any corners," I said jokingly.

Laney rolled her eyes and let out a little laugh. "No, Mags is at home tonight."

Ramsey turned toward us and started talking about party supplies that were still in the car and asked if we could get them. We nodded our heads in agreement and headed through the small adjoining door to the garage.

Laney walked in front of me, and I caught the smell of lilac and vanilla when her long hair moved against her back. Same Laney. I ached to reach out and grab her, instead I shoved my hands into my pockets.

Laney opened the back hatch to the Tahoe and started rummaging through a few bags. "I think the balloons and the Ninja Turtle masks are in this one." She pulled out a party bag and held it up.

I smiled at her and reached for the bag. "Is this all she needs?"

Laney nodded her head, then went to shut the hatch, but I reached above her to grab it, causing our bodies to nearly collide. She stood in front of me, her back to my chest as I slowly brought the hatch down. I could tell she was breathing unsteadily and was still affected by me, just like I was by her. I moved a fraction closer to her.

"Laney?" I whispered into her hair. She didn't turn around, but she waited, so I continued. "Can I take you somewhere tomorrow after the party?" She still didn't answer, so I tried again, "It's not a date or anything, just something I want to show you."

She took in a deep breath and whispered, "Okay."

She walked back into the house, and I stayed put. Once she was gone, I let out all the air in my lungs that had been trapped by her being so close to me again. It was like my body was trying to remember how to function around her. I'd have to get used to it because tomorrow was going to be a big day.

RED, YELLOW, AND BLUE BALLOONS WERE PACKED INTO EVERY POSSIBLE corner of the house. Ramsey had rented a helium machine and put

Jasmine in charge of inflating all the balloons with Theo. I oversaw the moving of the furniture and securing the bounce house outside.

We were going to have sunshine today, for the first time in weeks. The weather was still frigid, but the sunshine would be nice, and the kids wouldn't care while they jumped.

Jimmy was preparing the BBQ for hamburgers and hotdogs.

Laney had arrived at breakfast, wearing a dark blue dress with red flowers, tall brown boots, and a long sweater. She looked beautiful, and I tried to stop watching the way the fabric of the dress kept stretching across her chest when she moved her arms while measuring balloon strings and folding table cloths. She also had her dog Maggie with her. Apparently, the kids adored Maggie, and since it was going to be a long day, Laney didn't want her to be alone.

There were twelve eight-year-olds in the house, all singing happy birthday to my godson. I was proud of my little man, he was growing like a weed and getting past that cute baby stage. I had bought him a skateboard with all the padding and even a pair of vans to wear while he rode it.

Ramsey was so emotional during singing happy birthday, she had to leave the room. Jimmy wanted to follow her, but I merely reminded him this was his kid's party, and the honeymoon phase they were still stuck in could wait.

Jimmy smirked and joked, "Just wait until it's your turn."

My eyes scanned the room for Laney. She was helping serve everyone cake. I wanted to help her, but the entire day, I had been trying not to overwhelm her. I caught her watching me a few times and tried to relax at the way her eyes kept roving over my body like she was thinking about what it was like to touch it.

Finally, things were winding down, and all the big stuff was clean and put away. Ramsey had her feet propped up on the chaise lounge and was softly snoring while she dozed. I waved Laney toward me from her spot near the kitchen.

She locked eyes with me and slowly made her way over.

"Time to go," I informed her.

She looked nervous, and a little pink had entered her cheeks. I wished she knew how nervous I was, there really wasn't any comparing the two. She made sure Maggie was all taken care of and followed me out the front door, through the dusk, and climbed into the passenger side of my car. The car ride was silent, and I didn't want to ruin anything by talking because what I wanted to show her would hopefully say everything she needed to hear. I received a text from Theo a few seconds into our drive,

Ready

Since it came through over Bluetooth, Laney heard it and half turned toward me.

"What did that mean?"

I smiled and kept driving. "You'll see soon enough."

I put on my turn signal and headed toward the edge of town. We passed the small town of Belvidere as the colors of the sky turned from a dark blue to light pink, then a burnt yellow. At last, we approached a small, private driveway and rolled down it until we came up to a large, white, two-story house with a giant, wraparound porch.

Laney peeked through the windshield to get a better look, her face twisted in confusion. There were small candles lit and placed along the path to the house and along the porch railing. Theo had come about an hour ago to come set up, claiming he had to go check on the bar, but really, he was helping me.

Laney opened the door and headed toward the house. Before she reached it, she pulled her sweater tightly around her and looked around. The house sat on five acres with a small grove of trees, a fenced in back yard, and a big, red barn at the edge of the property. She faced me, opened her mouth while looking around, then closed it and headed for the house.

Here goes nothing.

39

LANEY

THERE WERE CANDLES EVERYWHERE. I MEAN EVERYWHERE. I PULLED the door open to the gorgeous house, and more candles waited for us. I looked down at the hardwood floors, little lights and flower vases intermixed to form a path. I held my breath as I walked through the empty space.

There was no furniture, and the place looked like a bit of a fixer-upper, but it was beautiful. I walked through what would be the living room and took in the huge, bay windows that filled the expanse of the room and faced the fenced-in yard. Jackson followed closely but silently behind me. Something caught my eye on the wall to my left.

I walked up to the paper that was hung in place by tape and peeled it off the wall. It was a drawing, in colored pencil, and it was done by a child from the looks of it. The picture was of a large family sitting in a living room together, watching television.

Something inside my head kicked into gear, and my pulse raced. I kept the picture and walked into the space for the dining room and searched the walls, and sure enough, there was another colorful drawing, this one of a family sitting around a long table with turkey and all sorts of food. Each person at the table was a different color.

I smiled and moved to the kitchen. It had large, pop-out windows, an island, and a huge pantry space. On the wall near the space where a fridge might go was another drawing of two people making food together.

I turned around and found the stairs, taking them slowly as Jackson faded into the background. I didn't focus on where he went, I was after the pictures now. There was a picture taped to the banister of two siblings riding a carpet down a huge staircase, their multi-colored dog following after them. I added the photo to my pile. I started with a small bedroom. A picture of a young boy in a blanket fort, colored in shades of purple waited for me.

Another room had one of a family in a tree fort outside, stargazing.

Three bedrooms later, I had a pile of pictures.

Finally, I went to the master bedroom. It was large, spacious with big windows and an attached bathroom. There in the middle of the floor, by a candle, was the last picture in the house—a man and a woman hugging in what looked like a church, getting married.

My breath hitched, and I searched the room for Jackson but couldn't find him. *Where did I leave him?*

I ran downstairs, still holding the mass of papers in my hand. He was waiting for me at the bottom of the stairs with his hands behind his back.

I slowly took the last few steps until I was standing in front of him. He was so still and quiet. I held the pictures close to my chest and waited for him to say something.

Finally, he spoke in a revered voice.

"Laney, you are holding every dream I ever dared to have as a child. I wish I didn't know when I stopped dreaming, but I do, and I've lived with that feeling my entire life. But those feelings didn't and couldn't compare to the emptiness I felt for the first time I was without you."

He stepped closer, and my heart responded in rhythm. Like it was finally finding its home.

"I screwed everything up between us, Laney, but I know I'm ready to dream again. I want everything, and I want it with you." He stepped even closer.

"I want the big, noisy family, the dog, the tree forts, and farm. I want to live close to our best friends and watch our children grow up together. I want forever with you, Laney because you're it for me."

He pressed his forehead against mine as tears fell freely from my eyes.

"You are forever branded inside of me. So, if you turn me down, I'll understand, but you should know you've left your mark on my mind, body, and soul and now, no one will ever fill the empty space you've created inside of me."

He bent down on one knee and held up a box. My hand went to my mouth as the waterfall of tears saturated my face.

"Laney Laverta Thompson, will you marry me? Be my forever and grow old with me?"

I didn't look at the diamond on display in the box, my eyes sought out those sapphire gems that always kept me still. I lowered myself to my knees and closed my eyes as I repeated the words I had read a thousand times that morning on the very last letter he'd left me.

"I'll be in you if you promise to live inside of me. Dwell with me, heal me, help me, and hope with me. I want to love you, but sometimes I need aid. I'll guide you if you lead me. Be my forever, and I'll be yours. For better or worse, if marriage is in our future, then let it bind us together like fire."

JACKSON'S BREATHING CHANGED, AND I LIFTED MY EYES IN TIME TO see his expression transform into surprise and shock. He pulled me until I was flush against him and whispered into my ear.

"Is that a yes?"

I threw my arms around him and trailed kisses along his jaw until I got to his ear.

"It's a yes."

Jackson picked me up and walked me over to the side of the stairs where a small bed was made up with blankets and pillows and gently laid me down. There was a small duffle bag of clothes there too and a few empty boxes of cup of noodles. *Had he been living here?*

He hovered over me as he carefully brushed my hair aside and dragged his finger down my face, tracing my lips.

"You're so beautiful," he whispered before he kissed me.

It was a gentle kiss that turned frantic as I pulled him closer. His hands roamed my body, and we broke apart, so he could pull my boots off and my sweater. Then he took a painstakingly long time with my buttons, but once they were free, he carefully peeled my dress away until I was just in my underwear. The way he stared at me, in the dim flickering firelight, stirred something awake in me. He carefully leaned forward to press a kiss to my bare shoulder.

I closed my eyes as his gentle kisses moved to my collar bone and down.

"You're breathing hard," Jackson whispered into my skin.

I nodded, trying not to cry and ruin the moment.

He stopped kissing and looked up. "What's wrong?"

I swallowed the thick lump of emotion in my throat,

"This is everything I've wanted for so long... it's just hard to accept it's happening."

Jackson brought a finger to my jaw and drew a line down my throat, stopping at my heart. He leaned forward and pressed a kiss there.

Like a faulty dam, I broke open and asked him the questions that have burned inside of me from that awful day in May.

"Why did you pack my things? Why did you end it?" I whispered.

Jackson's blue eyes stared into mine.

"Because I had to let you go. I was selfish with you, Laney. I used your PTSD as a reason to stay with you. You may have agreed to stay as a non-labeled couple but in whatever capacity I could, I loved you enough to not do that to you." He shifted a fraction closer and gently pulled on the ends of my hair.

"I used to watch you sleep. I'd trace your lips and your eyes, right here." He pressed his finger to the corner of my eye.

"I was in love with you Laney, but I had no idea *how* to love you, so like a coward, I pushed you away."

He leaned forward and pressed his lips to that same place by my eye.

"You were meant for me. I was just delaying the inevitable."

He carefully watched me as he pushed my bra strap down and returned to kissing my skin. He carefully placed his palm behind my head and laid me flat on the bed.

"Let me love you, Laney. Let me keep you," he bent down and whispered into my stomach as he kept kissing lower and lower.

Happy tears made their way down my face as he tugged down the fabric at my core.

"Mine." He breathed.

Gently, he pressed the flat of his tongue against my already slick entrance. I jolted at the contact.

"Jax," I moaned as his tongue separated my folds with a delicate pressure.

"This is what I'll think about on our bad days..." he said, adding his finger, coaxing another moan from me as he buried his mouth into my heat.

"This," he sucked my clit into his mouth, "is what I'll think about when you get that angry look on your face and want to freeze me out."

I bucked against his face, unable to stop the climax already building inside of me.

"Forever, Laney...I want to do this forever."

He sat back watching me, like I'd disappear any second. Then he was moving over me. His skin burned mine in places he had touched a million times before, but this time it was new and it set me on fire.

His erection pressed into my core, and like other times, I had to look down to watch how beautiful it was to see that smooth tip pulsing in his firm fist.

My eyes bounced up, watching his reaction as I helped guide him in.

"Forever, Jax."

He pushed in, fast and unforgiving.

"So you'll always remember how this feels, you'll never forget the way it burned when I claimed you."

He pulled out and then pushed back in until his balls were slamming against my ass.

I moaned, loudly almost completely undone by how good it felt.

This was so different from any other time we'd ever made love, this was something entirely more perfect.

"You're mine," he whispered as he withdrew and slammed into me once more, "forever, Laney."

I had my arms wrapped around him, holding tight as we moved, in sync for truly the first time ever. I held firm to his arms and his neck as he abolished the brokenness between us. As he mended the hurt and the fear, the anger and resentment. I was tethered to him like a string and he used our intimacy to stitch us back together. We were like the tide, coming together only to crash apart. I found peace and perfection in the solace of his love. In the brush of his fingers. In the kiss from his lips. In the cadence of his strong body and powerful thrusts.

I let his hands cradle me, as we both finished in a peak of desperation and awe. Our bodies were slack and weary, all the hopelessness extracted from our limbs. Hope and anticipation filled its place. This was the way we were meant to love each other, how we were meant to be.

I WAS PULLED TIGHT AGAINST JACKSON'S CHEST AS WE LAID WATCHING the room. He was dragging his fingers, lazily down my arm as I finally took a second to catalogue where we were.

"Jackson whose house is this?"

He kissed my earlobe and muttered against my skin, "Ours."

I turned in his arms. "What?"

He searched my eyes and laughed. "I bought this house three months ago, a little after I started my franchise in Rockford." He pushed the hair off my face. I kissed him, and we were nearly off to another round when he stopped and jumped up.

"I almost forgot!" he shouted as he ran off.

I laid back down and looked at the exposed beams in the ceiling as hope and happiness filled me to the brim. There wasn't any room for more surprises.

Jackson came back, holding my ring box and an envelope. I took the ring box and examined the godlike gem that rested there. *Holy shit, that was a big diamond.*

He resumed his spot behind me and handed me the envelope. It was from my student loans office. Dread filled me; I hated seeing this stupid balance every month. But why did Jackson have it? Anxiety surged through me.

He didn't?!

I sat up as I pulled the paper free and turned it over. I skipped all the words and went straight for the numbers. Right there, under final balance, was a big fat zero. I cried again, for the thousandth time. I couldn't look at him yet because what he'd done was too much. I owed over ninety thousand dollars in student loans. How on earth did he pay this off, buy a house and a ring, and start a franchise? All the questions were right there, but he must have sensed my struggle. He tugged the paper from me and pulled me close.

"My father left me a large inheritance." He kissed my temple and continued, "The franchise has a financial backer, and I sold my condo in Chicago. With the funds left over, this place was practically free."

I kissed him again, still unable to form words. *How did this happen? How did I get here?* I was still kissing him when he gently pulled me back.

"Are you okay?"

He was rubbing my arms again. I sniffed and tried to explain.

"I can't thank you enough, you didn't have to do all that, Jackson."

I tried to keep my sobs down because when I talked and cried, my words came out high-pitched and squeaky. He rubbed my back.

"Baby, I'd do anything for you. I'm sorry it took me so long to put it all into place, but when you told me back at that coffee shop in Plainville about what you secretly wanted, I knew I was going to be the one to give it to you. I was too selfish to let you have this with some other lucky bastard." He kissed my forehead and pulled me close again.

"You're it for me, Lane. Forever."

I laid down and rested in the crook of his neck and breathed in deep. He'd been home to me so many times in the past, but it always felt temporary, fleeting, like he'd just fade away. I let my heart pick up the fragments of hope that Jackson offered and sunk into them.

He had me then, he had me now, and he would have me forever.

EPILOGUE

Five years later

Laney

THE CLOUDS WERE MOVING THROUGH THE SKY AT AN ASTONISHING pace. Clearly today was not the day to look for cloud animals with my four-year-old, but he didn't seem to care.

"That one is a snake." Clark pointed his chubby little finger at the heavens.

I giggled. "Clark, they all look like snakes right now."

He laughed. "You're right, mama. It's a sky full of snakes." He jumped up and attacked me with his hand, pretending it was a snake.

I laughed and turned the attack on him by kissing his face, which always made him give in.

"Clark what are you doing to your mama?" Jackson yelled from the porch. Clark and I both turned to see him. Clark, like usual, ran toward his father's voice and was hoisted up on Jackson's shoulders within seconds.

"I was attacking her with sky snakes, Daddy," he joked while wiggling into place on Jackson's shoulders.

I got to my knees and ever so slowly stood up. Jackson gave me a concerned look with a raised brow while he grabbed our four-year-old's hands to steady him.

"Babe, you could ask for help, you know!" Jackson yelled at me as I continued my pilgrimage to stand up.

"I got it, sweetie. Thanks though!" I yelled back.

I was eight months pregnant with twins, and yes, I was as large as a baby elephant. Ramsey consistently measured me then googled facts about baby elephants to compare. Research was what she called it, but she and Jasmine laughed and giggled every time, and I always rolled my eyes and then fed her youngest daughter, Lara, candy.

Lara was born two weeks and three days before Ramsey's mom passed away. Carla got her wish to hold her grandbaby before she left this world. Lara helped Ramsey get through the grief and loss she'd been expecting for so long. When that baby girl was put into Ramsey's arms, she knew immediately that she wanted to combine Loretta, which was Jimmy's deceased mother's name, and Carla's names together, hence Lara.

"I'm just saying you could go into labor any day now, and you need to have like a cane with you or something. And no lying down on the ground," Jackson scolded as he walked across the yard. He'd become insanely protective when I was pregnant with Clark four years earlier, but now, with twins, he was extreme.

"I'm not using a cane," I said plainly.

Jackson and I had gotten married six months after he proposed, right here in our back yard. We spent that year remodeling our little fixer-upper, then when I found out I was pregnant, Jackson turned into super-man. Really, he did. I can't even go into all the disgustingly sweet things he did for me during my pregnancy.

Jackson reached me and grabbed the checkered blanket Clark and I had used for our picnic from my hands. Clark was still perched on his father's shoulders, but that didn't stop Jackson from giving me his infamous "I need you" stare.

It wasn't about sex anymore with that look; it was just a state of being for us. We needed each other randomly throughout the day. Sometimes, if he was at work, I'd call him just to hear his voice, and if I didn't have anything to say, he'd just let the silence hang between us and say, "I know baby, me too."

"You sure you're up for this visit?" Jackson asked while helping me back to the house. I reached up and grabbed Clark's little fingers as we walked.

I let out a sigh. "Is anyone ever really ready for my brothers?"

Jackson laughed and shook his head. "Not in the least, but they wanted to come over here and help set up the twins' nursery as a gift."

Hilarious, this guy. I gave him a side smile back. "A gift? Seeing the four of them try to put together a nursery is going to be a gift alright. Ten bucks says within an hour, at least two of them gets into a fight and uses part of the nursery as a weapon." I laughed as I climbed the porch steps and headed inside.

Our home was beautiful, and after being here for five years, there were pictures all over the walls—of real family moments, not just colored pencil drawings. There were dried flowers, drawings from Clark and from Lara. The two of them were inseparable, only a year apart, and Ramsey and I were already praying to sweet baby Jesus about their intended future. Jimmy and Jackson hated when we joked about their future marriage, but we were pretty set on legitimately arranging it.

"Lawson will keep them in check," Jackson said with total confidence while he set Clark down and grabbed some green smoothie drink from the fridge.

I held back an eye roll. "Lawson will have already picked out what to use as a weapon once things get out of hand within the first five minutes of being in that room."

Jackson laughed as he tried to reassure me. "True, but I'll be there to oversee it all, okay?"

I smiled as he hugged me from behind. I loved when he wrapped his long arms all the way around my belly.

He kissed my neck softly and gently moved my hair aside. "I love you so much, it still hurts," he whispered.

My heart rate doubled, and I wished so badly these babies would just be born so I could have my body back and my husband back.

The pregnancy hormones were no joke, but at this size, it made it nearly impossible for us to do anything. I grabbed his neck, pinning him in place behind me, and ran my fingers over his arms. I loved how secure he felt, how perfect. I looked down at his forearm, at the place I used to grab when I'd try to come out of a dream. There, tattooed in black ink, were the words *Brave enough to live.* He'd gotten it to match my tattoo.

Jimmy made fun of him all the time because it was a sensitive, almost female tattoo, but Jackson held firm to his choice. I loved it because I knew he'd done it for me.

Every now and then when old demons would come back to visit, I'd grip his arm in that same spot and those words would remind me to live. To move on. To let go.

I felt the twins kicking and moved Jackson's fingers until they were directly over the little bumps. He laughed from behind me then slowly moved around and kneeled, so he was eye level with my belly.

"Little spit fires." He gazed up at me from the floor, his blue eyes sparkling with excitement.

I cupped his jaw. "You think they're girls?" I wanted them to be girls so badly, but we had agreed not to find out. We liked the thrill of the surprise.

Jackson smiled, moved his hands over the expanse of my belly, and felt two more hard kicks. "Oh yes, these are girls. I'm almost positive. Only girls would have this much attitude in the womb." Jackson laughed and stood up, bending down to kiss me just as the screen door opened and a chorus of loud men made their way inside.

"Hey, we're here!" Leo called out as he moved through the house.

"I think they know, moron," Ty joked.

Here we go.

Jackson

IT TOOK THE THOMPSON BROTHERS THREE DAYS TO PUT TOGETHER THE nursery. It should have only taken them a few hours, but trying to get the four of them to work together was close to impossible. Laney couldn't stop laughing because she won her bet—within ten minutes, Zane had grabbed a crib piece and tried to smack Leo with it.

Clark loved every second of it, and since Zane had brought his three-year-old son, the boys played together all three days, blissfully happy. Then Laney went into labor and everything went to hell. The guys were still there, thankfully, and were able to watch Clark while I rushed Laney to Rockford.

"You okay?" Laney asked me while I stared out the hospital window.

I turned to look at her. She had an IV taped to her hand and a belly monitor attached to her stomach. She was so beautiful, even now, huge as a house, her hair damp from contractions and pulled into a bun. I loved her so much it terrified me.

"I'm okay. How are you?" I asked as I moved away from the window.

She smiled and rubbed her belly. She'd been in labor for six hours already, and it wasn't looking good that she'd be able to have them naturally.

"I just want them to get here, safe and sound. I don't care how. I just want to hold them," she said sleepily.

I brushed the damp hair from her forehead. "I know, baby."

It was all I could say because I wanted them here safe too, but a large selfish part of me also wanted more than anything to be sure she would be okay, no matter what.

I couldn't live without Laney, which wasn't a healthy thing, but it was still true. Jimmy had learned how to be a parent first and sacrifice all else for his kids, but I had Laney first and she was my reason for waking up every day. I loved my son and my two new children fiercely, but I shared a soul with Laney.

"Okay folks, let's go have a baby," Dr. Lang declared as he swept into the room.

Laney and I looked at each other and then at him.

"I want to get these babies out safely, and within the last two hours, your blood pressure has spiked," he informed Laney.

"So, I need a C-section?" she asked.

Dr. Lang nodded his head yes and started taking us through the information we'd need to know regarding the surgery. It seemed straight-forward, and I texted Ramsey and Beverly, who were on their way, then I changed into a set of scrubs.

An hour later, I had a baby in each arm, cleaned, swaddled, and ready to see their mother. Laney had been wheeled back to her room and the babies were set to be rolled down as well, but I needed a second with my girls. I was right—they were two baby spitfires. I brought each girl up to my face and gently kissed their foreheads.

The reality of the situation hit me: I had a family.

Three children, a wife, a house. This was my life now, and it felt better than anything I'd ever imagined. I wished my father could be here to meet my children and see how full and bright my life had become. I set my daughters in their rollaway cribs and let the nurses wheel them down to our room as I followed.

Toward my future, my hope, my life.

HAVE YOU READ LANEY & JACKSON'S ORIGIN STORY?

'At First Fight'? It's the prelude to Fade, so be sure you go snag it here for Free!

Enjoy Fade? Please take a moment to leave a review, it means so much to hear your thoughts.

Be sure to read Jimmy and Ramsey's story in Glimmer

OTHER BOOKS BY ASHLEY MUNOZ

ACKNOWLEDGMENTS

Always and forever, my number one spot of gratitude will go to God. He developed this love of stories within me and helps me through each and every grueling step.

To my husband and kids, thank you will never be enough. You guys cringe at the word deadline but still bring me coffee, dinner, and color me pictures while I'm glued to my computer and I couldn't be more thankful to you for it. Jose, thank you for holding down our lives as I create these books. This book was a rough journey for us. Through financial sacrifices and Dave Ramsey plans- I know investing in me wasn't an easy choice but it's one you made just the same. Thank you for believing in me and for protecting what's ours and for always dreaming with me. I love you for eternity and I will forever choose you.

To my beta readers who were the first to go through my book and give me confidence to keep pushing.

Courtney Wyczawski, Gladys Aviles, Leah Weybright, Lehua Stingy Hoarder Knight, Kassie Dedmond, Jennifer Taylor, Amanda Poppin, Mandee Frankfurter, Jessica N Davis, Ronita Banjeree, Michelle Heron, Brittany Taylor, Rebecca Patrick, Momma D. Several of you have continued to be apart of my street team, spreading things for me and encouraging me.

Gladys, a special shout out to you for always doing this without me even asking, you mean so much to me it's not even funny.

Marnie J, Kathleen Patt Matthys; both of you are such amazing fans and continue to me push toward success. I just wanted to say thank you to you both.

To my Sister Rebecca and my Mother Debra: Thank you both for getting excited about my work, for reading it and giving me ideas and helping me see things in this book that I couldn't see.

To my family: Eric, Mom, Daniel, Jass, Jon, Haley, Rebecca, Jonathan P, Amanda, Eli, Benjamin, Brian, Anthony, and Kevin. You are my life source tying me to normal and to what's familiar: thank you.

To my Dad: You're in heaven but there isn't a day that goes by that I don't think about you and wish you were here. I love you.

To Brittany Taylor: You are my person and I couldn't be more grateful for you. Thank you for reading Fade not once but twice and for always pushing me toward greatness. You took the brunt of so many harsh editing critiques and helped me to stay focused and on track, when all I wanted to do was give up. Thank you for making me laugh and introducing me to Jamie Frazier. I can't wait until I see you in April.

LK Farlow, thank you for being so amazing and giving me such a kick ass cover.

Amanda Edens, thank you for combing through this book and improving the content. Thank you for suggesting that I add in the actual break up.

C. Marie, thank you so much for your editing perfection. You gave this book the polish it needed.

Maria Vickers from Lip Service PR, thank you for helping me with yet another book, thank you for sharing, supporting and always answering my questions.

Book Beauties, thank you so much for posting, sharing and commenting. I love you guys so much and couldn't be more honored to have you read my work.

To my new readers, please send me messages and fan girl the heck out. I love it and need the encouragement much more than you might think.

Hayes Markham, thank you for answering my questions about Chicago and being willing to help this Oregonian with specifics of the city.

To all my author friends who help me share and post and interact with me; I love you all so much.

ABOUT THE AUTHOR

Ashley resides in the Pacific Northwest, where she lives with her four children and her husband. She loves coffee, reading fantasy, and writing about people who kiss and cuss.

Want to interact with Ashley?

Join her shutouts for exclusive excerpts and sneak peeks: www. ashleymunozbooks.com

Be sure to join her reader group: Book Beauties

Printed in Great Britain
by Amazon

79847391R00171